THE SCOUT
AND THE SCOUNDREL

What Reviewers Say About Barbara Ann Wright's Work

The Noble and the Nightingale

"Wright sets up the Sisters of Sarras lesbian fantasy romance trilogy with solid worldbuilding, a delightfully awkward couple who bridge social realms, and an entertaining adventure that leaves plenty of room to grow. ...By the end, Wright has established strong personalities for Adella's two sisters and taken the suspense plotline to the brink of war between Sarras and the Firellians, setting up strongly for the next volumes. Readers will be pleased."—*Publishers Weekly*

"Only Barbara Ann Wright can weave a satisfying romance from nothing more than looks of longing, stolen kisses, and hand-holding. ...*The Noble and the Nightingale* is an entirely satisfying addition to the shelves of Barbara Ann Wright, who somehow finds fresh ways to blend fantasy and romance with characters worthy of their settings."—*Beauty in Ruins*

"When I heard that Barbara Ann Wright was starting a new fantasy series about three sisters...I knew I wanted to read these books. *The Noble and the Nightingale* is a very intriguing beginning to this series. ...This novel has something for everyone. ...The tale is well-written. The setting and world building is superb. The characters are well developed and easy to connect with. The story kept my interest from the first page to the last."—*Rainbow Reflections*

"This book was a ton of fun. ...I think it is very approachable for all types of readers. ...I ended up reading this book until 3 [a.m.] because I had to know how everything would unfold and what would happen to all the characters. ...This is the kind of story to take you on an adventure and just have fun with. Not only could I not stop reading this book, but it put a big smile on my face. I'm a happy reader."—*Lez Review Books*

Lady of Stone

"Yet another stellar read from Barbara Ann Wright, *Lady of Stone* is a wonderful blend of magical fantasy and lesbian romance that had me eager to find out how it all ends, and yet reluctant to have it end."
—*Beauty in Ruins*

Not Your Average Love Spell

"Barbara Ann Wright mixes so much into her story—romance, comedy, drama, action, adventure—that it threatens more than once to collapse under the clash of themes, but those clashes and contrasts only serve to make it stronger and more engaging."—*Beauty in Ruins*

"…a solid little fantasy tale with a lot of really cool elements. …Wright plays to all the tropes…in a way that keeps the story fresh while preserving the surprises. …As for the romance, that was surprisingly sweet and amusing, with four women at the heart of the story who are entirely likable…the spark of attraction and the emotional connections are undeniable."—*Fem Led Fantasy*

"…a great story filled with magic, wondrous creatures and adventure but what I really enjoyed about the book was the way that the characters grew. …It is a great thing to read in these trying times and I took hope from it. The story pulls with enough magic to feel like a fully fleshed out fantasy world while keeping our heroes relatable and engaging. …I give it a full hearted thumbs up and you should definitely check it out."—*Paper Phoenix Ink*

"I thought this was a fun and entertaining adventure read…the fantasy aspects are very approachable. …The way the whole plot unfolded just felt different and I loved that. What also really impressed me was the amount of action this book had. It was one thing after another after another all keeping me completely glued to the book. …I could not stop reading."—*Lez Review Books*

"The adventures, as mentioned above, were plentiful. There are pirates and warriors, a yeti, giant spiders, a possible dragon, lizard people, and in general, a lot of tough-headed knights. The plot was definitely interesting, with a lot of twists and turns. The writing was seasoned with beautiful writing and truths. I highly recommend this book to lovers of fantasy and to those that want characters to be challenged to deconstruct what they know and learn how to live together. It's a beautiful book!"—*The Lesbrary*

"[*Not Your Average Love Spell*] is an entertaining...romantic fantasy adventure comedy? (I'm not sure how to categorise its Venn diagram of subgenres, either.) Starring an agoraphobic witch; a bright, curious, talkative homunculus; an archivist/scholar with a revolutionary bent; a knight who—at least initially—believes wholeheartedly in her order's mission to stamp out magic; and an invasion of genocidal warriors, *Not Your Average Love Spell* takes its characters on an entertaining ride and delivers all of them a happy ending. (Except for the genocidal warriors. Their happy ending would be terrible for everyone else.)"—*Tor.com*

The Tattered Lands

"Wright's postapocalyptic romance is a fast-paced journey through devastation. ...Plenty of action, surprises, and magic will keep readers turning the pages."—*Publishers Weekly*

House of Fate

"...fast, fun...entertaining. ...*House of Fate* delivers on adventure." —*Tor.com*

Lambda Literary Award Finalist—*Coils*

"...Greek myths, gods and monsters and a trip to the Underworld. Sign me up. ...This one springs straight into action...a good start, great Greek myth action and a late blooming romance that flowers in the end..."—*Dear Author*

"A unique take on the Greek gods and the afterlife make this a memorable book. The story is fun with just the right amount of camp. Medusa is a hot, if unexpected, love interest. ...A truly unexpected ending has us hoping for more stories from this world."
—*RT Book Reviews*

"The gods and monsters of ancient Greek mythology are living, breathing entities, something Cressida didn't expect and is amazed as well as terrified to discover. ...Cressida soon realizes being in the underworld is no different than being among the living. The heart still feels and love can bloom, even in the world of Myth. ...The characters are well developed and their wit will elicit more than a few chuckles. A joy to read."—*Lunar Rainbow Reviewz*

Paladins of the Storm Lord

"This was a truly enjoyable read...I would definitely pick up the next book. ...The mad dash at the end kept me riveted. I would definitely recommend this book for anyone who has a love of sci-fi. ...An intricate novel...one that can be appreciated at many levels, adventurous sci fi or one that is politically motivated with a very astute look at present day human behavior. ...There are many levels to this extraordinary and well written book...overall a fascinating and intriguing book."—*Inked Rainbow Reads*

"I loved this. ...The world that the Paladins inhabited was fascinating...didn't want to put this down until I knew what happened. I'll be looking for more of Barbara Ann Wright's books."—*Lesbian Romance Reviews*

"*Paladins of the Storm Lord* by Barbara Ann Wright was like an orchestra with all of its pieces creating a symphony. I really truly loved it. I love the intricacy and wide variety of character types...I just loved practically every character! ...Of course my fellow adventure lovers should read *Paladins of the Storm Lord*!"—*Lesbian Review*

Thrall: Beyond Gold and Glory

"Once more Barbara has outdone herself in her penmanship. I cannot sing enough praises. A little *Vikings*, a dash of *The Witcher*, peppered with *The Game of Thrones*, and a pinch of *Lord of The Rings*. Mesmerizing. ...I was ecstatic to read this book. It did not disappoint. Barbara pours life into her characters with sarcasm, wit and surreal imagery, they leap from the page and stand before you in all their glory. I am left satisfied and starving for more, the clashing of swords, whistling of arrows still ringing in my ears." —*Lunar Rainbow Reviews*

"In their adventures, the women must wrestle with issues of freedom, loyalty, and justice. The characters were likable, the issues complex, and the battles were exciting. I really enjoyed this book and I highly recommend it."—*All Our Worlds: Diverse Fantastic Fiction*

"This was the first Barbara Ann Wright novel I've read, and I doubt it will be the last. Her dialogue was concise and natural, and she built a fantastical world that I easily imagined from one scene to the next. Lovers of Vikings, monsters and magic won't be disappointed by this one."—*Curve*

The Pyramid Waltz

"...a healthy dose of a very creative, yet believable, world into which the reader will step to find enjoyment and heart-thumping action. It's a fiendishly delightful tale."—*Lambda Literary*

"Barbara Ann Wright is a master when it comes to crafting a solid and entertaining fantasy novel. ...The world of lesbian literature has a small handful of high-quality fantasy authors, and Barbara Ann Wright is well on her way to joining the likes of Jane Fletcher, Cate Culpepper, and Andi Marquette. ...Lovers of the fantasy and futuristic genre will likely adore this novel, and adventurous romance fans should find plenty to sink their teeth into."—*Rainbow Reader*

"Chock full of familiar elements that avid fantasy readers will adore…[*The Pyramid Waltz*] adds in a compelling and slowly evolving romance. …Set against a backdrop of political intrigue with the possibility of monsters and mystery at every turn, the two women slowly learn each other, sharing secrets and longing, until a fragile love blossoms between them…"—*USA Today Happily Ever After*

For Want of a Fiend

"This book will keep you turning the page to find out the answers. …Fans of the fantasy genre will really enjoy this installment of the story. We can't wait for the next book."—*Curve*

"A fun, unique story with a distinctive world. This series doesn't imitate other popular fantasy novels. It stands on its own. The writing is well paced and Wright incorporates a more modern or colloquial language which makes the books easy to read. Overall, *For Want of a Fiend* was an enjoyable read and I think you would like it if you are a fan of books like Game of Thrones or a TV series like Reign." —*Lesbian Review*

"If you enjoyed *The Pyramid Waltz*, *For Want of a Fiend* is the perfect next step. If you haven't read either, know that you'd be embarking on a joyous, funny, sweet and madcap ride around very dark things lovingly told, with characters who will stay with you for months after. The plot still moves at a fast clip. Characterisation continues to deepen—and I love that. I love seeing a passionate, adoring romantic relationship flanked by friendships."—*The Lesbrary*

A Kingdom Lost

"There is only one other time in my life I have uncontrollably shouted out in cheer while reading a book. [*A Kingdom Lost*] made the second. …Over the course of these three books all the characters have blossomed and developed so eloquently. …I simply just thought this whole novel was brilliant."—*Lesbian Review*

The Fiend Queen

Visit us at www.boldstrokesbooks.com

By the Author

The Pyradisté Adventures
The Pyramid Waltz
For Want of a Fiend
A Kingdom Lost
The Fiend Queen
Lady of Stone

Thrall: Beyond Gold and Glory

The Godfall Novels
Paladins of the Storm Lord
Widows of the Sun-Moon
Children of the Healer
Inheritors of Chaos

Coils
House of Fate
The Tattered Lands
Not Your Average Love Spell

The Sisters of Sarras
The Noble and the Nightingale
The Scout and the Scoundrel

THE SCOUT
AND THE SCOUNDREL

by

Barbara Ann Wright

2021

ISBN 13: 978-1-63555-978-1

This Trade Paperback Original Is Published By
Bold Strokes Books, Inc.
P.O. Box 249
Valley Falls, NY 12185

First Edition: November 2021

Credits
Editor: Cindy Cresap
Production Design: Susan Ramundo
Cover Design By Tammy Seidick

Acknowledgments

Thanks to everyone at BSB, most of all Cindy, the best editor a fantasy writer could hope for. Thanks also to Rad and Sandy for continuing to believe in my work. And thank you, Tammy, for my wonderful covers. Plus, thanks to Ruth, Carsen, Paula, Stacia, and all my fellow BSB writers for your unwavering support.

Thanks to my fabulous writing groups. It's been a slog of a year, but you're sticking with it. Sarah, Deb, Angela, and David, I couldn't have done it without you.

Same goes for my mom, Linda Dunn. It's because of you that I know anything about perseverance.

Dedication

For Deb. The way you handle life
has always been an inspiration.

CHAPTER ONE

To Roni, there was only one thing worse than sitting in jail after getting caught stealing: sitting in jail after getting caught stealing from some uptown nob with a vendetta against hardworking criminals. And on a feast day at that, when the constabulary were out of sorts for being forced to work while everyone else was having fun.

When the penalties for thieving were harsher.

After Roni had already been caught twice that year.

Okay, a few things were worse than just getting caught, but even while sitting in a jail cell, she couldn't regret her night's work. She blocked out the sounds of coughing and the murmurs and whimpers of her fellow inmates. She couldn't see much in the dim light of two lanterns hanging in the hallway outside. The constables shouldn't have bothered with light at all. It made the huddled forms sprawled on the floor or leaning against the wall seem like lurking ghouls. And the stench of cheap lamp oil seemed to make the stink of unwashed bodies that much worse.

Roni made herself ignore all of it and concentrate on the future. The loot she'd claimed to have thrown in the canal while being pursued by the constables had actually been carefully hidden. It would see her through the next few months, even after paying the exorbitant fees to the Newgate Syndicate for thieving in their territory. Well, the fees plus a few late charges from her last job. After she sold the jewels, she should still have more than enough.

Probably.

As Roni leaned against the wall in the corner of the dark cell, she tried to figure out how much profit would come out of the evening after everyone got their handful. Maybe she'd get lucky, and the syndicate would forget some of her old debts.

The devils watching from hell weren't so kind.

"Fuck," she whispered as she added in the fees she'd have to pay to get out of jail. With two other ticks under her belt, it was bound to be a bundle. Gods and devils, it was getting to the point where it wasn't even worth the effort to be a criminal.

Especially when a nearby drunk stumbled into her corner and retched all over her boots.

Like everyone else, Roni scrambled to get away. She rubbed her boots along the wall to clean them, but that no doubt added to the general funk coating her shoes. And judging by the noises coming from her new corner, she'd be moving again soon. Most of the other inmates were surrounded by an alcoholic haze and were probably in jail for causing a ruckus, or they'd gotten themselves arrested because they had nowhere else to go, and the temperature had dropped overnight.

Fucking weather. The only reason she'd been caught was because the constables who were *supposed* to be on patrol had ducked into a doorway to warm up and had seen her climbing down the wall of the rich nob's house. Not fair. Such lying in wait should have been illegal.

And she'd been so happy at that moment. She'd gotten in and out without a single person in the house waking up. Even the dog had slept through it. When her toes had touched the street, she'd almost frozen at the cries of, "Halt," and "Stop, thief!" Luckily, she'd recovered her wits enough to run. It was a sloppy end to a perfect job.

Roni jammed her hands in the pockets of her too-thin jacket and leaned her back against the wall. She ducked her head, pushing her face under her collar to cut out some of the smell. Sleep had just begun hovering around the edges of her consciousness when someone shouted, "Veronique Bisset?"

Roni straightened and dragged herself out of the haze of pre-sleep. "Here." She threaded through the bodies toward where a jailer beckoned from the cell's open door. It was her turn before the night magistrate, no doubt Jasper Olyphant, and she needed all her wits, ready to be charming or contrite or sympathetic or whatever the jumped-up little asshole might want.

The jailer led her to a gloomy little room with thick stone walls and a wooden desk at one end that looked so pitted and worn, it could have been here since the Kingdom of Sarras began hundreds of years ago. Roni stumbled when she saw that a tired looking woman sat at the table instead of Jasper. Her long gray hair had been twisted in a braid that circled her head before hanging in a tail down her shoulder.

And it had a couple of jewels in it, the sign of another rich nob. Gods, Roni was in the shit now. Nobs stuck together.

The magistrate glanced up and scowled, her eyes glinting like a devil's in the lantern light. Roni's stomach shrank at the glut of contempt in that leathery face. No amount of charm, contrition, or sympathy could move a hunk of granite.

"Charges?" the magistrate asked.

The jailer stepped past Roni and tilted a piece of paper toward the light. The magistrate didn't even look at him as he read the constables' report, adding—quite vindictively, it seemed—that the stolen goods had been dumped in the canal and had yet to be recovered.

Roni decided to try for contrition. She shuffled her feet and hung her head, wanting a break from the magistrate's eyes if nothing else. Any speaking without being asked would earn her a cuff from the jailer. She'd never wanted a lawyer to speak for her more than now, but who could afford that?

The jailer finished his bored recitation. Roni glanced up, ready to hear the fee, the damn tax on a hard night's work. Then one of her friends could post the fee, go with her to retrieve and sell the jewels, and she could repay her friend's kindness.

With a suitable tip to keep their mouth shut.

She'd be lucky if she had enough left over for a decent meal.

The magistrate seemed to be studying the report. She leveled a glare Roni's way that spoke of more than just the resentment everyone felt for having to work on a feast day. When she smiled, it had all the charm of a badger. "You're no stranger to this place, Veronique."

Roni shivered. What the hell kind of game was this? Keeping up the contrition act, she winced and nodded weakly.

The magistrate laid down her pen, cruel smile in place, her metallic gaze steady, waiting.

"No, Magistrate," Roni said, adding a quiver in her voice. It wasn't difficult. She'd felt less malevolence from syndicate bosses armed with brass knuckles. "I'm sorry, Magistrate."

"No, you aren't, you odious, thieving piece of filth."

Roni gritted her teeth and fought to hide her shock. Even Jumped-up Jasper had never called her names.

"If I give you a simple fee and let you out, you'll continue thieving until one of your equally odious acquaintances eventually knifes you in some back alley and leaves you to die in squalor." Her smile never slipped.

Even after a deep breath, Roni couldn't keep up the contrition act, nob or not. She made herself meet that basilisk stare, knowing she shouldn't speak, but... "Pretty high and mighty talk for a fucking night magistrate dragged in to work on a feast day."

She braced herself for the cuff from the jailer and leaned forward slightly to lessen the blow. Still, she staggered when the hit came, the back of her head smarting, until the jailer pulled her upright again. The magistrate's smile widened, and Roni scowled, wishing for that lawyer again. The kingdom didn't have the right to charge her for possible future crimes.

Or for simply existing, for the gods' sake.

The magistrate scribbled something on the report. "How does a fine of five thousand sovereigns sound?"

Roni nearly barked a laugh. That had to be a joke. She'd never even seen so much money. That was far more than she'd get for the jewels and was one hundred times the normal fee besides. "You can't be serious."

Another swift slap to the back of her head made her swear and stumble, her head throbbing now and anger burning inside her.

"You're opting for the prison sentence, then?" the magistrate said without looking up. "Very well. Five years."

Roni's ears rang, and her heart tried to beat out of her chest. This couldn't be happening. She tried to protest, but her throat felt clogged, her tongue like ash. When the magistrate smiled again, Roni spat, "Fuck you."

The jailer dragged her around and shoved her out the door. "Maybe some hard labor will change your future," the magistrate called. "An interesting experiment."

"I'm not your damn experi—" Roni gasped as the jailer twisted her arm behind her back and marched her along. She walked on tiptoe, forgetting everything but agony until the jailer shoved her into a small cell, and she staggered into the far wall. She turned, ready to hurl some insults at any target, but the heavy door banged shut, encasing her in darkness.

Roni scrubbed her hands through her hair and paced, finding all four walls after only a few steps. Gods, this couldn't be real. Prison? With murderers and thugs? Hard labor? If they wanted her to die, why not kill her now?

The magistrate's smile had said it all: the devils wanted her to suffer first.

She shouted, beating on the walls, acting just like those prisoners she'd tutted over on her last visit to this place. If they'd kept their heads, presented whatever the magistrate wanted to see, they'd be set free, but if they acted like raging monsters...

She couldn't stop until her voice failed her, and her throat felt ragged. Rage felt like all she had left, but as she sagged to the floor and buried her head in her arms, she discovered despair waiting for her. Tears welled, and her chest felt hollow. She shook her head, telling herself not to give in. She'd lived on the streets since she was ten. She could survive this and whatever else these bastards wanted to throw at her. Prison was just like any other community. She could create a niche for herself, be whoever she needed to be. She could make allies, avoid enemies, keep her head down.

Nodding, she stood. She just needed a plan. Step one...

She had no idea.

"Ah, fuck." She dropped to the floor again and wept.

CHAPTER TWO

Zara strode through the Sarrasian army base with barely a look to either side, trusting that everyone and everything was in its place, from the canvas-covered barracks to the stone buildings housing arms and offices. One of the things that made the army perfect was its clockwork efficiency.

The fact that having a place here was also fulfilling her duty as a noble to serve her kingdom was an embarrassment of riches.

Several lower ranking soldiers fired off salutes, standing straight in their crisp brown uniforms with one fist over their hearts and murmuring a greeting as she passed. She returned the gesture without slowing, wondering if enough people now knew her rank that she could forego the gold helmet and jewelry while on base. The ornamental pieces were completely impractical, and her younger sister, Gisele, often teased her about them, but the honor of being a squad leader at twenty-six had the unfortunate side effect of people mistaking her youth for inexperience and not giving her the right amount of courtesy.

Military law decreed that squad leaders received salutes and salutations from common soldiers, so salutes and salutations she would have. It was the order of things. She would never understand why people like Gisele found that logic amusing. But then, most people were strange.

Not here, though. Zara smiled at the thought. She knew exactly how her day here would go. She'd been on one reconnaissance mission to the border of the Firellian Empire already. She and her squad had found nothing to indicate a Firellian invasion force, so now they were back to resupply, rest, then head out to another spot on the border and scout again. Today, she would receive knowledge of their exact target and so plan her route.

And visit with the Vox Feram, of course.

Zara sighed and slowed as anticipation flowed through her. She glanced at the sky. Her superiors had told her to report between twelve and thirteen bells for her new orders, and she'd planned to appear right at twelve to combat the anxiety of possibly being late, but perhaps she could arrive exactly halfway between twelve and thirteen. That way, she could see the Vox now.

And she still wouldn't be late.

Or early.

And no one would chuckle at her timeliness.

She switched direction, heading for the armory. Gisele would tease her for her "lack of discipline," while their older sister, Adella, looked on indulgently, silently siding with Gisele, but Zara wouldn't let that spoil her excitement.

Besides, they didn't know about the Vox. Her prize, her honor, her secret, the only thing in her life she would never have to share, not even if she wanted to.

Inside the armory, the desk clerk only had to see her to fetch the box. Zara gave him a nod, appreciating the anticipation of her needs before she set the box on another table and took a moment to center her thoughts.

The surface of the metal box had been discolored by time, but it still fitted so tightly together that there was no seam, no hinge. It was light, almost flexible, and impossible to break or cut. Like the Vox Feram, it had been made by ancient people with knowledge long forgotten. Such magic barely existed anymore, even for the greatest mages.

She placed her hand on top of the box, moving her fingers just so without having to think about it. Ever since the Vox had chosen her, she'd known where to touch this box to open it, even if she couldn't recall exactly how she'd done it afterward.

Her skin tingled, and a seam appeared in the box as it opened for her and her alone. A bright yellow jewel the size of her thumbnail waited inside, the many facets dazzling her like always, and she couldn't help picking it up, its golden chain slithering after it. Why would anyone want to resist such a thing of beauty? Such a treasure demanded to be looped around her wrist and fingers in a precise pattern—still without her remembering how—creating a glove that caressed her skin like a golden spiderweb, with the jewel nestled against the pulse in her wrist.

Deceptively strong, the chain and jewel were treasures beyond price on their own, even without the greater prize they now tied her to.

From a small room to the side, Zara felt the Vox Feram stirring. "You're early," the Vox said in her mind, their many voices coming together in a happy chorus.

Zara stepped through the door, stopping to stare as a ray of sunlight passed through a high window in the small room and lit the Vox's eagle form in sparkling, breathtaking radiance.

"Flatterer," the Vox said.

Zara chuckled. "It's not flattery if it's the truth."

The Vox shook out their wings, creating a rustle of delicate, tinkling metal. Their clawed feet clinked against the perch, and were it not for the sunbeam, an ignorant observer might think the Vox an ordinary golden eagle, except their body gleamed in the sun, metal in more than name.

Each of the hundreds of feathers had been cast from gold or silver or other metals even the most gifted blacksmiths couldn't identify, and each looked as real as any bird's. The beak and talons functioned as a flesh and blood bird's might, but they were cunningly sculpted from metal as well and were sharper than any blade.

Ancient, beautiful, intelligent, deadly. What a pity that the secret of the Vox's construction was lost to time. Even the faintest voices inside the Vox didn't know how old they were.

And Zara had their favor. She shivered through a wave of pride. Even the way the Vox functioned by using her life force was an honor. She understood now why Gisele sacrificed her body to magic.

Well, she understood more. She still didn't approve of that painful way of life. The Vox didn't cause her pain, and most of their forms only took a little of her life energy to function.

The Vox lifted their wings, and the tiny pieces of metal that made up their body shifted and flittered like minute scraps of paper caught in a maelstrom, rearranging the eagle's body into the smaller form of a falcon before they hopped upon her gloved wrist.

"Shall we?" they asked.

Zara nodded and took them into the sun. Everyone she passed gawked as the Vox gleamed like a precious jewel. Zara straightened her shoulders, just as she had the day the Vox's former partner had died, and the Vox had chosen her out of everyone in the Sarrasian army. They'd said she possessed the same sort of heart as them. At the time, she'd been proud but also fearful, as the Vox's former partners had never been able to adequately describe what it felt like to merge with the ancient object. The fear had fled the moment she'd looped the chain around her wrist as if she'd been born knowing how.

And afterward…she couldn't even think of the right words to describe the bond. Maybe the words didn't exist. Complete connectivity, that came close. Words like best friend and soul mate acquired meaning for the first time.

And the Vox had agreed. She'd felt them doing so. Not struggling to understand someone or make herself understood had been the best feeling in the world.

"Look out," the Vox said. "It's your newest annoying hanger-on."

Zara changed direction even before she glimpsed Keelin Hoffman through the Vox's eyes. She'd met and loathed Keelin even before she'd bonded with the Vox, but it was nice to know they didn't like her either. Zara had never had to interact with her much, until her father, a colonel, had promoted his daughter to the same rank as Zara.

And Keelin was two years younger.

And useless.

And now that she and Zara were the same rank, she thought they were friends.

"We should be grateful she works a desk instead of leading soldiers to their deaths in the field," the Vox said with a sigh. "She's seen us. I take back the gratitude."

"Zara," Keelin called.

"Is she far enough away that we can pretend we didn't hear?" Zara asked softly.

"Maybe. If she doesn't…no, she's running to catch up." The Vox spoke softly, too, even though no one else could hear them. Probably habit, the same reason Zara usually spoke out loud when the Vox could hear her thoughts. At least the mind communication left the Vox free to mumble the true but uncharitable thoughts they shared about other people.

"Keelin," Zara said as she turned.

Keelin jogged to a halt, her red curls bouncing around her face when they should have been tied back or under a helmet. Her entire being exuded a joviality inappropriate for a military base.

"I didn't know you were back," Keelin said. "You never come by to say hello."

Why the hell would she? "Hello," she tried now. "Well, if that's all." She tried to turn toward the practice field again.

Keelin guffawed, though nothing was funny. "When are you marching out again? We should have lunch before then."

Zara clucked her tongue. "My schedule is classified, as well you know, and I usually lunch with my squad or at home."

Keelin continued to twinkle at her. "I wouldn't mind eating with your squad." She stepped closer. "Or seeing your home."

"Gods," the Vox said. "She's being very obvious today about wanting a space in your bed."

Ah, so that was it. Zara fought the urge to shudder. She had enough trouble reading the people in her own house; she did not need that extra complication in the one place she felt most at home. She liked being romantically pursued about as much as she liked chewing glass. "I'm afraid we must be going."

"I'll walk with you."

Zara and the Vox sighed in unison. If only Keelin was a rank lower. Then Zara could order her away or ignore her. Instead, she began walking, hoping an escape would present itself.

"Is it true he can turn into any kind of bird?" Keelin asked, nodding at the Vox.

"They. The Vox has no gender, nor do they wish for one. And yes, they can turn into any kind of bird."

Keelin's eyebrows lifted. "Any bird? A hawk? A vulture? A chicken?"

The Vox stirred, metal feathers tinkling, many voices darkening in anger. "Chicken, indeed. I should disembowel her for that."

Zara snorted, hoping that was a joke. Having a commander disemboweled by an ancient artifact would require a lot of paperwork. "They have no wish to become anything besides raptors." At Keelin's questioning expression, Zara added, "Eagles, hawks, falcons, vultures, and owls, the birds of prey."

"Pity. It would make such a pretty songbird. Or a peacock, or a pheasant, really." She laughed. "My mother would give quite a lot for even one of those feathers in a new hat."

"Disemboweling and decapitation," the Vox said. "The only cure for such an acute case of witlessness."

Zara smoothed their cold feathers. "Please stop making terrible suggestions, Keelin. They can hear you, and they do not approve."

Keelin gave her a dubious look. Zara kept down a wave of frustration, telling herself to be a little compassionate. A talking metal bird had been hard to believe in before she'd experienced them for herself.

"I suppose I must take your word for it," Keelin said. "It's not like you can prove it by asking a question only a bird would know the answer to. Even if I could think of one, I wouldn't know the right answer, either."

As she began to chatter about what birds might know, the Vox continued to groan, and Zara wished she could join in. She halted on the edge of the practice field, just down from the obstacle course. Other falconers were training a short distance away. Zara threw her gloved arm up to give the Vox some lift, and they leaped into the air, wings outstretched, then flapping rapidly to propel them into the bright blue sky.

Zara wanted to close her eyes and fly with them in her mind, but Keelin said, "You will be careful, won't you?"

Zara blinked out of the Vox's senses and scanned the field for possible danger before staring at her.

"When you leave for your next mission," Keelin said, smiling.

Zara frowned. "Of course. What a silly question."

"It's not silly for someone to worry about you," Keelin said with a frown.

After thinking for a few moments, Zara decided it was. "I'm very good at my job." She thought of what Adella might say about trying to see things from another's perspective and hit upon the answer. "Ah, but we've never been on a mission together, so I must forgive you for not knowing how skilled I am." She tried to look understanding and hoped it worked. "But my rank and the fact that the Vox chose me should tell you something."

Now Keelin stared as if Zara had lapsed into another language.

"She doesn't understand," the Vox said, their voice fainter with distance.

"Right," Zara said, thinking fast until she uncovered the obvious reason again. "I see why you're confused. I earned my rank through skill, you see, which is how many people earn it. But you have yours because of who your father is."

Keelin stepped back, her mouth open, and her cheeks darkening as if Zara had struck her. "You...how dare you?"

Oh hell. Something had gone wrong. Zara replayed the conversation, looking for an error, but it was all true.

"It was the part about her only having her rank because of her father," the Vox said, sounding amused.

"I didn't mean that as a joke," Zara said. "Perhaps it's supposed to be a secret?" She looked around to see if anyone could have overheard. "I've heard it mentioned many times, so I assumed it must be common knowledge."

Keelin darkened further, and tears glittered in her eyes. "How could you say that to my face?"

Now that was just absurd. "Which part of you should I have said it to?"

Keelin barked a humorless laugh. "You won't be seeing any of my parts anytime soon."

That couldn't be literal. Was she rescinding her earlier offer of lunch or lovemaking?

The Vox laughed. "The latter one. Or probably both."

"Oh," Zara said, relieved. "Good. That's okay. I'm not attracted to you, so you don't have to worry."

By the way Keelin's face shifted from red to purple, that had made things worse.

"I'm sure someone else will find you attractive," Zara tried, hoping her smile conveyed positivity. "Perhaps…" She looked around for someone to ask.

"Don't do me any favors," Keelin said. "I may only be as *attractive* as the ugliest of cows, but I can find my own lovers, thanks." She stalked away before Zara could wonder aloud how one judged the attractiveness of cows.

The Vox was still sniggering when they returned to her and explained why Keelin had been offended, though Zara still couldn't see the sense in any of it.

"Why does she care what I think? And why can you understand her better than me?"

"Experience," the Vox said. "Maybe if you had more than one lifetime behind you, you'd get it."

She doubted it, but one good thing had come out of the afternoon. Keelin was gone, and Zara had a few minutes left to fly in peace, far above the petty concerns of those below.

CHAPTER THREE

R oni expected to stay in the company of the constabulary for one more night, given how slow the wheels of law usually turned. She was fine with delaying her trip to prison. It gave her more chances to dream of escape. She had just had her gruel and moldy bread breakfast and was about to engage in some serious planning when her door flew open.

She scrambled to her feet in confusion when a shadowy figure beckoned from the doorway. "But I thought—"

The shadow grabbed her by her shirt front with one beefy arm and dragged her into the dimness of the hall.

"Nice to meet you, too," Roni mumbled as she got her feet and breath back.

Out of the shadows, the guard's body proved as meaty as that one arm. Her expression was so stony, her face seemed made of crags, and her pale hair wasn't even an inch long, perfect for showing off what little remained of her left ear and the wealth of studs adorning her right.

Roni glanced toward where another guard was fitting leg irons on the first in a line of four other prisoners. Unlike the city jailers in their uniforms of gray wool and bad attitude, these guards wore leather armor. Roni swallowed as her hideous breakfast threatened to reappear. What the hell kind of place was prison if the guards needed armor?

Gods, she was going to need all the help she could get.

She tried a cheeky grin with the beefy guard. "You don't have to bother with the irons for me, serrah. I don't steal lives, only valuables." She winked. "And hearts."

The guard's expression matched the wall so exactly, Roni bit back a joke about not being able to tell them apart.

The second guard was finished with the first prisoner and moved to the second. Roni's heart picked up speed. She could bolt, hoping she found the way out before anyone caught her and try for freedom.

But the way that arm had shot out just now…Beefy was large, but she wasn't slow.

Roni's emotions bubbled like a pot of stew. She licked her lips and wanted to stay quiet, but she had to do something. "Who cuts your hair?" she blurted, knowing the question made no sense, but she didn't care. She ran a hand through her own shoulder-length locks. It still had a few pins keeping it out of her face. "I like to keep mine short, too. Well, not as short as yours, as you can see."

The manacles made a loud *click-clack* as they went around the third prisoner's ankles, and the sound echoed inside her. Why had they let her keep the hair pins? Because they couldn't do a damn thing to armored guards? Maybe they wanted to give her a small chance against the vicious killers in prison or the option to do everyone a favor and kill herself.

And why the hell wouldn't this woman speak?

"Um." The leg irons rattled as the guard lifted them. He stepped closer. Roni told herself not to weep like someone ahead was doing. She couldn't be weak. "There's been a mistake," she whispered, unable to just shut the fuck up. She shifted as the guard kneeled at her feet, and Beefy put a hand on her shoulder. Roni clamped her teeth on a scream as that horrible clicking sound echoed around her. She could feel the cold iron through her trousers, and the weight was as heavy as her despair.

As the second guard began to lead them out, Roni turned to Beefy again, desperation screaming inside her. "Please help me."

The very worst thing to say where she was going, but there it was.

Beefy tilted her head and frowned. "Just keep your strides short."

Her voice was beauty incarnate, and when she turned Roni to face the backs of the others and gave her a gentle prod, Roni obeyed, letting those words flutter in her mind. They weren't just instructions on how to walk in leg irons. They were a mantra for her life right now. Little steps through life, taking each situation as she found it. She didn't have years in prison ahead of her. She had months, weeks, days, a series of mornings, noons, and nights. She held on to that through the jail and into the light and onto a wagon where another chain connected her to her fellow inmates.

Roni breathed deeply of the fresh air, feeling giddy, still nauseated, detached from herself, but drawn to Beefy, who drove the cart with her fellow guard. Perhaps her cart-mates might all feel such connectivity, forming a bubble of safety before they even reached the prison walls.

She looked at the man next to her and smiled.

He leaned back, frowning. "Keep your eyeballs and your teeth to yourself, or I'll rip 'em out of yer head."

Well, there went that bubble.

Roni lowered her chin to her chest and let despair settle over her like a cloak, tempted to end her life before any parts of her were ripped from any others.

And she hadn't even gotten to prison yet.

The admission process at the prison felt like a nightmare. She didn't dare look up as they searched her for weapons, covered her and her clothing in stinging delousing powder, and shepherded her through hallways filled with crying, muttering, and swearing. She was just getting used to moving through life like a downtrodden sheep when the pushing stopped at last.

Now what?

She could see her breath, so it was cold, but warm light hit the top of her head. She dared to look and found herself outside again, though stone walls encased this small yard made of dirt and rocks, and other prisoners wandered around, some eyeing her curiously but most seeming to focus on their companions.

Roni was frozen for a moment, unsure of what to do, where to go. Uncertainty got a person caught or killed. *When in doubt, blend in*. It was one of the first lessons she'd learned. A quick glance around revealed several loners leaning against the walls near the guarded doorway she'd just come through. Fantastic. She copied their stance and tried to project their aura of anonymity, too, finding comfort in the chameleon-like powers she'd always possessed.

Ignore me. I'm one of you.

Her ability to act however someone wanted her to would no doubt come in handy later.

Or sooner, judging by the way several people were now staring at her boots. They were secondhand and were almost worn through near the toes, but they seemed better than most of the footwear she could see. Roni tried to summon Beefy's stoic, no-shit-taking attitude and had to hope no one could hear her pounding heart. One person she could get away from, but an entire gang? And there wasn't anywhere to hide. She was probably safe near the guards, but they wouldn't be around all the time. She needed more of a plan. Damn, why hadn't she been paying attention when they'd marched her out here?

She kept her head low and scanned the people watching her from under her lashes. When everyone finally left off coveting her boots and went about their business, she thought maybe her badass bluff had worked.

Until she felt the heat of someone beside her.

She told herself not to look, but when the someone said, "It's Veronique, isn't it?" Roni started so hard, she squeaked.

This woman gave her a kind smile. She wore a dalmatica like a nobleman. It draped from throat to ankle and looked warm and snuggly…and was as pristine as her face, where everyone else bore a hint of dirt. Her salt-and-pepper hair was slicked back and cascaded over her shoulders like a shimmery waterfall. Her pale face brightened further as Roni stared, her smile highlighting laugh lines and making her dark eyes twinkle.

"I'm sorry," she said. "I didn't mean to scare you." She glanced around. "This can be a fearsome place."

Roni was so happy to hear a friendly voice, she almost whooped or wept and everything in between. "It is." She bowed. "My friends call me Roni, Serrah…" As the woman nodded regally, Roni tried to place her and failed, though the face and bearing were nagging at her mind.

The woman cocked her head. "I'm not surprised you don't remember me. You were barely more than a child when we met. I imagine you've dealt mainly with my sister's subordinates. Or my brother's, perhaps."

Pieces fell into place with those words. She'd only dealt with one family who could claim subordinates. "You're Julia Esposito." The eldest member of the Newgate Syndicate, the criminal overlords in charge of Roni's thieving ground.

"You do remember." Julia's smile was warm, matronly. Roni wanted to believe it, but there were too many stories about how Julia Esposito ruled her family even from prison. They said she could even leave these walls whenever she liked, but it was safer for her here, surrounded by allies, and with the head untouchable, the Newgate Syndicate would never fall.

Not even to her siblings.

If Roni stayed close to her…

She put on her best fawning smile. "Thank you for coming to my rescue, Serrah Esposito. I feared for my safety on my first day." Well, feared for her boots, but she needed all the sympathy she could get. "You must let me repay you." Surely, Julia would have some use for her. She could do laundry for three years or cook or clean, whatever got her out alive.

"How kind. And you don't have to worry. No one will harm you now."

Birdsong and choirs of angels sang in Roni's mind, exulting so loudly, she almost missed Julia's next words:

"Not after I've made it clear I want to kill you myself."

The birds and angels died, and Julia's smile never slipped.

"P…pardon?" Roni had to have misheard, could barely hear now through the rushing in her ears.

"My contacts tell me you weren't arrested with any money, and you are very late with your tithes, yet you continued to work our patch."

"I have the jewels."

Julia *tsked*. "On the outside. I'm afraid it's now or never."

Roni swallowed hard, her throat like sand. "I hid them. Someone could get them. I'll tell you where."

"Oh, Roni." Her sympathetic look seemed to steal all the air. "Now, how would it look if I let you keep breathing after you've broken our trust? I'll tell you what." She rested an elegant hand on Roni's shoulder. "Tell me where the jewels are, and you'll die peacefully in your sleep." Her grip tightened. "Instead of any less pleasant options. And," she added like a street merchant offering a bonus, "I'll give a few coins to your next of kin to make up for taking one of their breadwinners."

Nope, that still sounded awful, even with no kin to worry about. Through the panic jangling in her head, Roni saw the night magistrate's face and wondered if she'd been set up, how long the syndicate had been looking for her.

And like the night before in jail, she wanted to keep her mouth shut, but it took off without her, and she said, "Where did I stash the jewels? Hmm. Did you try looking up your ass?"

Gods and devils, that smile slipped now.

Ah well, if she was going to die, best to piss off as many people as possible.

CHAPTER FOUR

The rest of Zara's day went as planned, starting with sadly putting the Vox Feram back in the armory, then meeting with Colonel Lopez, her commanding officer, to get her next scouting location. She'd been to the Firellian border once already, visiting the first in a series of watchtowers that lined the Sarrasian side of the Kingfish River. They'd reported seeing nothing suspicious on the river below, but the rest of the border had to be checked, even though a tall cliff ran along the Sarrasian side of the river, protecting it until the mountains and their unpassable heights rose on one end and the other sloped gradually down until it met a well-defended plain and forest.

As part of the force protecting all of it, Zara felt a jolt of pride. She was happy to have a destination, a duty. She didn't even need to be told about anything specific to look for. Everything out of the ordinary would be noted in her report. Colonel Lopez had once told her that her reports were legendary. Gisele had said that was sarcasm, but she didn't know what she was talking about. Anyone who chose the constant pain of the mages' guild over the army wasn't using all the brain power she should be.

After she'd gotten the location, Zara was dismissed, her duties at the base done for that day as her sergeants were off-duty and resting, and the rest of her squad was taking their time off among the group of waystations on the way to the border, closer to their families.

Adella had said it was very generous of the army to have scouts patrol close to their homes. Zara didn't see the generosity angle.

Rather, she suspected scouts were posted near their homes so they had all the more reason to do their job properly.

Not her squad. They felt the same duty as her. But other, more undisciplined squads might need an incentive.

If Keelin ever got a squad of her own, it would no doubt need even more inducement than that.

Zara paused along the sidewalk and took a deep breath. She didn't need to think of people and why they did what they did. She was on her way home, would hopefully be the only one there, and let her internal map loose in her mind, thinking through the various routes. She knew most of them by heart anyway, but there was nothing better than examining each and weighing the options.

Smiling, she strode homeward again, staying to one side of the snow-encrusted streets, the one that had spent the most time in the sun. The wide avenues of the Oligarch's Ward always caught more daylight than most other streets. As she watched several people go skidding or sliding on the other side, she bit her tongue. She'd learned early on that pointing out illogic in most people's actions rarely earned her a thank you.

If only she could take the Vox home. Then someone could at least listen to and agree with her imaginary scolding. But even knowledge of it was forbidden outside the army. Probably for the best. If she took them home, no doubt Gisele would try to dismantle them to determine how they worked. The Vox would wound her, and that wouldn't make anyone happy, especially Adella, who would then want to take revenge on the Vox. She'd convince her lover, Bridget, to help her, and…oh, it would be a giant mess. Emotions would be flying about all over the place, and people would be shouting, and Zara wouldn't know which way to turn, and she didn't want her sisters maimed or upset.

Best if the Vox stayed put.

Though she would have loved to look through their eyes as they soared above these cobbled streets, winged through the knots of carriages and cloaked pedestrians, and dodged between the noble houses.

Then they could both see everyone's illogical actions. Like the amblers she was now forced to slow behind. They gawked at the houses, pointing and remarking. Zara changed her mind. It was hard enough navigating these streets when she wasn't half-out of her body. Repressing a grumble, she stepped into the street during a gap between the hustling carriages and leaped back to the pavement in front of the slow-moving clog so she could walk at a decent pace again.

She put the irritating thoughts from her head as she turned onto her home street, where the traffic was much thinner. She rubbed her hands, looking forward to some nice orderly task while she planned her route. She was supposed to be resting. "Idle," Colonel Lopez had said. Higher-ranking officers always used words like *idle* and *rest* for these times between missions. "Take a load off," she'd heard. And, "put your feet up." No one ever explained what she was supposed to put her feet up and do. Stare at the wall? Nap? She shuddered. Was that what her squad did with their time off?

She'd never bothered to ask. So far, most of them seemed to reserve slacking for when she wasn't around, so everything worked as it should.

Just outside her front door, Zara stopped and breathed deep again, letting her mind truly shift from work to home, where no one saluted, but there was still peace to be had, especially when Gisele wasn't there.

The foyer was quiet, and she heard nothing from the kitchen or upstairs. Blissfully alone. She hurried past the one sitting room Adella left open—and furnished—while the other sitting room still stood closed. Adella had wisely not wasted the money she'd lately inherited on more furniture, at least not yet. Zara approved of that. There were only so many places a person could sit in a day, and they'd done without most of the rooms in their ancestral home for much of their lives.

The kitchen, the heart, was as furnished as it needed to be, with a high table where everyone ate, and the chairs and bench sitting next to the giant fireplace on the kitchen's farthest end. She paused as she caught sight of the other chair that had joined the three that always sat there. This chair had been there for weeks, but she'd been gone when it had arrived, and it still gave her pause.

Bridget's chair.

Zara couldn't contain another shudder. She had no quarrel with Bridget Leir, not anymore, after Bridget and Adella had worked out their differences. More than that, Bridget's company was often pleasant. She didn't chatter, she helped around the house, and she oftentimes played soothing melodies on her mandolin. Better than all that, she made Adella happy, and Adella's hard work to keep their family afloat deserved to be rewarded.

But Bridget was another person in their space, and sometimes, that felt like a seed caught between Zara's teeth that she couldn't quite reach.

She laid her helmet on the table, took off her uniform jacket and sword belt, and tied an apron around her waist. She had just enough time to make some bread to go with the soup simmering in the oven for dinner. She smiled anew as she worked. Baking and cooking brought order to chaos, raw ingredients to their destiny. She dug in the pantry and paused again, frowning.

Someone had moved the salt.

It had to be Bridget, no doubt an accident, but Zara couldn't help a ping of annoyance. Gisele had stopped mischievously moving her things when they were children. Adella had threatened to cut off Gisele's allowance after Zara had nearly cried because the flour and baking sugar had been swapped.

That had been a hard day. Zara had spent two days after that in her room, willing the world into order again.

Now she simply swallowed her aggravation and put the salt in the correct spot. She'd have a word with Adella, unsure of the protocol for berating one's sister's paramour. If that didn't work, she might start leaving notes. Or labels. She looked to the pantry. Yes, labels might do very well. Then if they had visitors or if Gisele found a live-in paramour one day, Zara wouldn't have to keep repeating herself.

Nodding, she made a mental note to work on these labels after her next mission. Everyone would no doubt appreciate it.

The air shifted in the kitchen. Someone had opened the front door. Zara cocked an ear in that direction. Voices, Adella and Bridget. They shut the door quietly, as Zara had asked them to, so when they came into the kitchen, she gave them a smile.

"Something smells good, Zara," Bridget said.

She nodded. "Thank you."

Bridget wasn't in her patchwork coat, so she hadn't been out fulfilling her nightingale duties, and Adella wore a simple dress with no official badges, so they hadn't been to any political meetings. It was far too late for lunch and too early for dinner, so that left...

"How was shopping?" Zara asked.

Bridget thumped the table and grinned. "How does she know? We don't even have any bags or parcels." She laughed, her tanned cheeks rosy from the cold outside, and her short dark hair was damp with a bit of snow.

Zara handed her a towel and gave one to Adella for good measure.

Adella winked. "Our Zara is just that sharp." She wore her blond hair in a tail down her back and with a simple row of pearls braided into the sides and across her forehead. She'd adopted a simpler style since being dismissed from her ambassadorial job. Her bright blue eyes were merry, though she looked pale under the bloom of pink on her cheeks and nose. Maybe now that she was unemployed, she would be able to get a bit of sun.

While looking for a new job, of course. Adella wouldn't last long as a noble of leisure. She liked to stay busy, one of her most admirable qualities.

"But how do you—" Bridget started.

Adella made a strangled noise that sounded like, "No, don't ask," but all hurried together.

Zara didn't know why. She was happy to answer. "Through a simple process of deduction."

With a small groan, Adella put her head in her hands as she sat at the table. Bridget looked between them curiously as she sat, too. Zara frowned. She didn't need the Vox to tell her that Adella disliked her lectures on the deductive process. But Bridget had *asked*.

When Zara was through explaining, Bridget's eyes were wide, as if she was stunned. Zara didn't blame her. It was a lot to absorb for the uninitiated. She thought an ex-spy would understand deduction better than anyone. Maybe her lack of understanding was why she was a spy no longer. Hmm, a sensible decision on her part, then.

Adella hadn't lifted her head. Zara bit back an offer to teach Bridget some more, at least until Bridget had a chance to absorb what she'd already said.

"Coffee?" Zara offered.

"Thanks," Bridget mumbled just as Adella said, "Oh gods, yes."

They must have had a tiring day. She filled two mugs and set out the cream and sugar. Bridget and Adella shared a look she couldn't read before Adella said, "I told you not to ask."

Zara rolled her eyes. "You never want to learn, Adella."

"That's not true," Adella said around her mug. "I just learn better…with hands-on instruction." She shared another look with Bridget and chuckled, both of them turning even redder.

Even if the hands-on learning remark was true, the blushing and giggling told her they'd veered into sex joke territory, so she didn't respond, going back to her pantry where things made sense.

"Did you get your new orders?" Adella called.

"Yes, and you know I can't talk about them."

"I was just asking if they existed, not for specifics."

"You were going to ask that next." Zara brought out some cookies that paired well with coffee.

Adella had the grace to look a little guilty. "Maybe, maybe not."

"Are we allowed to guess?" Bridget asked, her smile friendly, not mocking.

That deserved an honest answer. "Guess all you like, but I won't say if you're right or wrong."

"Well…" Bridget dunked a cookie and stared at the ceiling for a moment. "If I was your commanding officer, I'd be sending you to the border, naturally, and with all the kerfuffle about the Kingfish River before the Firellian ambassador was escorted from the kingdom, my guess is there. Unless that's where you just were." She took a bite and glanced at Zara.

She shrugged. Correct, but she couldn't say that.

"Forget it," Adella said. "She won't crack."

Bridget nodded. "I would have hated to try to get information out of you in the old days."

The type of day didn't matter, but Zara turned away instead of saying so, letting Adella's words say it for her. She'd already told one person today that she was good at her job, and that hadn't gone well, so she wouldn't risk it again.

They had an easy evening, with Gisele joining them fresh from her duties as a mage. She needed Adella's assistance to climb the stairs and change from her black robe and headdress. Her magic often caused her incredible pain. Zara bit her tongue on another lecture about how the military would suit Gisele better if she wanted to serve her country, and it wouldn't pain her like this. Gisele never listened anyway and usually resorted to childish name-calling, which never failed to get Zara's blood up and force her to say that if Gisele wasn't her sister, they would duel. Then Adella would be angry, and...

Zara dismissed that thought since Gisele was so obviously in pain.

Maybe once she was feeling better.

Zara made another mental note.

Supper was jovial enough. Zara tuned out the conversation, thinking of routes to the border, then dismissing them and considering others. She'd whittled her choices down to two when someone knocked on the front door.

Everyone froze, staring at one another. Adella's face turned fearful, and Bridget paled. "The sentinels?" Adella asked quietly, the words shaky. The sentinels had put her through a lot just three weeks ago, grilling all of them about Bridget and her last job as a spy.

Gisele made a fist, then whimpered and frowned. No doubt she wanted to use her magic if it came to a fight, but she was clearly tapped.

Zara dabbed her lips with a napkin and rose. When Bridget stood, too, Zara waved at her to stay put. She grabbed her sword belt and drew her saber on her way to the door. If it was the sentinels, they could damn well explain themselves to her satisfaction before she let them inside. If it was anyone else looking for a fight, she'd give it to them.

She kept the saber up as she swung the door open, the portal wide enough to give her time to brace before whoever was outside could attempt to come through.

A young woman in army brown with the stripes of a courier and the badge of a private stood on the doorstep, her salute faltering as she looked at the saber. "C...Commander?"

Zara lowered the weapon, and her heart eased back into its normal rhythm. "It's all right, Private. Something for me?"

"Yes, serrah." She handed over a sealed envelope. "I'm to await an answer."

Zara waved her in with the saber, then pointed to a spot in the hall for her to wait. Adella had relaxed her rules about visitors in the house, but Zara wanted as few people in her space as possible.

Before anyone could come check, she shouted, "It's just a courier for me," and broke the letter's seal in the light of the lantern by the front door.

As per protocol, it didn't have her name or her commanding officer's name, but she knew the neat handwriting. After a brief greeting, it told her to report back to the base tomorrow to begin training potential new members of her squad, conscripts chosen from Haymarket Prison.

Zara blinked and read that again, then a third time.

It didn't change. Haymarket Prison.

She looked to the courier to see if it might be a joke, but the girl was still staring apprehensively at the saber. Zara shook her head and read the letter again.

Prison.

Even Gisele wouldn't find this funny.

There were more words on the page. Zara read them hurriedly, desperate for some sanity. A new program, it said, in case more soldiers were needed in a hurry. She knew what that meant. The field marshals feared not having enough bodies if war broke out. But prisoners?

Yes, it said, scattered among squads and regiments, and her squad had been chosen as an experiment to see if the scheme had merit.

A criminal.

In her squad.

Her vision went blurry.

"Serrah?" the private asked. "Your response?"

She wanted to tell the private to go back to her commanding officer and laugh bitterly. That was her response. Or to refuse. But, no, she couldn't disobey an order. Her heart pounded, and she had no idea what to do. They expected her to serve with someone who not only eschewed order itself but who spit on the law?

"Serrah?"

"Zara?" Adella called from the kitchen. "What's going on?"

"I…" The words wouldn't come. A rushing noise filled her ears, and the air seemed heavy, thick enough for her to feel it rotating around her, twisting her stomach. She shut her teeth around a rush of bile.

When Adella approached her, worriedly looking at the courier, Zara almost shoved the letter at her but stopped herself at the last minute, dimly recalling that orders shouldn't be shared.

Adella reached for it anyway. Zara moved it away.

"It's okay, serrah," the private said brightly. "It's not top secret. In fact, the brass hopes it'll build some goodwill with those people arguing for rehabilitation instead of imprisonment."

Such people existed? And since when were any military orders not a secret? Zara was so confused that she didn't resist when Adella finally took the letter.

"Oh shit," Adella said quietly.

"Language," Zara mumbled woodenly, the words Adella always said to them.

Adella ignored her. "Um, tell them she'll be there." She handed the letter back to the courier, as per protocol. When the courier looked at Zara again, Adella waved her out the door. "Don't worry about her. She's…making a plan. She'll be there tomorrow. Good night."

"A criminal in my squad," Zara said once they were alone. "A criminal. In my squad."

"I know," Adella said softly, her touch light on Zara's elbow. "You'll find a way to work with them. Let's get you some water."

"Work with a criminal? How? Why?" Her world wouldn't fall into order. This couldn't be happening.

"Or maybe we should put you to bed." Adella's face loomed large in her vision, peering into her face. "Yep, I'm taking you upstairs."

Zara let herself be led up the steps as Adella called to the others to finish without them. Memories flashed in front of Zara's eyes of the last time Adella had taken her upstairs in order to explain things to her, cutting out any noise or people, any distractions. She'd said it was necessary when Zara's mind "went off the well-worn path."

Deep down, Zara was ashamed that she still needed something like this, a childhood remedy, but that shame couldn't get through the wall of confusion. A prisoner. In her squad. She could not make the ideas mesh no matter how she turned them. All she could do was put herself in Adella's hands and wait for the world to become clear again.

CHAPTER FIVE

Roni rested her head against the cold wall of her tiny cell. She didn't have to share, thank the gods, because the cell was barely three feet wide and six feet tall and *almost* deep enough to fully lie down in. The walls and floor were cold bricks, except for the bars that made up the door.

The sight of the cells lining both walls in this section of the prison had reminded her of a series of mail slots, and she hadn't believed people could fit in them until she'd done it. So much about the building was unbelievable and also depressing and frightening. She'd heard that it had once been a fortress, dating from Sarras's early history. It had clearly kept all the charm of an abandoned military outpost. It even had a tyrant to run it.

After Roni's oh-so-incredibly smart remark earlier, Julia's face had gone as cold as ice, but she hadn't threatened Roni or fired off any angry words. She'd simply turned away, strode between the guards, and disappeared through the door that led inside. Everyone else had to wait until one of the guards blew a whistle before they could enter.

So the rumors about Julia Esposito having the run of this place were true.

The next few hours had been a mixture of berating herself and jumping at shadows. She'd received yet another bowl of revolting slop, had been assigned an overseer and work gang for the hard labor that began tomorrow, and had been put to bed early in her wall slot because as the guard said, "You'll need all your strength in the morning."

Because she'd probably be dead by afternoon.

Julia had no doubt taken the day to cement her murderous plans, and part of Roni wondered if she'd even wait until tomorrow when she had all night.

No, surely Julia wouldn't interrupt her own sleep to kill some lowlife, even if said lowlife had mentioned hiding things up Julia's ass. Tomorrow would work just as well.

If only Roni could really believe that. She sat against the back wall on the pile of straw that served as her bed. She didn't want to lie down, couldn't be caught off guard. And as one chatty neighbor kept reminding her, if she lay down, she had to decide where to keep her toilet-bucket.

"Near your head, and you'll have to smell it all night, of course," the chatty neighbor said yet again. They hadn't given a name, and the voice was too raspy for her to tell anything else about them. "You clean it every day, but you can't ever get rid of all the smell." They clucked their tongue. "Make sure you hold on to your own bucket, mind. There's some that'll try to switch out dirty for clean."

Roni fought down a surge of bile and pressed her forehead into the cold bricks. "Please stop talking."

"But if you put the bucket by your feet, you risk kicking it over in your sleep." They cackled, the horrid sound ending in a coughing fit. "Bet you wish you were shorter, eh?"

Roni felt like praying for the first time in ages. Not for her life— she accepted that she was doomed—but that Chatty Neighbor would fall asleep and leave her be. Maybe Julia Esposito had arranged for them to be together so Roni would welcome death when it came.

Eventually, someone down the row threatened to cut out Chatty Neighbor's tongue the next day, and they fell silent.

"Gods," Roni whispered. Why in the hell was she always getting herself into this kind of shit? Why couldn't she keep her fucking mouth shut? Her fellow thieves often praised her acting skills, but the minute she got angry…

Well, she wouldn't have to worry about her failings much longer. Maybe it would be best if Julia caught her asleep.

She closed her eyes and wriggled down a bit, still with her back against the wall. But sleep came in fits and starts. She jumped at every noise. All she managed were half dreams of knives in the dark that left her shaking, her heart pounding when she woke and had to remember where she was all over again. By the time the sounds of people stirring filled the hall, her back was full of knots, and her head throbbed in time with her heart.

Chatty Neighbor serenaded her with another coughing fit before saying, "Which did you choose, newbie? Head or feet?"

Roni rolled her eyes as she stretched but decided that talking sounded better than trying to get more restless sleep. "Feet. I didn't lie down."

"Ha. That's another way of doing it. I'll add it to my list."

Roni rubbed her temples and wondered if Julia Esposito was already waiting in the hall, if the gods were cruel enough to make this Roni's last conversation. "I won't have to pick head or feet much longer."

"Planning on breaking out? I'll keep you company."

She considered keeping mum, but what the hell. Her comment about Julia's ass had no doubt signed her up for the most painful death imaginable. She couldn't make it worse by telling everyone of her impending doom. "Julia Esposito is going to kill me."

The silence from next door stretched for several minutes. Maybe Chatty Neighbor wasn't so keen to talk to someone in Julia's bad books. "That's unfortunate," they finally said.

Roni had to laugh so she wouldn't cry, but she kept the noise to a minimum, too tired to shriek. "At least you'll have someone new soon to give the bucket speech to."

"That *is* a bright side."

Now that she had admitted her fate aloud, Roni couldn't control her fear. Desperation crawled up her throat, operating her mouth much like it had in jail. "Can you help me?"

Pathetic. She cringed. And when Chatty Neighbor didn't say anything, she wanted to cling to the bars and take back her plea and then scream for Julia to come fight her. Gods and devils, she had to be strong until the end.

Except...she didn't want to die here. She wasn't certain about what she wanted out of life, but it sure as fuck wasn't to be murdered in prison after an inflated sentence for stealing from a family who could damn well afford it.

The swirl of emotions left her grinding her teeth. Maybe she could shout. She'd scream the place down and wake everyone so her misery would have some company.

"No one can help you," Chatty Neighbor said.

Roni exhaled, her anger evaporating like morning mist and leaving room for despair to come creeping back.

"I would if I could," Chatty Neighbor added. "You seem smart, bucket-wise."

Roni laughed again, long and loud this time, with only a few sobs between guffaws. Several voices yelled for her to shut up, but she kept going. Maybe if she pissed off enough prisoners, there'd be a mob fighting one another to get to her. They'd get in Julia's way, and since inconveniencing Julia Esposito seemed the only thing Roni could manage in here, she'd take it.

Her damn mouth getting her into trouble again.

By the time the guards came to open the cells, everyone was awake and talking, most grumbling at Roni and Chatty Neighbor, who'd joined in the laughing at some point. She stood as the door to her cell opened, surprised and oddly pleased to see Beefy the guard again.

Beefy held up a hand as she tried to exit, the exact opposite of the last time. Roni frowned, curious, but as usual, Beefy's face gave nothing away. "What is…" Roni's mouth went dry as she realized that the guards probably worked for Julia Esposito, too. "Is this it?"

Beefy didn't seem to hear as she looked back and forth down the hall. The other prisoners filed past, shepherded by guards, and none stopped to look. Roni licked her lips. Maybe she could make a mad rush. Beefy was a slab of stone, but everyone had weak points. Roni could dive through her legs and run like hell.

Ha. To where? She was in a gods-cursed prison.

Roni took a step, and Beefy glanced at her again. "Wait," Beefy said.

Roni clenched a fist. She couldn't just stand here and die like a—

"Warden wants a word with you."

What? Roni sucked in a breath, wondering if she'd heard right. The…warden was going to kill her?

Beefy finally gestured for her to walk into the empty hall. She wished someone had lingered, even Chatty Neighbor, but she didn't see anyone as Beefy guided her off the cell-lined corridor and up a narrow circular staircase. The occasional arrow slit still adorned the walls—leftovers from the fortress era—but when Roni paused to relish the fresh air or try to get a glimpse outside, Beefy gave her a prod in the back.

The warden, a tired-looking man with all the vitality of a corpse, waited at the top of the stairs in a turret-turned-office. He sat behind a small desk and only glanced up as they entered, reminding Roni of the night magistrate but without the malice.

"Prisoner Veronique Bisset," he said with a sigh.

"Yes, Warden," Beefy answered. She pulled Roni to a halt on a threadbare rug with a nice view out the lone window. This one was large enough to lean out of, the shutters thrown open, though the breeze was so cold, it made her shiver. When she craned her neck to try to catch a sunbeam, Beefy's hand on her shoulder made her face forward again.

She wanted to bark, "Where do you think I'm going to go?" but her sense won out over her mouth for once. The warden shuffled some papers, still not looking at her. Should she say that Julia Esposito planned to kill her? Would that help at all, or would he have the same answer she'd gotten from her neighbor?

It couldn't hurt to try.

She opened her mouth to speak, but the warden seemed to find what he was looking for. "You've been selected for the army conscription program." He sighed again, maybe tired of his job or tired of life. She could relate. She was...

Wait. "What?" she asked.

Beefy gave her another prod.

"Nonviolent, first sentence, fits the given skill requirements. It's a good match." With yet another deep exhale, he moved a paper forward. "I suppose the army doesn't think it can control prisoners who are violent? I would think they'd be better at killing enemy soldiers. Ah, well." He looked up at last, his dark eyes infinitely exhausted. "If you are approved by your new commanding officer, your prison sentence will be transmuted to a term of military service lasting no less than a year. Sign here."

Roni couldn't move, too busy replaying his words. Military service? Her? She tried to picture herself in an army uniform and failed.

But outside, she could escape Julia and anyone else in here who wanted to kill her.

"Sign the paper, stupid," Beefy muttered.

Roni started into action, lurching forward and reaching for the pen. She half expected Julia Esposito to swan in from nowhere and snatch freedom from her fingers. She signed so fast that she couldn't read her own name.

When Beefy led her from the room, Roni was tempted to kiss her, but all the prodding didn't leave room for that. She settled for humming with joy. Julia's goons couldn't get to her on an army base. And after enough time had passed and the Newgate Syndicate's anger had cooled, she could escape from the army, too.

It couldn't be that hard.

CHAPTER SIX

Zara marched to the base in the morning light, endeavoring to keep her stride brisk despite the heavy weight of embarrassment dragging behind her. Adella had to put her together again last night. Years of learning how to deal with any situation life could throw at her had been blown away by one stupid letter, one unfathomable decision on the part of her commanding officers.

"How does this happen?" she'd asked Adella last night. The shadows had seemed much too large in her tidy bedroom, grown since the night before, as though she had shrunk back into childhood.

"They're your superiors," Adella had said calmly as she'd brushed Zara's hair, another calming gesture that hadn't had to make an appearance in years. Zara hadn't been able to summon the voice to say she didn't need it. "You usually trust them to know what they're doing, so trust them now."

True. If her trust crumbled, the soldiers under her command could lose confidence, too, like a tower with the bottom blocks removed. "But...criminals?"

Adella had sighed. "I suppose it won't help to know that many people think their boss's decisions are stupid now and again."

"I'm not most people," they'd said at the same time, but Adella's light squeeze on Zara's shoulder had conveyed that the words were said with affection.

"I'm proud of you," Adella had said.

How or why hadn't made sense, but Zara hadn't forgotten how to take the emotion and leave the questions behind, at least as far as her sisters were concerned.

Sometimes.

"Think of it this way," Adella had said. "After our parents died, you trusted me to make the decisions, even after all the mistakes I made early on." She'd chuckled. "And even after you'd toyed with the idea that you should have been in charge."

All true. "You were learning without instruction. Mistakes were bound to happen."

"Perhaps that's the case with these orders to train criminals. It's a new scheme. It has no textbook. Mistakes will happen. You only have to trust that your superiors will choose someone suitable, criminals capable of being reformed, whose skills will suit the army. You're always telling Gisele that the army has a place for everyone. Here's your chance to prove it."

Another truth. Zara had held on to them like lifelines, forming a structure in her mind that could at least contain both criminals and the army, even if she still got a headache when she tried to connect the two.

In the morning, the shame of shutting down had bothered her more than the oxymoron of a criminal army. The humiliation helped her in one way and depressed her in another, more emotions that refused to mesh. Adella would tell her to embrace anything that made her work troubles easier, but embracing her embarrassment felt... wrong.

The thoughts were enough to distract her until she reached the base. Zara blinked at the fact that she didn't remember most of her journey, but she hadn't fixated on the criminals' problems, proving Adella right.

Once again.

That thought was only a tad grating, much less so than when she'd been a child.

So she held on to that as she marched to Colonel Lopez's office. She wasn't a child anymore, didn't have to surrender to the feelings that threatened to overwhelm her. She could deal with anything that came her way. More than deal with them, she could defeat them.

Just being on the base made her insides settle. The orderliness felt like a warm blanket wrapped around her shoulders. And no matter what else happened today, she would get to see the Vox Feram, a soothing balm to all these damnable emotions pinging around in her skull.

Inside the officer's command center, Zara removed her helmet and breathed in the strong scent of old leather and the faint whiff of smoke coming from the large hearth just past the grand staircase. The lieutenant manning the desk in the marble foyer stood and saluted. "This way, Commander. They're waiting for you." He gestured behind him down a hallway rather than at the stairs Zara usually climbed to report to Colonel Lopez.

But this anomaly soothed her rather than sending her spiraling again. The criminal army endeavor was a unique circumstance, so it made sense that everything surrounding it would also be unique. She wouldn't have to keep trying to incorporate the usual and the abnormal that way. She followed the lieutenant down the carpeted hallway, her surprise growing when he passed door after door until he finally stopped at a pair of ornate double doors bearing the inlay of a golden eagle clutching four arrows in each claw.

General Antonia Garcia's door.

Zara's unease retreated further into growing excitement. She'd only met the general once, right after she'd been promoted to commander. The general was the highest-ranking officer and leader of the base, and she reported directly to the field marshals who stood by the oligarchs' side.

Once the lieutenant knocked and opened the door, Zara strode past, her posture as straight as she could make it. She kept her eyes respectfully on General Garcia as she saluted, dropping her fist from her heart only after the general's gracious nod.

"Commander." In the light streaming from the window, it was easy to see every weathered line in the general's tanned face. Her elaborately braided hair led back into a tidy bun, and only a few strands of silver stood out from the black, making it hard to judge her age. But age didn't matter with such a legendary gaze. Some said that those eyes, one blue and one green, could penetrate to one's very soul.

Zara's soul seemed fine, but it *was* a very masterful gaze, one she didn't want to look away from. When General Garcia motioned to the other two people in the room, Zara had to look and repeat her salute.

"Colonel Lopez you know," General Garcia said, nodding to the tall, deeply tanned, bald man Zara normally reported to, who compiled all the information from the scouting units and passed that on to the general. "And this is Colonel Hoffman."

Zara repeated her salute for the very thin, redheaded man who frowned at her. His pale skin and coloring combined with his name triggered a memory. This was Keelin Hoffman's father.

He had gotten Keelin her position as a commander.

And Zara had offended her.

By accident, but experience had taught her that such excuses didn't normally matter. No doubt people had been acting very irrationally about that whole incident.

"Your squad has been selected for the army's new conscription program," General Garcia said. "And we've called you in today to meet your possible recruits." She gestured to the two colonels. "While I have my doubts about the program itself, Lopez and Hoffman seem to believe you'd be a good fit for this experiment."

"If anyone can turn a convict into a soldier, it's Zara," Colonel Lopez said with a faint smile.

Flattering, she supposed, but the idea of criminal soldiers still twanged inside her like a broken cog. She looked to Colonel Hoffman, but he only smirked, and she didn't need the voice of the Vox to explain that look. He was punishing her. For a non-crime she hadn't even realized she was committing at the time. He should have been punishing his daughter for being so emotional or for pursuing a sexual relationship with a fellow officer, but she supposed that was too much to expect from someone who'd promoted his unqualified daughter to commander in the first place.

Zara's temples tingled in anger, but she kept up a litany that Adella had given her long ago: Most people were irrational, and she couldn't expect that to change.

She kept saying it to herself while General Garcia explained about soothing the public regarding prison reforms and bulking up the army's numbers in case of war and finding a use for prisoners who showed unique talents in certain areas.

None of it made much sense. Why would the public care about prisoners? They were being punished because they'd broken the law, and that punishment should be severe enough to deter others from doing the same. And if the army needed numbers, they should recruit in a more efficient way. Also, as far as she was concerned, the only talents a prisoner needed was with whatever hard labor they were assigned.

But most people were irrational, and she couldn't expect that to change.

At last, she was turned over to the colonels, and she tried to hold on to the happiness of meeting the general again as they departed.

Outside, the colonels turned to one another, Hoffman frowning. "Don't you have somewhere else to be, Lopez?"

Colonel Lopez shrugged as he donned his helmet. "I'm interested."

Hoffman frowned harder and nearly slammed his own helmet on his head. He turned and strode away, gesturing for them to follow. Zara glanced between them and wished she was better at figuring out what was going on under the surface. Hoffman didn't seem pleased that Lopez was still with them, but he couldn't simply order someone of the same rank to be elsewhere. That much she knew, but the animosity confounded her. She knew why Hoffman was irrationally angry with her, but what did he have against Lopez?

"I tried to get you out of this assignment," Lopez said.

Aha. "Thank you, serrah."

"I knew it would upset you, Zara, but I was telling the truth in the general's office. You can train a former criminal if you put your mind to it."

Zara suppressed a shudder. If they hadn't served their time, how could they be a *former* criminal? That implied that being in the army was some kind of punishment, but...she took a deep breath. She could not chase the logic because there was none.

Most people were irrational, and she couldn't expect that to change.

"I helped whittle down the list of prisoners," Lopez said softly. "Mostly nonviolent thieves and burglars. I figured they might have some skills compatible with scouting. If left on his own, who knows what Hoffman would have stuck you with." He sighed. "What did you say to his daughter?"

Zara opened her mouth to give a recitation, but Lopez shook his head and held up a hand.

"Never mind. I don't think I want to know."

"Yes, serrah." In his place, she wouldn't have wanted to know either. She tried to keep her breathing deep and even and not let her distaste show.

Too much.

❖

Nothing had ever made Roni want a bath more than seeing a beautiful woman after she'd gone four days without a good scrub. And two and a half of those had been spent in jail or prison, neither up for the award of "cleanest place in town." At least she didn't have a mirror to see how awful she looked.

As if she would have been able to look anywhere but at this fit military officer with dark eyes, cheekbones for days, and the confident stride of a hunter. That whiplike gaze said anyone who didn't hop to her orders would be up for some serious punishment.

Yes, serrah, sign her up.

Roni tried to stand a little straighter among her fellow inmates, hating the weight of the leg irons that kept her from adopting a more confident pose. She did what she could to push her hair back, tucking some behind her ears and shifting the hairpins in an effort to flatten the top. She would have loved to wipe her face but suspected her hands were among the dirtiest bits of her person. If she was going to impress this hunter, she'd have to do it with charisma alone.

Good fucking luck. She forced down a sigh.

Two men with officer's badges stood by the hunter, and they conversed softly with each other, one holding a sheaf of papers. Two other soldiers watched Roni and her fellow convicts with intense frowns. What she wouldn't give to see Beefy's face, but the prison guards had abandoned them at the gates of the base.

When Beefy had helped her down from the prison cart, Roni had given her a smile that hadn't been returned, and Roni's, "What, no hug?" had been answered with a snort. She hadn't even gotten a chance to promise to visit before Beefy and her fellow guard had taken the cart a short way from the gate to wait for anyone who didn't make the first cut.

A snide-looking base guard had told them that some of them would be trained on an accelerated timetable, and that the prison cart would be back every morning for whoever failed. Well, Roni wouldn't be on it again. Whether that meant working hard and passing through this training or escaping at the earliest opportunity, she didn't know, but she wasn't going back to the short life that awaited her in prison.

She squared her shoulders. Now to pass the initial inspection of her soon-to-be commanding officer. Gods, she hoped it was the hunter. They were made for each other: nearly the same height, both tanned, used to working outdoors, and the woman had a fucking golden helmet. Who else but the perfect partner for a thief came with their own loot?

But how to play it?

The only army personnel she'd seen before were those who liked to slum it in the "bad" part of town where she lived. Drunken louts looking to throw their weight around. They appreciated "sass" but not a direct challenge. But the hunter didn't swagger like some cocksure bravo. She was composed, neat, above it. Until the redheaded man started gesturing to the prisoners, the hunter had ignored them, but now her face held a hint of disapproval if not outright disdain.

Damn, that was tricky. Meekness wouldn't help, not in the army. Eagerness could be doubted or misinterpreted. Something told her that flirting would get her ass thrown back on the cart faster than brandishing a knife. As the hunter walked down the line, eyeing each of them, Roni tried to mimic her, stiffening her spine, keeping her face attentive but uncaring, hiding her attraction.

If she decided to stay, there would be time for flirting after being sufficiently impressive.

The hunter examined Roni with the same half frown she'd given everyone else. Then she turned so abruptly, her long dark ponytail fluttered behind her. Roni's fingers twitched, but she resisted the urge to reach for it and run her fingers through those silky strands.

"How am I supposed to tell?" the hunter said to the other officers.

The redhead smirked, clearly enjoying the fact that she seemed confused. Some grudge there, useful to know. The bald man shrugged minutely and said, "Talk to them?"

With a sigh for the ages, the hunter looked down the convict line again. "My name is Commander Zara del Amanecer. I lead a scouting unit that will be taking on two of you." Her mouth twisted slightly. Commander del Amanecer was not happy at all.

"Besides the chance to get out of prison"—the commander's lip threatened a sneer—"why do you want to be scouts? How are you qualified?"

Leg irons jangled as everyone shuffled. "Spent some time in the woods," someone down the line said. "I can light a fire, set snares, that sort of thing."

The commander nodded. "Anyone else?" When no one answered, she began pointing at them one by one, asking "You?" over and over. She got various qualifications like small, muscled, sneaky, and one "Fuck you," who was pulled out of line and hauled back toward the gate.

Roni *tsked*. Even with the promise of freedom, some people just couldn't bear doing as they were told.

Wait. Gods and devils, that was the answer.

"I can follow orders," Roni said. When the commander fixed on her with lightning quickness, she added, "I don't know how to be a scout, but I'm smart enough to learn."

The commander nodded again, and she didn't sneer. Roni held on to the most fragile hope. The angels might not be dead. Someone in the heavens had smiled on her enough to bring her out here. They couldn't cast her to the winds now.

Please, please, please.

Her heart nearly stopped when the commander picked her. She'd train with four others, only two of which would make the final cut.

"Oh, thank you, gods," Roni whispered, hearing the angels sing once again even as a head rush nearly made her collapse.

Thankfully, the commander stalked away before Roni had a chance to fall at her feet and kiss her boots.

CHAPTER SEVEN

Zara now had prisoners training to be in her squad. She still couldn't quite reconcile that in her mind, so she put the felons firmly in a new category. They were recruits like any others. She had to tuck the prison part as far back in her subconscious as it would go.

Never easy. Just like her desire to bring back honest dueling. It would never happen, but she couldn't stop hoping, so it popped out of her mouth frequently. Especially when Gisele was around. If only they weren't sisters...

She shook her head as she marched back toward the command center with Colonel Lopez. She left the training and billeting of the new recruits to her returning sergeants, trusting them to do their duty. Colonel Hoffman had already left, smirking as he went. Zara hoped this spelled the end of his vendetta, even if she didn't tear her hair out or weep or whatever else he no doubt wanted for his revenge to be complete. Choosing prisoners for her squad had shocked her, might even continue to do so, but she wouldn't let him see it.

But he definitely would have gone on the dueling list.

If only he didn't outrank her.

Although...she shook her head again as the specific rules on different ranks dueling one another wouldn't immediately come to her. She'd have to look that up later.

When they reached the command center, she saluted Lopez, and he returned the gesture along with a smile and nod, perhaps an acknowledgement that she'd handled herself well. Part of her was pleased; it was always nice to be recognized. But another part was annoyed that he'd thought she might behave any other way.

Zara sighed after he left. Her own emotions were hard enough to sort without worrying about other people's. She needed someone who always saw clearly. She needed the Vox Feram.

Zara hurried to the armory. She nearly tapped her foot while the sergeant behind the desk fetched the box, but she couldn't hurry opening the box or winding the chain and jewel around her wrist and hand. As usual, those happened almost without her thinking, leaving her again with no real memory of how she'd done them in the first place.

"Back so soon?" the Vox said in her mind, their many voices speaking at the same time, a comforting chorus in her head.

As she strode into the room to see the Vox perched in the sun, waiting for her, she relayed her memories of the new recruit convicts, seeking the Vox's clarity.

"Hmm," the Vox said when Zara's memories had flashed through her mind's eye. "I'm embarrassed to have missed so much. I had a feeling that Hoffman woman wouldn't go away quietly."

Zara wished she had the Vox's wisdom all the time, though they had never tried to speak through her, never offering exact words unless she asked. With a shudder of metal feathers, the Vox became a hawk-owl, a symbol of wisdom. Zara smiled, appreciating the attention to detail. They hopped onto her wrist, and she ran a hand along the cold metal feathers. They truly were a work of art.

The Vox's eyes went half-lidded, and they radiated delight at her praise. She walked outside with them for a while, reveling in the feeling of connectivity. The Vox studied her memories and delivered their verdict on each prison recruit and laid odds on whether they would make the cut.

"They certainly are a scruffy bunch," the Vox said.

Zara snorted. "I'm hoping some of that washes off."

"The tall one, the one who said she's good at following orders, looks the youngest. She looks stiff, like she's holding herself at the ready. Athletic, at least, if with fewer muscles than the meathead down the row. Her odds are good. Why didn't you get their names?"

"Why would I need them before they make the cut?"

"I don't suppose you would."

She nodded. "Jaq and Finn will take care of them." Her sergeants, siblings from the string of islands off the coast of the Kingdom of Othlan, had taken all recruits in hand since Zara had become a commander and was able to assemble her own team. Finn was good at "putting the fear of the devils in 'em," as she put it. She had a powerful voice that seemed to terrify as much as it motivated. And then Jaq was there to be their first real comrade, a sympathetic man who inspired loyalty and was more than happy to serve as a recruit's confidant.

"You might want to take a more active role with these particular recruits." the Vox said.

Zara frowned hard, but she bit back the urge to respond, knowing the Vox must have a reason. People might be irrational, but the Vox didn't suffer from that deficiency.

"For a few reasons," the Vox said, and Zara smiled at being right. "One, the accelerated training. They need to focus on some skills more than others if they're going to be ready for our next mission, and you're the person to name those skills."

Reasonable. But still…she'd never fussed with recruits. She wasn't about to start with those from prison. Most recruits needed to be molded a bit before she could even stand them.

"And," the Vox said, stressing the word, picking up on her thoughts and seeking to keep them on track. Zara shrugged and listened. "Loyalty is another thing. You don't have time for them to build loyalty to Jaq and then transfer that to you when they see you two interacting for a long while. You need them to be loyal to you from the start."

True enough. But…

"And last, we have respect. My memories tell me that a great deal of behavior in prison revolves around respect. These recruits will need to see you as someone tough and capable, someone able to do every task they're told to do."

Zara shook her head, seeing the flaw in their logic. "You're speaking of the way prisoners interact with one another. I'm more like the prison warden. They will do as I say because I'm in charge."

The Vox chuckled. "That's not why prisoners do what the warden says." They shared flashes of an older memory: prisoners being cowed by well-armed guards. As with most of the Vox's memories, this one was slightly hazy, as if she was squinting while she watched it. But Zara didn't really need to see. If the Vox knew it and shared with her, she knew it, too.

And the thought of abusing her troops, even recruits, disgusted her. "I won't beat anyone except in combat, and I won't keep any recruit who initiates infighting."

"You won't have to if you gain their respect much as a fellow inmate might. They might have obeyed their warden, but I doubt they held much esteem for anyone who was just another guard."

Her objections were crumbling, and she had to admit that sometimes, logic could be damn annoying. "You're right. And they need to trust me and my orders. They need to know that I want all my troops to come home alive and well."

But…later?

The Vox chuckled. "Well, we should give Jaq and Finn some time to get rid of anyone else who answers questions with, 'Fuck you.'"

True. Rough edges could be smoothed, but jagged ends could cut anyone who came close.

Roni had never run harder in all her life, not from the constabulary, rival thieves who'd rather spill blood than share, or syndicate members who wanted a piece of her hide. And she did it all to prove herself slightly better than the other convict candidates and secure a position she didn't want, in an army she didn't respect, to keep her away from a prison sentence she didn't deserve and a syndicate boss who wanted to murder her for her big mouth.

If there was a better reason to run her ass off, she didn't know it.

So she hauled herself around the track several more times as Sergeant Finn Aquino, a sergeant in the squad she hoped to join, shouted incentives and obscenities. At first, Roni had been disappointed that the hunter commander wasn't going to do the yelling, but as she huffed and panted and sweated, she was happy Commander Zara del Amanecer was nowhere near the field.

Roni had been hoping for a shower after being accepted as a recruit, but instead, a shouty monster had told them she wanted to "get an idea of how fit they were."

Or she wanted to see if she could kill any of them "accidentally" and save herself the trouble of training them. Roni wanted to be the best candidate, but maybe she could catch Commander Zara's eye instead. Any officer would want to keep their lover around for some much-needed stress relief.

Zara. Roni imagined moaning that name. Yes, serrah.

She grinned as she huffed, then quickly sank into misery again as the stitch she'd been trying to ignore in her side grew to a pain-filled roar. When she dropped to her knees and heaved her guts out, she heard the rush of the ocean. She'd read about the sea in stories, had always wanted to see it.

She fell onto her back, and a face drifted into the long tunnel she'd somehow fallen into.

"Breathe," the face said. It was a nice face, dark brown with pale patches, just like Aquino, but this face had a dark beard to go with his black hair and eyes. "Watch me." He inhaled and exhaled slowly, and Roni breathed with him, rising from the well after a few moments.

And remembering where she was and why. A trill of disgust went through her at the thought that she might be lying in her own puke. When the nice-faced man offered his hand, she grabbed it quickly, and the world tilted crazily as he pulled her up before clapping her on the shoulder.

"You did all right, chickling. You outlasted the others." He gestured over his shoulder to where the other recruits lay in the dust, all except the one farthest away, who was being shouted back to consciousness by Sergeant Finn.

"Oh. Good." She felt wrung out, hollow, and didn't really give a crap how she'd done against her fellow inmates. She could have fallen asleep on the edge of a sword. She managed a weak smile for this rare person who actually had an encouraging word for her. "Thanks, serrah."

"Sergeant Jaq Aquino, but you can call me Jaq." He nodded at Finn. "It's my sister who likes being the sergeant."

Good information. She shouldn't complain about one to the other. She shuddered. Not that she'd ever be sharing anything with Sergeant Shouty.

Jaq gave her another of those shuddering shoulder claps, but she managed to stay on her feet. "Come on, chickling. It's food and baths for you all."

Roni would have followed him into hell after a promise like that.

They were given the best lunch she'd had in years and a bath and a trainee uniform. They were told their old gear would be returned if and when they went back to prison, but Roni was more than happy to leave her old clothes behind. Even her old boots couldn't compare to army issue.

When she returned to the sleeping quarters of their guarded barracks, she was still toweling her hair, still blissfully high from the food and bath, but she stopped short when she saw all the other cons along with Finn and Jaq Aquino standing at attention before the hunter.

Commander del Amanecer.

Zara.

"Shit," Roni whispered. She jogged to her assigned bunk, spurred by the disapproval in those dark eyes, draped the towel over her shoulder, and stood as straight as she could manage.

Zara slowly stepped toward her, eyeing her hair with a frown. She lifted the towel from Roni's shoulder with a hand gloved in gold chains and nodded at Roni's hair. "Purple? I don't remember that."

With a grin, Roni touched the underside of her hair where a friend had dyed it so the purple only showed when she pulled the top half into a ponytail. She'd had her hair down when she'd first arrived; no doubt the purple was only showing now because it was so tousled.

Or because she'd been so grimy before.

Roni fought the urge to flinch. "Done with berry juice, Commander. I know it's probably not regulation, but it'll be gone after a few washes."

Zara stared, utterly impassive, and Roni wondered just what it would take to crack that facade.

No, she had to let those thoughts go and concentrate on keeping herself out of prison.

Zara finally gestured toward the baths. "You're dismissed to take care of it."

"Um, you want me to go wash my hair until the dye's gone, serrah? Now?"

"It's Commander. And, yes, now."

"Commander, I…" Roni opened and closed her mouth a few times. Zara wanted her to wash her hair three or four more times now? Maybe more? Earlier, she might have jumped at the chance, but after she was already clean? Way to take a good thing and make it tedious as hell.

"What's the problem? Do you need assistance?" Zara asked.

With anyone else, that offer would have been met with a leer or a snide twist of the lip, but Roni managed to keep her face still. And yet her mouth said, "You offering?" without consulting the rest of her, and as usual, she couldn't spit her foot out quickly enough to stop it.

The rest of the barracks went absolutely silent. Even the sergeants hushed, staring at Zara, waiting. Roni had been around enough syndicates to understand what was going on. She'd just challenged the boss, albeit slightly, and Zara's response would determine whether or not the crew lost their respect.

Roni expected anger, thinking a laugh or a come-on out of the question, but Zara only moved a chair to the center of the room and gestured to it. "We can provide assistance if required."

Roni bit her cheek. She couldn't hesitate now, or she'd be the one losing face. Besides, her head swam at the idea of those long, sure fingers teasing through her hair, brushing her neck, her ears. She couldn't remember the last time someone had washed her hair. She'd have to fight the urge to lean into it too much with everyone watching. Maybe that was the test?

When Zara put the towel around her shoulders, Roni barely suppressed the urge to lick her lips.

"Hold absolutely still," Zara said.

The words cut through Roni's lurid fantasies. "Why, Commander?"

"You might get cut," Zara said. Before Roni could wonder what that meant, Zara added, "As a matter of fact, hold her."

The sergeants leaped up, reminding Roni that they weren't part of a syndicate at all but an army unit, trained to obey. Finn grabbed Roni's shoulders, pushing her back against the chair, and smirking into her face. Finn and Jaq hadn't been waiting to see if the boss was still worthy of their respect. They'd been waiting to see how she'd school the newbie.

Jaq went around her and held her head still. Roni heard the *snick* of scissors. She stiffened, pushing slightly against Finn. "Wait."

"The commander ordered you to hold still," Finn whispered.

Roni so wanted to call her an asshole, but she managed to keep her mouth shut when movement might get her gouged with scissors. She swallowed hard and thought of all the reasons a haircut didn't matter so much. It was only hair, and obeying could win her points with everyone. She closed her eyes as strands of purple and her natural red fell around her. It wasn't the hair-washing fantasy of her dreams, but Zara was still back there, maybe brushing the hairs from her neck and collar, and she could imagine those hands coming down to caress her shoulders before moving lower.

"The razor now," Zara said.

Roni's eyes shot open. "Razor?"

"Just the purple bits," Finn whispered. The smirk grew, showing teeth.

Asshole.

Oh, well. It wouldn't be the first time her head had been shaved. It was a regular move at foster homes to cut down on lice. She breathed shallowly as a razor eased over the lower half of her scalp. When it was done, Finn released her. Roni breathed deep as she turned, wanting to make a smartass comment about the sureness of Zara's hands but hoping she could restrict herself to, thank you, Commander.

Her words dried up when she saw Jaq with the razor. Zara stood off to the side, head tilted as if assessing the work that she hadn't done. Roni should have known better. Her commanding officer was never going to cut her damn hair when there were grunts to do it for her.

"Perfectly acceptable, Jaq," Zara said.

"Thanks, boss."

Roni moved back into line, feeling the breeze on the lower half of her head. Jaq had even put the top part in a short ponytail for her.

With the uniform, she bet she looked a proper numbskull recruit now. If her old friends ever saw her like this, they'd laugh their asses off for weeks.

Zara turned on her heel and left, leaving Jaq and Finn behind.

Finn grinned. "Don't ask the boss for help if you don't want it."

Asshole, asshole, asshole. It was a struggle, but Roni kept her mouth shut. The more she looked like a recruit, the better her chances of staying.

Yeah, how long would saying that work?

Jaq and Finn dismissed them back outside and ran them through all sorts of shit Roni had never attempted: laying snares, tying knots, basic tracking, how to stay hidden. It seemed a general knowledge test just like the running had been general fitness, but she absorbed all she could. Finn even congratulated her on her ability to remain unseen. At least, Roni took, "Well, look who's not completely useless," as a compliment.

Hell, from Finn, that was probably a marriage proposal.

And Roni was able to speak with two of her fellow cons as they worked together. Leo was a short, squirrely man, a fellow thief, but they'd never worked the same patch. He was good with knots and staying unseen, but he had an unfortunate twitch, always smoothing his short brown hair. Roni wondered if he'd even done it while running.

Tati, the third member of their group, blurted, "I was in for attempted murder, but I didn't really do it," after Leo admitted his crime.

Roni wasn't about to argue with her. Tati was even shorter than Leo, almost reaching Roni's shoulder, but she carried enough wiry muscle for all three of them. Her bright blue eyes seemed permanently bloodshot, no doubt indicating some drug use in her past. Another reason not to contradict her. Depending on what she'd used, she might no longer be in her right mind. Still, she picked up tracking like a bloodhound, her shaved head inches from the ground as she scanned for footprints.

The three of them made a good team, but Zara only wanted two. Roni couldn't get attached. She wouldn't sabotage them, but she had to beat them.

And then? After she was an official member of the squad, security wouldn't be so tight. The Aquino sergeants wouldn't be watching them so closely. The barracks was surrounded by a fence, but she could scale it easily. And they weren't that far from the city proper. She could lose any pursuers once inside the dimly lit streets of the nearby Haymarket.

She glanced around as Leo and Tati finished setting a snare. The fence here at the back of the base stood flush against a forest. If she got out that way, she could follow the line of it toward the river. Even Tati the bloodhound wouldn't find her once she'd waded through the water for a bit.

Maybe she wouldn't even have to wait to pass or fail these tests.

Finn's bark of, "Time's up," brought her attention back to the moment, and after everyone's snares were rated from, "utter crap," to "slightly less crap," Finn and Jaq let everyone have a short wander while they carried on a whispered conversation.

Roni moved away from her teammates, avoiding the fence but trying to study it from afar. The wooden slats had upright gaps between them, not at all defensible, more a boundary marker. She couldn't squeeze through, but she could easily leap and get hold of the top. Her hands would fit between the sharpened tops of the slats. Then all she'd have to do was pull herself over, and…

Movement from beyond the fence caught her attention. She glanced at the others, but no one else was looking in that direction. She took a few cautious steps closer. Something moved again between the fence and the dark, barren trunks on the other side.

It was too tall for an animal, had to be a person. A guard? No, why would a guard be wandering out there in the frosty forest when they could be walking the cleared path inside the fence. After she took another step, a shadow moved again, and she caught a glimpse of a face peering in at her. It scowled, cheeks and chin dark with stubble and mean, piggy eyes glaring from a prominent brow.

It tickled a memory that faded before she could recall it, but she was left shaken, with icicles dripping through her core.

"Recruit Bisset, where in hell do you think you're going?" Finn yelled.

Roni whirled, and Finn took a step back, dark eyes narrowing at whatever she saw in Roni's face.

"Get back with the others." Finn continued staring as Roni hurried back.

She couldn't get the face out of her mind, memories flooding through her until she had it. Hacha, one of the Newgate Syndicate's enforcers. Someone had once told her that no one could identify all the victims of his last slaughter. They couldn't figure out which pieces went with which person.

"Gods," she whispered as Finn barked at them about something else. "Gods and devils."

Tati and Leo looked at her curiously, and Jaq was staring at her, a frown on his dark and pale face. Roni made herself breathe deeply and willed her heart rate to calm. She couldn't tell anyone about this, or they might decide she was more trouble than she was worth. One thing was clearer than ever before. She needed to make it into the squad, and she needed to stay put once she joined.

CHAPTER EIGHT

Zara was surprisingly pleased when after only a week of training, some of the recruits adapted to their new roles and showed some skill more quickly than promised. She and the Vox observed them several times over the course of that week, and by the end, she'd nearly made up her mind about which ones she planned to select for her squad.

And she had to admit, some of those who weren't going to make her cut might be a good fit for someone else's squad. Someone who wasn't as selective, perhaps, like Colonel Hoffman, whose idea it was to put prisoners in her squad in the first place.

As she watched the recruits practice digging latrines and setting up camp near the back of the base, she was happy to note that those she'd probably select also got on well with Jaq and obeyed Finn in a timely fashion, although...

"Yes," the Vox said from where they perched on her shoulder as a peregrine falcon. "The tall one, Veronique Bisset, does seem jumpier than normal."

"Strange for one so cocksure at the outset." Zara had noticed her swagger during the hair incident. She'd suspected the plea for help with the dye wasn't genuine, but it had served as a good demonstration of teamwork, finding clever solutions to problems, and the fact that no matter what, Zara would be obeyed. And the fact that Recruit Bisset had finally submitted without complaint showed that she could bend enough to follow the rules. Unlike at least one of the others, who seemed as if he was going to snap. Fragility was never a good quality for a soldier. Better that the breakable stayed home.

But now Bisset appeared fearful, and that also wasn't good. If she was jumping out of her skin before they even got into the field, she'd be utterly useless when facing the enemy.

"She keeps looking toward the fence," Zara said. "If she didn't seem so afraid, I'd think she was planning to escape."

"Perhaps she fears the wilderness," the Vox said.

They both said, "No," at the same time. That seemed a vague dread, and something about Bisset staring at one point on the fence was more specific.

"Take a look," Zara said. The Vox hopped onto her chain-covered wrist, and she flung them upward to wheel into the cloudy sky. The smell of snow was in the air, but it hadn't started yet, so there might not be footprints if something or someone was prowling the woods. But if there was something to find, the Vox would spot it.

With a sigh, Zara leaned against the building behind her and shut her eyes, seeing through the Vox, noting some broken branches along with animal trails farther into the trees. Could be human, could be deer. Might even be a bear who'd awoken early, but that seemed far-fetched. The Vox dropped to just above the treetops and flew in wide circles, never getting so far that she couldn't hear their mental voice. They had to remain close to the jewel that powered them, the one on her wrist which siphoned small amounts of her energy.

They saw nothing moving, and by the time they returned, the first snowflakes were falling, and dusk was approaching early in the gloom. Zara opened her eyes as Finn jogged up to her and said, "Shall we call it a day, Commander?"

Zara considered. If Bisset was afraid of a specific person or thing, it likely showed itself at dusk, or it would have been spotted by someone else. "Let them go a little longer. See how they deal with being caught out in bad weather and approaching darkness."

After a quick salute, Finn was off shouting again. The recruits groaned at being kept at their work, but that would be true of any recruits, and Jaq pitched in to help them. The Vox landed on a point farther down the fence from where the recruits worked and shifted to the form of a tawny owl, best able to pinpoint movement in low light but small enough to remain unseen.

THE SCOUT AND THE SCOUNDREL

Zara strolled closer to the recruits but hung back, staying where she could see them all and their view of the fence and forest, so any watchers might think her as preoccupied as Jaq and Finn.

The Vox detected something scurrying through the undergrowth, and Zara tensed.

"A mouse," the Vox said. Their soft laughter eased Zara's mind. "I don't even eat them, and I nearly pounced."

She hid her smile behind a cough. "We'll set a bad example if we jump at shadows, too."

"It's the lack of field time. It's making everyone edgy. Luckily, we'll be out there in two weeks. After you've made your choice."

Recruit Bisset looked up from where she dug a latrine and wiped her brow. It was a good sign that she was working up a sweat despite the cold weather. But as Bisset glanced toward the fence again, Zara guessed that any perspiration might also be due to fear. Still, Bisset carried on with her work and seemed well-suited to the task with her lean, muscular frame. She had an easy smile. The other recruits seemed to like her. Her dark red hair—though better than the purple—would stand out in winter, but not when she had her helmet on. Her skin was nicely tanned, almost dusky against the hair, which meant she'd spent some time in the sun and had less of a chance of getting crippling sunburn should they be caught in the open for days at a time.

"There's a lot to admire there," the Vox said, their tone slightly teasing.

Zara didn't take offense, not from someone who knew her so well. "I have observed her relative attractiveness, if that's what you're implying. It is an asset when it comes to getting along with others."

"Of course. And it's always nice to have a good-looking squad. Makes it easier to stare at them for days at a time."

She shook her head, knowing they were of the same mind despite the joke. Ability mattered more than beauty even if beauty had its place.

It just wouldn't affect her decision in the slightest.

When night had nearly fallen and nothing had shown itself, Zara called a halt, sending the recruits indoors, but she didn't like a mystery to go unsolved. She lit a lantern from the practice gear and called, "Recruit Bisset, a moment."

Bisset broke away from the others, a bit of trepidation on her face that transformed into something hopeful when everyone else filed inside, leaving them as alone as they could get on an army base.

Zara sighed, determined to quench any romantic feelings right now. "I didn't ask you to stay behind for any sort of dalliance, Recruit. Put that out of your mind and keep it there."

Bisset's dark eyes widened, and she nodded, but a small smirk still graced her lips. "Are you certain, Commander?"

Zara sucked in a breath to tell her off, but Bisset winced as if her own words pained her.

"I'm sorry, Commander," she said. "Sometimes my mouth runs off without my permission, and I blurt out things I know I shouldn't. I am working on it, I promise." She chuckled, but it sounded more embarrassed. "It doesn't help one's career as a liar when you keep blurting out the truth."

Zara paused in surprise, satisfied by the apology, sympathetic about saying the wrong thing, admiring the pledge to change, and flummoxed by the admission that Bisset still desired some kind of assignation.

"That is a lot to go through," the Vox said.

"I see," Zara said. "Well, good that you're…trying." She held up a hand before Bisset could speak again. "I would like to know why you are so anxious."

Bisset straightened as if slapped, and though she didn't turn toward the fence, her eyes jerked that way as if attached to invisible strings.

"I've seen you watching the forest and have observed your obvious nervous reactions, so you needn't bother trying not to blurt out the truth this time."

Bisset's jaw worked as if she was gnawing at her cheek. Zara could almost see her thoughts tumbling between lies and truth. She'd just admitted she was well-acquainted with both, but if Zara sensed a lie now, Bisset was not going to make the cut.

For a moment, she tried on a cocky grin. Zara kept her face impassive, and the grin stuttered and fell. "I can handle it, Commander. I'll pay strict attention from now on."

Zara sighed. She hated to get involved in anyone's personal life, especially a former criminal turned recruit, but... "Bisset, in a squad like mine, problems are shared. Not out of some childish need to cuddle one another but because we trust one another with our lives. Danger to one is danger to the many." She pointed to the fence. "And we will have enough danger out there without being blindsided by the troubles carried individually. Such an individual must remain behind, unworthy to join my squad."

Now the tendons in Bisset's neck stood out like steel bands. "I swear, I am not more trouble than I'm worth, Commander. Any old problems of mine are sorted. It's just a matter of forgetting them for good." Her gaze shifted to Zara's lips, possibly her neck. "You call your sergeants Finn and Jaq. You can call me Veronique. Or Roni, if we're going to be working together."

Zara could dismiss the flash of lust. She'd never been a fan of such obvious displays. But the offer of intimacy—and not just a first name but a nickname—startled her. Confidence was normally something she admired, but the way Roni...*Bisset*...seemed certain she would make the squad set foreign feelings bubbling in her stomach, especially when combined with the familiarity.

And the fact that there was...much to admire about Roni's, Bisset's, form.

Even the Vox seemed speechless.

The wind picked up, speckling Roni's—*Bisset's*, by the gods—hair with snow in the falling light. No further truths seemed forthcoming, even under the threat of falling temperatures. It seemed *Recruit Bisset* knew something of living in the cold.

"Dismissed," Zara said, elated that none of her confusion seemed to color her voice.

Bisset saluted—only a little sloppily—and marched into the barracks. Zara breathed in the cold air, letting it sear her lungs and burn these feelings out. Her mind still wobbled between Bisset and Roni, and she couldn't get it to settle, so perhaps she'd think of her as Veronique. They did often use first names in the field.

For everyone but Zara.

The Vox returned to her shoulder. "What do we think?" they asked.

"That the ranking of the recruits has shifted a little in my mind." If Veronique wasn't careful, she could find herself at the bottom of the pack. Secrets could be just as bad as troubles in the field. And so could any damn feelings.

❖

Roni tried to put thoughts of Hacha and Zara out of her mind as she bathed and got ready for bed with the other recruits. Worrying about Hacha had given her a permanent knot between her shoulder blades, one that wasn't helped by whatever she'd just shared with her commanding officer.

But she hadn't *really* lied to Zara. Even if she had, why in the hell did she care? Maybe because Roni wasn't in the habit of lying to people she worked with, no matter that some of them had lied their asses off to her a time or two. But the few partnerships she'd ever had were based in honesty.

Though she'd never had a real partnership, one built on complete trust.

And then there'd been the *moment*. Roni hadn't been able to keep her eyes from wandering to Zara's lips and neck, and something had passed over Zara's face. Not desire, exactly, but her lips had parted slightly, her eyes had widened just a tad, and an adorable little line had appeared between her eyebrows. Either Roni had confused her or the feelings had, proving the commander could be moved from her usual stoic state to…something else, if only little by little.

Not that any of that mattered now.

Roni sighed as she climbed into her narrow bed. Tati dimmed the lantern, throwing the small bunkhouse into darkness. The nightshirt the army had provided was a little coarse, as was the blanket, and the mattress and pillow had too many lumps to count, but Roni had gotten used to them over a week, especially since they were a step above the bed in her usual accommodation and leaps over the scattering of straw and stone floor of the prison. Being safe and warm should have made her happy, if only the safe part wasn't in question.

She'd seen Hacha at least three times over the week and thought she'd glimpsed him a few times more. He had to be waiting for the chance to kill her. And an army base wouldn't stop him for long.

Then why the hell didn't she tell someone? She'd asked herself that question time and again. Hell, Zara had given her the perfect opportunity that evening, but something had stopped her from speaking. Zara's insinuation that she might be trouble had angered her. If the army thought she came with too much baggage, they would never choose her to be one of them. Why pick a soldier who came with enemies already? The army found enough of them on their own. They didn't need Roni's troubles following them into the field.

As Roni tried to settle amidst the snores and movements of the other recruits, she prayed that Hacha would finally break into the base where he'd be caught or killed, and Roni wouldn't have to think about him again.

But what if only the first part happened? Hacha could easily kill the one soldier who'd been left to guard this barracks, as well as any others he encountered who were alone at the time. Roni was certain he had as much experience in a fight as any soldier. And he was used to sneaking through the shadows rather than on the field of combat.

The soldiers would think themselves safe on their base, in their beds.

What if Hacha found Zara's room?

Nonsense. Roni flipped over. She didn't even know if Zara lived on the base. Some officers didn't, she'd heard. And even if Zara lived here, the odds that Hacha would stumble into her quarters were as high as the moon. Hacha probably wasn't planning to break into the base at all. He was no doubt watching to get an idea of Roni's routine and progress, and then he'd try to grab her when she either failed out and was sent back to prison or when she succeeded and left the security of the base for the forest.

And wasn't that a comforting thought?

It didn't do anything to relieve the knot in her back, that was for damn sure.

Roni sighed and turned to stare at the dark ceiling. A few streaks of light came through gaps in the shutters on the far side of the room, proof that someone was still on guard outside. Maybe Roni and whoever was chosen with her would have their own guards amongst the squad. Perhaps they'd be watched over until they were well out of the city of Sarras, but that would be a waste in the wilderness. Even Roni hadn't considered running away after days in the middle of nowhere. She had no doubt that she'd die on her own out there.

Another incredibly comforting thought certain to send her to sleep in no time.

A creak came from outside. Roni held her breath, her heart leaping into her throat despite the fact that her mind supplied infinite possibilities for the noise. After a few seconds of silence, she breathed again, her pulse just coming down from the heavens when another noise jolted her again.

Scratching, scraping.

Mice? She hadn't seen any on the base. It seemed too cold for them, and the army kept several cats around to take care of any vermin. She'd envied those cats while they'd lounged in the sun. And the dogs used to patrol the edges of the base would scare away any other animal intruders.

When someone snored loudly, Roni sat up, hand to her heart in fear, before she called herself a fool. Still, she stayed sitting up for a moment, especially as another sound came from closer to the doorway.

The streaks of light flickered as if someone walked between them and the building.

The guard walking to warm themselves, maybe a change of guards or one of the cats she'd just thought of or a late-year moth or bird or a fucking angel from heaven. It could be anything.

Then came a scrape and a noise between a gasp and a gurgle. And she knew it was him.

Roni scanned the room. No one else seemed awake. Shout and rouse them? What if it was nothing? She shot from bed, padded the few steps toward the door, and leaned against it, listening. She didn't hear anything outside. It could have been a cough.

But it wasn't a damn cough.

She bit her lip and shook her head. She didn't know that, couldn't know that. Something or nothing? Either could brand her a troublemaker and send her straight back to prison. From Hacha's arms to Judith Esposito's.

No, she had to call for help, tell them she'd heard something, then they'd catch this madman, and she'd lie, lie, lie—

"You there, rat?" A harsh whisper, like sandpaper over stone, drifted through the door, just loud enough to send a shard of ice through Roni's guts.

The door shifted as if someone on the other side was trying it. Roni braced it with her back, toes curling into the planks of the floor. Her voice seemed caught in a vise of terror. She'd heard that voice before, oh gods.

Hacha made a small wet sound, and she imagined him sucking his teeth while biting his lower lip and making his demented version of a laugh. "I know you're there, rat, can feel your heat through the door. I'm waiting for you, rat, come out, come out."

That childish notion that he'd forget about her if she didn't speak overcame her, and she squeezed her eyes shut hard.

"Got your friend out here, rat," Hacha said. "Alive but not for long. Not unless you come out. Ain't going to kill you. Just got a message."

Like hell.

His voice seemed farther away when he spoke again. She could barely hear. "I backed off, rat, come on. You've got time to scream to wake the damned if I try anything." Another of those gasping gurgles came through the door, proof that the guard was still alive and a threat that they wouldn't be alive much longer.

Maybe she didn't quite feel like the soldiers were her comrades yet, but she couldn't stand by and let someone be murdered. After a few deep breaths and a hundred rounds of calling herself a fool, she cracked the door and peered out.

Hacha grinned lopsidedly. The left side of his face never did seem to cooperate with the rest of him. He held the unconscious guard by the throat but let him slip loose. "There you are."

"So talk," Roni managed, a strangled whisper. Any minute now, one of her fellow recruits would wake, or another guard would walk by on their rounds. She lined up a few stories in her head, but none seemed ideal.

"I was gonna kill you, rat. But the boss thinks differently after what I told her."

Roni frowned. She should have been happy to hear that she wasn't going to die, but no doubt she'd only be spared for something worse. "What?"

"Your commander's got something the boss wants. The gold glove, the metal bird."

"Metal what?"

"You get on that squad, and once you're well out of town and in the woods, you steal the glove and the bird, and you give them to me. I'll be following. I'll be watching. You do it before your squad comes back, or you all die." He touched his hand to his heart in a mock salute and pointed at the barracks. "Time for beddy-bye. Go on, now."

Roni had a thousand questions, but more than that, she wanted to embrace the opportunity to close the door in this monster's face and go hide in her bed.

But…

She nodded at the guard while calling herself a fucking moron. "What about them?"

Hacha tilted his head like a dog puzzling over something new. "He's coming with me."

Roni was trying to gather enough saliva to object when Hacha flicked his fingers as if dismissing her fears.

"They'll find him at daybreak. Alive. If you keep quiet." After another crooked grin, he hoisted the guard over one broad shoulder and motioned to Roni like a parent shooing their child to bed before he faded into the darkness with his captive.

Roni's hands shook as she pushed the door closed, and she sagged against it, lost and breathing hard to keep from collapsing into sobs.

CHAPTER NINE

Zara stared at the kitchen table in her home and imagined the new recruits as game pieces. Her three weeks to train them were almost up. In her mind, she kept sorting and moving them, ranking them based on who was better at which skills, who seemed the healthiest and fittest, and who took orders well.

The largest, bulkiest recruit, Emil, lagged at the back in every contest. Strength was his only real asset, and scouts didn't need that as much as some other squads did. Still, he seemed content to do simple tasks with plodding efficiency, and she planned to recommend him to the infantry.

The other four, though...

Everything about Cortez was average. Not just in height and build, but the soft brown tone of his eyes, skin, and hair could be labeled average as well. He seemed happiest alone and went only by his surname where the other recruits embraced informality. He was handy with a saber rather than a truncheon or a bow, and he was a master of staying unseen, one who could probably hide in the open just by being...nondescript. Zara preferred that word to Finn and Jaq's label of "boring as hell." He might be good at some aspects of the job but might not mix well.

Leo was small and slight, useful attributes if Zara needed someone to watch an enemy encampment, but he had an unfortunate hair-pulling twitch. Maybe it would be countered after a few weeks spent wearing a helmet. He was also handy with snares and knots and obeyed orders without question, though he needed a great many things explained to him twice and was terrible at weapon craft. Still, the others seemed to get along with him.

Particularly Tati. She was short and muscular and had proved to be a fair hand with a saber. She also seemed to develop loyalty early on in relationships. She was already tight with Leo, and even Finn seemed to like her, though Tati would likely never know it. Her tracking skills grew stronger every day. She didn't need to be told to do something more than once, but she often did things incorrectly. Like Leo, she wouldn't be winning any intellectual prizes anytime soon.

If Zara wanted brains, there was Veronique. Tall, which could be a detriment to a scout—though it had never stopped Zara—she was also wiry and could run like the wind. She did better with a truncheon than a saber. She couldn't sneak as well as Cortez, didn't track as well as Tati, and wasn't as handy with a rope as Leo, but she was average at all of those skills. More importantly, she was smart enough to learn how to get better. She got along with everyone.

And there was something in her eyes, something that went beyond intelligence.

Zara stood to get another cup of tea. She shivered as she thought of the night she'd prompted Veronique to speak about what had her so anxious. Veronique had declined, but as she'd promised, she'd stopped watching the fence and had started paying attention to her training. That showed she was a person who kept their word, another plus.

And as uncomfortable as Zara was to admit it—even to herself—she liked having Veronique around.

Unfortunately, that was a mark against her. Zara couldn't have distractions in the field, even if she wasn't quite sure what it was about Veronique that distracted her. Besides the rebellious spark Zara sometimes glimpsed.

The day after Zara had confronted Veronique, the guard assigned to watch the recruits' barracks had gone missing. Not for long. The base patrols had found him in a dark corner behind some utility sheds. He'd reeked of booze, though he'd claimed—in a drunken slur—that he couldn't remember touching a drop. Zara had been outside with the recruits when the patrol had brought him shambling past, and she'd turned away in disgust.

Veronique had been standing there, face pale, watching with undisguised sympathy. When their eyes had met, she'd said, "It... maybe it wasn't his fault."

Zara had cocked her head, confused. She hadn't yet heard the full story of how he'd been found, but she'd been able to smell liquor from fifteen feet away and had heard his slurred protests. "Not his fault that he drank while on duty?"

"He didn't...I mean, what if he..." She'd breathed deeply, nostrils flaring, and the look she'd given Zara before turning around had said she would defend the disgraced guard to the grave.

"Wait," Zara had said. When Veronique had continued walking, Zara had lifted her voice a little. "Stop, Recruit."

Veronique had turned stiffly, anger still blazing in her eyes. Zara had marveled at her, wondering when she'd had the time to develop loyalty toward one of her guards.

"Maybe she doesn't like anyone being judged without a hearing," the Vox had said in Zara's mind.

A sense of fairness, Zara could respect that. Still...

"You will wait until being dismissed when speaking with your commander," Zara had managed, but a strange part of her had wanted to see what else Veronique would do.

After a somewhat sarcastic salute, Veronique had said, "Yes, Commander. May I be excused, Commander?" And while they were the right words, it wasn't the right tone.

Zara had stepped closer, the beginnings of anger rumbling inside her. "You may, Recruit." Before Veronique could get far, Zara had added, "There are some laps that need running." Then she'd gestured to Finn to give Veronique some very loud encouragement.

The whole incident had left Zara a little scattered, and even the Vox couldn't help her process all her feelings.

Since then, Veronique had seemed the model recruit, with only a few flippant words that made Zara's anger spike. Thankfully, there were always laps to be run.

In the deepest part of her mind, Zara acknowledged that she enjoyed watching Veronique run, too. Such exercise showed off her lean curves. Her game piece moved a little farther forward on the board in Zara's mind.

Until one of the others outpaced her, and Zara had to start over again.

Zara sighed and put her head in her hands, happy the house was quiet. Today was the deadline. She would announce her picks, then head out on their assignment soon after, gathering the rest of the squad as they went.

If only she could make her picks. She took another sip of coffee and sighed.

"What are you thinking so hard about?" Gisele asked from the doorway.

Zara held in a groan. She'd hoped to make a decision and be out of the house before anyone else stirred, particularly her little sister. "Work."

"Work doesn't normally give you such a constipated look."

Zara glared. "Must you be crude?"

Gisele grinned, her eyes sparkling. "Yes."

"You know, if you weren't my sister—"

"Oh, learn a new tune already. I'm so sick of that one, I can't even mock you by repeating it."

Zara boiled with the desire to say something cutting, but she held her tongue, unwilling to lecture Gisele yet again when she needed to direct her intelligence to far more important matters. She stared at the table again and tapped a finger against her cup so the vibrations would roll through the liquid. Now, which recruit had been in the lead?

"You won't even argue with me? You must be troubled." Gisele poured her own cup and sat, always attracted to the situation where she was least needed. "What's going on?"

Zara spared her a glance. "Nothing you can help with."

"How do you know if you don't try me?"

"Years of experience."

Gisele stuck her tongue out, but her dark eyes didn't seem angry yet. Her dark hair was down, flowing in waves over her shoulders. "I mean it, Z. I will help if I can, you know that. Give me a chance."

Yes, during any emergency, Gisele would lend a hand and not just out of sisterly duty. Zara was the same. But if those emergencies required them to speak to one another, it always seemed to go the same way: quickly downhill.

But if she gave the problem to Gisele to consider, perhaps she could sneak out of the house while Gisele pondered.

A happy thought.

"I must select two recruits to join my squad today. Out of the five I've been training, one is out for certain, but the other four..." She shrugged and gave Gisele a quick rundown of their abilities.

As Zara hoped, Gisele stared vaguely at a spot on the other end of the kitchen, her lips working as she mumbled to herself. Zara slid out of her chair, determined to start for the door unnoticed.

When the front door slammed, they both jumped, and Zara frowned hard as Bridget and her handler, Jean-Carlo, walked into the kitchen. Bridget's tanned cheeks were rosy from the cold. She took off her cap and ran a hand through her short black locks but paused when her eyes met Zara's. "Oh, I didn't expect anyone else to be up yet."

"Then why slam the door?" Zara asked, unable to keep the irritation out of her voice.

Bridget had the courtesy to look sheepish. "Sorry, the wind caught it. I'm not used to such heavy doors."

Swallowing her ire, Zara inclined her head. Jean-Carlo did not look sheepish from where he stood behind Bridget. His long pale face was as stoic as usual. He shook his long black braid out of his cap and removed his gloves, telling Zara he was staying awhile.

Oh, well, maybe they would all distract one another, giving her another opportunity to get away.

"You're just in time," Gisele said. "Z and I are working on a problem." Before Zara could offer a protest, Gisele had laid all before them. Zara gave her a look that she hoped conveyed her displeasure. By the wink Gisele gave her, the message had been received but was deliberately misunderstood.

"Hmm," Bridget said after she'd gotten mugs for herself and Jean-Carlo. "That's a tough one. I'd pick whichever two are the most adaptable."

Jean-Carlo shook his head. "Definitive skills are more important."

"But so is loyalty and amiability," Gisele added.

"Perfect," Zara said. "That clears everything up." She put her cup in the sink, telling herself she couldn't be angry. She hadn't wanted their help in the first place.

"I suppose none of them fits in all those categories?" Bridget asked, her smile sympathetic. She held up a hand. "Don't answer that. The choice would be easy if that were true."

"Well…" Zara cocked her head. "One of them comes close. Veronique seems able to learn and adapt quickly. Her skills aren't the best, but they are the most varied, and everyone seems to like her well enough."

"One down," Gisele said smugly.

"Leo and Tati sound like a pair who'd work best together," Bridget said. "You could always send them to another scouting unit and take Cortez."

"Or take the first two and send Veronique and Cortez away," Jean-Carlo said. "As you said, they have no trouble with loyalty, they have the skills you need, and a little stupidity isn't a bad thing in someone who simply has to follow orders."

Gisele gave him a sweet smile she usually reserved for bouts of extreme sarcasm. "Are you someone who fits that description?"

He returned her look without batting an eye. "I'm best when my orders are to observe, adapt, *and* act intelligently."

"And kick people in the face as needed," Bridget added, cutting the tension.

Zara sighed. "I'm glad to know every single choice in front of me is still valid."

"What about your commanding officer?" Bridget asked, jumping in just as Gisele opened her mouth but before she could make a sound. "Couldn't they help narrow it down?"

Colonel Lopez could no doubt help her, but he'd left this in her hands. How would it look if she returned to him unable to make a decision?

"Z wouldn't ask him for help," Gisele said, showing rare insight. Then she added, "She's too stubborn," throwing all hints of insight into the trash.

Zara glared at her. "I'm quite capable of making this decision on my own." Well, she'd run it all by the Vox again, but they were practically the same being. "So I'll thank you for your useless input and take my leave." She strode to the closet for her cloak.

"You didn't actually thank anyone," Gisele called after her.

Gods, if they weren't sisters...

By the time Zara made it to the base, she was still moving the recruits around in her head, gnashing her teeth whenever Veronique came wandering to the forefront. She wavered between capitulating to whatever her mind was trying to tell her and rebelling against it right up until the moment she spied Finn and Jaq taking the recruits through their paces one final time.

As she stood and watched, the recruits continued to switch rankings in her mind. She told herself to stop waffling and make a decision even as her eye kept finding Veronique. With her long legs, she ran the obstacle course in easy, controlled movements. She'd rolled up her shirtsleeves in spite of the cold weather, and the muscles in her arms hinted at the lithe strength in the rest of her. Again, a lot to admire, but Zara had many reasons not to admire any of it.

Better to turn her down, send her to another squad with one other and choose—

"There you are, Commander," Colonel Lopez said from beside her.

Zara tamped down a flare of surprise and turned, snapping off a salute and chastising herself for not seeing him coming. "Colonel." She should have retrieved the Vox before coming to watch the recruits if she couldn't pay attention to her surroundings.

"Have you made your choice?" he asked.

She took a deep breath, but before she could respond, she hit upon one factor that could help her decide. "Emil should go to the infantry. The other four are good candidates. Who's going to get the two I don't choose?" She knew some of the strengths and weaknesses of other squads. If she could choose a good fit for them...

Lopez's mouth turned down a bit. "No one, I'm afraid, though I might be able to get the last one into the infantry. They're less picky than the scouts."

Zara took a moment to process. "Aren't the other scouting squads involved in the prison reform initiative?"

"They are, but the commanders want to start from scratch like you did."

Zara didn't bother to hide her frown. "Begging your pardon, Colonel, but that is idiotic. All four candidates have some training now. They could easily fit into any squad."

He was silent for a few moments. Damn, she really should have gotten the Vox to help her figure out what was going on. Lopez had a look of disapproval, but it wasn't directed at her. So he was unhappy with someone else, probably those who insisted on "starting from scratch" with another batch of prison recruits.

She joined in that disapproval, but she also knew a bit about military politics and its unchangeable irrationality. "They...don't want recruits trained by me?" With her service record, that went beyond idiotic to bizarre or antagonistic.

"That's not how it was put to me," Lopez said with a smile. "They argued only that they want to train their recruits themselves."

Some people always had to do things the hard way. "What's going to happen to the recruits I don't choose?"

"They'll go back to prison."

That didn't sit well with Zara, not after the past weeks. While it was true that the idea of a prison recruit still didn't completely fit in her mind, Cortez, Leo, Tati, and Veronique had worked hard and behaved themselves. They all did have time left on their sentences, too, so it shouldn't have bothered her so much, but as she watched them train, they seemed to fit here, and making it this far in their training had to count for something. It couldn't simply be a colossal waste of time.

But orders were orders.

Colonel Lopez gave her an understanding smile, as if he could read her thoughts, and she envied his ability to glean information from an expression, though she thought herself a little better at it than she used to be.

"Well, give me your choices by the end of the day, Commander."

After they'd saluted again, he strode away, leaving Zara to look back to her recruits. Veronique was looking her way, with some of the others glancing around occasionally, but it was Veronique's dark eyes that caught her. She seemed apprehensive, and why not? Zara had her future in hand.

She was a criminal. She didn't deserve this kind of careful consideration.

Yet she'd worked very hard, come very far.

When compared to her crimes, her effort was irrelevant.

And the fear in her eyes? The potential in her stance? Zara straightened her shoulders and gestured for Veronique to join her, nodding to Finn and Jaq when they glanced over. Veronique jogged instead of ambling, and there was no trace of impishness in her salute. More points in her favor.

Irrelevant as they were.

Still, she had to ask, "Why so nervous, Recruit Bisset?"

Veronique's lip twisted slightly, but she pulled the corner down between her teeth and seemed to swallow whatever she'd been about to say first. "Commander, I was just...I was curious about..." She sighed deeply, her eyes closing for the briefest moment. "I have to know...we have to know, what's to become of us?"

She said it as if Zara might be sending her to the gallows, though that had never been an option. "The idea was for me to choose two of you for my squad, and I was under the impression that any others who had potential would be shifted to other squads. Unfortunately, that impression was erroneous." Zara held in a sigh of her own, fighting a bad taste in her mouth.

Veronique's face tightened as if she'd just eaten a lemon. "Those who don't make the cut are going back to prison." Before Zara could respond, Veronique took a step closer. "Please, serrah, Commander, please don't send us...them...anyone back there."

Zara fought the urge to move away, unwilling to show how much this proximity unnerved her. "Recruit—"

"You don't know what it's like." Veronique's voice had dropped to a ragged whisper. Her nostrils flared as she breathed hard, and fear seemed to radiate off her. Zara didn't know whether to place a comforting hand on her arm or ask her to step back or dress her down for interrupting an officer.

Luckily, Veronique spoke again before Zara had to decide. "There's a woman. Judith Esposito." Veronique spoke so quickly from there, Zara could barely keep up with the tale about a criminal with free run of the prison who could kill when and where she wished. This Judith Esposito had already targeted Veronique, she said, and would murder her upon her return.

Preposterous.

Zara's face must have shown some of her skepticism because Veronique pressed on to tell stories she'd heard from Tati and Leo about bullying and violence.

"If they're sent back, they won't be able to watch each other's backs," Veronique said. "They were in different blocks. Cortez and Emil haven't shared any horror stories, but I'm sure they have some, too."

Zara held up a hand, reeling under the weight of the words and what it meant if they were true. Criminals sent to prison were denied their freedom; that was their punishment. To be abused and threatened on top of that? To live under the threat of death because of guards who'd been bought? "That's obscene," Zara said. And hard to credit, but she couldn't say that to the blatant fear on Veronique's face.

Veronique stood tall, as if Zara had said it all the same. "I'm a thief. I'll cop to that, and I have lied a time or two, but with all the gods as my witnesses, I am not lying now. My life will end in prison, and the others might be in more danger just because they were able to get out of that shithole for a time." Her cheeks went a little darker. "Begging your pardon, serrah, Commander."

In a world where prisoners could also be army recruits and prove their worth by training hard, a prison could be run by convicts, Zara supposed. It was still a topsy-turvy world she did not want to live in, and she had to conjure the image of Adella saying, "Most people are irrational, and you can't expect that to change," to keep her brain from stuttering or getting sucked into a logic-less morass that she would need help escaping from.

Veronique was watching her with a confused expression, and she wondered how much of her emotional state was playing across her face. Veronique couldn't seem to *stop* displaying her feelings, a detriment to someone who wanted to be better at lying.

But good for someone who didn't.

"You're afraid," Zara said, unable to keep the wonder from her voice. "I believe that."

Veronique frowned a little and swallowed so hard, her neck trembled. Zara had the strangest urge to stroke that smooth skin. "I'm terrified, Zara."

"Commander." Zara corrected her without thinking. "Or boss, like Finn and Jaq say. Serrah will do if nothing else comes to mind." She was rambling a little, but the sound of her name from Veronique's mouth put her in another spin.

"Does that mean I get to stay?" Veronique asked with so much hope in her eyes, it was almost blinding. Then her expression shuddered. "But...the others?"

Thinking of others as well as herself? Zara swallowed again, finally conceiving of a way to banish the bad taste and all of Veronique's fears. "I'll send Emil to the infantry and take the rest of you."

Veronique rocked back, eyes wide. Zara felt somewhat shocked herself, but the decision felt right in spite of that. She'd been told to pick two but hadn't been forbidden from picking more. And she nodded now, certain she could convince Colonel Lopez to accept her decision.

She'd leave it to him to argue with anyone else.

Veronique beamed, her shining smile taking her from attractive to beautiful, something Zara had heard about herself but hadn't understood until now. She hadn't been exactly pleased to hear those words before, so she decided not to repeat them now, especially since Veronique's smile eased back a little, and her eyes roamed Zara's face as if memorizing it, lingering here or there.

Zara's stomach buzzed, a not altogether unpleasant sensation, but one she didn't have time to ponder or explore at the moment. She put her hands behind her back and hoped she looked as stoic as she intended when she said, "Back to training, Recruit."

Veronique's smile returned, and her salute had a bit of impishness again as she jogged back to her training. Zara tore her eyes away and marched toward Colonel Lopez's office, in a hurry to get that meeting over with so she could tell everything to the Vox.

CHAPTER TEN

The gods in heaven were smiling, and choirs of angels sang to Roni as she ran through the obstacle course again. She climbed a net, skittered across a thin log, dangled from various bars, and swung on a rope, all over a pit of muddy water. Even Hacha and a legion of devils couldn't depress her at that moment.

Three of her fellow prison recruits were going to join the squad, and Roni felt as if she'd managed to convince Zara to pick them.

And she'd managed to swallow her anger enough to speak the truth without swearing.

Apart from a minor one.

And at the end of her argument, Zara's expression had opened a little, and she'd seemed almost awed by what Roni had said, and if Zara had been anyone else, Roni would have kissed her.

As it was, she'd barely controlled herself.

That was probably one of the reasons she was still here.

And staying here. The angels were still singing until her thoughts looped back around, and she realized that even in her elation, she'd thought of Hacha.

The angels weren't quite so loud now.

Instead, Roni thought of a golden glove and a metal bird that she'd have to steal in order to stay alive. What would Zara's face look like then? With a shake of her head, Roni forced herself not to think about that part. The future had possibilities now besides "looming horrific death," so she had to work with what she had.

She leaned on her knees and breathed hard while the others ran the obstacle course. She hadn't noticed any gloves on Zara today, especially not golden ones, but she sometimes had a golden chain looped around one hand. Roni had thought it might be some mark of rank, but she hadn't seen it on anyone else. It could be considered a glove, but what about the bird? She cast an eye over the trees beyond the fence, but with winter not yet over, there weren't many birds around, not that there were any metal ones around in other kinds of weather.

Something tweaked Roni's memory, a sight from days ago: something resting atop a roof near where Zara stood. She hadn't been able to tell much at a distance, but it had a bird's silhouette. She'd thought it a statue or gargoyle to scare smaller birds or vermin.

What the hell did Judith Esposito want with that?

Roni glanced around but didn't see it now. Maybe Zara had put it away. Roni couldn't fathom why, and the thought of Zara lugging around a gargoyle like a kid with her favorite toy made her chuckle.

"Something funny, Recruit?" Finn asked from her place near the obstacle course.

Damn. Finn had finally stopped yelling at everyone to get their lazy asses across the course, and now Roni had given her something new to bark at. "No, Sergeant."

"Does the obstacle course amuse you in some fashion?"

"No, Sergeant." Though the news that she'd be staying mixed with a rush of adrenaline made her giddy enough to find Finn amusing at this moment. She hoped to the gods she could hide it.

"Perhaps you don't find it challenging enough," Finn said.

Oh, shit. Mission failed. "No, Sergeant."

"No, you don't find it challenging?" Finn asked, and before Roni could argue, Finn turned to Jaq. "Recruit Bisset is laughing at our course, Jaq."

He gave Roni a sympathetic look, and she gave him one that she hoped said she knew she was screwed anyway. "Better have her run it again," he said.

Roni couldn't even be mad as she jogged to the beginning, waiting until Tati and Cortez finished their final runs before she began again. The muscles in her legs twanged like bowstrings as she climbed. Her head swam when she reached the top, the rushing in her ears nearly enough to drown out Finn's braying. Okay, maybe she was a little irritated, but that was because she felt like she might drop at any moment.

She paused before the log, trying to find the balance that seemed to have fled before she'd even started. She gripped one of the support beams and half turned, trying to say she needed a moment.

"Get on with it, you lazy shit," Finn bellowed.

Roni froze as something gleamed in the distance. It was Zara, her helmet shining in the sun like always, but now it had competition, something gleaming from her hand as she walked. Finn's cries faded to nothing as Roni squinted. "I'll be damned," she whispered. It was a fucking metal bird perching on that golden chain like a real bird might.

It seemed smaller than before.

All Roni's thoughts of what and why and how tumbled together as the platform shook slightly. Finn was climbing, mouth working all the while. "I swear to the gods, Bisset, if you haven't moved by the time I get up there…"

The shaking added to her vertigo, making the world tilt sideways, but Roni managed to hang on to the beam.

Until the metal bird statue turned its head to look at her.

Then she fell into the muddy water below.

The cold water hit her like a slap, stealing her breath more than a short fall ever could. Jaq pulled her from the water while Finn bellowed from the platform above, asking if she was all right.

She managed to nod as she looked for Zara again, but Jaq sent her in to change right as Zara joined them with the metal bird, its head swiveling to look at everyone. Roni cursed her clumsiness and Finn's attitude and even the cold that made it essential for her to rush in to change rather than wait around to find out what was up with the bird.

By the time she returned, the recruits were celebrating the fact that they were all going to be scouts, all except Emil, who had been pointed to another part of the base. Zara and her metal bird were gone.

Damn, damn, damn. Roni had finally seen the metal bird Judith Esposito and Hacha were so interested in, and she'd missed getting an introduction. She nursed a slightly sore shoulder and listened to Jaq and Finn walk them through how to pack their kit when they left the next morning.

Roni thought about the bird as she gathered all the things the army had given her. It looked like a hawk or eagle or something—her bird education was sorely lacking—and it did seem to be made of metal by the way it glinted, but it was so...detailed. And it moved, even flew if that had been it she'd seen on the roof. The wind didn't blow its feathers around. She wondered if it breathed. Or blinked. The thought of an inhuman, non-blinking stare made the back of her neck itch.

When Jaq walked around to supervise the packing, Tati asked, "What was that metal bird, Sarge? The boss didn't say much besides calling it the Vox...thingy."

"Feram," Jaq said.

Roni turned in their direction. Maybe she hadn't missed a detailed discussion after all.

"The Vox belongs to the commander," Finn barked from where she stood by the door. "That's all you need to know."

Shit. Why couldn't Finn take the stick out of her ass just once?

Jaq chuckled and winked. "Best to leave the Vox alone," he said quietly. "Or it might take a chunk out of your finger with that big beak."

Perfect. Roni sighed. Well, at least that was information she needed to have when she stole it.

"Just keep your minds on the task at hand," Finn yelled, and that was that.

The squad rode out at dawn the next day. Even with long underwear, shirt and trousers, a heavy jacket, leather armor, stout boots, fingerless gloves, a cloak that went over everything, and a helmet, the cold managed to seep in. Roni shivered on her horse, happy that she wasn't walking, at least, and that her horse carried her pack for her. They rode single file down a well-worn road, passing towns and villages that lay between the city of Sarras and the wilderness that preceded the border. Zara set a quick pace. By the time they stopped that evening at an army waystation to rest and change mounts, Roni was too saddle sore and exhausted to think about much of anything, let alone speak. Along with everyone else, she fell into bed after dinner and slept like the dead.

The next morning was much the same, except they picked up two other veterans of the squad at the next waystation, corporals who introduced themselves as Ernesto and Claudia. They could have been siblings with their tanned skin, dark hair, and dark eyes. They were nearly the same height, too, an inch or two taller than Roni, nearly six feet. Jaq informed Roni and the other recruits that Ernesto was their primary medic, with Jaq serving as backup.

Roni tucked that bit of information away, but Leo seemed to brighten and followed Ernesto around as if the very presence of a medic would keep him safer.

It was agony to get back on a horse again, but Jaq told them they'd miss the transportation after the last and final waystation that evening, after which the wilderness truly began, and they'd have to walk. Disbelieving, Roni almost fell to her knees that night when they reached the final waystation—that also served as an outpost—and praised the gods and even the devils. Ana, the final corporal on the squad, joined them there. She was small, darker than Finn and Jaq, and she lacked the pale patches that ran across their faces, but when she smiled, it seemed to light up the room. Tati took to her much as Leo had taken to Ernesto, only Tati blushed like a kid every time Ana grinned at her.

Something about the sight made Roni look for Zara, but she was discussing something with Finn and Claudia. When their eyes met, Zara gave her another of those confused looks before diving back into her conversation.

Roni tried to tell herself to forget it. Zara wasn't interested, and the reasons why ultimately didn't matter. But though she agreed with herself there, her eyes didn't seem likely to stop looking. Maybe they'd taken disobedience lessons from her mouth.

In the morning, the horses remained at the outpost while the squad would cut through the ass-end of nowhere on foot. "I've never been so happy to walk before," Tati grumbled.

Roni had to agree.

Now that they were three days away from the city, Roni hoped to walk near Zara and work up the courage to ask about the Vox, but the three corporals stuck close to Zara now, speaking quietly. Jaq followed just behind them, then came the four recruits, and Finn marched at the rear to growl at any stragglers.

A dense forest in winter was the quietest thing Roni had ever heard, and it gave her the creeps. That combined with the cold and the weight of her gear—much more difficult to tote without horses—quickly sank her into a funk. They were damned with horses or without. And unfortunately, her funk did not stop her from thinking nearly as much as a saddle-sore ass had. The squad wasn't alone in the woods. Hacha was out there somewhere, waiting for her to steal the Vox now that she was on foot.

She should tell everyone. Right now. She was surrounded by a military squad, people who could overwhelm Hacha with numbers if not skill. She should confess that he'd threatened her, that he'd been responsible for the guard accused of drinking on duty. She'd already told Zara about Judith Esposito. Why not take this final step?

Hacha's face loomed in her memory. His voice echoed in her skull, saying he'd kill them all. And he wouldn't be easy to find, not even by this lot. He wouldn't run if they began to look for him. No, that bastard would wait in the shadows. He'd pick them off one by one. He'd enjoy it, probably saving Zara for last so Roni wouldn't have anywhere to turn. She'd just have to watch.

An all the biting metal birds in the world wouldn't stop him.

Roni swallowed hard as the image of the squad lying mangled and broken brought her out in a cold sweat. She'd met them all now, knew their names. She even liked some of them. And as for Zara... well, she couldn't watch her die. Ah, who was she kidding? She wouldn't be able to watch any of them die even if she didn't know or like them. She didn't like seeing people get hurt. That was why she'd never gotten into muggings and never broke into houses where anyone was still awake. She couldn't take a swing at even the richest of nobs, didn't lift a finger to anyone unless they came at her first. Even then, she'd never killed anyone.

And it had been a gamble telling Zara about Judith Esposito in the first place. Roni kept thinking of Zara's comment about the troop sharing problems because they only had one another to rely on out here. The last thing Roni wanted to do was be another problem. If they knew a killer had followed her, they might leave her to deal with him alone.

Gods, why couldn't the cold and the gear and her sore body be the only things she had to worry about? They hadn't even gotten to the enemy soldiers and scouting part of their little adventure, yet, and she was already tied up in knots.

Beside her, Tati groaned. "They didn't prepare us for all this walking. We practiced on ropes and logs and went for short runs. Where's all that now?"

Roni tried to laugh, but it came out a wheeze. The obstacle course did sound better than this monotonous, foot-breaking stumbling. A light cover of snow and frost hid all the loose limbs and tree roots and whatever else that seemed determined to trip her. "At least we're not on horseback anymore."

"The horses lugged all this shit for us," Cortez said behind her.

"Sore back or sore ass," Roni said. "That's the trade."

They snorted laughs until Leo said, "Not just sore. All the skin on my thighs is gone," and then they laughed a little harder, everyone sounding punchy with fatigue.

"Quiet," Finn said, low and growly. She didn't seem tired at all. She was probably powered by an inexhaustible supply of anger.

Zara called a halt soon after, and Roni sat in a circle with the other recruits. Now that they were part of the squad, that title didn't seem to fit anymore. But no one had given them another. Zara stood with the corporals and sergeants, looking over a map. Finn jerked a thumb toward Roni's group, and Zara stared in their direction with a frown.

Great. What could Sergeant Asshole possibly want Zara to do with them? Probably have them up front as arrow fodder.

When Zara and the others marched over, the recruits fell silent. Tati and Leo leaned forward eagerly while Cortez stiffened and caught Roni's eye, looking as wary as she felt. Zara glanced at each of them, and her gaze seemed to linger on Roni, though that could have been her imagination.

Ever hopeful. Like a chump.

"Finn has reminded me that as members of my squad, you should be privy to what this mission is about."

Roni wanted to frown at the fact that Zara had to be reminded to include them, but she was equally flabbergasted that it was Finn who'd suggested involving them instead of, say, suggesting they be thrown into a ravine. But Finn did seem to care about her job and would no doubt yell through it as expertly as she possibly could.

Zara turned the map around to show them. Roni guessed some of the squiggly lines were trees, but beyond that, it meant nothing to her. "We're here," Zara said, pointing, "and our objective is this point along the Kingfish River, across the border with the Firellian Empire. We're to scout the area, make note of any Firellian activity, and report back."

Roni glanced at the other recruits to find them all looking at one another.

"That's it?" Tati asked.

Finn made a little noise of disapproval. "You say commander when speaking to her. And don't speak unless spoken to."

Tati flinched. "Sorry, Sergeant, Commander."

Ernesto, Claudia, and Ana looked away or covered their smiles, but their expressions didn't seem cruel, more like they were remembering being dressed down by a sergeant a time or two.

The rest of the briefing was a discussion about which routes were best, with the three corporals having more up-to-date information than Zara and the sergeants. Roni strived to pay attention, but she had little to offer since no one wanted to know the best cheap restaurant on Bond Street or which nob lacked proper security.

But when the meeting broke up, Roni got an idea. If they weren't going to resume marching immediately, it was the perfect time to find out more about the Vox. She nearly leaped to her feet. She'd try the top first, see if Zara would give her any information.

It wasn't just that she wanted to be close to Zara. Well, not entirely. "A moment, Commander?"

Zara nodded from where she stood a slight distance from the others but closer to where the Vox perched like a statue on a low tree limb. "What's on your mind, Veronique?"

The sound of her first name was enough to make Roni shake off some discomfort from those unblinking golden eyes. Well, Jaq had said things got a little informal out in the sticks. Roni took a deep breath to buy time. She saw two paths in front of her all of a sudden: ask about the bird and so prepare to steal it or confess her deal with Hacha and make a plan to get rid of him.

"What are we?" came tumbling out of her mouth instead.

Zara blinked slowly, and Roni knew that question was meaningless without context. Unless, oh gods, what if Zara thought Roni was asking about their relationship status or something stupid like that? The completely absurd third option: make her commanding officer so uncomfortable that she'd leave Roni out here for the wolves to find.

With her cheeks burning, Roni held up a hand while it looked like Zara was trying to puzzle out her question. "Sorry, my thoughts got a little ahead of my mouth. I meant, what should we former recruits call ourselves?"

A relieved expression passed over Zara's face, and Roni was so happy to see anything that wasn't anger or disgust or any other emotion that would have frozen Roni's innards. Gods, she had to get ahold of herself.

Zara opened her mouth but tilted her head before she spoke. "I suppose you're…associates? Jaq and Finn are sergeants, and the others are corporals, but you…" She shrugged. "You didn't enlist, so you don't have a rank. I suppose we could call you specialists for now."

Roni stiffened, not well pleased at the idea of being nothing. "What does that mean for us when this mission is over?"

Another head tilt said she didn't know. "I suppose you might be given the option to fully enlist and take all the necessary training—"

"Why didn't that happen in the first place?" Roni snapped.

Zara frowned, probably at being interrupted. "I don't know. I was ordered to find a place for some of you on my imminent mission, so I did." And she didn't sound too thrilled by that, either.

Roni fought the urge to cross her arms. She had to keep her cool, even while discussing her entire future so casually. After all, she hadn't thought about the army in terms of forever, so why should anyone else? "Who'd you piss off to get those orders?" she said, trying to joke her way to a better mood but making sure to add, "Commander," this time.

"A colonel's daughter."

"You…what?"

Zara put her hands behind her back and nodded with a faraway gaze. "Oh, the prison reform idea was already in the works, but some unfortunate words to a colonel's daughter meant my squad was chosen first."

Emotions warred in Roni's chest. A spat between officers—no, no, an officer and an officer's fucking kid—had given her a way out of certain death, but no one had given a thought to her future beyond that. She was less than nothing, just an idea, an experiment to see if prison scum could play nice with the brave, morally upstanding, thoroughly bloodstained killers of the army.

The only thing that kept her from exploding now was the fact that Zara had chosen all four of the remaining recruits instead of sending them right back to hell. But gratitude only went so far.

Roni met the eyes of the Vox again, forced herself not to flinch, and dredged up a smile. "Well, then, I'd like to meet the last member of my squad if that's allowed." She nodded toward the Vox, gratified by Zara's warm smile in return.

"Veronique Bisset, this is the Vox Feram. The Vox already knows who you are," Zara said, gesturing between them.

Roni seemed a bit unnerved by that, but everyone found the Vox disquieting at first.

"They can't know me like you can," the Vox said in Zara's mind, and their many voices sounded pleased. They chose who they were bonded to, after all. "Please tell her I said hello."

"They say hello."

Roni blinked. "Um, hi," she said, first to Zara and then to the Vox. She gave Zara a careful, slightly doubtful smile. "Is it saying anything else?"

Zara rolled her eyes, used to this reaction, too. "Them. And I'm not having an auditory hallucination. The Vox communicates telepathically with their chosen partner."

Roni nodded slowly, and she seemed to be trying to keep her expression pleasant, but her smile seemed a touch artificial, and her eyes still flashed with doubt.

"Don't worry," Zara said. "Everyone has the same thoughts upon meeting the Vox. That's why I don't mind telling my squad about them, even though the Vox's existence is a secret outside of the army. I doubt anyone would believe you if you rambled about a living metal bird that only talks in one person's head."

Now Roni's smile seemed a bit more genuine. "That is a hard sell, yeah. And it's…sorry, *they're* alive?"

Zara's estimation went up a notch. She usually had to correct pronoun usage two or three times where the Vox was concerned. She nodded. "Much older than you or me and not subject to the same deficiencies, but alive, yes."

"Deficiencies?"

"They don't need to eat or sleep. They don't feel the need to seek out company."

"Thank the gods," the Vox said.

Roni's head tilted. "I rather like those deficiencies. Particularly the company one."

Gods and devils, was she flirting again? Granted, the thought wasn't as stomach-turning as Zara usually found it, but this wasn't the time or place, and she didn't know how to respond, and now her mind was sliding down unanticipated tracks, and—

"Easy," the Vox said. "She might have been simply stating a fact."

With a deep breath, Zara thanked the Vox as she held on to that thought, stopping her mind from wandering too far.

Roni was watching her with wide eyes. In fear?

"You have been quiet for longer than necessary," the Vox said.

Ah. "Um, yes," Zara said. She looked to the Vox again, desperate for some way to get this conversation back where it belonged. "The Vox can shift into any bird." The Vox graciously picked up on her invitation, and with a flutter of metal, they turned from a hawk to a horned owl.

Roni took a step back, her mouth open. "I knew they'd gotten smaller than the first time I saw them." Her face lit up with unmistakable joy. "That's amazing."

Zara felt a bit of heat in her cheeks, as if she had received the praise, but she was only happy someone else recognized how incredible the Vox was.

They soaked up the compliment. "I am amazing, yes." They inched a little closer along the branch. "She can touch if she wishes."

Zara passed that on, and Roni extended a careful finger, staying clear of the beak and stroking the feathers atop the Vox's head before she withdrew with a shudder. "Beautiful but so cold." Her gaze flicked to Zara, as if she was afraid this statement would be accepted badly.

With a wave, Zara dismissed the comment. It was nothing more than truth.

Roni nodded at the chain wrapped around Zara's hand, over her cloth glove but with the jewel resting against her bare wrist. "And that glove? Do you only wear it when the Vox is around?"

Interesting. She was very observant, but in this instance, Zara wasn't sure if that was a mark in her favor. Learning surface details about the Vox was one thing, but when it came to how to operate them, well, that should stay between the two of them. "It's time we were moving again." She gestured for Roni to fall back with the other specialists.

"When we were just getting acquainted?" Roni asked. She winced a little as if her mouth had run off with her again.

Zara glared, but her stomach twisted at the thought of them truly getting to know each other, of maybe being alone together. She shuddered and shook her head, fighting the urge to lash out harder than she needed to. "That's enough of that, Bisset. Back in line." Zara turned away and nodded at Finn to bark everyone else into order.

The Vox resumed a smaller shape and perched on her shoulder as Zara began leading them down a game trail once more. She tried to keep her focus where it belonged: their location and the distance they'd have to march before they angled northwest and began the gradual uphill journey. But her attention kept drifting to Roni's reactions, to her mention of company, and how Zara's mind had wandered, and her body tingled in ways she was unaccustomed to.

"She was talking about you," the Vox said, thankfully interrupting her thoughts.

"About becoming acquainted? I know."

"With the beautiful and cold remark."

Zara frowned and went back over the conversation. "But she touched you."

"Then looked at you."

"But…" That made no sense. She was a hell of a lot warmer than the Vox just because of the blood flowing through her veins.

The Vox chuckled. "Personality-wise."

Hmm. That hurt a little. She wasn't cold. She just didn't like any feelings that got in the way of the job. She was cautious and thought things through. Just because she didn't go around spewing emotions like lava didn't mean—

Zara shook her head again and grumbled, speaking even softer than before. "This is why I didn't want to bring her along. She is a distraction. I shouldn't care what she thinks of me."

"You should have sent her back to prison, then."

"No, not if it's the death sentence she claims, and I may not be an expert on feelings, but I know fear when I see it." And why couldn't Roni be grateful and leave it at that? She could become a loyal, valuable specialist, go through basic training when they returned to Sarras, and then she could rejoin Zara's squad with a rank of her own, and they'd have some much-needed distance.

If not that, Roni could start a romance with one of the other squad members, and then Zara could resign herself to that fact and get on with her life.

Or be so envious she ground her teeth to powder.

"I know you're not cold," the Vox said, their many voices softer, too. "But not everyone gets to see inside your head. Would it be so bad if you and she—"

"Yes," Zara said, a little too loudly. She cleared her throat. She couldn't see any relationship of that kind as more than a distraction, one even more dangerous than the small amount she felt now. The feelings, the sensations she imagined, they'd all be new. If Adella and Gisele were to be believed, she'd be swept away and turn into a moony, sighing creature like they sometimes did.

Gods, what a repulsive thought.

"Maybe it doesn't have to be that way," the Vox said. "You operate in unique ways, think in ways others sometimes find strange. I can't help but think you'd find a unique way of being romantically involved, too."

True. She didn't do many things the same way Adella and Gisele did. She often did them better, though they became quite snotty when she pointed that out. But what would it be like…

No, that didn't matter, not now, not when she had a mission to complete.

She forced herself to think about small details, a coping mechanism from her younger days. She felt the cold and compared it to another winter mission she'd undertaken. The frost wasn't seeping through her boots like the snowdrifts of last time, but the wind was stronger now, forcing her to hide her chin in her cloak. Crunching footfalls provided the only sound in the forest, and the trail was hard to determine with even a keen eye.

Thus distracted, Zara kept Roni out of her thoughts until they reached their first campsite. Then she was free to stand back and observe while the others set up tents, gathered firewood, and prepared the evening meal. With the Vox beside her, Zara tried to find fault with Roni, forcing herself to be hypercritical in order to stop…whatever it was happening inside her. If she discovered all of Roni's faults—and no doubt there were many—this early in their association, Zara could more easily brush off any feelings as if they were stray cobwebs.

But Roni seemed to be performing all her tasks adequately. And what was more, both the old and new members of the squad seemed to like her. Finn even gave her the occasional compliment, a rare jewel, though those were still embedded in sarcasm. Indeed, as everyone gathered to eat, some seemed to gravitate toward Roni, and she told a story that had them all laughing.

Zara frowned as a cord of jealousy wound through her. She'd never known that easy familiarity, had never drawn anyone into her presence the way Roni did. Neither her squad nor her family sought her company like that.

"She's a flash in the pan," the Vox said. "New and exciting. They'll soon become used to her and so will you, and any power she has over all of you will fade."

"You were drawn to her, too. You even let her touch you."

"And that didn't make you jealous. So why should this?"

Zara didn't have an answer, but she couldn't stop the feelings that seemed determined to haunt her. Finn brought her a share of the dinner but only stayed long enough to ask if she had everything she needed before going back to the others as Roni began another tale.

"So go join them," the Vox said, but they didn't sound particularly enthused by their own suggestion.

Zara could relate. She didn't like gatherings. Though she understood most jokes, she didn't find them funny, and that usually made her stand out for the wrong reasons. She'd never had a knack for being the life of the party.

"Is that something you want?" the Vox asked, their voices hesitant, doubtful, as if a greater decision rested on her choice.

"No." But just for a moment, she wondered what it would be like.

She snorted a laugh. Well, all she'd have to do was meet a group of people just like her, and then she could find out. Though a group of Zaras wouldn't have to tell stories and laugh loudly. They'd be comfortable sharing silences.

The Vox made a noise of agreement, and Zara retired to her tent to bask in her own quiet.

If her mind would shut the hell up for the night.

CHAPTER ELEVEN

After spending the night shivering in a tent in the middle of nowhere, Roni was ready for the horses to appear out of thin air so she could ride back to civilization, sore ass be damned. But the squad only walked deeper into forested nowhere and would continue to do so until they neared the Firellian part of rocky *and* forested nowhere, where anyone they encountered was likely to kill them.

And as every creaking branch or gust of wind had reminded Roni the night before, someone was out to kill her now, no waiting for the border required. At least when they were marching and she was cold and tired and miserable, she didn't fear death so much as long for it. If Hacha had appeared in one of her miserable moments, she might even have cheered.

As if summoned by her dark thoughts, something whistled out of the trunks and dense bracken, the rush of air tingling Roni's cheek like a butterfly kiss. She looked behind her. Tati dabbed at a streaming cut on her cheek, staining her fingertips red.

Roni frowned. "What was—"

"Archers! Get down," Finn cried from the rear of the column.

Roni's meager training kicked in, and she dove for the underbrush, her cloak and pack catching on the spiny leaves like little fingers. Fear coursed through her in tingling waves. Gods, she hadn't meant it; she didn't want to die. She clamped her teeth shut on an apology to no one and forced herself to think. She was not some green kid committing their first burglary. She could handle herself. Several arrows whistled out of the trees. The rest of the squad had scattered from the trail, except for Tati, who still stared at the blood as if she'd never seen anything like it.

"Tati," Roni said, a high-pitched whisper. "Get over here."

Tati looked in her direction. She seemed confused, almost astounded.

"Gods," Roni said. "Move your ass, Tati." Damn it all to hell, she was going to get killed. Roni couldn't just lie there. "Fuck." Her stomach heaved, but she prepared to leap on Tati and probably vomit at the same time.

A cry came from ahead, and she whipped her head in that direction, straining to see through the branches. People were darting through the trees like sparrows, and metal clanged amidst cries of pain.

Fighting. Her squad was fighting.

Shit. She had to help. And maybe get shot. "Fuck it all, then." With fear twisting inside her, she drew her truncheon and clambered from the brush. She couldn't spare everyone from Hacha only to let them be killed by some random bastards in the woods. She started for Tati, who still stood frozen on the path.

A figure in dark leather armor came for Tati from the other side of the trail.

Roni shouted through her fear to get the newcomer's attention. A war cry like a dying cow drowned her out, and Leo leaped from the woods. He charged the newcomer, who sidestepped his clumsy lunge and shoved, sending Leo's spindly body flying into a snarl of brambles.

Tati started as if waking, and she drew her saber so quickly, it seemed to appear in her hand. She came at the newcomer with frenzied strokes. Roni tried to remember her combat training, but she'd been getting into scraps since she was a child, and no one needed to teach her how to fight dirty.

When the newcomer struck back at Tati, putting their weight forward, Roni crept up behind them and bashed the side of their knee. They howled and crumpled backward, kneeling, and Tati buried her blade in their neck.

The sounds of combat faded, and Roni stared at the newly made corpse. A gout of blood obscured their features. She'd never really seen what they'd looked like alive. She shifted her stare to Tati, who also watched the body with wide eyes, her face blanching to the color of old parchment. Roni had seen death, but she'd never…participated in making it.

A cry from behind made her turn. More of the squad was fighting ahead. Right, they weren't done yet. Claudia pointed at someone and yelled. Roni glanced around wildly and saw someone half-hidden in the trees with an arrow pointed in her direction.

"Oh." No time for fear. She'd never outrun—

Something fell on the archer with a metallic shriek that rattled through Roni's head and brought her terror back in a rush. She tried to decipher what was happening, but the parts of her that weren't screaming in terror were yelling at her to move. She grabbed Tati's arm and hauled her into the trees.

"Archers, archers," Roni managed as she scanned for more.

"Where?"

"Don't know." She had to find them, to warn everyone. She crashed through the brush toward the downed archer in time to see a golden eagle tearing their throat out.

The Vox glanced up at her before leaping into the air and taking wing. The light glinted off their bloodstained beak, their gore-covered claws and wings. How could she have ever thought to steal this flying collection of blades? She followed their progress back to the path and saw them alight above Zara, who scanned the battlefield in all directions, saber in hand.

"Sound off," Zara called.

As the squad began calling out their names, Roni took a deep breath and realized the fight was over. Seconds had gone by, but they were etched in her memory like hours. Shaky and jumbled, she couldn't manage her name until Tati said hers, then prodded Roni's shoulder.

"Bis…Bisset," Roni said.

"You okay?" Tati asked.

"I might throw up."

Tati nodded. "Aim into the trees." With one more grimace at the corpse, she started back to the path.

Ernesto circulated among them, checking for injuries, but Tati's cheek was the worst among cuts and bruises. She sat on the ground with a bandage pressed hard against her face. Once he'd been freed from the brambles, Leo rested beside her, his helmet off and his forehead leaning on her shoulder.

Roni stood beside them, feeling adrift. They hadn't covered the aftermath of battle in her hurried training, and that thought added anger to her growing ball of emotions. She couldn't keep her eyes away from the spot where the Vox had torn that archer to pieces.

"Bisset," Zara barked.

Roni felt her feet leave the ground before she even realized she'd leaped. She staggered, her hand going to her truncheon even as her mind screamed that the fight was over.

And that attacking Zara would be a grave mistake.

As if she could pull that off. Zara grabbed Roni's arm and her opposite shoulder and stepped into her space so quickly, Roni was hypnotized by the light smattering of freckles across her nose. Her dark eyes were calm and beautiful and had the world under control.

Roni relaxed in her grip even before she spoke.

"Veronique," Zara said softly but without a hint of softness. "The fight's done. Get a grip. You're fine. We're fine."

Roni nodded, comforted in a strange way. "Y…yes, serrah."

"Right." She stepped back quickly. "Go help Cortez search those bodies."

"But why? For…coin?" That sounded like something any hard-up denizen of the Haymarket would do if they found a corpse in the snow.

Zara frowned. "For anything that tells us who they were, where they were from, or what they were doing out here."

Finn stepped up to her side, frowning. "Coins count as clues, but we are not some band of petty thieves." Even when she was keeping her voice low, she seemed to be shouting. "Report anything of note."

Roni stepped woodenly to where Cortez was going through the pockets of the dead with sickening efficiency. She could only watch for a moment, following hesitantly in his wake until he directed her action-by-action. With her stomach rolling over, she patted the clothes of one of the deceased attackers. Her gaze kept trying to drift to the open eyes, the bloodstained face, but she knew she'd throw up for sure if that happened, and Zara was still watching, and oh gods, Roni did not want to throw up in front of her.

"Anything?" Zara asked, kneeling beside Cortez. When she looked at Roni again, she drew back as if shocked. "Take a break, Veronique. You're nearly green."

Roni stood and breathed deep, hoping the embarrassment would settle her stomach. "Thank you, Commander."

After a nod, Zara turned back to Cortez, who gestured to a small pile of items. "Nothing telling, Commander. A few canteens and trail rations. A length of twine and some other miscellaneous bits. No money. No markings on the weapons or armor."

Zara moved to the face of the corpse and bent low, her brows puckered as she tilted her head to stare at the very sight Roni wanted to forget completely.

She swallowed as her chest burned with bile.

"Too bad you can't tell if someone's Firellian just by looking at them," Zara said.

"Think that's who they were?" Ana asked as she joined them. A white, bloodstained bandage stood out against the dark skin of her arm. She tossed a few bits of flotsam into Cortez's pile.

Again, nothing seemed unique, but focusing on the things did wonders for Roni's calm.

"Who else?" Zara said as she stood. "Brigands would hunt closer to the road, and these all seem too well-fed and healthy to be vagrants."

Cannibals, maybe, living in the wilderness, eating whoever they caught. Well, that made the breakfast want to appear again. Roni clenched her fists and told herself to shut it.

"They're not carrying enough supplies to have been out here for long," Claudia said. "They have to have a camp nearby." She studied the woods, her handsome, squared profile so much like Ernesto's.

If Roni could just stay fixated on small details like that...

"All right," Zara called. "Listen up." Everyone gathered around, giving Roni more details to look at, and she almost shouted with glee when Zara said, "Spread out, look for tracks. We need to know where they came from."

And she couldn't possibly focus on the dead while bent double, searching for clues amidst the churned-up mud and frost.

And it would have been nice if that was true, but her mind only managed to work its way back around to the torn archer and the person she'd helped Tati kill. It hadn't seemed to matter in the moment. Tati was her squad-mate. Roni had to help, even if she'd only acted after Leo had burst from the trees like a deranged ox. But she couldn't shake the feeling of her truncheon against that leg or the sight of Tati's saber poking out of their neck.

Gods and devils, why did everything about this whole adventure make her feel so many damn things?

As she thought of the dead, she couldn't help wondering what would have happened if she hadn't helped Tati or if the Vox hadn't helped with that archer.

"You all right?" a quiet voice asked from behind her.

Roni jumped again and cursed herself as she put a hand to her heart and faced Ana. "Sorry, um, serrah. Yes, I'm fine." She tried a smile and felt it wobble. Maybe she'd get lucky, and Ana would put any shaking down to the cold.

"You can call me Ana." Her smile was small but confident. "You've been staring at nothing for a few moments."

"Looking for tracks," Roni mumbled, embarrassed to be caught out.

"It's all right to be upset after your first battle." She stepped around, also searching the ground.

Roni couldn't stop herself from saying, "I've been in fights before." She wasn't sure why she was feeling snappy. Maybe because she usually worked alone, and having to look after people freaked her out.

Not only that, she had to rely on them to watch her back, too. That thought made her extra anxious and more than a little angry that she'd been forced into this position. She didn't need a damn nursemaid.

"A street fight is different from a battle," Ana said with the same steady voice. "I grew up in the Haymarket, too, you know."

Roni hesitated as a cold feeling rushed through her. "How did you know that's where I'm from?" A list of who this woman could be spying for raced through her even as Ana gave her another smile.

"That swing to the leg. Old mugger's trick."

Roni bristled. "I was never—"

"Or a good move for helping a friend in a sticky situation."

That was more like it. Roni took a deep breath. Her suspicions about Ana being a spy were probably incorrect, but she'd keep a few cards close for a while. "The street fights I was in didn't yield many corpses." Or any at all.

Ana nodded. "That's what I mean. Here, try this." She took a deep breath. "Inhale, count to five, exhale, repeat." She led Roni through it a few times.

The anxiety in her chest eased a little, and she ducked her head, a bit embarrassed by her suspicious thoughts. As if Zara would have a spy in her midst.

Was Roni any better?

No, damn it, that was different.

When someone found the attackers' tracks, the time for censuring herself was over, at least for the moment. Everyone went quiet as they followed Zara, with Claudia ranging far ahead of the rest of them and Ana halfway between her and the squad, gesturing for them to follow, stop, or stay low.

Roni crowded with the others and ended up near Zara as Ana called a brief halt. Little lines of fatigue gathered at the corners of Zara's eyes, and her forehead hadn't lost its intense crease. Her breathing seemed a little labored, too, and Roni wondered if she'd been wounded but hadn't bothered to tell anyone.

Typical for the strong, mostly silent type.

But though the thought of Zara being wounded worried Roni more than it should, she hesitated, certain any concern would be met with recrimination or stony silence. She shifted slightly as they waited by a clump of trees for the signal to come ahead. Zara didn't have any bandages that Roni could see, nor was there any blood. But she could have twisted a joint or something. Maybe if Roni said something to one of the sergeants, they could speak where she couldn't.

She glanced around to find Jaq already looking in Zara's direction. Good. He and Finn could convince Zara to belt up and take help if she needed it. When he stepped closer, Roni stared ahead at Ana as if she wasn't paying attention to Zara. She had to hold her breath to hear Jaq say, "You're using the Vox too much."

Zara made a small noise of disagreement. "They were useful in the combat."

Too true.

Jaq stayed silent, and eventually, Zara sighed and said, "They agree with you, it seems. I'll start putting them to sleep at night."

Interesting in more ways than one. Roni glanced out of the corner of her eye and saw Zara rub at the chain glove right where a jewel nestled against her wrist. So the Vox did sleep in spite of being made of metal. And if the glove and the bird went together somehow, Zara would probably take that off at night, too. That would be the time to steal both and give them to Hacha.

And if the Vox was needed in battle again, someone would die like she almost did.

Roni squeezed a fist and cursed herself, Hacha, and the whole fucking world. Maybe she'd get really lucky, and they'd find Hacha's frozen body if he'd stumbled on these same attackers earlier.

The devils would never allow her a boon like that.

Ana gestured for them to come ahead, and they creeped slowly until Claudia appeared in the distance, waving them in. They picked up speed, and Roni's breath caught at the scene opening in front of them.

Three tents flapped idly in the breeze, standing open. One had been slashed down the side, and various items had been strewn through the snow as if tossed around in a quick search. But what drew the eye more was the crimson trails frozen in the snow, streaming across the gently fluttering tents and nearby trees. Roni followed them as she would a river across a map to three bodies lying like so much garbage on the frosted mud.

Roni couldn't hold back a whimper as her heart lodged in her throat. Three bodies? Well, three heads, at least, with throats cut so deeply, one head lay almost flush with its shoulder. One corpse's belly stood open, a red and black pit lightly dusted with snow like icing sugar.

Beyond that...who could tell? Limbs and gore and bits of flesh had been cast around as if their insides had been searched like their tents. This was frenzy, the work of an animal, but Roni knew it was an animal that walked on two legs.

Hacha's work, his legend becoming terrible reality.

CHAPTER TWELVE

"What in the gods' names?" Zara said, aware that she'd already said it once, but as she stared at the carnage in front of her, she could only say it again. She licked her lips and swallowed, but that only forced more of the heavy scent of blood and offal down her throat.

With a cough, she turned to find most of the squad either equally affected or vomiting into the bushes. Even Cortez, who hadn't flinched at the bodies in the road, looked upon this butchery from the side of his eye while frowning deeply.

Zara tried to speak and coughed again, swallowing bile. "Search the tents," she said, counting on a volunteer to emerge. "And the…" She couldn't say bodies because that couldn't be true. Human beings couldn't be reduced to so much carrion.

The Vox landed in the blood-covered snow and shimmered as they changed into one of their larger forms, a harpy eagle. Zara took a deep breath as her heart pounded, and she felt even more light-headed. Jaq had been right. She needed to remove the glove that connected her to the Vox more often. The larger forms took a toll on her during normal times, and after days of nonstop connection, this shift made her stomach cramp.

"Sorry," the Vox said, radiating sympathy. "I'll be quick. No one else seems to have the, um, stomach for it right now."

Zara sensed the slight humor in the Vox's many voices as they regarded the corpse that had been disemboweled. She clucked her tongue and winced. The Vox didn't furnish her mind with any other images as they picked at clothing and detritus, searching for clues along with those who looked through the tents. "Your sense of humor can be rather dark," she muttered.

The Vox only chuckled in her mind.

"Commander?" Roni was staring, her face tight with worry or horror and her skin the color of ash.

Zara stepped toward her, unsure what Roni was asking about but sensing she needed words, at least. "Bisset." She took a breath and made her voice softer. "Veronique. Are you all right?"

"I…are you?"

"Of course." Zara begged her roiling stomach not to prove her a liar. "You can wait on the path." She nodded toward where some of the others lingered. "You don't have to touch anything. Try…try to put it out of your mind." That had been her advice to a few recruits after seeing their first dead bodies, but it sounded lame after witnessing this. Who could put such a nightmarish tableau from their thoughts?

"This is…they're…" Roni still couldn't seem to form a thought.

Damn. Zara patted her awkwardly on the shoulder and looked for Jaq, but he was busy counseling some of the other specialists. "It'll be all right." Adella would say to give her a hug, but the army wasn't that kind of world. She dreaded to think what Gisele would say. Probably something about kissing her to distract her, bloodshed be damned.

"Firellian coins," the Vox said. Zara got a flash of one in the massive talons of the harpy eagle. Blood sat in the coin's etching. In such a place, blood could be in every breath.

Zara coughed again and pressed a hand to her mouth. She steered Roni farther from the bloodbath and stood between her and the scene. The others slowly migrated toward them, and Cortez and Claudia produced more items of Firellian origin, though nothing that indicated their purpose in these woods.

"The weapons and armor are similar to what we found on the others," Claudia said. She kept her normal stony expression but had a sheen of sweat above her lips. Even the calmest of them seemed to be boiling inside. "By the look of the place, they've been camping here awhile before they were killed."

"But what happened to them?" Ana said in a harsh whisper. She glanced at the Vox as they landed on Zara's shoulder in the small shape of a falconet.

"The Vox didn't do this," Zara said before that suspicion could take hold of anyone else. When Ana didn't seem relieved or even convinced, Zara frowned. "The Vox doesn't act without my direction, Corporal. Or do you think I ordered this?" She jerked her head backward.

Ana whipped her head from side to side so fast, her helmet wobbled a little. "No, Commander. I'm sorry, serrah."

Zara nodded, mollified for now. The Vox muttered something about not being an animal except in shape.

"Was it an animal?" Ernesto added, voicing Zara's sudden thought.

"Animals don't use knives," Finn said, one of the few who'd managed to get close to the bodies. "Only a knife can slice a neck like that."

"Infighting?" Leo asked quietly.

Claudia shrugged but shook her head. "I've never seen this level of violence even in a mutiny." She sneered and waved as if to banish a bad memory. "I suppose they could have all gone rabid or something."

"The ones who attacked us weren't rabid," Finn said.

"They could have left before these went mad." Claudia shrugged again as if to say she wasn't convinced by that idea herself.

"Who could do this?" Zara said. "Rabid or not?"

Cortez made a small noise and rubbed his forehead, pushing his helmet up slightly. When Zara nodded at him to speak, he opened his mouth, then sighed. "It's probably nothing…I mean, it *is* nothing. I was just remembering a bogeyman from the Haymarket, a story that started around, oh, fifteen years ago. The Hatchet?" He looked at the others.

Ana snorted without humor. "Don't be stupid. The Hatchet is just a story, something to scare your siblings with on dark nights."

Cortez shrugged. "I said it was nothing, but cutting people up with a big knife? It fits the story."

"Wouldn't he use, um, a hatchet?" Ernesto asked as he scratched his eyebrow, hiding a mocking smile.

"I just said it *sounds* like the stories," Cortez said. "I knew I shouldn't have said anything."

Zara nodded, understanding the mockery but also the comparison. Scenes like the one behind her should have been reserved for horror stories.

"Back me up," Cortez said to Roni.

She started as if someone had grabbed her, her horrified look deepening as she trembled. Jaq grabbed her elbow as if afraid she'd pass out, but she waved him off with a humorless, twitching smile. "I'm all right." She took a shuddering breath. "I've…heard the stories. Everyone has. Everyone." She wouldn't meet anyone's gaze.

Zara opened her mouth to ask if there was more, but the Vox said, "Ask her later," just as Zara thought of that, too. Whenever Roni had voiced concerns about anything, they'd been alone. She probably preferred that setting.

"Even if someone decided to make this Hatchet real," Zara said instead, "they surely would have started in the Haymarket, not all the way out here." She drew herself up, not wanting to linger. "Form up. We need to be well away from here before any hungry wolves stumble upon it."

That made them hop. Zara consulted her map and led them away. She tried to turn her thoughts away from what she'd seen and back to what Firellians were doing this far inside the Sarrasian border. The camp wasn't big enough to be an invasion force. Scouts? But why so far away from home? And something else about that camp bothered her, too.

"Probably the mutilated corpses," the Vox said. They continued to ride on her shoulder rather than tax her by flying. She was grateful, even though they couldn't function unless she could. They pecked lightly on her helmet. "And I care about you, of course."

Zara smiled lightly. "Of course. I wasn't thinking about the bodies." Yet they flashed into her mind again, making her wince. "As Claudia pointed out, that camp had been there awhile. The firepit was well used, and the ground only had a light dusting of snow." As did the bodies. Seemed she wasn't going to get rid of that image anytime soon.

"And so?"

"Scouts keep on the move."

"You think they were, what, guarding something?"

Zara gestured around. "There's nothing here."

The Vox shifted slightly. "Something that was taken by whoever killed them?"

She shook her head. Right now, they were assuming that the Firellians had killed one another, and if that was the case, the squad would have found this object that had to be guarded. And why in the gods' names would the Firellians bring something this far into their enemies' territory to guard it? "Not a thing," she said softly. "A place?" Before the Vox could speak, she tapped her chin. "Not for itself, but for the path." This wasn't a well-worn track to the border, but it was still a path, one of a few that Zara knew about. And one of a few the Firellians might be watching. Perhaps they didn't want anyone getting anywhere near their border.

Guarding the border itself? Or was it something at the border?

Zara was still pondering when she called a halt for the night. The sergeants set watches as well as directing the setup of the camp. Zara didn't share all her suspicions, wanting to let them stew in her head for a bit. Everyone seemed on edge enough to be hyper vigilant.

Especially Roni, who seemed to jump at every thump of snow sliding off a bare branch. She still shivered, and Zara bet it was from more than cold.

"Veronique?" Zara called softly, trying not to startle her further, but she still whipped around at the sound. She then sighed and chuckled as if laughing at herself, but her eyes were still wide, face taut. Zara motioned her away from the others, but she stared at the shadows among the trees as if they might come alive.

Zara frowned. She wouldn't hug Veronique, and she damn sure couldn't kiss her, no matter what her hindbrain thought about that. Time to fall back on the brusqueness she knew best. "Out with it, Bisset."

Roni blinked for several moments as if Zara had switched languages. "Co...commander?"

"You've been jumpy since that camp, which I can understand to a point, but unless I miss my guess, it affected you more than the others. I want to know why." This might constitute prying into the personal lives of her squad, but instinct said that wasn't it. If Roni had seen something significant back there, Zara needed to know.

It was also nice to have someone to focus her frustration on, but that was neither here nor there.

Roni took a deep breath, and her haunted look gave way to something stonier. "I'm sorry, Commander, if my…*jumpiness* is interfering in some way with my duties. I'll do better." She turned as if to leave.

"I didn't dismiss you." Zara welcomed the fresh rush of irritation. "Did you spot something significant to our situation at that camp? Do you have an idea of who did it? Are you afraid of the bogeyman? Out with it."

Roni's jaw tightened, and her eyes flashed. "You do not have command of my thoughts, serrah, or a right to my past." She blinked as if realizing who she was speaking to, then winced. "Commander," she added, a bit more respectful.

Zara couldn't be angry, not when it felt like she was finally getting somewhere. "You were right when you said your mouth sometimes runs before your thoughts. Do you remember what I said about how a squad carries the burdens of all its members?"

"I'm not the only one who doesn't tell you everything."

Interesting. That left Zara's footing a little uncertain, and she had to admit to a smattering of jealousy, even though she didn't want to sit around the campfire and delve into everyone's personal business. But if they had problems, why didn't they ask for her help or advice? She was good at a lot of tasks and knew about even more. "Such as?" Zara asked.

"I don't betray confidences." Now Roni was looking away like a petulant child, which made her admirable statement seem like so much nonsense. She couldn't say anything because she didn't know anything.

Or she was very good at making it seem that way.

Zara stepped closer, staring hard, a look most people backed down from. Most started babbling at that point or gave ground, but Roni met her eyes quickly and matched her height, her own gaze hard and unrelenting, not about to surrender.

Desire stirred through Zara's core, surprising her, almost shocking her enough to back away. Defiance should have made her angry, but all her "should-haves" seemed miles away at the moment. She licked her lips, and her breath hitched when Roni gave them a glance before meeting Zara's eyes again.

"Soldiers follow orders, Veronique," Zara said softly. "You should know that by now." When Roni smiled arrogantly, Zara wanted to kiss the look off her lips.

"As you pointed out before, Commander, we prison rats aren't really soldiers." She leaned so close they were almost touching, and her voice was a husky whisper. "But I'll follow wherever you lead whether it's to the border...or to your bed."

The heat building inside Zara died like a fire under a snowfall. She stepped back as guilt wormed through her. She would never order someone into her bed, especially not someone under her command.

Roni blinked as if confused. This clearly wasn't the reaction she was hoping for, but Zara had no idea what that was.

"You're dismissed." Zara walked away this time, ashamed of herself for even entertaining such thoughts about one of her soldiers, for taking even a modicum of advantage in their imbalance of power. That was why she couldn't be romantically involved with someone in her squad, now or ever.

Damn, damn, damn, damn. Roni couldn't stop screwing up. First, she'd been so freaked out by Hacha's work that she'd made Zara suspicious, then she'd given Zara the come-on.

With predictable results.

Part of it had been emotional flailing on Roni's part. She'd been so nervous all afternoon that everyone had probably noticed it. Then when Zara had been close enough that Roni could have reached all the way around her, could have kissed her without taking a step, Roni had grabbed on to lust as a way to stop being afraid.

Well, that, and she really, really wanted to kiss her.

But damn, she'd known Zara would react badly to that sort of directness. She seemed to like being in charge too much for anything else. Maybe Roni's big mouth had been reacting to the fear, too.

As she helped set up the tents, she kept replaying the moment, deciding at last that Zara hadn't been angered by Roni's words or even tired by them. She'd seemed sad, guilty even. Damn again. Not only had Roni pushed Zara away, she'd said something to trigger shame in her.

About having feelings for someone under her command? Possibly. And there *were* feelings there. Roni had seen it in the flush in Zara's cheeks, the bloom of her pupils, and the shortness of her breath.

Until Roni had fucked it all up.

"Hey," Cortez said, interrupting her reverie.

"Huh?"

He frowned and plucked a tent stake from her hand. "These are supposed to go in the ground. Unless you're going to hold the tent up all night."

"Yeah, yeah." Roni moved to another corner and chopped a stake into the frozen earth.

"What's eating at you?"

"Nothing."

"Bullshit. You've been nervy all day."

Wonderful. Another person who thought themselves a mind reader. And she had no desire to distract this one with come-ons or kisses. "Mind your own business."

He *tsked*. "It's the Hatchet, isn't it?"

Roni shivered. Gods and devils, she did not want to talk about the bogeyman or the real man. She'd heard some of the stories, but most people didn't know those were based on a real person. And the bloodiest exploits of the Hatchet were nothing on Hacha himself. "No."

"I think I was ten when I heard the first story about him."

Roni sighed. Cortez would have gotten along well with the chatty bucket-man from the prison. Both babbled on despite what their listeners wanted. Hell, maybe Cortez *was* bucket-man.

"You know what?" He leaned toward her with a conspiratorial look in his eye.

"Does it matter if I want to know or not?"

He grinned. "The Hatchet's a real guy," he whispered.

Roni's belly went colder than the snowy breeze picking up. Cortez was still smiling at her, and she didn't detect any malice behind the look, but she couldn't be sure. If he knew Hacha, chances were good that he'd worked with the Newgate Syndicate. Well, he had been in prison. Not everyone there could be as innocent as Tati claimed to be. But was he in Judith Esposito's gang? Watching Roni on her or Hacha's instruction?

Roni looked away, her heart hammering, though she told herself not to be paranoid. "Oh yeah?"

"It's the truth," he said, "but you shouldn't tell Ana or the others."

She tried to laugh, but it came out like a bray. She swallowed instead. "Why not? Don't you think they should know the real... Hatchet is out here?" She almost said Hacha, but she wanted to give him a little more room to spill what he knew before she declared anything.

Unless he already knew it all.

Shut up, shut up, shut up.

He stared into the dark woods. "Well, if the Hatchet's out here, it must be for a reason."

Was that a warning? She had to move her tongue around to work up enough spit to talk. "Like killing random Firellian soldiers?"

His grin was back. "Maybe he's the secret protector of Sarras."

She let out her breath in a rush, relieved that he was just messing around. "Maybe." She tried to chuckle, but it transformed into a yawn.

"Unless he's after one of us, and the Firellians got in his way."

"Damn it, Cortez." She almost barked that he should spit it out if he was working for Hacha, but she managed to stop herself. She lowered her voice. "Did my *nerviness* make you think I needed *more* to worry about?"

He held up a hand. "Sorry, sorry. Just thinking out loud."

Roni couldn't decide if he was an enemy or an idiot. But she would not be sharing a tent with him tonight, not unless at least two other people lay between them. She shivered as she looked at the dark trees. She also had to avoid sleeping by the tent wall, or she'd get no sleep at all.

As if being away from the wall would keep Hacha from reaching her.

Best to not sleep. She would take a watch, give Zara time to go to sleep, then steal the Vox and the chain glove. Then she'd be safe from Hacha, at least.

If he was feeling charitable when she handed them over.

Roni groaned and shook her head. Charitable for Hacha was probably killing someone quickly. Whatever she decided, it was going to be one hell of a long night.

She decided to take the last watch instead of the first. Everyone would be deeply asleep by then except for Ana, her watch partner. It would be easier to fake a visit to the latrine, then sneak into Zara's tent and steal the Vox and the glove.

Acid churned in her stomach at that decision, but it was a relief to have a decision, a plan. She hoped it would make her sleep easier, but she only lay awake next to Tati and Leo, staring at the darkness. Stealing the Vox was the right decision, even if it hurt some people in the short-term. At least she'd be alive to make it up to them.

But would anyone let her repay the theft? No, this new life would be over. Even if she managed to sneak back and protest her innocence, the squad would devolve into a nest of suspicion, with the veterans standing firm against the prison recruits. Tati and Cortez wouldn't take that lying down, and Roni could only imagine what would happen when angry words or even fists started flying.

The truth would come out. It always did. Oh gods, the disappointed look on Zara's face would kill her. Roni wasn't quite sure what Zara was feeling after her mysterious withdrawal, but the theft would not only anger her, it would hurt her deeply.

Perhaps literally as well as emotionally. Taking away such an efficient killing machine would leave the squad vulnerable to attack.

Great, that thought again. She'd be lucky if she ever slept again.

Still, when comparing all that to her own bloody murder…

Roni sighed. Death might be preferable to these rapidly multiplying consequences. She gritted her teeth, angry at herself, at the circumstances, at Zara, even at Tati for snoring softly while blissfully asleep. But mostly at Hacha, the murderous bastard who deserved to be carved up with his own knife. If only she stood a chance against him.

Roni gasped as she thought of the Vox pouncing on that archer like a bundle of blades. Who said she had to hand the Vox over once she had them? From what she'd heard, the glove controlled the Vox or let Zara communicate her wishes. Roni could put it on and either command the Vox or plead with them to end Hacha for good. They were metal, not flesh. His knife would be useless against them.

Grinning, Roni had to suppress the urge to leap from her bedroll. Gods and devils, she had the answer, killing two birds with one stone. Or one terrible murderer with one bird. Whatever. Then she'd return the Vox without Zara ever knowing, and all would be well.

When it was her turn to take watch, she nearly ran out of the tent in eagerness. Ana gave her a strange look as she yawned and took up her own position on the other side of the campfire.

Even with the odd look, Roni couldn't contain her smile. "Just… happy I finally get to pee," she whispered, nodding toward where the latrine waited in the trees.

Ana's lips quirked up, and she gave a slow nod as if humoring a madwoman.

Roni ignored her, grabbed a lantern, and made herself walk carefully into the trees. She couldn't risk waking everyone by blundering around like an ox. Plans shaped rapidly in her mind. First, she would leave the lantern in the woods, then creep to Zara's tent. That part would be easy. The theft would be more complicated, but she'd been taking things that didn't belong to her since she could walk. Putting it back later would be a definite novelty. But this plan was full of firsts. First time operating a metal bird, then asking said bird to rid the world of a monster, and finally convincing the bird to keep the whole adventure from Zara.

Tricky. Exciting. Gods, finally, here was something she could do. And she loved a challenge.

She nearly trembled as she set the lantern down and glanced back the way she'd come. Ana and the campfire were hidden by dark tree trunks. Good. Roni forced a few deep breaths, waiting for her limbs to still and her mind to quiet, just as she always did before a job. She found her center quickly, and calmness spread through her. She could do this, was good at this. Soon, everything would be all right.

When a hand clapped on her shoulder and turned her, she didn't panic, wondering which of the others it was, already lining up the lies she could use to send them—

Wide, panicked eyes met hers as the point of a knife introduced itself to her belly just below her leather armor.

Roni gasped, but the knife went no deeper, hesitating inside her jacket and shirt and just beneath her skin. Her world narrowed to the trickling sensation down her stomach, to those wild eyes and bared teeth. The feminine features were smeared with mud and blood. She whispered something unintelligible, and it was a heartbeat before Roni realized she was speaking Firellian.

A Firellian soldier, one who'd survived the massacre by the look of her…and the fact that this close, she stank of blood. She said something again, and the knife jabbed a fraction harder. Roni gasped anew, and the hand on her shoulder tightened.

"I don't understand," Roni whispered. Her calmness fled, but she forced herself to stay still through the pain. She'd be gutted before a scream even left her mouth. But it seemed like this soldier wanted to talk, and gods and devils, Roni wanted that, too, anything to keep that knife from moving. "I don't speak Firellian."

"You," the soldier whispered, her accent thick. She muttered a few more words, and her eyes filled with tears even as she frowned, looking somewhere between enraged and amazed or terrified. "Why kill? Kill so…much?"

Thinking of the soldiers who'd ambushed them on the trail, Roni said, "They attacked us."

The soldier sneered again and leaned forward slightly, turning the knife just a fraction, but the sharp ache echoed throughout Roni's core. "No…no."

The urge to argue rose in Roni, but the look on this soldier's face unnerved her too much, never mind the blade. No, she wasn't talking about the ambush. She meant the camp, thought Roni and her comrades had slit those Firellian throats and turned that clearing into a slaughterhouse.

"No," Roni said, trying to put all her denial into her features, her voice. "That wasn't us. That was Hacha. Hacha, not us."

Whether the soldier understood or not, her face didn't change. She spat something that sounded like, "Bastards," but Roni couldn't be sure. Gods, this was the end. Of all the ways Roni had recently imagined her death, being disemboweled near the latrine hadn't topped the list.

"I'm sorry," she whispered. And she was, not only for this soldier, whose comrades had been killed by Hacha *and* Roni's squad, but for leaving her own comrades just as she was starting to get to know them, to like them, to briefly consider them as a path forward and a new life.

And she was sorry she hadn't kissed Zara when given the chance. They could have been so good together.

The Firellian soldier drew in a sharp breath, her mouth opening. Roni grabbed for her hand without thinking, but the soldier was already falling backward, her eyes rolling up to the whites as she crumpled.

Cortez stood behind her, his own bloody knife in hand. "You all right?"

"I…" Roni put a hand to her stomach, digging under her clothes to see the wound. She couldn't think of any one thing, the past few seconds playing over and over. When she bared her belly, the cold air hit her like a brick, and she put a hand over the shallow but aching wound. Her legs went to jelly.

"Whoa." Cortez put a hand under her elbow. "You're wounded? Let me see."

She jerked away from him, stumbling to one knee. "What are you doing out here?" She clenched her teeth, fighting tears or vomit or screaming or any of the hundred other things she wanted to do.

He leaned back, his expression hidden in shadow. "The same thing you're doing out here, I'm guessing."

Planning to steal the Vox to kill a murderer and then almost getting killed? She had to breathe deeply to keep from saying the words or laughing hysterically or passing out and letting someone else deal with this situation. "Lucky…lucky for me."

"That I have a small bladder?" He shrugged. "If that's the way you want to look at it." He kneeled, still staying out of arm's reach and looking at her as if she was a wounded animal. "It's all right, Roni. No one's going to hurt you now."

Oh, how she wanted to believe that, but if tonight had proved anything, it was that she couldn't let down her guard. Ever.

CHAPTER THIRTEEN

Zara hoped Veronique knew how lucky she was that she and Cortez had visited the latrine at the same time. Otherwise, everyone might have been standing around staring at two dead bodies.

If only they could have questioned this Firellian soldier. She'd clearly thought the Sarrasians had killed all of her squad, and Zara would have loved to know why. At least they had one question answered: the Firellians hadn't turned on one another.

And Zara could understand why Cortez had killed her instead of trying to capture her. Doing anything else might have resulted in Veronique's death. Any loss in her squad would have been a blow, but she had to admit that Veronique's death would have been…different than the others. Like the end of personal possibilities instead of just a life.

Nonsense. All deaths saw an end to possibilities. But even logic couldn't argue that Veronique's death wouldn't have been harder to take. Gods, she wished she was wearing the glove so the Vox could help her sort through some of this emotional mire. But she felt better for spending a night without her body having to sustain the Vox as well as herself.

She glanced around at the darkness and knew it would be dawn soon. "Pack up," she said. "It's no use trying to get another hour of sleep." Everyone went about their tasks, leaving the dead Firellian in the snow. Her family would never know what had happened to her. Zara shivered as she imagined her sisters in the same predicament.

After a sigh, she turned to her own tent, hating how the pre-dawn darkness always led one to melancholy thoughts. She caught Veronique's eye and nodded to her abdomen. "All bandaged up?"

With a nod, Veronique lifted her shirt enough to show a white bandage. "Ernesto gave me a few stitches but doesn't think the knife cut any deeper."

"Getting sewn up in the cold is never fun."

"I imagine it wouldn't be fun any time of year, Commander." She hadn't cried out or made a fuss during the procedure, another sign in her favor.

"I'm glad you're all right, Veronique."

Her head whipped up from where she was examining her wound. "Are you?"

"Of course." Zara nearly took a step back, flabbergasted. "Why wouldn't I be?"

"I don't…you can call me Roni, you know."

Zara frowned and went over their recent interactions, trying to glean where she'd given the impression that she didn't care if Veronique—*Roni*—got hurt. Surely, Roni didn't think her withdrawal from their last conversation meant she had ceased to care?

In fact, when Zara switched to the nickname in her thoughts, she cared a little more.

How strange.

Roni avoided her eyes for a moment before sighing. "I'm sorry."

"What for?" Another confusion to add to the pile.

"I just…am. Commander." She nearly ran to help the others.

Zara stared for a few seconds, wondering what in the gods' names that had been about. Well, she didn't have time to wonder now, nor did she want to run after Roni and demand an explanation. She went into her tent to pack and took the chain from her pocket, looping it around her hand until it was a glove. As always, she couldn't quite recall how she'd done it. The pattern always seemed to appear in her mind and disappear as quickly. And when the feeling of the Vox's awakening flooded her senses, she couldn't even wonder how they worked. She was just so happy that they did.

"I missed a lot, I see," the Vox's many voices said in her mind as she thought about what had happened in the night.

"Any ideas about what Roni said? About being surprised that I wanted her to be safe?"

"Humans are a mass of contradictions, that's what I know."

Zara nodded. They were of the same mind there. "We'll have to ponder as we move. Scout the area for more Firellian stragglers while we pack."

The Vox shivered in a whirl of metal until they became a snowy owl. They didn't need the real bird's protection from the cold, but the silhouette was good camouflage from anyone who might catch sight of them.

Unless any watchers saw them glint in the light. The Vox ruffled their metal feathers in a tinny sound like tiny bells. "For anyone to see me, I'd have to be close, and then it would be too late for them." They hopped outside and flew into the sky.

Zara shivered in pleasure but paid only half a mind to the data the Vox sent to her. She began the march while it was still dark and called a halt two hours later so the squad could have some breakfast in the gray daylight that managed to filter through the wall of clouds.

Everyone ate quietly, many staring into the woods or casting nervous glances over their shoulders. Zara sat because some of the others would remain standing while she did. Jaq made a round, checking on everyone before he came to sit beside her on a log away from the others.

"They're worried about the enemy scouts, boss," he said quietly. "And whoever slaughtered that camp since they know it wasn't a Firellian soldier now."

Zara frowned. "It still could have been Firellian soldiers, just not anyone that particular soldier knew."

He gave her a mild smile, and she guessed that particular point of deduction wouldn't comfort anyone. He leaned closer. "A couple of the veterans are even looking at the newbies and vice versa. They think someone could have sneaked away from camp at night, done the deed, and been back before sunrise."

"Damn. I hope you put a stop to that."

"As much as I can, but when people are scared, they look for someone to blame."

Zara shook her head. "Nonsense. Such a person would have been covered in blood, doused in it by the look of that camp. Someone would have noticed that in the morning."

"I don't know if that will help, but I can try reminding everyone of that."

"Do your best, Jaq."

"Boss." He gave a small salute and began to mingle again as everyone finished eating.

Zara tried not to frown at her squad too hard, but she would not tolerate ludicrous suspicions. She hesitated to say anything before someone started pointing fingers aloud. If they knew that Jaq reported much of what they said to her, they might stop speaking to him, especially the new members.

But suspicion could get a squad killed, especially one that had to trust one another as much as hers. To be on the safe side, she had Finn adjust the walking order, mixing new and old and having the veterans teach quietly as they walked, pointing out various plants or animal tracks or how to spot a good place for a snare or a camp.

Zara took point again, the Vox still scouting, and it was a good four hours of marching before the Vox's many voices sounded in her head.

"A Firellian camp."

Zara raised her hand, fist closed, and everyone behind her fell silent and stopped as she did. She waited, heart pounding in her ears while the Vox circled and reported.

"Fifteen at least," the Vox said. "Looks like they've been here awhile, same as the others. They seem relaxed. Maybe the other camp was supposed to send word of any trouble but didn't get the chance."

Gods and devils, the forest was crawling with enemies. "What are they doing here?"

"I could try to get close enough to listen."

"No, maintain your distance." Up close, they'd see the Vox's metallic nature and might follow or attack them. Contrary to appearances, they were not impervious to weapons.

They acknowledged that thought with a mental huff.

As the Vox continued to scout, Zara called everyone into a huddle and imparted the news as calmly as she could.

"Fifteen's too many to attack," Claudia said.

Zara nodded. "Agreed."

"Even in an ambush?" Tati asked.

"That's more difficult when they're dug in," Finn said. "They could have snares, perimeter guards, the devils know what."

Zara held up a hand. "Our orders were to scout the border and report back," she said, meeting everyone's eyes. "Not to engage every enemy we see. We mark the camp on the map, and we go around."

She wasn't happy about leaving an enemy encampment on this side of the border, but the infantry could clear it out later. She left Jaq and Finn to explain that while she copied the Vox's report in her journal, and when the Vox returned, she steered the squad directly north, leaving the path and heading for one of the tributaries of the Kingfish River that could guide them to the Firellian border. Maybe such a detour would keep them away from any other Firellian camps.

If the woods weren't filled with them.

They had to go slower in the forest proper, circling deadfalls and snowdrifts. After an hour of marching that hadn't gotten them far at all, Zara called a halt and examined her map again. Maybe it would be faster to actually go around the camp and take to the trail again.

"If you keep scouting, that might work," she said to the Vox as they hopped from her shoulder to a nearby branch.

"Not if we come close to them while making this much noise."

She scowled even though she agreed. The veterans made enough of a din going cross-country, but the others? As Adella would say, the dead might have heard them.

Impossible, but it was a comparison that quieted groups of people quickly, perhaps because of the inference that if they weren't quiet, they might not live that long.

"We breaking for lunch, boss?" Finn asked.

Zara glanced around and nodded. It was as good a place as any and would give her more time to ponder. Everyone began to spread out when Leo fell over with a little cry.

Zara turned, looking for the cause, but noise exploded around them, deafening screams and animal cries that echoed between the bare trees like a chorus of devils.

Everyone had their hands over their helmets as if that would stop the sound. Zara fought to think through the noise. It could only be a magical tripwire. "Run," she yelled as loudly as she could, but the sound was lost amid all the others. She waved or shoved everyone into motion, pulling Roni along as she took off at a breakneck pace.

When they'd come far enough from the noise to speak, she stopped and pulled the gasping squad into another huddle. "Magical tripwire," she said. The sound was already fading, but the Firellians would be coming.

"Firellians don't use much magic—" Claudia started.

Zara spoke over her. "No time to ponder. We'll split up to confuse them. Ana, you're coming with me and the Vox. We'll lay an obvious trail for the Firellians to follow, then double back toward the trail to lose them. Finn, take Ernesto, Roni, and Cortez. Jaq, you have Claudia, Leo, and Tati. Go more carefully along two separate lines and keep to the north until you hit the tributary. Got it?"

"Yes, boss," the sergeants said.

They began to split up, and Roni's worried gaze caught Zara's again. She tried to give her a reassuring nod, hoping to convey that if she trusted in her sergeant, everyone would be all right.

Gods, she willed it so.

Roni panted, her breath a white plume as she ran. Finn ordered her, Cortez, and Ernesto to run far apart, just within sight of each other, in an erratic pattern. When possible, they had to avoid breaking the snow while going as fast as they could. Roni reached for low-hanging branches and swung where she could, trying to break up her trail, but any competent tracker would be able to follow her. But she knew the idea was to get the Firellians to split up or follow only a few squad members. Anything to cut down on casualties.

Gods. Roni started to glance behind but stopped herself. She knew better. In the city streets or out here in the woods, she'd only slow herself down and would no doubt slam into something harder than her head. She forced herself to run faster, reckless, fearing for herself, for the others, for Zara and the *obvious* trail she was laying.

Zara wanted the Firellians to chase her so her soldiers could get away. If she was caught, she'd no doubt fight to the death rather than be captured.

"Fuck," Roni muttered, but it came out as a wheeze. She was going to lose Zara, to lose the first new friends she'd made in years, and then she'd freeze to death in this gods-forsaken nowhere. When someone shouted in the distance, Roni's darkest thoughts seemed to be coming true. Finn whistled from off to the right, one sharp note, and Roni remembered her training enough to leap for cover. She dove over a snarl of fallen branches, her arms flung up so she could catch herself and roll into a somersault on the other side. One palm connected with the snowy earth, but the other landed half on a rock, her wrist twisting painfully, and a line of fire cutting through her glove into her hand. She hissed and fell, heard the crunch of ice, and then the world went spinning as she rolled down a sharp incline.

Roni clamped her teeth on a cry and grabbed a root that stuck out of the frozen slope. Her cloak caught on something, choking her, and she reached up to tear it away. Even with her heart hammering, she managed to get her feet under her and tried to find a place to stand, but the ground around the root seemed frozen solid. The little spit of wood she clung to made a horrid cracking sound, threatening to give way.

Devils help her. She tried to see what waited below but couldn't twist enough to look. Moving as quickly as she dared, she shrugged one arm out of her pack. The root groaned again. Forcing herself to breathe slowly, she switched to holding on with her injured hand and breathed through the pain. She freed her other arm to send the pack sliding down to join her cloak in hell, for all she knew.

She switched hands again. The root held. Roni breathed in and out, risking a look this time. Beyond the patch of ice she lay in, the ground seemed a little firmer, as if she'd had the misfortune to fall in the middle of a little creek. Figured. The wounds on her stomach and hand ached. She couldn't stay here, freezing her ass off and waiting for the Firellians to find her. Slowly, carefully, she reached a foot toward more stable ground.

The root snapped.

"No," Roni squealed, trying to grab at the slick ice or other roots, making her wrist sing out again. Her heel caught on something and sent her swinging sideways, sliding under a clump of spiny-leaved bushes.

When the world didn't tilt or slide or reach out to hit her for several minutes, she opened her eyes before rolling onto her back. She forced her breathing to slow again and flexed her limbs. Nothing broken, only sore as hell. A mass of small twisted branches hung a foot above her face, and she felt one bush's small trunk against her hip. She raised her head enough to see that the plant covered her whole body and then some.

Well, her wrist ached fiercely, her palm throbbed, and the stitches in her belly let her know they weren't happy, but at least she was hidden. She put the injured hand on her chest and glanced at the long-frozen creek. How the hell was she supposed to get out of here and find the others? Fear rose again and kept pushing into her throat, wanting to make itself known, wanting her to run again.

Finn would have told her to muzzle that urge. She'd been given the signal to hide, and that meant someone was on their trail. And Roni had no doubt just left a very obvious path to follow.

She drew her truncheon slowly and tried to listen past her chattering teeth. The Firellians might only find her, a strangely comforting thought. Now she knew why Zara put herself in danger. If they just found her, she wouldn't have to watch anyone else die.

Great. Only her own messy death to come, then.

Time dragged by agonizingly slowly as she lay there, the cold seeping past her armor and clothing, into her skin, her blood. The branches she'd broken when she'd slid under the plant emitted a strong, spicy smell that made her eyes water. How long had she been here? She had to be safe now. Even if someone found her, she couldn't just stay—

Footsteps.

Roni froze, all thoughts of revealing herself gone in a rush. She tensed as if that would make her hear better.

A twig snapped, closer now. Someone walking down a slippery hill couldn't be as quiet as on flat ground. Roni turned her head and stared at the path she'd taken under this bush, her neck aching as she waited for the sight of a boot.

Or maybe they'd start randomly stabbing the bushes.

She licked her lips, swallowed, and the spicy plant scent went down her throat, making her stomach roil. Telling her damn mind to stop screaming, she tilted her head, trying to see farther up the path. Nothing yet.

Someone whispered words she didn't understand.

And someone else responded.

Two of them? Maybe more. Gods and devils, she was doomed. She should run, right? They'd be as hampered as her by the terrain and snow, and maybe Finn and the others would hear and come save her ass.

She tensed, getting the feeling that these plants wouldn't be as easy to get out of as they were to get into.

Someone gasped, and a wet gurgling sound rattled through Roni's ears. A shriek of terror cut off with another of those awful sounds. Roni flopped onto her stomach and looked up the slope. A body fell, sliding gently on the icy creek, its throat a ruin of red, and its eyes wide in terror. The jaw worked once, steaming gently before it went still.

Roni clapped a hand over her mouth, tasting ice and mud, but she had to keep it there to stop from screaming. A pair of boots stepped to the side, revealing another body. Its throat would be the same; she didn't even have to see it to know.

"Come out, rat." Hacha's sandpaper voice. "I saved your sorry life. Come out and say thank you."

Roni trembled, her fear as sharp as the first time they'd spoken, but at least there had been a door between them and an army base surrounding them. He'd find her, and oh gods…

He made that same wet sound as before, his devil's laugh. "I was born near these woods, rat, raised here. Can find you as easily as I found these. You want proof? A jab for your troubles?" He chuckled again. "I don't recommend it. Once I start stabbing…"

With a final shudder, she wriggled out from under the bush and forced herself to stand, leaning awkwardly on the slope while she tried to avoid the ice. Staring at his boots and the corpses was bad enough, but hell, if he was going to kill her, she was going to look at his fucking face when she spit in it.

He grinned lopsidedly as if impressed or maybe happy to see her. Gods, the thought made her sick. He had a full beard now after a few days in the wilderness, and his small dark eyes gleamed like a predator's in its element. "That's better, rat." He gestured at the two corpses with a bloody knife.

She had to swallow several times before she managed, "Thank you, Hacha."

He put a hand across his waist and bowed. "At your service, serrah." He sucked his cheeks and bit his lip and made that awful laugh again. The merry look faded as he took a step toward her. "Where's my merchandise?" He looked fondly at the corpses again. "Not that I ain't enjoying my vacation in the country."

Why did the gods allow such people as this? Devils should have to stay in hell. "I'm trying. I...would have had them last night, but one of the Firellians almost killed me." She couldn't seem to speak above a whisper when she wanted to cry for help.

No, he would kill her squad, too. She had to face him alone.

"Maybe I should get the glove and bird myself." He wiped the knife on his trouser leg, adding to an already substantial stain. His heavy leather coat and hood was covered in dark splashes and blobs.

"I'll get them."

"Slit that commander's throat—"

"I said I'll get them," she said, taking a step toward him, surprising herself, her idiot self.

"Oh?" His overhanging brow puckered as if processing new information.

"She wears the glove at night sometimes," Roni said hurriedly. "And that means the bird's awake. They'll kill you." Gods, she could just picture his death, but it couldn't take place in Zara's tent. No one else should have to come face-to-face with a bogeyman.

He tilted his head, no doubt wondering how he'd fare against the Vox. Then he pivoted on one foot, far faster than such a large person had a right to, and stopped beside a leaning tree trunk, looking back up the slope as if hiding from someone there.

Ernesto stepped into view, his saber in hand. "Roni?" With a glance at the bodies, he started down. "Who are you talking to?"

"No," she said, her voice catching. She threw herself forward.

Hacha was faster.

Ernesto tried to backpedal and raised his saber. Hacha didn't bother to try him blade to blade. He fell forward and grabbed Ernesto's leg, yanking him down.

Roni stumbled and clawed at the frozen ground with her injured hand to try to gain speed. She swung her truncheon, trying to connect with anything, distract Hacha just long enough.

Too far away, by the gods.

Hacha pushed up on his knees and dragged Ernesto toward him. Inside Ernesto's reach, Hacha batted his sword arm away.

"No," Roni cried again, lunging.

The knife flashed, a red fountain erupting close behind it.

Hacha shifted out of the way so Roni fell onto Ernesto. She dropped her truncheon and pressed her hands to his neck, trying to contain the flood, but it was too much. She sobbed, forcing herself to meet Ernesto's gaze, to let him know he was not alone. She prayed as the life faded from his light brown eyes, asking for forgiveness from him, from the others, from the universe itself.

She couldn't stop her sobs. "You didn't have to…you didn't… oh gods."

"Don't be silly, rat. We can't let the others know who you're really working for. You're welcome. Again."

Roni grabbed Ernesto's saber and clambered to her feet, but Hacha was already disappearing into the woods at the bottom of the slope. She wanted to charge after him, but anger deserted her for fear and anguish as someone else softly called her name from above.

CHAPTER FOURTEEN

Cortez stepped onto the slope and looked from Roni to the bodies. She followed his gaze to the corpses and spotted the similarity in three slashed throats. Devils take it, she was doomed.

But Cortez said, "Oh gods," and sheathed his saber as he shuffled closer. "Are you all right?"

"I didn't kill them." Roni realized she was still holding Ernesto's saber and dropped it, unable to stand the feel of it. She had to get her head together.

"I know that." He gave her a long-suffering look. "You've got scratches on your cheeks and a big hole in one of your gloves. Are you hurt anywhere else? Where's your cloak and pack?"

She pointed down the slope and reached for her cheeks. She hadn't even noticed getting scratched, and the hole had to have been caused by the rock that started this whole mess. Her wrist and stomach still ached, too, and she stopped herself from touching her face when she saw that her arms were covered in Ernesto's blood. She was shaking even harder than before, feeling colder and emptier than she'd ever felt. "No, I...I..."

Damn it. She couldn't fall to pieces, not now. She had to think up a lie about how the Firellians and Ernesto had killed one another, especially now that Cortez had kneeled by Ernesto's corpse.

Gods, poor Ernesto. His blood was literally and figuratively all over her hands, freezing but still tacky. She kneeled on the slope to try to wipe them clean with snow.

"Hacha killed them all, huh?"

Roni froze, her heart beating like a hammer and threatening to spring from her chest. Could she blame the Hatchet? Would that work? But he hadn't said the *Hatchet*. He'd admitted he knew the legends were based on a real person, but to know the name...

She looked up at him slowly, half expecting him to come for her, but he went from Ernesto to the Firellian bodies and started patting them down. Without a word, he clambered down the slope much easier than she ever could and came back with her pack and cloak. When he met her eyes, something in her face seemed to set him back on his heels.

He sighed and continued holding out her gear until she took it and put it on, having to tie the strings of the cloak as best she could after she'd torn them. The weight helped push back the cold a little.

"You're a thief, not a killer," Cortez said. "So why are you hiding Hacha's presence from the rest of us?"

She was afraid to speak, afraid to move. One foot was already sliding a little. Maybe she should follow it, scramble down the hill and run like hell.

Straight into Hacha's arms.

Cortez's look wasn't accusing, only calculating. "You don't seem like someone who'd work willingly with a butcher. Is he threatening you? Bodily harm or blackmail? What's he doing out here?"

Gods, was he reading her mind? No, he'd have those answers if he did. "Who are you?" she whispered. "Why were you in prison?"

He tilted his head. "Are you separating each of us from the pack so he can kill us one at a time?"

Anger boiled within her, fighting past some of the grief and guilt. She couldn't stop a snarl, more than ready for a target.

"Nope," he said, one lip quirking as if amused. "So this death wasn't planned." He glanced at Ernesto again. "And you can't be responsible for the Firellian presence or for them giving chase." His expression turned thoughtful. "Unless you're a spy. But I highly doubt that."

She almost laughed at the sheer absurdity, but if she began an outpouring like that, it would quickly shift to sobs, and she couldn't have that, not without knowing what the hell Cortez thought he was doing. "Are the others coming?"

"No idea. But if you have something important to say, you'd better say it now. The others might not believe you innocent of Ernesto's death or Hacha's presence." He waved vaguely into the distance. "What should I tell them?"

Fear and grief still wormed through her gut, but she stared him down. "Do you know so much about blackmail because you're good at it?"

He seemed to think for a moment. "Perhaps. But I don't want money, only answers."

"Why? What's it got to do with you?"

Cortez glanced at Ernesto again as if saying knowledge might save his life.

Damn. He was right, but...

She shook her head and fought down her emotions. "It would be more dangerous if you did know. Count yourself lucky."

He sighed again and rubbed his face. "Okay, I can see we're going to have to do a give and take. I know something that you don't want getting out. If I share something I don't want getting out, can we work together?"

"If one goes down, we all go down?" She'd worked that way often enough. And gods knew she needed an ally. "Okay."

His smile seemed genuine enough. "To answer your question, my name is really Cortez, and I've never actually been inside a prison. I was inserted into the prison recruitment scheme by a Sarrasian intelligence agency that wants firsthand knowledge of events happening at the border."

Roni barked a laugh this time. Of all the crazy shit she'd heard in life, that took the biscuit. But was it the truth? It couldn't be. When he kept his simple smile, she gawked. "But...the government is going to get a report from the army already. Isn't that how it works?"

He gave another of those enigmatic little head tilts. "This is how firsthand knowledge works."

"So you don't trust the army?"

He shrugged.

"Or you don't trust Zara's reporting skills?" Insane as that sounded.

Another shrug.

Gods and devils, everything he said was way above her level. She just wanted to get out of Hacha's clutches. "And why would you help me hide the fact that Hacha is out here because of me?"

"Isn't it better to have allies?"

She'd had the same thought. And answering a question with a question seemed like a government thing to do. The only Sarrasian *agents* she was used to working with were guards and magistrates, and she'd loathed almost all of them. But Cortez had saved her life. And he wasn't running to tell the others.

But he hadn't balked at Ernesto's death, which made him efficient but damn creepy.

Who to trust? She'd never felt pulled in so many directions at once.

"Come on," Cortez said as he kneeled by Ernesto's shoulders. "Grab his feet." When she hesitated, he sighed. "Look, I don't like covering up a death, particularly not of someone I actually liked, but you've got to put sentiment aside right now."

She frowned and didn't know if she could do that. "So you're going to dissolve into a puddle of tears when you have a free moment?"

He shrugged. "It wouldn't be the first time."

He said it as matter-of-fact as everything else, and she couldn't tell if he was using whatever words would get her to cooperate or what. Or maybe he'd lost enough comrades that he had learned how to mourn only when he wanted to.

"We've got to take him back to the others and spin a story about how he died," Cortez said, not unsympathetically. "And we've got to do it before we're discovered. I will look suitably sad, believe me."

She obeyed, wincing when she had to touch the body. Her hand ached, but the pain was nothing to Ernesto's death. "Some of us won't have to fake our sadness."

"Good for you." He only sounded a little snarky when he said it. "And later, you're going to tell me what's going on with Hacha."

He didn't have to add what would happen if she didn't. She could well imagine. He'd spill her secret, she'd spill his, and Zara would kill them both.

Gods, Zara was going to be so sad and angry about Ernesto. She might want Firellian blood, might forget her orders to observe and report and tear off on a quest for vengeance.

No, not calm Zara, even with all the ways this particular mission would hurt her. At least she'd be spared one kind of pain: Roni was not going to turn the Vox over to that pig-faced bastard. She'd use them to kill him, and maybe Cortez would help. Then maybe someday, Roni could tell Zara that she'd claimed vengeance for all of them when the Vox had torn Ernesto's murderer apart.

As Zara crouched behind a deadfall with Ana and the Vox, she racked her brain for reasons why the Firellians were in this forest in such numbers. And why in the devils' names did they have a magical tripwire so far from their camp?

At least ten had come after her and Ana. That was a good sign, really. It left fewer Firellians to chase the others. The Firellians had to have laid tripwires along any part of the forest that even resembled a trail, which meant there were more than she had thought. And they were using more magic than anyone had ever considered.

Gods, she had to get back to Sarras with this news.

But not until she saw what the devil they were guarding out here.

"Any sign?" the nearest Firellian called to his fellows.

Another called an answer, the words too garbled by distance for Zara to translate. They yelled something else, and the nearest one frowned and shook his head. "No one wants that...out here. She would...us, too."

Zara bit her lip, trying to translate the two words she wasn't as familiar with. She wanted to cast her mind back to her Firellian lessons, but she had to remain alert right now. They were coming closer, searching methodically, and the time would soon come to flee again or fight. But even the Vox couldn't handle this many.

Not in any of their usual shapes.

The Vox tilted their head up from where she'd hidden them against her chest. "Are you sure?"

"What choice do we have?" she whispered.

Ana glanced at her.

Zara leaned closer. "The Vox is going to use a mythic shape."

"Commander..." Ana's brows pulled together, her face full of doubt. "You'll pass out. You didn't wake for a day last time."

"I'll be more careful," Zara said, though her stomach roiled a bit. The mythic shapes had no counterparts except in legend. And they used all her energy in one go. "We won't hold it so long."

"Seconds," the Vox said. "I'll be as quick as I can."

"After I pass out," Zara said. "Cover me and the Vox with branches and head for the others."

Ana gripped her arm. "You've been using the Vox for days, boss." She licked her lips. "If I use the glove now, I can take the strain. Maybe I won't pass out."

She had no idea what she was volunteering for, no idea of the toll this would take. Still, Zara considered. It was possible for other people to use the glove and speak with the Vox. How else would they make their choice for a new wielder after the old one died? But this was Zara's burden to bear. She had been chosen.

"No," Zara said. "You have your orders, Corporal."

"What shall I be?" the Vox asked. "Phoenix?"

Zara shook her head. They didn't want to light the forest on fire. "Roc."

They clambered onto her hands. "Throw me right in the heart of them."

With her heart thundering in her ears, Zara watched the Firellians, waiting for those in the rear to come closer. She tried to clear her mind. Once the Vox took a mythic shape, she would try to hold on to consciousness for as long as she could. Best not to expend energy with even stray thoughts.

But her mind kept turning over.

Kill, that was what that second word in Firellian had been. "She would *kill* us, too," he'd said.

Who? A soldier? A commander? The mage who'd laid the traps?

The Firellian searchers were moving closer, almost in a clump.

"Get ready," Zara whispered.

Why would a Firellian attack her own people?

Ana tensed, one hand on Zara's arm. "Boss—"

"Steady," Zara said.

Unless these weren't her people, whoever she was. Maybe a captive, someone the Firellians had threatened or cajoled into compliance.

Ana shifted slightly, but the Vox was a still weight in her arms. "Now?" Ana asked.

"Wait." The Firellians were pulling in tighter, but they needed to be as close as possible if Zara didn't want to spend the rest of this mission out cold.

A captive mage, someone alone, frightened, and injured. A mage like Gisele.

Zara's worry boiled into rage, and she flung the Vox into the clearing where the Firellians had gathered.

The Vox shimmered, bits of metal turning over one another until they filled the clearing with a wingspan of over forty feet. Zara sagged, feeling as if she'd been punched in the gut or bled dry. She barely heard the screams in the clearing as the Vox lashed out with seven-inch claws and snapped with an even longer beak. The golden wings buffeted the Firellians into the trees or slammed them into the ground.

Zara fell to her knees, losing sight of the battlefield. Her vision swam in and out of focus, and Ana seemed to be calling her from a great height. The sound of a clanging bell filled her ears. She couldn't hold on, clutching the frozen ground as she sagged lower, her eyelids like weights. Were the Firellians dead? It didn't matter. She had to... she had to...

Her cheek pressed to the cold ground, and her eyes fluttered open once more. Monster, that was the other word the Firellian soldier had said: "No one wants that monster out here. She would kill us, too."

But they'd died anyway. Zara closed her eyes and fell into darkness.

CHAPTER FIFTEEN

Zara's arm hurt. She'd been asleep, out like the dead, but now a pain like tiny needles stabbing her was building in her arm. No, her shoulder. If the damn thing would quit hurting, she could... There, the pain subsided. Sleep called to her again.

Now the other shoulder hurt.

A scraping sound filled her ears. Harsh crunching mixed with the sound of snapping wood. And someone was grunting and puffing as if they were lifting weights. Or hurrying. Or both, hurrying while carrying something heavy. Or dragging it.

The sound paused, and the pain in her shoulder dimmed once again, but she couldn't enjoy it. Her back was growing cold now. Was she sleeping on ice? Then her back lifted, and both shoulders groaned, and the grunting started again.

And her ass was frozen solid.

Zara's eyes fluttered open to the sight of dark branches against a cloudy sky and something bulky hanging over her. A backpack. The pack stayed in view, but the branches and the sky stuttered past as her body jerked along. And that dragging sound was coming from...her. Someone was dragging *her*. By the arms. Memories fell into place: the clearing, the roc, falling into darkness. The Vox must not have killed all the Firellians, and now one had taken her prisoner.

Or so they thought.

Zara closed her eyes again and tested her muscles, bringing herself more awake, forgetting aches and pains and her frozen posterior. She listened but heard nothing except her captor. Maybe only one Firellian had survived to take her prisoner. As unfortunate for him as it was lucky for her.

When another break came in the pulling, Zara slammed her arms downward. The captor cried out and released her. Zara pushed up, shaking loose the backpack that had been laid on top of her. She curled one leg underneath her and kicked the other around and behind, catching her captor's shins while they were still off-balance. They fell with an *oof.* She drew the saber they'd foolishly left her and prepared to plunge it into their heart when they rolled over, hands up.

Ana.

Zara held her breath for a moment, letting her training and adrenaline fade before she sheathed the saber. She now saw the Vox's legs peeking out from the top of the pack with her cloak. Irritation replaced her surprise. "Corporal, I thought I told you to hide my body with the Vox and head for the rendezvous point."

Ana put her arms down and sighed. "Yes, boss. You did. But even though the Firellians in that clearing were dead, I thought I heard more in the distance and couldn't risk you or the Vox falling into their hands."

Zara nodded, too tired to argue for the moment. "I suppose the court-martial can wait." Ana helped her stand, and she lifted the pack. The Vox was as still as an eagle statue in their sleeping state. Zara winced as she untangled them from her cloak. A few of the feathers looked damaged. They were always more vulnerable in such a large state. They could repair themselves when awake, but that took quite a jolt of energy, too. She donned her pack and slung her cloak around her shoulders. "The glove?"

"In my pocket." Wordlessly, she handed it over.

With another nod, Zara put the chain and jewel in her own pocket, then staggered along at Ana's side. Her legs felt as if they were filled with jam. She couldn't power the Vox right now, and she didn't want anyone else to, either. They would have to wait until she'd recovered. "How long was I out?"

Ana glanced upward as if judging the light. "A couple hours."

Good, much better than the last time the Vox had taken a mythic shape. Still... "I apologize for being a burden all that time."

Ana gave her a crooked grin. "I apologize for nearly yanking your arms out of their sockets."

Zara managed a chuckle. Now that they could pick up the pace, they'd make the rendezvous well before nightfall. Gods willing, everyone would be waiting for them, and her slightly aching shoulders would be the only injuries.

When they'd walked for another hour, and Zara heard the gentle gurgling of the tributary ahead, she whistled, imitating the call of a snowy owl. Another owl answered, and she led the way into the open. The squad came out of hiding to greet her.

But not all of them. Her stomach shrank as only four came forward. Finn, Roni, Cortez, and Ernesto were not among them. "Report."

"A few soldiers chased us, boss," Jaq said. "We managed to lose them in the trees." He nodded toward Claudia. "Only one injury."

Zara took a good look. Claudia limped out of hiding and sat on a log. Leo and Tati helped her elevate her left foot, which was wrapped in a hasty-looking splint. Her face was pale and pinched, and her forehead was covered in a sheen of sweat, far more than would be explained by a sprain.

"Broken?" Zara asked.

Jaq nodded. Claudia turned her head to the side and cursed before looking at Zara again with fierce determination. "I can go on," she said.

Zara cocked her head. That wasn't true, but she appreciated the will it took to say it. Still, willpower wouldn't help anyone walk on a broken foot. "You can't, Corporal, and you know it."

Zara smiled a little after Claudia looked away and cursed again. She clearly didn't want Zara to think the curses were for her. Oddly touching. "I'm sorry," Zara said as she sat by Claudia's side. "I want you with us. I hope you knew that before I said it."

Claudia gave her a tired smile, too. "Thanks, boss."

"Someone will have to walk back with her," Jaq said.

Now Claudia glared at him. She tensed as if to stand, but Tati put a hand on her shoulder while Leo looked nervously from face to face. After a deep breath, Claudia said. "I will not rob the squad of another member, Sarge."

Zara rubbed her forehead. A headache had been lurking near her left temple, and now it began to bloom. She let Jaq and Claudia argue, knowing Claudia would eventually see sense. She had to begin limping back to the last waystation, and she had to have an escort to help her get there. Zara considered who it would be. Ernesto would be the best choice. The most experienced medic should be with the most injured person. Jaq would have to patch up the rest of them as they continued toward the border.

When the arguing died down, Zara stood and stretched. A deep ache had settled in all her muscles, and she wondered if this was what Gisele felt like after overusing her magic. She really would have been better off in the army. Then she wouldn't be in pain all the time. But she never listened to sense, especially from those who loved her.

If they weren't sisters, they probably would have come to real blows long ago.

Zara shook off her reverie and glanced at Claudia. She was staring into the trees, frowning, with a bit of color in her cheeks. Jaq nodded when Zara looked at him. Good, they'd settled it.

She nodded to Tati and Leo, too. They sighed, seeming relieved. Everyone felt better when a plan had been ironed out. She set her pack with the others and gestured for Jaq to follow her a few steps away where they could talk quietly.

He nodded toward the hand that usually wore the Vox's glove. Like Ana and the rest of the regular squad, he knew about the mythic shapes and how they taxed her. "Was it a big fight?"

"Successfully resolved. And the Vox was only slightly damaged."

"And you? If you're injured, you know you have to tell me, boss."

It was the same reminder of duty she'd leveled at Claudia, and it worked just as well. "Tired and achy but no injuries." She glanced up. They didn't have much daylight left. "But I might have to send the Vox looking for the others."

She worried for all of them, but she wasn't foolish enough to deny to herself that one stood out from the others. Roni reminded her of Gisele at times with the way they both wanted to do everything the hard way without any help. But she couldn't even guess why such an aggravating trait in Gisele would be strangely enticing in someone else.

"I don't think that's wise, boss," Jaq said. When she looked at him again, he held his hands up as if surrendering, and she softened her glare. "You know your own limits, but I must remind you of the last time you used the Vox soon after waking up from a mythic shape...nap."

She had to give him credit for not saying coma or faint or any other debilitating terms. "I do remember feeling like someone was splitting my skull with an ax, Jaq, thank you."

He crossed his arms and shrugged, too tactful, it seemed, to remind her that she'd almost passed out again, too. Then he crossed back to the log to fuss over Claudia's foot.

Zara took a slow look around the clearing. The others might come from any direction if they'd had to shake pursuers. She doubted any of them would leave the others behind, so they'd probably arrive in a clump. But gods, how long would it take?

That ill-fated near kiss popped into her mind. She knew she shouldn't be thinking of it, not after she'd decided it couldn't happen, but if Roni had been injured, or worse...

No. She clenched a fist. She understood the real world, where people couldn't act on every thought that came to mind. Nor did she see the sense in keeping one's problems cloaked in secrecy when others could easily help, another trait that Roni, Gisele, and sometimes Adella had in common.

Gods and devils, aggravation wasn't helping the headache.

And even more frustrating, part of her still wanted to kiss Roni. She knew which damn part it was, too, and that made her angrier because that side of her normally didn't give her any trouble.

Maybe she should send Roni back with Claudia and Ernesto, out of harm's way and out of reach.

The call of a snowy owl came from the south. Zara sighed in relief as Jaq returned the call. Zara marched in that direction but stuttered to a halt as Finn, Roni, and Cortez emerged, carrying Ernesto between them.

Gods...he was...was he injured?

But they didn't bear him with any sort of care.

"Oh gods," she whispered. She'd never lost anyone before. She strode toward them, anger overtaking her, silencing the others' questions with a slash of her hand. "Report."

They lowered him gently to the ground. Finn's face was an angry mask as she nodded to Cortez, who seemed calm if out of breath.

Zara couldn't look at Roni, not yet.

"Ernesto and Roni were caught by Firellian soldiers, Commander," Cortez said. He lowered his and Ernesto's packs to the ground. "I got there toward the end of the fight and saw Ernesto go down. Roni and I finished off the last Firellian."

Zara looked at Roni finally and saw the scratches on her face and the bandage peeking out her torn, bloody glove. She didn't meet Zara's eyes, and her face seemed to shudder with emotions, too many for Zara to parse. They'd all lost a comrade today, but to see it happen…

Zara kneeled by Ernesto's side, hearing the others crowd around. His face was slack, mouth open, his chin and armor stained with blood from his torn neck. Confusion fought through her anger and sadness. It was a precise cut, done by a very sharp blade, and it matched some of her memories of that horrible campsite massacre.

Had a Firellian done that after all? Maybe someone from the group that had chased the squad that afternoon? But why, in all the devils' names? A memory came floating up from just before she'd passed out. The monster that the Firellians feared would kill everyone.

Was this her work?

Staring at his body wouldn't force the answers to come. She stood, grinding her teeth to keep from shaking or screaming or tearing off into the woods looking for revenge. "Are the rest of you uninjured?"

Finn and Cortez said yes, but Roni only mumbled something as she stared at Ernesto with tears dribbling down her cheeks. Zara understood. It was hard to lose someone, even if she didn't know him well. Ana was crying, too, and Claudia looked even more ashen where she stood propped between and towering over Tati and Leo. Jaq slowly shook his head, his hand resting on Finn's shoulder.

Zara took a deep breath, knowing what she had to say, what she'd learned in training and from the advice of others. She forced down the fact that she'd have to report Ernesto's death, that she might have to tell his family that he was never coming home. A harsh lump tried to lodge in her throat. She cleared it several times before she could speak. "I know what you're feeling. I'm feeling it, too. Ernesto was a good soldier, a good person. And we have to carry out the mission for him and Sarras, just as he would have done for any of us. We'll lay him to rest here, then we'll continue on."

She didn't wait for the newcomers to protest or give anyone a chance to completely dissolve into tears. They needed tasks. Digging into the frozen ground wasn't an option, so she told them to gather stones for a cairn and clear some space beneath a large felled tree. Ana sewed Ernesto's body into the blanket from his pack.

Zara pulled Jaq aside. A hollow feeling kept rising in her chest, but she pushed it down yet again. No tears, no rage, no outbursts, not yet, not while there were still things to be done. "You'll have to help Claudia back," she said.

He nodded slowly. "That leaves you without a medic."

"We know enough to patch each other up." A dark voice inside said any other injuries wouldn't matter. Broken bones or rattled skulls or anything serious would have to be left behind. The mission was everything. She gestured for Jaq to rejoin the others.

The hollow feeling remained. Her thoughts had been a lie. She wouldn't simply abandon anyone. Ever. She'd keep them close, keep them safe. She wouldn't send Roni away to be hurt again.

After a deep breath, she joined the others.

To Roni, every tree in the forest seemed to have eyes. She knew Hacha was nearby, listening if not watching, and Cortez seemed to be keeping her in sight ever since he'd confessed his true identity.

If people like him even had such things.

She cringed and kept her own eyes down, trying to shake the nerves that added to her fear and anger and turned her insides to mush. If anyone had offered her food at the moment, she would have had to run into the trees and retch.

Zara was looking at her, too, her expression wavering between angry, concerned, and something that could have been guilt or sadness. Roni had always been good at reading people and then putting on a show, acting in whatever way she thought they wanted in order to get what she could from them. But with an expression like Zara's, she didn't even know where to start. Whenever Roni met her gaze, she looked away, but Roni could still feel Zara watching the rest of the time, yet another set of eyes. A caring glance or two should have made her feel better, but at the moment, it just made her neck itch all the more.

At least Ana had sewn Ernesto into a blanket so Roni didn't have to feel his dead stare along with the others. As she helped lower him into the shallow depression beneath a felled tree, she whispered, "I'm so sorry. Gods, I'm sorry." Someone patted her shoulder, and it was all she could do not to shake their hand off. She did not deserve any pity. She'd helped kill this man.

Roni placed a few rocks on top of him before ceding her place to those who'd known him better, those who had a right to sadness.

Roni backed away from the grave until she knocked into Zara, who grasped her arm as if to steady her. Roni glanced at her face, but the mix of emotions made her look away again. Still, she felt as if she had to say something, anything that might turn Zara's attention from—

"I'm glad you're not badly hurt," Zara said, then cleared her throat. "Well, not worse than the scratches and your hand and…the wound you had before in the, um, the stomach. How is that, by the way?"

Gods, she sounded so nervous. Most of the others were sniffling; a few seemed angry. All this outpouring of feeling had to be throwing someone like Zara for a loop, if their past interactions were anything to go on. Roni patted her midsection where the small wound she'd gotten was healing nicely. It sure as hell hurt less than the cut and bruise on her palm. "I'm good, Zara, thanks. Commander," she added hurriedly. "Boss."

Zara's grip tightened on her arm, forcing Roni to confront the fact that she hadn't moved her hand. Maybe she needed the steadying contact. Gods and devils, someone else should be providing that, someone whose hands were metaphorically clean.

But if Zara needed it…

"You're doing a good job," Roni said softly. Her cheeks warmed. Maybe this mess was making her ill, too, or maybe comforting the woman in charge would be enough to embarrass anyone. "I mean, I know that's not for me to judge, but I…just wanted you to know." She tried to put on a hint of her old confidence and met Zara's gaze. "You're the best commander I've had."

The only one she'd had, but for fuck's sake, this was not the time for jokes, especially lame ones.

Zara seemed a little relieved, smiled just a bit, but it seemed like one of those looks someone got just before they burst into tears. Zara didn't go that far. She continued watching the cairn being built, her hand never leaving Roni's arm. At last, she whispered, "Jaq and Claudia are heading back toward the last base. Do you want to go or…" She shook her head. "No, I'm keeping you near, keeping you safe." She seemed to be talking to herself until she turned her gaze on Roni again, and her dark eyes held such weight that Roni nearly stumbled.

All her experience deserted her. Her guilt and sadness seemed lighter, and in their place was a feeling of being lifted, something she couldn't quite put words to, but she'd never felt so safe in all her life. "Thank you." She put a hand over Zara's and squeezed, and Zara— *gods love her*—didn't squirm out from under her touch.

Zara nodded before finally withdrawing her hand in a lingering motion and moved toward the cairn. As she began to say a few words about Ernesto, Roni could barely breathe. How could she have kept secrets from someone like Zara, someone who'd just vowed to protect her with such force of will that Roni believed it in her soul?

The hasty funeral finished, and Roni prepared herself to walk with Zara at the head of their new short column and confess all, but Cortez handed Roni her pack. Ernesto's gear had already been distributed among the rest of them.

"Let's walk near the back, and you can fill me in," Cortez said.

Her soul died a little. She nearly blurted out the truth to Zara anyway, but who knew what Cortez would do if she tried. Even if he did nothing, she wanted Zara to hear the truth without him adding something to make her look bad.

If that was even his plan.

Her insides fell into turmoil again.

When Claudia and Jaq were gone, everyone else continued north in pairs, searching for tripwires as they went. Cortez volunteered himself and Roni to take up the rear, and Zara and Finn agreed. Zara even seemed relieved, maybe that Roni would be farthest from any ambushes, and Roni felt like a faker again. It was almost a relief to spill her story to Cortez as they walked, though she would have much rather told Zara…if she could ever bring herself to do so.

Still, she had to take whatever was on offer. And it did lighten her guilty load a smidge.

At the end of her story, Cortez nodded as they continued to go slowly, checking for tripwires while the others did the same ahead of them. "If you can convince the Vox Feram to kill Hacha, we should attempt it tonight when we know the commander will be too exhausted to have them awake."

Roni frowned at the offhand way he described Zara and at the way he and Roni were now a "we." Though it might be nice to have some backup. "What makes you think I won't be able to convince them to help?"

His smile seemed more than a little smug. "My organization knows far more about the Vox than the army does."

"Oh?" She waited for him to elaborate and forced herself not to grind her teeth when he didn't. "Well, anyone can *say* they know something."

He snorted. "Nice try."

"So you want to risk me failing because I don't have all the facts? You're either malicious or ignorant, serrah."

With a sigh, he glanced at her. "I'm not in the habit of handing out information."

"I'll pay you later," she said with a sweet smile. "Put it on my tab."

When he looked ahead again and walked closer to her, he had a gleam in his eye. He might not be in the habit of giving out information, but he seemed to enjoy doing it. He pitched his voice low like someone gossiping with a neighbor. "The Vox is ancient, a thousand years old or more, and they started out as an it, a simple tool that anyone could use and that would obey commands without question, but over the years, they've retained bits of their owners' personalities and gained a sort of consciousness."

That last part fit with what Roni had heard about the Vox picking their wielder. "How did the Vox retain…bits of the old users?"

"That chain glove doesn't just allow someone to control the Vox. It drains the user's vitality in order to *power* the Vox."

Roni frowned, that piece of info turning her stomach. "Does that mean they'll eventually kill Zara?"

He shook his head. "Not if she's careful. The user can replenish themselves with rest, but if she uses the Vox too often or relies on the larger, mythic shapes they can turn into, she risks her life as much as someone does when pushing themselves for days without rest. Luckily, it seems that if the user is drained to the point of unconsciousness, the glove drops away. But if the user is exhausted to begin with and keeps trying to power the Vox…"

"They could drain what's left of her life," Roni said. Cortez nodded, and Roni chewed her lip. Pushing herself to death for a mission or for the lives of others seemed the exact sort of thing Zara would do. "But if the Vox has a consciousness now, if they like Zara enough to bond with her, surely they wouldn't use all her vitality."

He shrugged. "I don't think the Vox can just stop taking energy from her if she wants to give it."

So there was still something of the mindless tool left in them. But all Cortez's facts contained one bit of happy news. "Then the Vox can't stop me from powering them, too."

He offered another damn shrug. "True. You can wake them up, but they don't have to obey your commands."

"I can talk them round." She was certain of that even when Cortez gave her a skeptical look. "I'll tell the truth. Killing Hacha will save Zara since he's determined to get his hands on the Vox whether I hand them over or he has to take them himself."

"Tonight it is, then. I'll follow you when you leave camp with the Vox in case you need assistance." He raised his eyebrows when she gave him a look. "Having a killer lurking about jeopardizes my mission as well as Zara's. And yours?" he asked, tilting his head. "Once Hacha's out of the frame, do you intend to stay or run?"

Run into the woods? He had to be joking. What the hell did she have out here? Or was he asking about her long-term plans? What if he decided she jeopardized his mission just by knowing who he was? "I plan to stick to Zara's side," she said slowly. "And not mind anyone's business except my own."

After another nod, smile, and shrug combo, he seemed to turn his full attention to the tripwire search again. Roni tried to shake off her nervous feelings, maybe focus on the irritation. If Cortez shrugged at her once more, she'd have to restrain herself from kneeing him in the balls.

The thought made her chuckle, and she tried to hold on to that image or even the feeling, but the future kept weighing her down like wet sand.

CHAPTER SIXTEEN

When they stopped to camp that night, Roni felt so many butterflies in her stomach that the smell of dinner cooking made her gag. She happily took a turn digging the latrine, the solitude giving her time to go over her plan yet again.

Spawning a whole new host of jitters.

They calmed a little when she was back in the camp. But then she saw Zara sitting by herself near a tree, hidden from most of the camp and staring at nothing. No one looked at or approached her, perhaps kept away by the differences in their rank.

With a sigh, Roni walked over. After all the trouble she'd caused, lending a shoulder felt like the smallest price to pay. And being near Zara still made her feel safer than she'd ever been.

Damn it all, she couldn't be so selfish. Zara needed *her*, not the other way around. Who the hell could they depend on if they both needed the other? Roni shook her head at herself. Maybe the key to not falling down was that they'd lean together, into each other.

If Zara *could* lean, that was.

When Zara looked up with that sometimes inscrutable but always dependable gaze, Roni's mouth ran away on its own. Again. "I was going to ask if you're all right, but I know you're not." She winced. She'd wanted to ease into this conversation, but what the hell? She was over the cliff now. "And from what I've seen, well, it seems like you don't like sharing your feelings with your squad or maybe with anyone, but there's no one else here."

She plonked on the log at Zara's side and stared at the darkness, telling herself the lack of eye contact would help Zara open up. In reality, she didn't want to face the fallout of having just eaten her own foot.

Again.

Zara's silence stretched on. Roni risked a look from the side of her eye. Zara had taken off her helmet, and her normally tidy ponytail was askew. A few strands blew across her face. Roni forced herself not to tuck them behind Zara's ear. This situation was too delicate for casual touching. So far, no one was storming off, so that had to mean this was going better than some of their other conversations, but the length of the silence was starting to get ridiculous, and why—

"I've never lost anyone," Zara said quietly. "Not under my command. For some reason, I keep thinking of when my parents died, though that had nothing to do with me."

Neither did Ernesto's death, but Roni couldn't admit that, not yet, not with Zara's voice so confused, as close to fragile as she probably got. Roni risked another look and saw her face open, hurt, as lost in emotion as she never would be in the wilderness. She seemed far from the confident woman who'd made Roni feel safe a few hours earlier and yet with the same strength underneath this shell, one she shouldn't have to break through alone.

Roni told the calculating part of herself to shut the hell up. She put an arm around Zara's shoulders. Zara stiffened. All of Roni's suave glibness disappeared as her mouth took over again. "I'll move it if you want."

The silence stretched again. Finally, a bit of the tension left Zara's body, but she still whispered, "Commanders shouldn't hug their soldiers."

"Even when their soldiers need it?" Or when it was the other way around?

"It's not standard procedure, no." She leaned against Roni a fraction. "But I'll overlook it this time. As you're still learning."

Roni risked a small caress on Zara's arm and felt her shiver slightly before she leaned fuller into Roni's side, her cheek ghosting across Roni's shoulder. The feel of Zara's breath near her ear sent a different kind of butterfly fluttering inside her. She turned her head a fraction, her desire building, but this was another eggshell, and Zara had to want to break through it just as much as Roni did, or it wouldn't work.

Their gazes caught from mere inches away, and still, Zara didn't run.

"What about people who were soldiers, who fulfilled their service, then became civilians?" Roni asked. "How do commanders feel about...touching them?"

Zara's breath hitched, and Roni felt the small movement all the way to her core. "Is that how you see your future? As a civilian?"

A small amount of glibness slipped when Roni couldn't take her eyes off Zara's lips. "I'm practically one already."

Zara smiled slightly. "Even I can tell that's an invitation."

"A gentle one. One you can decline with no hard feelings." She met Zara's gaze again and so hoped for acceptance, but she wouldn't, couldn't push. More than anything, she wanted Zara to know she meant what she said.

Well, more than almost anything.

A look of wonder passed over Zara's face, and she whispered something in a rush, words that took Roni a moment to understand as, "You're telling the truth," but then her lips were touching Roni's.

Everything else ceased to matter. Zara's kiss was hesitant, as if she was unsure what to do after contact had actually been made. But now that she'd broken the barrier, Roni was happy to be her guide. Still, Roni kept it soft, taking each of Zara's lips between her own and kissing them gently. She really wanted to lean in, deepen the kiss until even their moans entangled, but they were still in the woods, with the squad, and they had a job to do.

And Roni didn't want to always be pushing until Zara had to run away. Roni leaned back, letting her arm fall away slowly but keeping eye contact. "I'm always here if you need me."

Zara gave her a smile and another of those wondering looks before she leaned back, too, and shook her head, taking her long dark hair out of its ponytail before pinning it back again with almost brutal efficiency. "Thank you, uh, Roni. Yes, thank you. I..." Her mouth worked a few more times, and her look held affection. And also a strong desire to return to normalcy. "You...thank you."

"Anytime," Roni said before Zara could go on thanking her for the comfort or the kiss or maybe the offer to be there whenever Zara needed her.

As if that was even the truth.

Roni's heart sank again as Zara strode toward the campfire. She had been telling the truth, but what she had in mind with Cortez, with Hacha, might make a liar of her after all. Gods, if Zara ever found out, she'd never trust Roni again.

Roni used the rest of the evening to try to get into the mindset she preferred before she did a job. She tried to let the nervousness flow down her body, out her feet, and into the ground. She breathed deeply to calm her heart and pictured the job at its successful conclusion. The only thing missing was the mantra she normally used: rich nobs didn't deserve to have as much as they did while other people were starving.

She'd starved enough in her life that it usually worked.

But this situation was different. She tried to think up a new line. She was doing this to save Zara's life, all their lives. It was a necessary evil. And it wasn't even that evil, not really. Sure, it had been when she'd been planning to give the Vox to Hacha, but now that she planned to murder him, everything was for the greater good.

Roni fought not to sit with her head in her hands and warn everyone that something was on her mind. She switched tactics yet again and tried to convince herself that the Vox was going to kill Hacha, not her. No blood on her hands, by all the devils.

But after everything Cortez had told her about the Vox being a tool at heart...

Fuck, she was not getting out of this clean.

As she watched Zara chatting with the squad before finally going to bed, she thought it okay to get a little dirt on her soul for someone like Zara. When they caught gazes, there was a hint of softness that hadn't been there before, and it both elevated and crushed her. If Zara found out what Roni was going to do that night, would that look and everything that came with it be lost to her forever?

Gods, why couldn't she have had feelings for someone when everything had been calm in her life?

Because she always did things the hard way.

She and Cortez volunteered for first watch. Roni guessed that Hacha would stay up to watch them, too. Or maybe the Vox would find him asleep and kill him. In an odd way, that thought made Roni feel a little better.

Cortez didn't say anything as they sat near the campfire, and Roni was grateful. Silence was best for keeping her mind on the job. She gave Zara about an hour to go to sleep. Then it was time, but she couldn't move. Cortez finally looked at her with raised eyebrows.

"Shit," she muttered. Yeah, it was then or never. After a few deep breaths and a swift kick to her feelings, she moved toward Zara's tent. She told herself those were Cortez's eyes she felt and not Hacha's. She couldn't afford distractions. She took off her cloak and shook her shoulders out.

Kneeling, she closed her eyes. The crackle of the fire was the loudest sound, and she tuned it out, listening harder, catching the slight breeze clacking through the bare limbs of the forest and the gentle crack of settling ice. She ignored them, too, once they'd been identified, and listened for a sound she'd heard many times: a person sleeping.

Most people she'd spoken to about sleep noises claimed they didn't make any, but everyone did. And they didn't have to rumble like pebbles in a can. Most snoring was gentle, intermittent, and mingled with the sounds of shifting or a dreamy word or chuckle. There was a randomness to it that people didn't seem to embrace while awake.

And she heard it now in Zara's tent. Gods, she'd been hoping Zara would still be awake, and she could drag her feet some more.

No such luck. She slipped a finger through the gap in the tent flap and worked loose the strings Zara had tied from the inside. She went slowly, patiently, and the soft sound of fabric sliding against fabric seemed to echo in her ears. When the flap was untied, she paused again, listening to make sure the sounds of sleep hadn't changed to the more rhythmic sounds of someone waking up.

Again, no such luck. Still, Roni paused to take more notice of how the breeze blew, not wanting to wake Zara with a sudden gust. But the weather was helpfully and damnably still that night. She opened the flap near the top where stray light or cold would have less of a chance to wake Zara and peered inside, leaning so the light from the fire could trickle in over her shoulder.

Once her eyes adjusted, Roni scanned the tent. Zara was a lump in the middle, her belongings smaller hills around her. Everything seemed orderly and neat, everything packed and ready to go. Roni couldn't help a smile. She should have expected nothing less. She watched the lump and wondered if Zara was dreaming of their kiss, if she hadn't been able to get it out of her mind. Everything about her said she wasn't used to romantic entanglements, so she had to be wondering what it had all meant, what she should do.

She should stay sleeping so Roni could do this damn job.

After censuring herself, Roni took another look at the objects closest to the front of the tent. She didn't spot any glint of metal, but it was too dark to really tell. Still holding the flap closed in the middle, she eased a hand inside the floor of the tent and felt around gently. Leather, fabric. Something hard inside a bag. Metal? Yes, but the shape felt like a cup or a plate. Nothing as large as the Vox.

They had to be on Zara's other side, guarded by her sleeping body.

Of course they did.

Roni froze, considering. She could cut a hole in the back of the tent, but she was hoping to pull this off without Zara ever knowing. She made sure the breeze was still blowing softly before she eased through the flap, staying low and keeping it closed around her as much as possible.

Once in the tent, straddling the bag at the entrance, she let her eyes adjust again, savoring the warmth of the small space and wishing she could just cuddle up at Zara's side. She leaned closer, grateful she couldn't see Zara's face in the gloom, or she might have lost her nerve. She reached over the sleeping lump, freezing whenever Zara made a small noise, and trailed her hand along until she encountered a cold swath of metal that couldn't be anything but the Vox.

Hating herself a little for smiling in triumph, she tested the weight and found a good place to grip. When she lifted them slowly, Zara made another noise, and Roni froze, her wrist and stomach aching from the weight of the Vox as she held them in midair. When Zara made no other noise, Roni nearly sighed in relief.

One down.

She put the Vox just inside the tent flap. Now she needed the chain glove. It wasn't wrapped around the Vox, and Zara hadn't been wearing it when she'd gone to bed. Well, the Vox would be awake if she was. Where would she keep something so precious? Not in her pack.

Roni looked at the lump again, barely able to discern it from the darkness. Gods, as much as she'd wanted to touch Zara since they'd met, she couldn't do it now. Disturbing the blankets and searching her would definitely wake her. Roni leaned across the lump again, fighting hopeful flashes of getting this close to Zara when they were awake, and gently patted around the area where the Vox had been lying.

There, right by a...

Warm hand.

Roni clamped her teeth together and fought the urge to yank her hand away, knowing sudden movements were the enemy here. Zara made another noise. It sounded somewhat contented. Or Roni was fooling herself. Either way, she stretched back, pulling the chain farther from Zara's hand before gathering it and sitting back again.

Now she wanted to sigh and whoop in victory and curse her admittedly excellent skills.

And she couldn't do any of that because she was still in the tent.

Again fighting the urge to hurry, she gently crawled out of the flap, bringing the Vox and the chain and tying the flap together again before she fell back onto the cold ground and breathed. Gods, she was good. And a complete bastard. Was it better to be a clever bastard than an idiotic one?

She'd work that one out later.

Cortez loomed over her, holding out a hand. She let him pull her up and swing her cloak back around her shoulders. "That took forever," he whispered.

"I doubt you'll live long in your job if you don't learn patience."

He rolled his eyes as he led the way back toward the fire and held out a hand. "I'll take them."

She clutched the Vox to her chest. "No."

"Why?"

She thought for a few moments but couldn't summon a good reason. Because they were *Zara's*. And she'd stolen them, but she could make damn sure no one else got their hands on them. "Because I said so."

He gave her a flat look. "Seriously? Are you pretending to be my mother now?"

"Whatever keeps your hands to yourself." She moved farther from him and sat on a log, the Vox in her lap as she studied the chain and the gem that sparkled on it. She'd seen Zara wearing it and knew the gem went on the inside of the wrist, but there were no clasps, nothing to indicate where to start. Maybe Zara just tied it on randomly?

Cortez sat beside her, peering at the Vox. Roni lowered her elbows onto them so he couldn't grab them, and he made a noise of irritation.

"Do you know how this wraps around the hand?" she asked.

He crossed his arms. "I'm worthy of giving you information about the thing I helped you steal but not worthy enough to touch them?"

"Funny, I don't remember seeing you in the tent."

"Well, I'm helping now, with this part of the operation."

"By…not giving me any info?"

"I'm your backup," he said slowly. "I'm going to follow you into the woods after you figure out how to use them." He stabbed a finger toward the Vox. "After you figure it out alone, apparently."

"If you don't know, just say so." She studied the chain again.

"I'm not going to be drawn into a fight with you." But his brow drew down, his eyes flashing.

Gods and devils, she so would have taken that challenge at any other time. "Just make sure you wait to follow me in case Hacha is watching. In fact." She dug in her pocket and handed him a few coins, then pointed to the fire. "Here, I'm bribing you and telling you to stay put," she said softly. "Just for Hacha's benefit."

With a slight grumble, he took the money. "And I'm accepting your bribe."

"Good." Well, if the gem was the only feature she could spot, and she knew it went on the wrist like—

As soon as the gem touched the flesh of her wrist, Roni's mind seemed to slide to the side. Her hands took on a life of their own, twisting the chain around her uninjured palm and fingers, and though she was watching, she couldn't remember what she'd just done, nothing able to stick in her slippery thoughts.

Panicky thoughts rose up but slid away just as quickly. She couldn't stop, couldn't acknowledge Cortez as he spoke, couldn't do anything but wrap the chain around until she reached the end.

Her mind came back to her in a rush, but even under the threat of death, she couldn't have told anyone what she'd just done. She froze, staring at the chain that had become a glove until a wind seemed to blow through her, carrying layer upon layer of voices.

"Well, well," they said. "This is unexpected." They sounded... intrigued.

Roni moved her arms to the side. The Vox still reclined in her lap, but the head had turned, and one incredibly realistic golden eye regarded her intently.

CHAPTER SEVENTEEN

Zara knew at once that she was dreaming. It was a typical day, filled with comforting, ordinary tasks. Most of the dreams she could remember went this way. She'd get up, get dressed, eat breakfast, and go to work, but the difference was that everyone in her waking life rarely appeared in her dreams, and no one irritated her with chaotic thinking or unreadable faces.

The last part starkly denoted the difference between dream and reality.

Sadly.

And as soon as she realized it was a dream, she began to wake, curious about why she'd never had the ability to control her dreams like her sisters claimed on occasion. But how would she change dreams that were already perfect?

Well, maybe she could explore some of her unusual feelings in a safe environment, where she didn't run the risk of upsetting everyone and confusing the hell out of herself. Roni could make an appearance.

Her senses came back with the return of rational thought. It was still dark, with not even a hint of light coming through the back of the tent. If she went back to sleep, maybe thoughts of Roni would enter her dreams somehow if she held on to them while drifting. Though it hadn't helped last night when she'd analyzed that kiss over and over again.

That entire encounter was hard to find fault with, a miracle in itself. But an even greater miracle was that Roni seemed to know that Zara needed time to analyze everything from every angle. Based on what Zara had seen and heard and read of love, she'd thought she would be expected to change on some fundamental level, or she would remain unlovable.

But what if that wasn't the case? Most people were irrational, and she couldn't expect that to change, but what if she and an irrational person could sort of…bend around each other, adapting. Even loving.

She smiled, her eyes drifting closed. She couldn't wait to share these thoughts with the Vox tomorrow. Lazily, she felt around for the chain that she always kept close on missions.

Not there.

She opened her eyes again, frowning. Had she batted it away in her sleep? She'd never done that before. She supposed one marvel could have followed another this evening. Maybe she'd even rolled over and dropped it on her other side, a further deviation from the norm, but—

Zara sat up when her searching hand didn't find the Vox, either. The lack was as disturbing as finding a burning brand in her tent. It had to be a mistake. She reached to her left and found the match pocket in her backpack without even looking, proving yet again the value of always keeping one's things the same.

But she couldn't even feel the smugness of justification when she struck the match to find the Vox well and truly gone.

Zara had her boots on and was out of the tent in a moment, shivering in her long underwear. The campfire sat abandoned. It could have been first watch or well into second. She spun in a slow circle, listening, trying to think through her confusion. Someone had taken the Vox. Maybe their mere absence had woken her. But the thief hadn't bothered to kill her, though they could have killed Roni and Cortez on first watch or Finn and Tati on second. Zara's heart lurched, beating harder, and it shamed her a little that one name hurt more than the others.

No time for that. Business first.

She pulled on her trousers and shirt, then carried her leather armor to the other tents and quietly roused those inside. When Ana, Finn, Tati, and Leo emerged, Zara's insides felt colder than the air in the dark forest, but she bit those emotions off, too, and told everyone to dress and arm. Before they could ask questions, she held up a hand.

"I don't know what's going on," she said quietly, "but we're going to find out."

Finn nodded once, sharply, and disappeared to dress. After glancing at each other, Leo and Tati did the same. Ana gave Zara a long look before ducking into the tent she shared with Finn.

Zara donned her armor and cloak and walked the length of the camp, spotting the footprints of Roni and Cortez as they crossed from the camp into the dark forest. No one else seemed to be with them, so they hadn't been forced out.

Lured into the forest by something or someone? Possibly.

Or…they'd stolen the Vox and fled. They were both convicted thieves, after all.

Zara searched for a reason why they'd want the Vox and found nothing, but a voice inside her reanalyzed her interactions with Roni and her conclusion that she'd found someone who wouldn't demand she change herself at the core.

Had everything Roni said and done been a ruse?

Gods and devils. Zara should have known better. She curled her hand into a fist and fought that notion down, too. She needed evidence, could not reach a decision without it. When the others emerged, she ordered the tents emptied and discovered Roni's and Cortez's backpacks with the others.

She breathed easier. They wouldn't have fled into the wilderness with nothing. Still, that voice she'd roused deep inside wasn't convinced, as if now that she'd allowed one unfamiliar feeling in, all the rest were flooding behind it.

Gods, she couldn't start doubting herself now. She fought the leaden feeling that wanted to take over her limbs, that disconnect from reality that forced her to stop functioning and led her brain off the well-worn path. This was a mission, and the mission had to be completed. After all, this was her domain.

Her insides settled. If something disappeared into the woods, she could track it. If it threatened her, she could fight it. If it hurt those under her charge, gods help it.

She wouldn't lose anyone else.

This was her domain.

"Roni, Cortez, and the Vox are missing," she said. "Bank the fire, light the hooded lanterns, and follow me."

❖

The Vox had listened to Roni's story without comment. They'd perched on her wrist as an owl and stared at her. She'd stumbled several times, unnerved by the inhuman face that regarded her unblinkingly. She couldn't read them at all.

When they had told her to start into the woods while finishing the story, she'd been grateful just to be able to look somewhere else, and the Vox had taken up a position on her shoulder, their claws sinking into the cloak and leather armor as if they were no more than silk, a reminder of what the Vox could do to her if they wished.

"I'm not going to hurt you," they said in her mind. "I do need some repairs, so apologies for the drain."

Roni grimaced and not just from a small jolt of dizziness. It had always been a comfort to her that no one could truly know her thoughts. Bang went another fact of life she'd taken for granted. At this rate, nothing from her former life would make sense anymore.

A tendril of amusement came from the Vox, and Roni wondered which of their users they'd absorbed a sense of humor from. She winced, not knowing how the Vox would react to that thought even if they knew of their own creation, and then she censured herself for thinking that on top of everything else.

"Relax," the Vox said. "I might not remember being some *ordinary tool* in my past, but I do know my personality is an amalgamation of experiences. But what else is a personality? I have shared in all the experiences of my *users*, after all."

"No offense intended," she added.

They scoffed in her mind. "I know."

Right, they were in her head, and she was not going to think uncharitable thoughts about that right now. Damn it.

There came that amusement again.

"Are you finished talking to yourself?" Cortez asked softly behind her. "Because I don't want to wait out here forever."

Roni glanced back, but his face was hidden in shadow, the hood of his lantern pulled nearly all the way down. "You were supposed to wait to follow me."

"I did. But you were standing there muttering so long, I thought I'd come give you a prod. Now get on with it."

"You know I'm not talking to myself," she muttered as she started walking again. He was just pissed that she hadn't let him handle the Vox. And she did need to get ahead of him so Hacha wouldn't find them together. She steeled herself, the weight on her shoulder reminding her that she wasn't alone.

It was several steps later that she realized she'd forgotten to grab a lantern, but she'd had no trouble making her way through the near lightless forest in the dead of night.

"That's because I'm seeing for you," the Vox said.

She gasped, wondering how in the hell she hadn't noticed earlier, but it was true. The forest wasn't lit up like midday but maybe early morning or dusk. The Vox had shifted to an owl when they'd first entered the woods, but she hadn't realized what that meant until now. She lifted a hand to her face to find the angle slightly off and almost panicked when she realized she was seeing the world from a few inches to the right of where she expected it to be.

"Breathe," the Vox said. "We're synced. I'm turning my head with yours. You can fight the input I'm sending you, but you shouldn't right now."

Roni took a few deep breaths, fighting fear and a dash of vertigo as she realized she could see through her own eyes again if she wished, though it made the world tilt and descend into darkness. With a shuddering breath, she forced herself to relax, to enjoy a world few others would ever get to see. She had to fight the urge to think of herself as being controlled and focus on what the Vox had said about being synced. Sharing, not controlling.

"Exactly. Now, about Zara…"

A great many emotions fluttered through Roni's mind, but she forced all thoughts and memories to the side. Mind reading on that topic was the last thing she wanted, especially now that there had been some progress—

"Aha! A kiss," the Vox said, their many voices shrill with glee.

Gods fucking damn it. "None of your business," she said with a growl.

"*Tsk*. I'll find out when Zara and I are reunited."

"You can't tell her about any of this," Roni said. "Otherwise, you might as well not cooperate at all." Speaking of, they hadn't said they would kill Hacha for her. They'd only listened, as good at getting information out of someone as she used to be when she'd had enough coin to soften someone up at the bar.

The Vox remained silent, and Roni wished she could manifest their knack of keeping their thoughts entirely to themselves. She knew the Vox heard that, too, but they didn't offer any tips.

But even that *confirmed* that the Vox could keep things from Zara if they wanted to.

Nope, not a peep, even when goaded. She might as well have been talking to a stone.

Still nothing, not even that jot of amusement.

That finally got a chuckle. "I don't mind getting rid of this Hacha creature for you. Seems the world would be a safer place without him."

"Definitely. And as for telling Zara?"

Not even a whisper, devils take them.

Roni spotted movement ahead, the slight shift like a beacon to the Vox's eyes. She paused, her heart accelerating. She didn't know how much Hacha knew about the Vox, and she didn't want to give away that they were synced by walking perfectly through the dark. Something shifted again, human-sized, but she didn't see a light. If it was Hacha, he'd probably doused his light when he'd heard her coming. His night vision might be excellent, but it couldn't match hers at the moment.

Gods, it felt good to finally have some advantage over him.

"Stay here," the Vox said. With a flutter of metal wings, they were gone from her shoulder.

Roni gasped as the ground seemed to fall out from under her feet. She lighted on a branch above herself before taking to the air again. Dimly, she felt her real legs wobble. Flying, she was flying. The rush, the air, the sudden burst of freedom. Gods, her heart soared. How could Zara stand not spending every moment like this?

Her joy evaporated when she saw Hacha leaning against a tree, waiting, a shuttered lantern near his feet. When the Vox flapped their wings again, he started and jerked the lantern up, dropping the shutter and blinding the Vox just as they dropped toward him.

It wouldn't matter. Their claws were outstretched, beak open, but more than that, the heavy metal body would fall on him like a stone and—

Pain ripped through Roni, and she fell, her own senses coming back in a rush as the Vox screeched in agony. Something was wrong, oh gods, and she could barely think straight. She stumbled upright and through the dark, hitting branches, snagging undergrowth, and slipping on hidden patches of ice. She struggled for the light ahead, fighting off the Vox's suffering. They were made of metal. How the hell could they feel pain?

Roni pushed past the last tree and saw the Vox splayed on the ground, one of their wings pinned by a large metal spike as long as a dagger. Hurt seared through her own shoulder as the Vox fluttered, their tiny metal pieces rolling over and over one another as they sought to reform, but the area around the spike stayed the same, as unmoving as stone.

Hacha laughed and stood from the Vox's side. The light shining from the ground made his face even more ghoulish as he smiled and licked his lips. "Oh, good try, rat." He chuckled again and wiped his forehead as if he'd done a hard day's work. "Though I'm a little insulted you'd think I'd come unprepared." After a deep breath, he held out a hand. "The glove."

She was tempted, hoping he'd put it on and share in the agony, but when she removed it, the Vox would lose all life, and he'd be able to carry them back home without a fuss. No, she had to keep it on, had to find a way to free the Vox and hold on to that spike so they could tear Hacha to pieces.

"Yes, get it out," the Vox screamed in her mind, shrieking aloud, too, and Roni almost dropped again.

Hacha stepped closer. "Take it off, or I'll do it myself."

She backed away, circling behind the tree. "F...fuck off." With a gasp, she pushed the Vox's pain away again, willing them to hold it in as best they could. She was coming. She'd help them, but she needed her wits.

The pain receded a little, the Vox's cries dying down.

Roni drew her truncheon.

Hacha sighed as if world-weary. "If I have to help you, the hand's coming off, too." When she stepped around the other side of the trunk, closer to the Vox, he eyed her truncheon and laughed. "You know what, rat? I'm almost gonna miss you." He drew his knife, but before he could advance, Cortez leaped from the shadows.

Hacha turned away quickly, still damnably fast, but Cortez's saber flickered in the light and caught Hacha across the upper arm. He didn't drop the knife, but he did back farther away, eyes darting between them. Cortez advanced cautiously, but Hacha stepped closer to the Vox.

Roni creeped forward, too. She couldn't take Hacha weapon-to-weapon, not even with Cortez backing her up. But if she could make him think she was going to attack and make him step far enough away, she could dive for the Vox and free them.

Her heart thundered in her ears, her vision shimmering with her pulse. She fought the urge to look at the Vox, not wanting to give her plan away. Time seemed to have slowed, everyone as taut as bowstrings, every step a strategy game. Roni thought she heard movement in the forest behind her, but she couldn't take her eyes off Hacha to look.

Someone cried out.

In Sarrasian.

Zara was coming.

Roni's heart stuttered before her body went cold. Gods, no.

Hacha's gaze flicked toward the trees. Cortez darted forward, blade at the ready. Roni made herself move, feinting toward Hacha to drive him back before she leaped for the Vox.

She landed just a few feet shy, but before she could move again, noise burst through the trees, the same kind of deafening screams and devil chorus that she'd heard once before on this journey.

Someone had set off a magical tripwire.

The Firellians would be coming, too.

❖

Zara didn't look behind to see who'd fallen over the tripwire. All that mattered was that they had to leave this spot as quickly as possible. And find the Vox. And Roni and Cortez. While leaving all their gear behind in the camp.

All of these thoughts ran through her mind in a moment, but she pushed ahead toward the light she'd glimpsed in the dark forest. "With me," she shouted over the noise, trusting that the others would be right behind her. She didn't know what awaited her ahead, but she'd be damned if she'd turn back now.

When she stepped into the light, the scene was chaos. A large man with a knife faced off with Cortez, but as Zara watched, he darted toward where Roni lay on the ground. He kicked, and she rolled away before tossing a handful of dirt and leaves in his face. Cortez pushed forward, but the large man stepped inside his reach. He ignored the dirt spattering his cheeks and elbowed Cortez's sword arm away, cutting into his other arm in the process where the armor didn't quite cover the wrist.

Zara stepped toward them, her own saber out, but something glinted from the ground, and she stopped in horror. The Vox, pinned to the ground by a long spike, squirmed and tried to shift, their metal pieces fluttering like paper. They screeched dully, and Zara hurried to them, barely remembering to keep an eye on the large man with the knife.

He swore when their eyes met, but before he could come for her, Finn was on him, Cortez at her side. Leo and Tati attacked one flank and Ana the other, leaving Zara to fall to her knees at the Vox's side.

She couldn't hear their voices. But they were active. How...

Zara glanced to the side and met Roni's horrified expression, her guilty eyes.

The golden glove on her hand.

Rage coursed through Zara. She used it to yank the spike from the Vox's wing. It came free with an ear-splitting screech, and the Vox sprang from the ground, metal twisting until they became a small falconet. They dove into Zara's lap, knocking her backward and almost stealing her air. She curled an arm about them and let her anger flow, determined to protect them.

She stood and held a hand out to Roni, who looked up at her with gratitude until Zara said, "Give me the glove."

Roni's eyes sparkled with tears, emotions they didn't have time for.

"Now," Zara snapped.

With shaky hands, Roni slipped the gem off her wrist, and the chain fell loose. Zara snatched it from her fingers, casting an eye toward the fight as the Vox went still in her arms. The rest of the squad had backed the large man into the trees, but he moved so quickly, they couldn't seem to surround him.

The alarm still sounded from the dark, and Zara hoped they had a few more minutes since it was still the dead of night. She donned the glove, and the Vox stirred again.

"Oh, I missed you," the many voices said.

"Do you know if he has more of these?" She lifted the spike, asking both the Vox and Roni.

Roni shook her head just as the Vox shrunk away. "I hope not," they said.

Even if he did, he was too busy fighting for his life to draw one. But Zara didn't want to take that chance with the Vox's safety.

"Be an owl. I need your eyes," she said. The Vox transformed, and she sent them up to wait in the branches. "Pick up that lantern and stay behind everyone," she said to Roni. Zara drew her blade and joined the fight, not knowing who this man was or even caring at the moment. He'd hurt the Vox. That was all she needed. She pressed him hard alongside the others, backing him farther into the trees. The squad had scored several hits against him, but they seemed shallow, and he was still slippery and lightning quick.

And now the Vox spotted lights in the forest, coming for them.

Zara went low, aiming for the large man's knees. He thrust his hips back, hopping out of range. Tati came at him from the right, and he blocked her swing with his long knife and scored a cut across her hand. She left off with a cry. The big man had opened up his left side in the process, and Cortez scored a long cut across his arm before he whirled away with a grunt. He wore no uniform, could have been Firellian or Sarrasian, but Zara knew he was from Sarras, part of some trouble Roni had kept a secret.

And Zara thought she couldn't get angrier than she already was. Fury drove her harder, swinging faster, edging Leo and even Finn out of the fight. Ana took Tati's place and added some mad swings, pressing from the right, and Cortez darted in and out, taking every opportunity. They had this man. It was only a matter of time before—

He vanished, gone with a crash and a cry.

Zara pulled up short, grabbing Tati and holding the flat of her blade across Cortez's chest to keep him from following the big man. She looked through the Vox's eyes and saw what her subconscious mind already knew: the man had plunged through a sinkhole, a natural pitfall this close to the border where the forest met the rockier terrain near the river.

And they didn't have time to see if he'd survived. Maybe the Firellians would finish him off.

Zara called the Vox to her shoulder. "Stay close," she said to the squad. She pointed to Roni, lamenting the fact that she didn't have time to kick her ass, too. "You bring up the rear with the light."

Using the Vox's night vision, Zara led the way into the darkened forest. They had no supplies, but they'd all trained for that possibility, and she was still going to complete the mission and get them all out alive.

Then she'd strangle Roni and Cortez.

CHAPTER EIGHTEEN

Roni thanked the gods that she was running. The gloom hung about the squad like a cloak, even with her lantern, and the cold bit at her as she staggered over brush and branches, but at least she didn't have to stare into Zara's blazing eyes.

Gods, she'd never seen someone so angry, so hurt, and people had actually wanted to kill her before. But Zara wasn't going to kill her, no. Roni had never feared that. She would ask and demand and punish, but worse than that, Roni had felt her walls go up with a bang, harder and higher than any prison.

And everyone's lives were still in danger.

The alarm was still blaring off to their left, though the sound was fading faster than they could escape it, dying out as if losing power. A call seemed to come from behind them, but that might have been Roni's own harsh breathing or the ringing in her ears. Gods and devils, how the hell was she going to explain?

Another noise came from in front of the column, followed by the ring of metal on metal. The Firellians? Hacha reappearing from the void he'd fallen into? Roni pressed forward, bringing the light with her, though if Zara was connected to the Vox, she could see well enough in the dark.

Would Zara ever forgive her just for sharing that experience? She didn't have time to think as several more lanterns bobbed through the dark forest, and the Firellians closed about them.

Roni drew her truncheon and stood shoulder to shoulder with Ana and Tati. She swung wildly, her heart thundering, and got several grunts and cries for her trouble. A larger person came for her, features hidden by dancing shadows, and she thought of Hacha. She cried out as she swung, desperate to banish that devil from her life.

When the enemy lifted their weapon to block, Tati stabbed them in the gut, and they fell, just another Firellian soldier. Damn.

Another soldier came for Roni and Tati, and the Vox fell atop him with a screech, tearing and rending. Roni couldn't look. When she wasn't in their head, they were too inhuman.

Ana cried out, and Roni turned to see someone jabbing at her thighs while taking cover near a clump of bushes. Roni pressed forward, but Finn was already wading in, swinging repeatedly. When Ana groaned, Roni turned to find her collapsing. Tati got there first and caught Ana's small frame across her broad shoulders.

Cortez and Zara turned from a pile of dead. She looked like a blood-covered spirit of vengeance, and when no other Firellians emerged, she held a hand up before anyone could speak.

The crashing sounds of pursuit still echoed from the darkness.

Zara's face set grimly. "Finn, take the others and head for the river. I'm going to lead the Firellians away with some noise."

Finn nodded once, her own expression like stone.

Roni wanted to smack them both. If this trip had proved anything, it was that the Vox and their wielder were not invincible. As Finn grabbed a fallen lantern and began to lead the others away, Roni stuck close to Zara.

Zara frowned at her and nodded to where Finn had stopped to call for Roni and Cortez, who also lingered. "Go, Bisset. Cortez."

Oh, they were back to Bisset, were they? Fuck that. "I'm not leaving you, Zara."

She bared her teeth. "I'm giving you an order."

"I don't care."

Zara rocked back, her eyes almost comically wide, as if Roni had said she was a giant possum or something else that made no sense.

And the Firellians were getting closer.

Zara seemed ready to say something else, but a strange whistling sound came from the darkness. Roni whipped around and half crouched, expecting arrows, but this sounded larger.

Zara gripped her arm. "Run! Everyone, run." She pulled Roni along, her breathing heavy. Cortez kept pace with them. Roni fought not to stumble, to obey the new fear in Zara's eyes. A wave of sound and heat and light rolled over them, and Roni pitched forward, carried along as the forest flashed like the sun had descended upon them.

She managed a look back to see a flash of fading fire that left their little battlefield a smoking ruin of blackened trunks and charred bodies. "What...the hell?"

"Keep moving." Panic still coated Zara's voice like tar. "It's the mage."

A mage could light up the forest brighter than midday? With a fire hot enough to incinerate with a touch, an inferno that faded just as quickly?

What the hell was wrong with mages?

And why didn't the army just recruit a bunch of them to do this shit?

"Where...did they get...someone who can do that?" Cortez said as they ran.

Zara didn't answer. The trees around them had begun to thin, making it easier to see. Roni was running on fear. Cortez was no doubt feeling the same, but they couldn't stop now. At least Zara had gotten some sleep, and Roni could trust her to lead them out of danger. She'd find them a nice hiding place, and Roni could rest her aching head and burning legs and bleary eyes and pounding heart.

Until Zara tore into her for the betrayal and disobedience. Shouting or a beating would be better than laying on the guilt or keeping up this silence.

Zara led them in a haphazard pattern, though she also seemed to be leaving an obvious trail, snapping off small branches and crashing through snowdrifts. Good news for the other group but not for Roni's plans for sleep. It didn't help that they were angling steadily upward. Roni glanced around when Zara had them jog sharply to the right and saw a large hole in the ground, black as a hungry maw, too large to be covered over like the one that had eaten Hacha.

And only the Vox's keen eyes kept them all from falling into it now.

Just another fear to add to the list.

Zara veered again, this time down a steep slope. Roni grabbed at the nearby trees for purchase, the lantern hanging over one wrist.

She thought Zara might be leading them into a cave or something, and a new sense of terror washed over her. If there were caves, Hacha was prowling them at this very moment, and Roni did not want to be immersed in darkness again.

She breathed easier when Zara led them under a massive overhang, the rock wall pockmarked with holes but none large enough to be called a cave. Zara waved for them to halt, and then they all leaned on their knees and breathed hard.

The Vox flew in and stood on a boulder, staring at Zara for a few moments. She nodded, and Roni fought down a wave of frustration at being left out. Strange what she could get used to after a taste. But the whole damn trip had been like that.

"We should be safe here for a moment's rest," Zara said. Her expression had closed itself to everything but anger again, and she stared at Cortez. "Tell me."

Roni shifted, but Zara couldn't seem to look at her. She bit her lip, afraid Cortez would only lie and make things worse. "He works for some kind of intelligence outfit," she blurted. "And I'm…a thief."

Zara's gaze moved to hers slowly, as if reluctant, and that helped pull Roni's story out in fits: getting caught, Judith Esposito, Hacha, the ever-changing plans to steal the Vox. Everything. She took every opportunity to say she was sorry, to explain how her feelings had changed from simply wanting to survive, to craving escape, to feeling trapped by Hacha and Judith, and finally, to wanting to kill Hacha when she feared he'd murder everyone like he had poor Ernesto.

At last, Roni took a breath and closed her eyes as tears threatened to come pouring out. She couldn't add that she never meant for any of this shit to happen. Zara would figure that out on her own. "I'm sorry," she said again, ashamed at the way her voice cracked. "I know Ernesto's death is on me. I wanted to tell you everything so many times, but Hacha said…" She took a deep breath, but the tears spilled out anyway. Blinking rapidly, she looked up, trying to stop them. "He said…that if I told anyone…he'd pick you all off one by one."

Her deep breaths shuddered, and she willed them to stop. She couldn't break down, not in front of Zara and especially not Cortez. She wasn't some mewling baby. "And he could do it," she forced out. "And I couldn't…I know you said we had to share problems, but…I care about everyone and…most of all you." Fuck. She rolled her lips under but couldn't keep the sobs inside. She shut her eyes again and clenched her teeth, putting a hand over her mouth to stifle herself.

"No one thinks for me," Zara said after a few moments of silence. Her voice was deep, still angry, but she wasn't spitting venom. Roni's stomach knotted as she sobbed again. Venom would be better. A punch to the gut would be better than this quiet anger. "Don't do it again."

Roni risked a look. Again? They were going to have an again? Of any kind? She swiped at her tears to try to see Zara through the blur, but now that the tears had started, they didn't seem inclined to stop. She smacked her chest to get the sobs to still, but that didn't work. When she tried again, Zara's iron grip closed about her wrist.

"Breathe," Zara said calmly. Roni tried and failed. The grip tightened, but the thumb worked back and forth over the underside of her wrist. "Look at me."

Roni lifted her head. Zara's face was calm now, as implacable as the tide.

"Breathe with me." She inhaled slowly, her chin lifting, and exhaled, lowering her head as she did.

Roni breathed with her. Sweat trickled down the sides of her face, and a few strands of black hair had escaped her ponytail and stuck to the sides of her neck. Her cheeks were flushed, and she had dark circles coming out under her eyes, but those eyes were bright, comforting wells. She looked tired but beautiful and more than that, she exuded competence. She was in charge, and nothing bad was going to happen while she remained that way.

That feeling of safeness washed over Roni again. Zara would protect her. Even after everything she'd done, Zara would see her home alive and well.

"Everything we shared was real," Roni whispered, not caring who might be listening. "I lied about a lot of things but not that. I care about you, Zara. I want…to get to know you better, in every sense. That was never false. You're the most honest, trustworthy person I've ever met, and I can see myself feeling safe with you for as long as you'll have me around." She swallowed hard. "However you'll have me around, whatever you'll let me be to you." Zara's gaze remained steady, her head tilting just a little as if she was trying to see into

Roni's soul. "I said I didn't care about your orders, but I realize that was another lie. I'll always come when you call." She had to breathe out and add, "Well, unless you order me to leave you in danger. It seems I can't obey that one."

Zara's eyes shifted to the side, to the Vox, and Roni hoped with all her might that the Vox was backing her up. They'd seen into her mind, could maybe know things she wasn't aware of herself. But after seeing the jealous anger on Zara's face, Roni didn't want to remind her of that fact.

Zara released her slowly. "I'll get you home."

Was that it? Roni wanted to ask but bit all her questions back. She'd said she'd be whatever Zara wanted. If she had to be just another part of the job, she'd have to live with that.

For now. But that wouldn't be the end. She'd never said she wouldn't try to be anything more. At least until Zara *said* she didn't want to be pursued. Then Roni would bow out. But she'd be damned if she'd give up the fight beforehand.

Zara turned her gaze on Cortez, and it hardened again. He'd moved off several paces and was winding a piece of cloth around his wounded wrist. "Is it my turn?"

Gods, Roni had hoped he'd be smart enough to realize that now wasn't the time for jokes, but no such luck.

"I'm not surprised to find someone like Jean-Carlo out here," Zara said casually. "I'm not even angry about it, just a little irritated that your agency thought my report wouldn't be thorough enough for them."

Roni watched carefully, more than ready to be on the receiving end of some new information for once.

Cortez frowned. "It's less about your thoroughness and more about making sure my *agency* receives the full report, something the army would no doubt try to keep from us." He put his hands on his hips. "And I'm nothing like that stuck-up asshole."

Well, well. So he had a beef with a colleague? Roni looked to Zara.

"I've met one of his kind before," Zara said to her. "They're like spy hunters, but they ferret out information about their own government, too."

"The better to put together an accurate picture of the world at large," Cortez said, still seeming a little peeved.

"I thought the government already did that," Roni said.

Cortez shrugged. "There are some tasks better left to unofficial channels."

"Ah. Illegal ones," Roni said. "So you operate like one of the criminal syndicates."

Cortez frowned.

Zara snorted. "Jean-Carlo certainly doesn't seem to care about the law."

"I am nothing like him," Cortez said slowly.

Oh, this was good. Roni would much rather sort his dirty laundry than confront any more of her own mistakes. "Do I sense some tension?" she asked.

Cortez glared at her and said nothing.

She smiled slightly. His rigid posture answered for him. "Did he show you up in front of the boss? Betray your trust? Break your heart?"

He chuckled at the last, but it had no humor in it. Aha.

Roni wanted to press more, but Zara only shook her head. Again, Roni would have given a lot to know what she was thinking, but before she could begin to wonder, Zara said, "Let's get moving."

Zara searched for food as she led Cortez and Roni toward the Kingfish River. For a moment, she'd been glad they'd had to leave their supplies behind. Surely keeping an eye out for anything edible *and* everyone in the forest who wanted to kill them would fully occupy her mind.

No such luck.

Having Roni on this expedition had fulfilled all her fears. Even if she put away all the unusual feelings like the lust Roni occasionally sparked or the strange hope that kindled in her every time she looked deep in Roni's eyes, there remained the unnecessary physical reactions like the fluttering in her belly…and the cold feeling of betrayal.

But most of all, Roni unforgivably distracted her. So much so that Roni had been able to steal the Vox as soon as Zara's eyes were closed.

"That's more down to her skills than your inattentiveness," the Vox's many voices said in her mind.

"Skills," Zara mumbled with a snort. "Thieving skills."

"Are still skills."

"And she's still distracting me," Zara said in a harsh whisper. "If I hadn't been so distracted this trip, maybe…maybe…Ernesto might still be—"

"That's illogical bullshit, and you know it."

Zara bit her lip. It was. Blaming oneself for circumstances beyond one's control and for knowledge one didn't possess was as bad as taking credit where it wasn't due. As for Ernesto and Roni's part in his death…

She sighed. Her training never involved untangling problems like these. She didn't exactly blame Roni for Ernesto's death, but what if—

No, she couldn't "what-if" herself or Roni to death. But the fact remained that Roni hadn't given her all the facts.

"Neither did Cortez, but you're not half as angry with him."

That was true. She wasn't really surprised to find out someone like him had joined her squad. Indeed, it made sense after a moment's consideration. And he wasn't dragging baggage behind him like Roni was.

"And he doesn't make you feel like she does," the Vox added.

Zara almost barked at them to stop taking Roni's side, but that was another bit of claptrap. The Vox was always on her side.

"Always," they echoed fondly.

A moment of silence passed between them, but it was comforting and gave her another chance to sort through all the other sounds around her, checking that two sets of footsteps were still following her, and no sounds of pursuit echoed through the rocky terrain surrounding them. The wind had picked up the closer they came to the river, and she caught the hint of rushing water, a sound that would only become louder from here on. Good, that would prevent conversation.

The Vox sighed.

Zara frowned at the irritated noise. "You spoke to her." She couldn't decide how she felt about that. Another betrayal? But the Vox wouldn't have been able to resist being linked to Roni through the glove.

But they could have refused to speak to her, could have tried to resist her scheme. Could have flown into Zara's tent and woken her.

"It's never easy going against the wishes of the wielder," the Vox said. "And her plan was sound. By removing Hacha, I was removing a threat against you as well."

"I don't need protecting."

"I *know*," the Vox said, stretching the word out. "But if you'd been awake, you would have tried to arrest Hacha or something, but I had to think of him the way Roni saw him, as a rabid animal. Such creatures won't be swayed by the threat of prison."

Zara didn't know whether she could trust that or not. Everything Roni thought was suspect, and the law should be the same for everyone. "She's influenced you." By their own admission, the Vox had been swayed a bit by everyone who had ever wielded them. Sometimes, that thought made her wonder if she was really having these conversations with herself.

"No," the Vox said definitively. "Though I admit to choosing people whose personalities align with my own as the years have gone by. That's why I chose you. And why I would never leave you for Roni or anyone else."

Zara had to smile. That helped ease one pain in her chest. But it still left the question of what to do about Roni. Zara still had a job to do, and she didn't need distractions. Now that Zara had let all these damn feelings out, they wouldn't just go back to hell where they belonged.

"You have to grant her some leeway," the Vox said softly. "Your feelings for her are not her fault. There's nothing evil in them. After seeing in her mind, I can say that she genuinely cares for you and the others, and she's let herself imagine a future with you, something she's never done before. Trust is a new feeling for her."

For both of them, though in different ways. Roni had all but admitted that she now trusted Zara with her safety where before she'd thought she had to fight Hacha alone. But could she be trusted with Zara's heart? The Vox said yes, and Zara was beyond grateful that she had a way to peer into Roni's mind. But…

"Did you share my feelings with her?"

"No," the Vox said, sounding a little chagrined. "I…" They sighed. "Is it wrong that I didn't want her to have the same kind of connection with you as I do? Even through me?"

Zara laughed softly. "I understand that feeling completely."

Even before the Vox had confirmed it, Zara had known Roni was telling the truth when they'd stopped to talk. When she'd looked into Roni's tear-filled eyes, she'd felt the same as just before they'd kissed. She knew Roni was telling the truth about her feelings.

Now if she could only stop lying about everything else.

Could she? To find out, Zara would have to keep her around, have to forgive her, even while knowing she wouldn't forgive more lies. If she wanted to know how trustworthy Roni was, if she wanted to get past finding these damn feelings distracting and find them normal instead, she'd have to give Roni another chance.

Like Adella had given Bridget.

Who'd lied about…pretty much everything in her life. She made Roni look like a paragon of truth. Zara would have to ask Adella how she'd managed to forgive all that.

Gods, then Adella would squeal about Zara "finding someone," and Gisele would mock her. They'd want all the little details and would *hoot* or *ahh* if she blushed or couldn't find the right words.

She'd rather go to hell. With a sigh, she asked, "So should I just tell her I forgive her?"

"No," the Vox said adamantly. "She has to suffer a bit more to remind her never to screw up like this again."

Zara would have to trust the Vox on that. And she had to admit that the decision to forgive made her feel a little better. Someone who touched her deeply, who tried to fight against or make up for their destructive patterns deserved a little leeway.

"After the suffering," the Vox added. They stirred on her shoulder, head bobbing.

Zara looked through their eyes and spotted some creature moving among the rocks. At her command, the Vox was on it in an instant, snuffing its life. Breakfast was served.

They ate in silence around a small campfire. Without the salt from their packs, the meal was tasteless, but at least it was filling. Zara threw the last of the bones in the fire and turned her attention to Cortez. "Do you know why the Firellians are out here in such numbers?"

He wiped his hands on his trousers and stared off into the distance. She'd always thought of his looks as nondescript, with average…everything, a perfect look for a spy. When he didn't speak for a few moments, she sighed.

"I know people in your line of work aren't used to sharing," she said, "but the more I know, the better equipped we are to finish this mission."

He looked at her as if calculating something.

"It's okay if he doesn't tell," Roni said with a shrug. She drew her knees up and leaned on them, staring into the flames. "We'll finish the mission, then this Jean-Carlo you know can fill you in when we get back."

Cortez gave her a flat look. "Nice try."

Zara watched them, sensing something else at play, something beneath the words. Subtext, fantastic, just what she was worst at. She fought the urge to sigh.

"Give Roni some backup," the Vox said.

Zara nodded. "Well, I am trying to keep us all alive, and I am the only experienced scout here, so it would be best if I had the information now. But if you refuse, Cortez, then, yes, Jean-Carlo will no doubt prove invaluable when it comes to writing my report."

Roni chuckled. "Bet your superiors will wonder why they sent you at all, Cortez, when they could have sent this other guy."

He bristled. "Stop trying to get under my skin. I'm twice the agent he is."

Roni gave him a flat look. "Okay, sure."

His lips flattened to a thin, bloodless line, and he turned his glare to Zara again. "Here's what I can tell you." His gaze slid to Roni. "And not because you goaded me."

She shrugged, not looking at him, giving Zara the barest glance and a quick wink.

Remarkable.

"We've heard rumors about the Firellians training special soldiers," Cortez said. "But I didn't expect a mage. I expected some kind of elite fighting unit. We thought there might be more Firellians than usual guarding their side of the border or maybe some on this side but not this many. I've been wondering if they're all here to guard the mage."

Zara shook her head. "A mage powerful enough to set magical tripwires and light an entire clearing on fire doesn't need that many guards." She rubbed her temples and recalled what she could of Gisele's stamina for magic. "They'd need to be protected when they're tapped, but that wouldn't take all these separate camps. And it might only be the one mage. When I was alone with Ana and the Vox, I heard some of the Firellians speaking about a monster who could kill them all. If that's the mage, they don't completely trust her."

Roni groaned and rubbed her forehead, pushing her helmet back. She stooped even while sitting and had stress lines at the sides of her face, paler lines through the dirt and sweat that no doubt coated them all. "I thought Hacha was the only monster out here."

Apparently not.

"The mage could be another guard," Cortez said. "For something else they don't want us to find."

And it probably wouldn't be something stationed out here in the forest. "When we get to the river," Zara said, "we'll know more." She would stake her reputation on that.

Cortez nodded. If he was tired or stressed, he hid it well, seeming clear-eyed as he watched her. She didn't want to waste his sharing mood, so she pulled the spike that had pinned the Vox from her pocket. She felt them shiver from where they rested on the branches overhead.

"A normal spike wouldn't keep the Vox from shifting its shape," Zara said. "Nor would it have caused such pain." She tried to pin Cortez with her gaze, letting him know she was talking about more than duty now. "What do you know about this?" His expression didn't flicker, but she continued to watch.

"And how does a thug like Hacha know about it?" the Vox asked.

Zara repeated their question and waited. If she sensed Cortez knew anything about the spike, she wouldn't bother to rely on Roni's tactics. Old-fashioned violence had its uses.

CHAPTER NINETEEN

It was nice to watch Cortez squirm for a change. Roni had seen more than enough of Zara's steely glare. But as he told Zara the history of the Vox, Roni suspected he was nervous because he hadn't known about the spike. That clearly upset him more than Zara's hawklike focus.

"As for Hacha having that spike or even knowing about it..." Cortez said, shrugging again. "I have no idea. His syndicate must be very well informed."

Zara's expression didn't change. "Clearly. They seem to know more than yours."

Roni wanted to laugh, then cover Zara's face in kisses, but that would needlessly piss everyone off, so she hid a smile behind a cough.

Cortez glared into the trees, his nostrils flaring. "So it seems, Commander," he said archly. Still, he kept up the niceties. Maybe he wasn't a fool after all.

"Well." Zara tucked the spike away and leaned forward to arrange some of the sticks and leaves dotting the rocky ground. "We're here, and the river should be here."

Roni stared in awe as Zara outlined the path she'd planned for them. How in the gods' names did she know exactly where she was? Even if she'd been this way before, what was there to denote one bit of forest from another? Or one rocky overhang? Did the squirrels make little signposts that only Zara could read?

Instead of trying to figure it out, Roni watched Zara, her confidence, her grace, her doggedness. She would have made an incredible thief, probably would have had her own syndicate by now.

And like her squad, her underlings would have followed her to rob the mansions of hell.

Cortez had some suggestions and questions, but Roni didn't care how the mission was done, just that she wouldn't have to leave Zara's side. And that was about more than her own safety—well, a *bit* more—Zara seemed to need someone to tell her that she didn't always have to risk herself. Her life wasn't less important because she was in charge. The Vox seemed to understand Zara, but she also needed someone who thought differently, who could think a little less...straightforwardly.

The leader of a syndicate needed a good lieutenant.

Roni sighed, warmed by the thought even though Zara would not agree. At least not out loud. Not at first. Shit, patience had never been one of Roni's virtues when she wasn't in the midst of a job. She couldn't sit back and wait for Zara to notice her value.

"What do you think?" Zara asked, her dark eyes boring into Roni's and pulling her out of her head.

Fuck. Roni studied the leaves and twigs while her mind raced, but she didn't even know which one she was supposed to be. It was on the tip of her tongue to make a smart remark or lie, but the idea left a bad taste in her mouth. So she let herself run along a different track. "Honestly, I don't know what to think. I have as much chance navigating out here as I do in the middle of the ocean. But I trust your knowledge and training, Zara. It hasn't let us down yet."

Zara's mouth twitched before she rolled her lips together, but the way she relaxed slightly and turned her gaze elsewhere said she was pleased. Then her brows arched, and their eyes met again, and Roni said, "Commander." There were still protocols that must be followed.

"Good," Zara said as she stood. "Let's get moving again."

And just like that, rest time was over. Roni swallowed a sigh as she stood and stretched. She hoped they'd get some time to sleep soon, or she really might drop.

"Commander's pet," Cortez mumbled.

"Jealous, Constable?"

He rolled his eyes. "Not a constable."

She shrugged and wiped her hands down the sides of her cloak before flexing her injured hand slightly, not wanting it to stiffen up.

The wound in her stomach was just a small ache in comparison. "Constables, sentinels, whatever you call yourself. You're all the same. Law-and-order types."

He barked a laugh. "You joined the *army*, Recruit Bisset. You can't get more orderly than that."

True. But she started walking after Zara rather than say it. It felt good to argue.

"A lot of people go from the army to the constabulary and vice versa," Cortez said. "Who knows? That could be you one day."

Too far. She turned and pointed at him. "Bite your tongue."

He grinned, and that was nice to see, too. She'd enjoyed talking with him when they were both just recruits. Gods, what was it, nearly a week since they'd departed Sarras? Four weeks since they'd started training? She'd cased places for longer, but this felt like an eternity.

When Zara stopped ahead and put her hands on her hips, Roni hurried to join her, but not before saying, "I'll look up your buddy Jean-Carlo when I get back and ask him what to call you."

Cortez made a noise between a huff and a squawk, but he clambered over the rocky terrain behind her.

Zara led them slowly, pausing frequently and kneeling, her head cocked as the Vox flew overhead. Roni heard nothing special, but her ears had begun to ring, and her vision blurred with fatigue. After another long pause, Roni couldn't keep in a groan.

With a smirk, Zara glanced back. Roni wondered if this slog constituted part of her punishment for stealing the Vox. She creeped closer to Zara's back. "Cortez is tired, too," she whispered.

"Cortez also deserves it," Zara said.

"Aha. I knew this was a punishment."

Zara sighed and shook her head. "But fatigue does make one clumsy." She glanced back. "Just a little farther and we'll stop."

Cortez mumbled something about not being tired, and Roni rolled her eyes. She did her best not to stumble as she followed Zara into another crevice. "Sleep," Zara said. "I'll keep watch."

Roni didn't bother to wait and see what Cortez did. She stretched out on the ground, rolled up in her cloak, and drifted to sleep, trusting Zara to watch over her.

When she awoke, the light seemed different, early afternoon, maybe. Whatever it was, it didn't feel long enough since she'd laid her head down. She looked to where Zara was rousing Cortez and got an approving nod as she stood.

"I was about to wake you," Zara said as she helped Cortez to his feet.

Roni only managed a return nod before a yawn overtook her face. She couldn't recall what had awakened her. Maybe Zara's mere proximity. As they started walking, Roni stretched to try to loosen her muscles. She wasn't refreshed, but she did feel a bit more alert, if only to Zara's presence.

It was idiotic to pay more attention to Zara than to her surroundings. She should be helping look for tracks or tripwires. When Zara called a halt a few minutes later, her raised fist lifted to signal them to stop where they stood, it took Roni a moment to obey, and she offered Zara an apologetic smile.

Yeah, so much more alert.

They began walking again, and Roni told herself to behave, but ever since she'd confessed to Zara, she'd felt more attached to her, more enthralled by her, a puppy in love with a new owner, not a very "lieutenant" way to feel.

And now she was feeling weird about her own feelings. Gods, they were like a runaway tap on a full keg, but she had to find a way to bottle them before they got her killed.

Or Zara killed.

She forced herself to take more notice after that thought. Cortez would have to look after himself.

Zara called several halts and had them hide from Firellian scouts or patrols. The Vox stayed high in the branches above. The river rumbled in the distance, and the enemy was as thick as the devils in hell. Zara stooped to examine the many tracks they came across, but those didn't tell Roni anything except that a lot of people had come through the area recently. Too many. And by Zara's worried face, Roni knew she hadn't spotted the tracks she most wanted to see: Finn and the squad.

Still, they continued creeping toward the thunder of the river. Roni wanted to suggest that the mission had become too dangerous, but Zara wouldn't leave it undone. And what could Roni say? That she'd often picked an alternative target if a house seemed too risky? Soldiers didn't get to be so picky.

And more than completing the mission, Roni didn't want to leave her comrades behind. Gods and devils, they'd really hypnotized her into being one of them.

After dodging a fourth patrol, Zara put a finger to her lips and led them back the way they'd come. She kept low and craned her neck as if searching for something, finally waving them to huddle by a large fir tree. The Vox glided down to rest on her shoulder.

"Look for a rock formation," she whispered, gesturing as she spoke. "A tilted column with a protruding edge. Jaq says it looks like a duck's head. It'll be near a sharp drop right around here."

When Cortez nodded at the Vox, Zara shook her head. "We're too open out here. If the sun glints off their wings, the Firellians will spot them."

They spread out slightly and searched until Cortez waved them over to the duck's head. Zara led them around the back of it and slithered down a shallow hole onto a narrow ledge below. Roni followed easily, well-used to climbing, then helped Cortez down when he stumbled.

"Need to build some muscles?" she whispered. The last few hours of silence had weighed on her, and it felt good to tease him.

"Shut up," he said, but he seemed relieved, too.

"We'll ask your friend to come next time."

He snorted. "He wouldn't deign to get his boots dirty."

She glanced back, and they shared a grin. "Sounds rich."

"He's a noble. They're all rich."

"Not all," Zara said from farther along the ledge. "Now keep up and keep quiet."

They made good time along the ledge, and whenever there was even a hint of a path going to the ground below or up to the rocks where they'd been walking, Zara nearly put her nose to the ground. Finally, she put up a hand for them to stop, then waved them forward to look at the ground where a steep path intersected it from above.

"Four people, one limping."

Roni couldn't tell the prints apart but could guess whose they were down on this hidden path: Finn, Tati, Leo, and the injured Ana.

Zara hurried under a sharply curving overhang and down a large hole flooded with light from the other end. The river practically roared nearby, but Zara gestured for them to lie down and belly crawl toward the light.

Roni squinted into it and gasped when she could see what lay before her. A cliff extended far below them to where the river roiled past. The forests of the Firellian Empire stretched away from the other bank, but Roni's eye was drawn to the tents dotting the shallow bank on the Sarrasian side and the scaffolding snaking up the cliff face, where people swarmed like ants as they hammered stairs into the rock.

Finn and the others were nowhere to be found.

Roni looked at Zara. Her eyes were wide, disbelieving, and her mouth hung open just a bit. "Impossible," she said. "There's no way this many Firellians would have gotten past the watchtowers upriver. This is impossible."

Cortez seemed just as surprised, staring at the Firellians as if counting them or memorizing what they were doing.

Roni glanced back, but there was no other way out of this shallow hole. "Where are Finn and the others?"

Zara was silent for a moment before she scuttled back and studied the ground again. Whatever she saw made her sit back on her heels and swear.

Roni moved to join her. "What is it?"

"The four we were following came in here," Zara said, pointing. "But a larger print follows theirs, someone on tiptoes." She gestured again. "Then they all went out together."

Someone large had followed the squad inside. A Firellian guard? Why would there only be one?

Because she knew who it was and didn't want to say it, didn't want to think it, wanted the relief she'd felt when he'd disappeared into the earth to stay with her. But only one person would be hunting the squad on his own.

Hacha was alive.

CHAPTER TWENTY

Zara wasn't sure which of the recent surprises was the most upsetting: the fact that Finn, Tati, Leo, and Ana were still missing; the evidence that Hacha was still alive; or the presence of a host of Firellian soldiers on the Sarrasian side of the border.

"And the army needs to know this as soon as possible," the Vox said from where they kept watch near the path that led up and out of this shallow cave.

Zara nodded. That was more than just a statement of the obvious. She might have to return to Sarras in all haste, leaving the rest of her squad to their fate. Gods and devils, how could she?

She looked to Roni, whose expression seemed stricken, but Zara couldn't say what upset her more. And for once, she appeared quite at a loss about what to say, even frozen, one hand clenched in a fist by her side, and one half-raised as if to reach out to Zara.

"Waiting for you to tell her what you need," the Vox said.

Touching. Perfect. Zara gave her a nod, not quite willing to put the lies behind them yet but happy to acknowledge when Roni did the right thing.

If only Zara could decide what that was.

She crawled back to the lip of the cave and looked out at the river again. Cortez still lay there, staring at the troops, the tents, and the construction on the wall as if memorizing everything. Good. Zara dug a small notebook out of her pocket and handed it over. He took it after one glance and then began writing furiously with the short pencil tucked inside.

"I was upriver a few weeks ago," Zara said as Roni joined her. "And there was no hint of anyone coming past. The Firellians couldn't have done all this since then. And it would have taken ships to bring in all this equipment."

"Maybe they used small boats and came straight over from the Firellian side?" Roni said.

Zara shook her head and pointed at the wide, turbulent waters of the Kingfish River. "The current is too deep and rapid for small craft and horses. And the river's too wide to hold a line taut enough to pull a barge across. That's one of the reasons the Firellians haven't been able to invade across the river before." Until now. She bit her lip, angry that this was happening during her lifetime, on her watch.

The Vox tried to argue, but Zara wasn't in the mood to hear it. She was too concerned with how the Firellians had done the impossible. "There are watchtowers along the river," she said, "watching for ships. This can't have happened."

"What if the towers were taken by the Firellians?" Roni asked.

Zara shook her head. "They report to each other regularly by signal fire, giving the all-clear along the border and into Sarras. Scouting groups like ours come this way regularly to watch the gaps." And there hadn't been any gods-forsaken gaps. This lot appeared to have popped up from a pit to hell.

"Could the Firellians have been giving the all-clear?" Cortez asked.

"Only with the right sequence, which is regularly changed." She set her chin down on her fist. Could there be a spy in that chain? When she caught Cortez's eye, he frowned.

"I know what you're thinking," he said. "If the watchtowers have been infiltrated, no one told me."

Zara wished she had his knack for reading expressions, especially as she thought she wasn't wearing much of one for him to read, though that wouldn't have helped her now. "This area of the river should have been safe since the cliff is so steep." She shook her head as she watched the Firellians build a staircase. The first ones here would have had one hell of a climb as they put the scaffolding in place.

But how in the devils' names had they gotten here in the first place?

"Look!" Roni gripped her arm, and Zara followed her pointing finger out to the river.

A shimmer hovered over the water, and Zara squinted, thinking it might be reflected light. She was about to ask the Vox to look for her when a large ship appeared on the water as if by...

Magic.

Zara's belly went cold. "The mage," she whispered. "But that's...it's...impossible." She thought of Gisele's pinched face, the exhaustion and pain obvious in her stooped shoulders and heavy breathing, and that had been after bending the light around three people for short bursts at a time. The way Gisele spoke about making objects or people invisible made the task sound not only excruciating but difficult, far too complicated for most mages. And no doubt Gisele was very powerful.

But this? An entire sailing ship with two masts, a great many sails, and a host of sailors? Even if they were just letting the river move them, they were speeding along, and Gisele had said that speed was the enemy of invisibility.

"Well, that explains how they made it past the watchtowers," Cortez said.

"It shouldn't be possible," Zara whispered. "One mage shouldn't—"

"What about more than one?" the Vox asked.

Zara searched her memory and had no knowledge of mages working together. Gisele had always made it sound like a competitive field, but perhaps among the Firellians... "Their monster has company."

Roni couldn't seem to take her eyes off the ship. "I never knew mages could do such things," she said softly.

No, mages were an elite bunch, and Roni was more used to the company of—

"Don't say that aloud," the Vox said.

"I know," Zara said with a grumble. Even though Roni was aware of her former station in life, she wouldn't want to be reminded. Zara had learned that after getting to know some of her fellow soldiers and where they'd come from.

And she'd learned it from the commander who'd started her adventure with prison recruits, Keelin, whose colonel father had pushed for his daughter to get a rank she hadn't earned. She certainly hadn't liked having that fact pointed out.

True as it still was.

"Easy," the Vox said. "Don't spiral. Keep your mind to the well-worn path."

Adella's magic words. Zara took a deep breath. The Vox was right. Too many choices, too many strange and new occurrences, and her mind jumbled, falling all over the place. She couldn't afford to become trapped in her own head right now.

Cortez stopped writing and put the notebook down. "We need to get this information back to Sarras now." When Zara glanced at him, he raised his eyebrows. "Right now, Commander, and you know it."

"Hold on," Roni said. "We can't leave the others here at Hacha's mercy. Or to be captured by the Firellians."

"We can't waste time," Cortez said.

Roni bristled. "Helping your friends is never a waste."

"Be quiet," Zara snapped. "That's not a decision either of you has to make, not while you're under my command." She took the notebook and crept back from the edge so she could stand. Roni and Cortez followed as she moved to where the light streamed in from the other side of the shallow cave. She still had two tasks: get the information back to Sarras and free the rest of her squad.

The solution seemed a simple one if the day contained room for more impossible things.

Zara turned to Cortez and held out the notebook. "If you can avoid the Firellians, you should be able to follow the river down to the next watchtower and alert them." She looked into his eyes, inviting the Vox to look with her, to help her read him. "Can you do it?"

He nodded gravely, and the Vox agreed that he seemed confident. And he'd proven his competence and his willingness to accomplish what Sarras needed of him. Though she would never go about fulfilling her duties by lying.

"I say trust him," the Vox said.

Zara let him have the notebook, then turned to Roni. "I assume that you're going to stay with me even if I order you to go with Cortez."

"Damn right."

Zara liked her look of confidence, too, even if she couldn't approve of disobedience.

"Go on and trust her, too," the Vox said. "Like you said, it's a day for the impossible."

Zara clasped Cortez's wrist, and Roni gave him a clap on the shoulder. "If you pull this off," Roni said to him, "I'll brag about you to your *friend* in Sarras until he begs me to stop."

He snorted a laugh. "I'll look forward to that."

"Be safe," she said. "I don't like you, but I don't want you to get hurt. Sorry I can't come and protect you."

He rolled his eyes, but even though what she'd said wasn't particularly kind, he gave her a little smile. "You'd only slow me down." As he clambered back onto the ledge outside, he said over his shoulder, "And I don't like you, either." But he was still smiling as he said it and as he offered a nod to Zara. "I won't let you down, Commander."

She nodded and was left wondering if he and Roni were friends or not. But now wasn't the time to ask, not when she had a job to do.

❖

After Cortez left, Zara paced a bit, staying in the shadows between the two shafts of light. Roni knew she should be quiet and let Zara think, but her lack of patience demanded she do something. Maybe Zara would even let her contribute to the plan to rescue the rest of the squad.

She was going to offer but ended up saying, "I'm sorry," again. "Hacha is out here because of me, and—"

"You're not responsible for anyone's actions but your own. I thought we covered that." She scrunched her face as if trying to recover the exact memory from the last time Roni apologized.

Roni shook her head. "Yeah, but see, I mouthed off to Julia Esposito, and that started this whole ordeal. My action, my responsibility." And maybe she could feel a little better if Zara reprimanded her again, anything to relieve some of the tension knotting her shoulders.

But Zara shook her head. "You can't know what Julia Esposito would or would not have done if your confrontation had been different." She sighed. "And I can't completely blame you for saying whatever's on your mind. I suffer from that habit myself. You might not have been part of my squad if I hadn't upset Keelin Hoffman and her colonel father. But the prison recruitment plan was already in the works, so who can say for sure where you would have ended up?" She waved a hand as if dismissing the entire argument. "We could play the what-if game back to our earliest decisions, and it wouldn't help us now."

Thoughtful and logical and strangely comforting as well. And, well, touching in a very Zara way. Roni sensed that Zara would never be angry at her for some made-up reason, would never transfer frustration and anger from another source. She seemed honest to her very bones.

"I want to hug you," Roni said softly. "I know it's not a soldier thing, but I think we'd both benefit from it. Who knows, you might make it standard practice."

Zara appeared to consider it. "That sounds like something Jaq would say." She sighed again, and the sound seemed to come from her boots. "I hope he and Claudia are all right."

Roni moved in for the hug, pausing only long enough to make sure Zara wasn't going to object. She held on tightly, Zara copying her, their chins resting on each other's shoulders.

"The action I can't apologize enough for," Roni muttered, still holding on, "is hiding things from you until they came to a head. I'm going to stay sorry for that awhile longer."

"You're still learning how to trust," Zara replied, her own voice muffled by Roni's helmet. "I can sympathize." Her grip tightened a bit. "I trust my squad to do their duty but not with my...feelings, my deeper thoughts. I can't seem to bond with them like you did."

Roni frowned, wanting to look Zara in the eyes, but she sensed this was something Zara needed to say from the safety of Roni's arms. "Why? Are you afraid they won't respect you?"

"No, I'm afraid they won't like who I am inside. People seem not to."

Her tone was matter-of-fact, and Roni's heart hurt for her as much as it grew venomous toward those who'd said they didn't like her. She pulled back, and Zara dropped her arms as if to end the embrace completely, but Roni pushed her helmet back and kissed her. She tried to put all her affection into that kiss, all the passion she could manage, hoping Zara got the idea that this was one person who liked her a lot no matter what she said or did or felt deep inside.

Zara made a little gasp before leaning in, letting her mouth open. Heat surged in Roni's chest as she took the invitation and kissed Zara harder, their tongues meeting. She felt more than just lust, putting all the fear and worry and every other damn feeling into the kiss so Zara would know she was in her life and not going anywhere.

Roni pulled away at last but kept her hands on Zara's cheeks for a moment, soaking her in. "I like you, and that won't stop."

Zara smiled. "I like you, too, but…you can't see into the future any more than you can see what might have happened in the past."

So Zara. "I'm willing to risk saying it anyway."

Zara pulled back slightly, still smiling. "I'm starting to like the way you distract me. That's a problem when we have a job to do."

Roni rolled her eyes. "I'll bet anything that part of your brain was still working on a plan to get the squad back during that kiss." She tapped the front of Zara's helmet. "I just quieted all the messy thoughts up front."

"Huh." Zara's eyes went wide. "You might be right." She nodded and looked away as if seeing the plan come to life. "The Vox agrees with you."

"You're cute when you're figuring stuff out," Roni said, her insides still warm despite the danger in their future.

Zara gave her a slight frown, as if trying to figure out the meaning of the words.

Roni lifted her hands. "No sarcasm. I meant it."

"Yes, well," Zara said, her cheeks darkening slightly. A blush? Oh, that was fun. "To business. I think we should merge our talents. I'm going to find the squad's trail, but instead of fighting to get them back, you're going to steal them."

Roni liked the sound of that, even if she couldn't imagine how at the moment. "What about Hacha?"

"If my plan goes right, there'll be no need to fight him. The Firellians will do it for us."

CHAPTER TWENTY-ONE

Zara knew her plan was a simple one: find where Hacha had taken her squad, draw the Firellians to that location, and rescue the squad while Hacha and the Firellians killed one another. Simple, elegant, and low-risk.

It should work, which was why she doubted it would since unexpected events never unfolded quite like she hoped. Priests and priestesses in Sarras preached that the gods had plans for the world that were too unfathomable for humans to see, but Zara doubted that. Surely there would be more logic to the world if that were true.

Unless the gods were idiots just like most people, a dark thought but a not unsurprising possible reality.

"If this all goes wrong, we'll have to adapt," Zara reminded Roni as they followed the squad's tracks along the ledge.

"My strong suit," Roni said, a smile in her voice.

Zara appreciated the confidence. She was coming to appreciate more about Roni as time went on. She made mistakes, but she learned from them. She was skilled, loyal, intelligent…and her embrace made Zara feel like parts of her body might burst with wonder and happiness and, well, lust, if she was honest.

And Roni had been right when she'd named herself the right kind of distraction. With her less manageable thoughts directed Roni's way, Zara's brain was free to be the efficient machine she'd trained it to be.

She'd have to remember that when assessing people from now on.

"Just don't tell them that," the Vox said from where they rode on her shoulder.

"I know," she muttered. She'd kept the Vox close all day, not wanting them to attract attention by flying in the light. As soon as evening faded to night, she could rely on their eyes again. She'd thought about coating their metal body with dust so they didn't gleam so, but she didn't want to hamper their ability to fly or transform.

"Much appreciated," the Vox said.

Zara smiled, happy with her two companions despite the current nature of their mission. What a difference a few weeks made in one's life.

But she didn't have time to ponder such things just now. The tracks didn't lead all the way back to where she, Roni, and Cortez had climbed down onto the ledge. They veered off into a small scattering of brush tucked against the rocks, then dimmed as the squad had no doubt scrabbled up a steep, partially hidden trail leading upward.

Zara took a few more steps down the ledge anyway to make sure it wasn't a false trail, but when she returned to the narrow path, she saw dislodged pebbles and a few broken roots that told of a hurried climb. The larger prints followed, so the squad had either been forced up this path or had managed to flee from Hacha.

She told all this to Roni, but as she explained, something tickled the back of her mind. "Something's wrong."

"What?"

She inched back toward the cavern, creeping, tracing each print in the air. "These are Finn's. Tati and Leo have newer boots, so this is one of theirs…and this." She scanned the ground. "Where is Ana?"

"You said that was this print, the limping one," Roni said, pointing.

"Going toward the shallow cave we were in, but she doesn't come back." Zara frowned and clenched her fist. If that devil had killed her…

No, she would have seen signs of a fight. There would have been blood or a mark where Ana had hit the ground. She studied the larger prints again. This was where Hacha had originally come down to the ledge after the squad first passed. He'd followed them, tiptoeing occasionally, then following them again when they'd come back this way, and *those* prints were deeper.

"He was carrying Ana," Zara said, rubbing her chin as she double-checked. "See here? The deeper heel marks?"

"Amazing," Roni breathed, looking at her in awe.

The praise felt nice, but she dismissed it. "Anyone can learn given time."

"I'm not sure about that."

Well, maybe she was right. But again, no time to bask in warm feelings.

"If he's bothering to carry her, she's alive," Roni said. "It's probably how he's keeping the others in line."

Sensible, but if Ana was unconscious when Zara found her, the rescue would be harder to pull off. "We might have to carry her once the fighting starts."

Roni nodded. "We'll manage. Tati's as strong as a mule. And she likes Ana."

Zara glanced at her in surprise. "How do you know?" Before Roni could speak, Zara held up a hand. "Never mind. You can tell me all the little things I never noticed once we get out of here."

With a crooked grin, Roni said, "I'll show you all sorts of things you didn't know when we get out of here." She seemed to chuckle at herself when Zara didn't know what to say. "I know you don't like come-ons, but I had to say it."

Zara would have pointed out that no one *had* to say anything, but since Roni had already remarked upon her runaway mouth, Zara only nodded. "There will be time for many things after the mission is done."

She turned from Roni's surprised face and hurriedly climbed the slope. The rocky ground above was harder to track through, but now that she knew exactly what she was looking for, she spotted the occasional smudge or broken bit of foliage. No doubt the squad had made the trail as obvious as they could, given the terrain.

Hacha had probably done the same, wanting her to follow so he could trade the squad for the Vox. As if he wasn't going to try to kill them all anyway. Anger burned through her at the thought. She'd give him more trouble than he could handle soon enough.

Roni hissed, the signal that she'd spotted something while Zara studied the ground. Zara followed her into a slight dip behind a jutting tor and crouched while a pair of Firellians crossed from one patch of trees to another in the distance. They seemed to be chatting, though they were too far away to hear. They were overconfident. Good.

Of course, if they had so many troops up here that they had a reason to be confident...

Well, that would be worse news for Hacha.

And no doubt it meant they were using fewer tripwires so their own people didn't become tangled in them. Zara frowned as another thought occurred: what if they were confident because they'd caught the rest of the squad and assumed they'd gotten all of them? The Firellians the squad had fled from had undoubtedly reported in by now, so the Firellians knew they weren't alone. But if Hacha had traded the squad for something—like safe passage out of the woods—the Firellians might think all their problems had been solved.

"There are too many variables to speculate," the Vox said.

Zara nodded. She often warned people about doing that very thing. She couldn't be a hypocrite now and ignore her own advice. When the Firellians were under cover again, Zara nodded to Roni and went back to the trail. At least it didn't lead in the direction the Firellians had taken.

Yet.

Roni kept swinging through all the emotions, so she'd given up trying to decide what they were or how to focus on one. She watched for Firellians and let her mind and her heart do whatever it was they were going to do.

At least until this was all over. Then she could go back to choosing between confusion, joy, and dread.

She watched Zara follow the prints like a bloodhound. A breeze passing through the forest wouldn't be able to hide from her. She muttered about the sheer number of Firellian prints—when one would have been too many—but that would help when they met Hacha. If this plan worked. Oh gods, not back to the ifs.

She steered away from those thoughts again, trying to take Zara's advice about them to heart. When she saw a hint of movement through a denser collection of trees ahead, she thanked the gods again for giving her something else to focus on.

Roni hissed, and Zara followed her behind some bracken as a trio of Firellians passed between trees in the distance. "We're all going to get caught at this rate," Roni whispered.

"More Firellians means more cover for us."

Unless there were enough of them to swarm Hacha, kill him quickly, then pursue the rest of them. Devils, she was back to dread again.

"Why does the empire hate us so much anyway?" she mumbled.

Zara gave her a wide-eyed look. "Are you joking?"

"What? I've always been told they're just assholes and that they think the same about us." When Zara opened her mouth and shut it again quickly, Roni smirked. "You were going to ask me why I didn't pay attention in school before realizing I probably didn't go, right?"

"Not…precisely."

"Then the Vox stopped you for that very same reason?"

Zara sighed. "Are all thieves so astute?"

"Are all scouts so evasive?"

"Our history with the Firellian Empire is complicated and bloody. Promises of marriage between ancient monarchs fell through, treaties were made and broken, alliances evolved with each other's enemies, etc. My elder sister was an ambassador to the empire and told me their disputes over the last couple of decades have been about trade. Maybe they think they're losing too much money in fees and tariffs since nearly everything they trade via the Kingfish River has to go through Sarras, and we make them pay for the privilege."

"That would piss me off, too," Roni said, frowning. "But if we have that much history with them, they'd do the same, I wager. It's like never being able to get clear of an ex-lover."

"I wouldn't know."

Roni had assumed Zara was inexperienced, but the comment still set her back on her heels. She tried to keep her mouth closed, but, "You haven't…" slipped out anyway.

"The Firellians are well past. Shall we?" Zara headed out again, searching the ground.

Roni wished she had a Vox of her own to tell her when to shut the hell up. The best way to deal with embarrassing Zara was probably to pretend it never happened.

But gods and devils, they had to have a long conversation when all this was over.

After a few more minutes tracking, Zara glanced at Roni over her shoulder. "Fresher tracks." She said it so quietly, Roni had to lean forward. She thought they'd been slow before. Now they really did creep, both staying low. Roni's back and knees started to ache. She'd had some slow climbs in her life and had inched through dark hallways on the balls of her feet, but she'd never tried to walk in a half crouch before.

Zara halted abruptly, and Roni had to lean against her as she tried to regain her balance. Roni tried to speak, but Zara turned, a finger across her lips. She pointed ahead.

Roni looked but saw nothing. When she tried to stand, Zara grabbed her, frowning. She pointed again. When Roni shook her head, Zara leaned toward her ear.

"The bark on that tree is torn near the bottom."

Roni shivered as Zara's breath tickled her, and she had to blink away the sensation before focusing. She thought she glimpsed a lighter patch of bark on a tree some fifty feet ahead but couldn't—

Zara mouthed something, then waggled her fingers as if mimicking someone walking. When she then gestured up, Roni realized what she'd said: "He's up the tree."

Oh, the clever bastard. Roni fought a shiver and looked upward, but as they'd come closer to the river, the leafier trees had been slowly replaced by pines and other spiny plants that kept their needles in winter. She couldn't spot Hacha, but with she and Zara so close to the ground, he might not have spotted them, either. And they'd been going so slow, she doubted he'd heard them.

Unless he really was a devil in human shape. No, she couldn't start thinking that way now. He'd bled. He could die.

Instead, she looked ahead for the squad but didn't see them. No doubt they were incapacitated or something nearby. But if she and Zara roused the Firellians now, Hacha could stay up his tree while the squad was captured.

Unless he'd already killed them all.

By the grim look on Zara's face, she was thinking the same thing. She waved Roni along and circled far around the tree, searching the ground and the brush. When Roni spied a pair of legs through a gap in the plants ahead, she knew what Zara was looking for.

She pointed, and Zara gestured for her to lie on the ground. Zara followed suit and carefully parted some brush in front of them.

Roni held in a gasp. Ana, Tati, and Leo sat tied together on the ground beside a pit similar to the one that had swallowed Hacha before. A huge gnarled tree sat on the opposite side from the squad, its protruding roots like a lumpy half wall. But the difficult terrain wasn't the only thing that made Roni gasp. Ana's head lolled against her chest, and she'd been bound so that her lower legs were dangling into the pit. If she hadn't been tied to the others—who leaned away from the pit—she might have toppled in and carried the others with her. As it was, Leo and Tati were lucky that more of Ana's weight wasn't poised above oblivion.

Still, a good kick would send them over, especially since their legs were also bound at the ankles. Maybe Hacha planned to swing down and deliver one if Roni and Zara got close. Roni shivered. She'd just have to rescue them before that happened. And maybe they'd know what had become of Finn.

"Circle around the other side," Zara whispered in her ear. "I'll use the Vox to distract Hacha or knock him from the tree."

"What if he has more spikes to hurt the Vox?" Roni said, gesturing to drive her point home.

Zara shrugged as if saying what other choice did they have? "Their shrieks will bring the Firellians. You go for the squad once you hear the Firellians in the distance. If he goes for the squad before then, I'll hold him off until you get the squad loose, then we can lose him in the confusion of battle." She passed Roni her belt knife.

Roni nodded, her heart thundering, but she tried to breathe through it, to quiet her body as she did before every job.

Zara plucked her sleeve and pointed back to several points in the small clearing near the squad. Roni squinted but saw nothing. Zara came in for one more word: "Snares."

Shit. Hacha had planned this trap well. Roni kept careful lookout as she edged around the pit and the gnarled tree. She avoided several snares, able to see them once she was nearly on top of them. She came to a stop on the other side of the tree, so it was between her and where Hacha waited.

The seconds dragged on, but Roni made herself wait quietly, flexing her limbs so she didn't stiffen up. When the Vox shrieked, Roni nearly jumped but made herself sit still and waited for the sounds of approaching Firellians. She had the knife in hand, but she'd need to pull them away from the pit before she cut them loose. Hacha must have raided a Firellian camp for supplies and rope. She wondered if a squad of Firellian scouts was out there right now, following a line of bodies and thinking a devil walked among them.

Zara's voice broke the silence. "He's not in the tree. It's Finn. Roni, watch—"

Roni lost the last of Zara's words in the sound of her own heart in her ears. She ran for the squad, certain Hacha would be doing the same.

He hauled himself out of the pit using the tree roots. He had the end of a rope in hand. Roni had a moment to follow it back to the tied-up squad before he flashed an evil smile and gave the rope a yank.

Ana tipped forward into the pit, pulling the others after her.

"No!" Roni leaped, catching hold of the rope that held Leo's arms behind his back and secured him to the other two. He cried out around a gag. She hauled back and grabbed wildly for another handhold so Tati couldn't slide in either. Her hand flared in pain as she found a place to grab, but she held on.

They stopped sliding, thank the gods, but she couldn't get any leverage to pull them up. She was stuck with her arms out, one leg underneath her as Hacha's shadow fell over her in the fading light.

CHAPTER TWENTY-TWO

S et Finn loose," Zara yelled to the Vox while she ran for where Roni was stretched out on the ground, Hacha looming over her.

As she leaped a snare, Hacha glanced at her and grabbed Roni's helmet. Quick as a snake, he had a knife to her throat while he pulled her head back at a cruel angle. Zara skidded to a stop, and Hacha grinned, his lips shiny with saliva, as if the chance to kill someone made his mouth water. "Give me the bird and the glove."

Zara hesitated, mind racing. If she could only—

Hacha flexed, Roni grunted, and a thin line of red appeared along the side of her neck as if by magic. "Call it, now," he said.

"Vox," Zara said, swallowing a lump of fear and dread. What could she do? There had to be a way to win this.

The Vox glided over. "I managed to loosen her ropes, but Finn is still tied up," they said in Zara's mind. They perched on the gnarled tree over Hacha's head.

He made a slurping, wheezing noise and smiled wider. "Take off the glove."

She couldn't.

"Do it," the Vox said. "I'll hop over the pit and fall."

Zara fiddled with the end of the chain, acting as if she was removing it while thinking frantically to the Vox. "You'll be destroyed, killed."

"Maybe not. We don't know how deep—"

"Hurry up," Hacha said, and a second thin line joined the first on Roni's neck.

"Better destroyed than in enemy hands," the Vox said, something so in line with Zara's own opinions, she swore she heard her own voice in their multitude. "Save Roni. Save them all."

She uttered a small cry of pain as the Vox hopped backward, over the pit. She yanked the glove off, and the Vox fell like a stone. Hacha turned his head at the movement. Zara lunged, holding the gem in her palm in the hope that it would be enough without the chain holding it in place.

Hacha stumbled to the side, avoiding her swing, but he let Roni go. Zara pivoted, the gem clutched in one hand while she swung with the other.

❖

Roni dropped her head, gasping for breath. The muscles in her arms burned, shaking so much she barely felt the sting of the shallow cuts on her neck or the dread in her stomach. She was free of Hacha, but how long could Zara last against him? And how long could she hold the squad up before—

She gasped as the weight seemed lighter. She didn't know if they were helping somehow with their bound feet or if she was having a surge of strength, but she heaved, taking full advantage and grunting at the pain in her hand.

A rush of air washed over her, and she cried out when the Vox rose from the pit, helping drag Ana back from oblivion. Their wings seemed to stutter, their movements jerking as if they had gone lame. Roni grunted as she pulled with what remained of her strength. Tati and Leo watched her with wide eyes as they leaned away from the pit. When they were back on solid ground, Roni pushed to her feet and forced her leaden arms to work. She grabbed the Vox so they wouldn't fall again and set them on the ground. Black spots danced across her vision. No, she couldn't collapse now. She had to help Zara, who was still fighting Hacha off to her right. And he had to die here, either from her and Zara or from the Firellians who were probably advancing toward all the noise of combat.

Roni took a step and drew her truncheon, but Zara threw the chain glove in her direction. She couldn't don it while her free hand was occupied with her saber and while barely keeping Hacha at bay.

"Fuck, yes." Roni placed the gem to her wrist, then willed herself to hurry as she again wrapped the chain around her hand without remembering how she'd done it. When she felt the Vox come alive in her head, she said, "Watch out for any spikes."

"Watch out for the knife," they thought back to her.

Roni pushed through the pain and darted into the fight. Zara had several slashes to her arms and one streaming wound on her hip. Hacha seemed to know the best way around armor. Roni tried to serve as a distraction, knowing she couldn't take him like Zara could. He gave ground but drew another spike from his pocket and slashed as quickly with that as he did with the knife. Still, the Vox flew past his head and hovered, snapping, clawing, and screeching, but something about the spike's very presence made them keep their distance.

"It's like a bubble of pain," they said in Roni's mind.

Hacha danced away from all their strikes, an evil smirk on his face. "I love a challenge," he said as he darted at Roni, forcing her to give ground, then retreated before Zara could take a swing. "I knew you were good," he said to Zara. "And I ain't been disappointed."

Zara scored a slash on his arm, adding to the blood still staining his jacket from the last time they'd fought. He laughed, a squealing sound like a pig in pain. The Vox flew at him, but he only had to lift that cursed spike, and the Vox careened sideways.

"Hanging around with this rat will get you killed," Hacha said.

He went for Roni again. When Zara moved to protect her, Hacha cut the back of her sword hand, making her gasp, but she didn't fall back, pressing her attack and gouging his shoulder. "I don't know any rats," Zara said. "She's a soldier."

Roni felt a surge of pride and anger. She took a glance to her right and thought to the Vox, "Drive him to his left. Fight through the pain."

The Vox seemed surprised but circled around.

Roni bared her teeth at Hacha. "You shouldn't underestimate me either, pig."

The Vox dove at him, and Roni lunged with them. The Vox screeched in her mind as they came close to the spike, but Hacha had to move to his left to avoid them both.

Right into the snare Roni had just seen.

The snare closed over his foot, and the bent sapling it was tied to shot upward, dragging Hacha's feet out from under him. He twisted as he landed hard on his back, slashing wildly, but the Vox pounced on his knife arm, talons sinking into his flesh.

Hacha's shrieks joined those of the Vox as he lifted the spike. Zara grunted as she dove and swung, knocking the spike away.

With a cry, she buried her saber in Hacha's chest.

Roni remained taut for a moment, disbelieving until Hacha gurgled his last. Gods and devils, it was over. "That was for Ernesto," she whispered. She began to shake, all the fear and dread and uncertainty of the past weeks washing over her. She couldn't hold it together.

Zara's strong arms went around her from the side, crushing her in an embrace, stealing her breath. Roni leaned into her, and when the Vox hopped onto her shoulder in a smaller form and wrapped their wings around them both, Roni barked a laugh that was still partially a sob.

They'd done it.

"We can't stay here," Zara and the Vox said at nearly the same time.

Roni laughed again. She felt dizzy, and the spots were still there, but Zara was right. And though they'd scored a great victory, the war wasn't won yet. The Firellians would be coming.

Roni passed Zara the chain glove without being asked and started for the squad, stopping when she saw Finn had already begun untying them. Finn's face was puffy, with a split lip and one eye swollen shut, but she looked ready to give hell. Tati and Leo seemed equally beaten up, but they stood without complaint, and Tati lifted Ana across her shoulders again. Gods, they were a sorry looking bunch. There'd be no running from the Firellians today.

"We have to hide," Roni said.

Zara had a faraway look on her face, and the Vox was gone, no doubt scouting. Zara nodded after a few seconds. "The Firellians are close."

So they'd have to hide nearby and hope the Firellians didn't spot them in the dark, but where? Zara moved to the pit and tied the rope around one of the roots of the gnarled tree, hiding the end in the brush. "Everyone tie on and get in."

The squad looked at her dumbly until Finn said, "Move your asses." They obeyed, Tati and Leo securing Ana between them.

Roni had her own doubts as she moved to the pit. In the gloom, she could just see a narrow ledge where Hacha must have been waiting. Below that lay yawning blackness. How far to the bottom? She swallowed, but the dread was back, sitting in her stomach like an unwelcome guest.

"Are you sure about this?" Roni whispered to Zara.

Zara's steely look was back, the commander who didn't hug her squad and certainly didn't give in to fear.

Roni sighed and tied herself on before helping to lower Ana down and then climbing in with the rest.

Zara's hands and arms stung from the many places Hacha had cut her. She could feel several of them oozing under her armor and clothing. Her hand and hip complained sharply every time she moved, and she knew she had to get a bandage on them soon. When dirt settled into the slash on the back of her hand, she cringed and predicted an infection in her future.

She'd be lucky to live that long.

Roni sat on one side of her and Finn on the other. The ledge was just long and wide enough for everyone to perch on even if it was extremely uncomfortable. A multitude of rocks dug into Zara's back through the cloak and armor, an affliction no doubt shared by everyone. She looked down the line, but the light was so low, she couldn't see the rest of the squad on Finn's other side and hoped Tati and Leo could hold Ana up until the Firellians left.

Or until they lowered lanterns into the pit. Gods, she hoped that thought didn't even occur to them.

"More are coming," the Vox said in her mind.

Zara closed her eyes and saw through the Vox's eyes from where they were hidden in the branches of a pine tree. The Firellians chattered to one another, exclaiming over Hacha's body before searching the surrounding brush. One fell with a cry, and after others moved to help him, one called a warning to watch out for more snares.

If things weren't so dire, Zara might have snorted at that.

Dusk had almost given way to dark, and the Firellians lifted lanterns and squinted into the gloom. Each was like a bonfire to the Vox's owl eyes. Several soldiers growled about how it was useless to search for intruders in the dark, and most seemed to agree. Zara clenched her uninjured hand in victory, especially since no one suggested camping on the battlefield above and waiting for morning.

"Get one of the monsters," someone said, a woman whose voice held an air of authority. Another soldier ran off, presumably to do her bidding.

Zara ground her teeth. If monster was indeed the word they used for their overpowered mages, she and the squad were in trouble. At least that confirmed that the Firellians had more than one mage. She just had to find a way to survive long enough to report that information to her superiors.

Zara drew Finn and Roni closer so she'd only have to whisper once. "They're bringing in a mage."

Finn grunted as if in pain, but Roni whispered, "So?"

"They read auras," Zara said, remembering Gisele speaking of that before. "They might be able to see ours in here or follow our trail." If auras even left a trail. Zara had no information on that, but she couldn't take the risk. Her training hadn't included dealing with enemy mages. The Firellians were rumored to fear or look down on magic, and a lack of mages in their military history had seemed to prove those rumors true. Even now that they obviously had their own mages, they still called them monsters.

If these *were their* mages.

Still, the training would have to be amended, another mental note.

The squad wasn't in any shape to fight or try to climb down, even if the rope was long enough to reach the bottom *without* all of them tied to it. "I'll kill them with the roc."

She could feel Finn's sharp gaze more than see it. "No, boss. You haven't the strength."

Zara jerked her close again. "I'll find the strength." She had enough to kill the soldiers out there, to free the squad, and if the Vox drained her completely, so be it. She turned her head to Roni, wondering what would be best said to her. Appreciation of what they'd shared, just in case she died? Regret that they didn't have longer?

No, she didn't have the time or the words. "You'll have to hang on to my...to me. When I go limp," she said in Roni's ear.

Roni stiffened. "Are you sure about this? You'll be helpless. You'll be..." She gasped. "Hang on to your what? What were you going to say first?"

Zara clenched her hand. "Not so loud."

"Your body, was that it?"

"Shh."

Roni breathed quietly for a few moments. "No," she said at last.

Zara waited for more, but when none came, asked, "No?"

"Finn might not argue with you, but I will. You need someone to tell you no on occasion, and I'm saying it now. The Vox can take a mythic shape, but you're not dying today. I'm taking the glove off you before that happens."

"That's not your call."

"Yeah? Stay awake and stop me."

Zara ground her teeth again. No, they were never going to work as commander and subordinate. And that was just as well because Roni's words did more than cause Zara to reconsider. They warmed her in a way that Adella's or Gisele's concern never did. As well-meaning as they seemed, her sisters' warnings and objections always held an air of control, as if they knew better than her.

But Roni just wanted to keep her around. Zara had never pretended to be someone else around her, had never moderated her personality in order to make a good impression, as nearly everyone in her life had wanted her to do at one time or another. And Roni still wanted her to stay.

Zara rested her helmet against Roni's for a moment.

"I think the Firellians heard you," the Vox said. "They're walking toward the pit, and the mage has arrived. Oh, and I'm glad you've decided not to die today. It makes my earlier attempt to sacrifice myself seem much more special."

Zara chuckled. At least she'd been distracted for the right amount of time. She gripped Roni's hand and bade the Vox transform into a roc.

As before, she felt her vitality drain as if someone had kicked her in the gut. Images from the Vox were reduced to fits and starts: screaming faces, running forms, flying lanterns, blood, and bodies.

Zara held tight to Roni and tried to keep her eyes open. Finn hauled her upright, and the pain in her hip made her gasp, giving her a jolt. She had to stay conscious, had to give the Vox more time. There were more soldiers, a flash of fire from the mage that blinded the Vox. Metal rang as several soldiers managed to score hits along the Vox's body. Stabs couldn't pierce them, but a swing from a mace sent vibrations all through them. A wing swipe took care of that attacker, but Zara could feel that the Vox had been damaged in more than one place.

The Vox began to repair themselves, and that took another surge of energy. Zara grunted, slumping but trying to give just a little more. Roni's voice came at her from a long tunnel, and Zara tried to say, "Not yet. There are more," but she couldn't. She just held on until she seemed to go weightless, her wounds and pains disappearing but her connection to the Vox still a deep ache in her chest.

Just a little more. She could take it. She wouldn't die. She still had a bit more to give.

"Fuck this." Roni's vulgar words, clear and bright in her ear.

She wanted to laugh or censure or something, but the deep ache in her chest disappeared as she slipped into unconsciousness.

Roni had to let Zara go as she donned the glove. It would be all right. Finn would rather walk merrily into hell than let her precious commander fall to her death. At that moment, Roni could have shoved Zara into the pit herself. Even after everything they'd gone through, Zara was still willing to sacrifice herself without a thought.

"It's her nature," the Vox's many voices said in Roni's mind.

"She's going to have to bend that nature if I have anything to say about it," Roni mumbled.

"What?" Finn barked.

"Never mind." Roni turned her thoughts back to the Vox. "Are you all right?" She saw through their eyes but quickly shut out the images of crushed and torn bodies. "Are there any left alive?"

"No, but you'd better hurry all the same. More will be coming."

"Right." Roni looked over Zara's head to Finn. She could barely see the pale patches on her skin in the dim light from a lantern above. "Time to go."

The Vox scooted the light closer, and then it was a matter of climbing and heaving and swearing to get everyone clear. Finn pushed Zara's limp body up while Roni pulled from the top of the pit. She tried not to jostle Zara too much, taking care not to aggravate any injuries, but she was still angry and frightened. When she laid Zara on the ground and caught sight of her unconscious face in the lantern light, Roni didn't know whether to kiss her or kick her.

That was a lie. She'd choose kiss every time, no matter how much Zara infuriated her.

"I'm the same way," the Vox said. "That allure is another part of her nature."

Roni snorted as she helped pull the others out of the pit. "Just don't try to kiss me with that beak."

"I'll give you a *peck* if you don't move faster."

A joke or a real threat? Maybe both. The Vox was still deadly for all their joviality. And they didn't seem in a hurry to reassure her after that thought.

Probably for the best. She could put her mind to helping Leo carry Zara while Tati heaved Ana across her shoulders. Finn picked up a lantern and took a quick look around, almost putting her nose to the ground like Zara had.

"This way," Finn said.

Roni stumbled after, her arms locked around Zara. With Finn leading and the Vox scanning for Firellians in the shadows, they hurried into the dark. Gods, they had to make it to safety now. The gods couldn't be so cruel as to let them be caught after escaping death four times. Or was it five? Devils take it, she couldn't count the number of times. That had to be a bad sign.

As she got a better grip on Zara, Roni sighed. She'd do all this shit again for her. That was some nature.

CHAPTER TWENTY-THREE

Zara awoke with a start, leaving turbulent dreams of capture and torture behind. She reached for her saber, and a flare of panic hit her when she didn't find it. Her instincts were telling her to leap to her feet, to run or fight, but thankfully, her rational brain took over.

She wasn't bound. Or wearing armor. An untidy looking bandage—that had probably been made from someone's shirt—had been wrapped around her hand. A campfire crackled nearby, and sleeping bodies surrounded it, some of them snoring softly.

The squad. They'd gotten away.

Zara rubbed her forehead as relief rushed through her. With the firelight, she could just see a shallow cave around them, the ceiling so low, she wouldn't be able to walk upright, but the tight quarters meant that heat lingered, and she felt warmer than she had in days.

Well, when she wasn't running or fighting, that was.

Someone moved in the mouth of the cave. Roni, her helmet off and her red hair falling around her shoulders. She stretched, no doubt keeping watch over the rest of them. Zara's heart warmed further. She eased out of her cloak. A flash of pain came from her hip, and she felt another bandage under her trousers and across her arm. She tiptoed around the sleeping bodies, bending double to avoid smacking her head, and sat beside Roni at the cave's entrance.

Roni smiled softly, and Zara was struck with the desire to lay her head on Roni's shoulder. She refrained, needing some answers first. "Where are we?" she asked softly.

"You're asking the wrong person," Roni said with a grin. The shallow cuts on her neck had dried into mere red lines. "Finn led us here. We're not far from where we fought Hacha."

Still in plenty of danger, then. Well, she hadn't really thought they'd be magically transported home.

Roni passed her some fruit and a bit of cold meat. "I saved these for you. The Vox and I went hunting, and Finn found some wild plums that weren't too damaged by frost."

Zara took them gratefully but also glanced at Roni's hand to see if she was still wearing the glove.

"The Vox is resting, too," Roni said, giving her a nudge. "I saw that look." When Zara ducked her head, trying to think of a way to apologize, Roni patted her knee. "It's all right. I know you can't help it. If I had a bond with someone like you do with the Vox, I'd make sure I knew where they were at all times, too." She leaned close. "And I'd be a little jealous if anyone else decided to stick their nose between us."

A very odd picture indeed, but Zara was relieved she didn't have to say any of that. She also didn't point out that Roni was getting to know her pretty well, too, though she'd have to examine her feelings around that later. Right now, it seemed an added comfort.

She ate while Roni filled her in on everything that had happened since she'd unleashed the roc. Roni had taken the glove and powered the Vox in their regular form. Clambering out of the hole and to this cave had taken quite a bit of effort, and then Tati had carried Ana, with Leo and Roni carrying Zara, and Finn finding the way here. By the time everyone had arrived, they'd been so exhausted that most had passed out after they'd bandaged one another and eaten. Finn had taken the first watch and Roni the second.

Zara touched the bandage on her hand. Quite a few undershirts had no doubt been sacrificed that night. They were going to be quite the ragged team when this mission was over, and they were safe in Sarras. Everyone except poor Ernesto, but he'd at least been avenged.

"There's a little stream nearby," Roni said. "So we can all get a drink in the morning before we head out." She sighed. "If we can with all the Firellians around. They've been stirred up like hornets. I think one of their mages died."

Zara nodded. She vaguely remembered the Vox killing someone who wasn't wearing the armor of a soldier. "One of their monsters," she said quietly.

"Yeah, why do they have such a downer on mages?"

Zara rested her elbow on one knee and put her chin in her hand. "I don't think these are normal mages. The Firellians were never that keen on magic. I've heard some say that mages aren't often born there, but I don't know if that's true. And these mages they have now…" She shook her head. "Making that ship disappear and making all those tripwires, not to mention that one fire blast we saw, all points to someone very powerful. Even my sister Gisele would be gawking at them, and she's a very good mage."

"But monster?" Roni said with her lip curled in distaste. "Why not something more flattering?"

"The Firellians I heard sounded scared or upset. These mages must have a tendency to get out of control, or there was something the Firellians did to them that made them…I don't know, violent or something." She shook her head as she straightened, wincing at the pain in her hip again. "Or perhaps that's the way Firellians always refer to mages if they're that wary of them. I'll have to lay it all out before my superiors, who will no doubt consult the mages' guild and see what they make of it."

"One thing's for sure," Roni said, "the Firellians don't want us to spread the word about their monsters."

"Or their new way into Sarras." Gods, she hoped Cortez had made it out okay, even if he wouldn't give as full of an account as she would. At least the government would know something of what was happening. "Why don't you get some sleep? I can take watch until morning."

"Because I want to take every opportunity I can get to be alone with you."

Zara felt a rush of heat on her cheeks, and she smiled, an expression she couldn't seem to help when Roni said such things. "I…I hardly think…" She tried to summon the rest of that sentence about now not being the time or the place for…canoodling of any sort, but an inner voice said that wasn't what Roni had meant. Just existing together could be enough sometimes.

But as Zara met Roni's eyes, she wanted more than a mere existence together. She wanted things she'd only heard of, encounters she'd merely read about, feelings she'd once dismissed as irrelevant. She quickly weighed the consequences of kissing Roni now, when the squad could awaken at any moment, and decided it was worth the risk.

Roni gasped as Zara pulled them together, but her surprise seemed to morph into enthusiasm in a blink. Remembering how Roni had kissed her before, Zara duplicated those movements, pleased when Roni yielded to her, letting her guide their path. She deepened the kiss, finding exquisite pleasure exploring with her tongue, her lips, following through on the urge to bite Roni's bottom lip ever so softly.

When Roni moaned and nearly crawled into Zara's lap, Zara knew she had to end this…for the moment.

She pulled back, breathless, beyond happy to see Roni's pink cheeks, half-lidded eyes, and parted lips. It didn't take the Vox to interpret that lustful look. And it turned disappointed when Zara stopped another kiss by holding her thumb against Roni's lips.

"I'm sorry to deny you," Zara whispered. "To deny both of us." She rested her forehead against Roni's. "But there will be time later."

Roni sat back with a slight pout. "Stupid mission that won't end."

Zara snorted, chuckling. "It will." She sighed as she glanced back at the sleeping squad. "But as injured as we are, it's going to be hard to avoid the Firellians when we flee. And we can't stay here undetected while we heal."

"If we can't stay and can't go, what do we do?"

Zara thought about it, and the answer came to her quickly. "A diversion. The squad can slip out if the Firellians are otherwise engaged."

Roni stiffened. "Let me guess, you'll stay behind to provide this diversion?"

Zara said nothing, happy Roni was at least acknowledging Zara's duty. It was on the tip of her tongue to order Roni to go with the squad while she did…whatever she was going to do. But the words wouldn't come. Perhaps she didn't want Roni to have to defy a direct order again.

Or maybe she wanted Roni to volunteer, silly as that sounded in her mind.

"Don't even think about ordering me to go," Roni said as if reading Zara's thoughts, albeit a little behind.

"No?"

"Whatever you've decided to do, I'm coming with you."

Zara cocked her head, not finding those words as upsetting as she once would have. "What if I said I could more easily accomplish whatever I'm deciding to do while envisioning you reaching a place of safety?"

Roni blinked at her. "If you expect me to believe you'd truly be happier on your own with just your *visions* of me, you're delusional." She sniffed. "The real me is way better than any mental picture."

Zara chuckled again. "I'm not delusional, and I never doubted you'd come with me."

"Don't tell me I'm becoming predictable." She put a hand to her chest and leaned back, a mockery of affront.

"You forget who you're talking to. I like predictable."

Roni laughed before glancing back at the squad and lowering her voice. "I'll keep doing it, then." She kissed Zara quickly before leaning back. "While also throwing in the occasional happy surprise."

Zara could live with that.

Roni watched the night slowly giving way to day with Zara by her side. Long silences often made her nervous, but with Zara, it felt different.

Everything felt different.

She gave it some thought but couldn't pinpoint exactly when she'd gone from wanting to get away from the army as quickly as possible to volunteering for dangerous missions when she could have been part of the escape party.

She'd never been a joiner; no syndicate was right for her. But then, she'd never met a person she'd follow to hell either. Not until Zara. Roni's desires hadn't changed at a single point in time. They'd changed for a single person. She'd never wanted to get away from Zara, not at first sight, when Zara had been the hunter of her sexiest dreams, and not now.

Even when it was going to be the two of them against an army.

When Roni said that to Zara in the morning, before they roused the rest of the squad, Zara tilted her head, frowning. "Not an army," Zara said.

Roni sat back and waved at the wilderness which seemed to have a Firellian hiding behind every tree. "Not enough enemies out there for you?"

"I concede that there are a lot, but an army usually consists of a headquarters, two or more corps, and auxiliary troops."

Roni stared for a moment. "Isn't that splitting hairs? There is still a boatload of enemy soldiers here."

Zara rolled her eyes. "Several boatloads, I grant you, but you said army, and I do not think they fit that definition."

So Zara. Roni threw back her head and laughed. She clapped a hand over her mouth to dampen the sound, but she couldn't help carrying on. Gods, some people just had to be themselves no matter what, and Roni fell a little harder for her in that moment.

Before the squad could go from muttering to truly awake, Roni leaned close to Zara, who was staring as if Roni had gone into hysterics. "I could fall in love with you, Zara del Amanecer. I could fall so hard that you'll never truly get rid of me, and I'd pine to death if you tried."

Zara gave her a long, slow blink, as if deciding whether she was friend or foe. Then her mouth opened slowly, and her eyes shimmered with a few tears as a blush darkened her tanned cheeks. "Roni…"

Roni held up a hand. If she'd just confessed her might-be love to anyone else, she would have been anxious as hell, hurt even, that her confession hadn't been returned, but this was Zara, who needed time for these sorts of emotions. Part of Roni knew she'd eventually come around to might-be love, too.

The rest of her was ready to be anxious and depressed at a moment's notice.

"I'll wake the squad," Roni said, not wanting to wait while Zara processed her words. She moved among the squad instead, checking on their injuries as she went. She wasn't a medic, but she'd been in enough scraps to tell if a swollen eye or fat lip were healing correctly.

And she'd seen enough knocks on the head to tell when someone was going to be all right or if their brains had been knocked a little loose. Everyone seemed on the mend if still slow and tattered. Even Ana woke up. She'd lost a lot of blood when she'd been wounded during Roni's last fight with the squad. Finn had sewn her up adequately if messily, but the stitches had broken when they'd been caught by Hacha. The new ones seemed to be holding, but Ana still looked ashen, her eyes drawn.

Leo and Tati went to fetch water in their helmets. Roni rejoined Zara at the front of the cavern. Zara stared into the trees, barely blinking. Roni chewed her lip. Gods and devils, she'd broken her. Maybe she should take back what she'd said?

No, Zara liked honesty, and Roni had spoken the truth. Zara probably needed to talk her feelings out, but with who?

The answer came quickly, and Roni took the gold chain and gem from her pocket. Zara didn't resist when Roni lifted her hand, but instead of just handing the chain over, Roni pressed the yellow jewel to Zara's wrist. Zara's free hand took the chain and began looping it around her hand. Roni tried to watch, to pay attention to how she did it, but her vision blurred, and after she blinked, the glove was complete.

She could see why magic freaked many people out.

The Vox stood from where Roni had leaned them against the wall. Their tiny metal plates shifted, the motion better than yesterday when they had to fix themselves, taking so much of Roni's energy, she'd felt winded afterward. They became a falconet and landed on Zara's gloved wrist.

She already looked more at peace.

The squad ate the leftovers from last night, and everyone had a sip of helmet-water—gods, she had to stop thinking of it like that—and by the time they were finished, Zara seemed herself again. She gave Roni a soft, kind smile and didn't seem nervous or uncomfortable.

Roni breathed a sigh of relief, so happy that the optimistic part of her had been right. It would have been terrible to have to make good on that pining to death thing.

The squad watched Zara quietly as she kneeled to address them. That was probably more imposing than if she'd tried to stand and had to hunch. "We can't stay here," Zara said quietly. "And we can't leave while there are so many Firellian patrols."

The squad watched her so intently, it was like her words sat on them like weights. Even Roni shivered under the intensity.

"Roni and I are going to create a diversion to draw the Firellians' attention, and you will use that opportunity to escape up the river, heading for the next watchtower. The Firellians will no doubt be giving the area around the watchtower a wide berth, and there will likely be fewer tripwires near the cliffside."

Roni nodded. It was a good plan. And they'd be heading in the opposite direction of Cortez, just in case he had anyone on his tail. But the squad did not look happy. Well, Finn never looked happy, but even Tati and Leo were frowning.

"Boss?" Finn said. "What kind of diversion? Because if you use one of the Vox's mythic forms right after recovering…"

Zara nodded. "I'm aware of the risks."

"And there's always me," Roni said. "As backup," she added quickly, not wanting it to seem like she was taking charge.

Finn still looked skeptical, and Roni had to breathe deeply to keep her temper in check. She'd just been happy that some people never changed. She couldn't be angry that Finn was one of them.

Even if she really wanted to be.

Zara didn't comment, but as her eyes shifted to the side, she smiled slightly, and Roni knew some inkling of a plan had just occurred to her. "Pack up what meager gear you have and get ready to move as soon as you hear the commotion." She glanced out the cave mouth as if thinking of their location. "You should be able to hear it even from here."

Even while grumbling, the squad still did as they were told. Roni donned her armor, helmet, and cloak while Zara did the same. They'd head out first, of course, and Roni tried to figure out what Zara had planned but knew she'd be told in time.

If she could wait that long.

Finn approached them slowly, giving Roni another scowl for good measure before looking anxiously at Zara. "You're sure about this, boss?"

"Absolutely." She stuck her hand out. Finn eyed it for a moment before clasping her wrist. "The odds are good that we'll see each other in the future, Finn, but in case we don't, I want you to know that it's been an honor having you as my sergeant." Her eyes flicked to Roni and back to Finn. "Do you...have you ever wanted a hug?"

Roni covered her mouth to keep from chuckling and was so proud of Zara for saying that aloud that she could have burst into applause.

Finn's mouth dropped open, and she kept shaking Zara's arm dumbly. "I...no, thank you, boss. And it's been my honor, too." She closed her mouth and swallowed several times before letting go of Zara's arm.

"I'll take a hug," Tati said from where she stood with Leo, both of their arms around Ana. They all nodded as one, and Zara moved awkwardly toward them, hugging all three at once.

Zara stepped back and patted each of their shoulders softly, as if afraid she'd hurt her own squad. "It's been an honor serving with you, too," she said, nodding at each. "Keep each other safe."

It was too much. Roni had to put a hand over her mouth to keep from tearing up.

Before Zara could walk away, Tati cleared her throat, glanced at Leo and got a nod, then turned back to Zara. "I didn't think you'd come for us, boss, you and Roni. Not because of anything you did or said or who you are," she added, lifting her free hand. "But because, well, no one's ever...rescued me before, me or Leo. No one's ever come for us when we've been in trouble. And we both wanted to say"—she looked to Leo for another nod—"we both hope to stay in the army, but we never want to serve under anyone but you. That'd be our honor."

Roni scrubbed away the tears that dribbled down her cheeks. Zara's lip seemed to wobble for a moment, and she couldn't seem to speak, though the way her gaze passed over them said she wasn't lost in her own head again, just at a loss for words.

Gods and devils, she'd better not ruin the moment and say something like, the squad would have to serve under whoever they were assigned to. The Vox had to stop her from saying that; they had to.

"I'll choose you next time, too," Zara said quietly.

Roni let out a slow breath and thanked the gods. She hugged everyone except Finn, too, but her good-byes had less "it's been an honor," and more "watch your ass." She was grateful for that. She couldn't afford to cry anymore after the only refreshment she'd had that morning was helmet-water.

She followed Zara out of the shallow cave and toward the sounds of the river. "I'm glad you didn't try one last time to get me to go with the squad," she said quietly.

"What good is giving orders if they're going to be disobeyed?" Her smile took any sting out of the words. "And I'm glad you're here. I'll always choose you, as well."

Roni squeezed her hand, her heart lurching. "If it wasn't for the fact that we're headed into danger again, I would say that's the most romantic thing I've ever heard." She thought for a moment. "No, fuck it, that is the most romantic thing I've ever heard."

"Language," Zara said softly.

Before Roni could complain that Zara couldn't try to change every aspect of her personality, Zara stopped and turned, glancing around quickly as if to make sure they were safely hidden. "I could fall for you, too, Veronique Bisset, though I'm still not sure I understand the expression. I wouldn't pine to death after rejection, but I would…I would…" She gave another glance around, maybe speaking to the Vox in her head. "I would be seriously put out. Disturbed, even. Incommoded—"

"I get it." Roni kissed her softly. "And I'm glad that you're you."

Zara cocked her head again, and Roni could almost feel her thinking, "Who else would I be?"

So Roni kissed her again. "I mean, I'm so glad you are the person you are, Zara. I wouldn't change a thing."

Zara's eyes became a little misty, and she wiped them with the heel of her hand. "Thank you. Now come on. We can't waste any more of the day on sentiment and tears."

Roni couldn't agree more. Although… "And you're happy I'm the person I am, right?"

After another look of utter confusion over one shoulder, Zara said, "I wouldn't have chosen you otherwise."

So perfect. So Zara.

"What's the diversion plan?" Roni asked, speaking even softer when they had to cross an open stretch of rock between patches of trees.

Zara didn't speak until they were under cover again. "One of us is going to power the Vox in their phoenix form and burn the scaffolding and ships to ash."

She said it so calmly, Roni thought she might have heard wrong. She turned the words over in her head several times. Could either of them hold on long enough to accomplish such a task? How close would they have to be?

And how could they even hope to escape after stirring up that hornet's nest?

Roni supposed they'd have to hurry up and be in love. They didn't have any more time to fall.

CHAPTER TWENTY-FOUR

Zara lay on her stomach, Roni by her side, and looked at the bustling Firellians on the ship below. It appeared to be anchored near the shore and was offloading supplies and troops, many of which were steered toward the scaffolding that scaled the cliffside and the staircase being constructed into the rock.

"There," Zara said, pointing to where the Firellians were hauling up people and equipment via a series of ropes and pulleys. "The Vox will start there as a phoenix, burning the scaffolding, before following the line of the cliff down to burn the ship." She nodded to herself, hoping she could hold out that long. Despite getting some rest the night before, she still felt exhausted.

"I have no doubt of your stamina," the Vox said, but she sensed them building to an argument.

Roni looked askance at her, having already arrived at her argument, it seemed. "And then I'll take the glove from you when you pass out and land them before they crash to the ground?" Skepticism coated her voice.

Zara nodded, pleased she was able to read Roni as well as she did. Though she also had to admit that Roni seemed much freer with her emotions than other people.

"Or," Roni and the Vox said almost at the same time.

"No," Zara said.

"I should take the attack, and you should bring the Vox home," Roni said, defying orders that hadn't even been fully given yet.

"You're better with the Vox than I am, faster with the glove. You could pull it off me, get the Vox going just by holding it, then don it, and have the Vox fully powered in the time it would take me to even grab the glove off your wrist. And I didn't have to power the Vox in a mythic shape yesterday. I just had to haul your unconscious body to safety after you almost sacrificed yourself." She gave Zara a flat look. "And you're more injured than I am."

"I'm well enough, thank you." But she shifted uncomfortably under the barrage of feelings.

"Zara," the Vox said softly. "Roni already said she likes you for who you are. She knows you're not weak. Letting her do this is not going to make her turn away from you."

Zara frowned, wondering how Roni and the Vox could be of the same mind when they couldn't even hear each other. She tried to line up logical arguments in her head, but they were deserting her as quickly as she could think them up.

"If I do it," Roni said, "the Vox will be able to function for longer and do more damage. Fact." She had the wisdom not to look at Zara as she said it.

Zara sighed. "I can't deny your logic." She caressed the chain and the jewel. "Be careful," she said softly.

"When am I not?" the Vox asked, but their voices had a soft, caring quality. "It'll all be over soon." They hopped closer, metal feet ringing against the stone. Part of their feathers still seemed a little dented, but everyone in the squad would be going home with a few dings.

Zara held out a finger, and the Vox curled their cold talons around it. She smiled as they shook hands.

Roni grinned, too. "If you're saying farewell for now, don't bother. You'll be reunited in a matter of moments, lovebirds."

Ignoring the name calling, Zara prepared to take the glove off. The thought of Roni merging with the Vox had made her jealous not long ago, but now she thought it a boon. Having the Vox peek into Roni's mind would help Zara understand her even better.

The Vox chuckled. With their laughter still echoing in her brain, Zara took the glove off and brought the Vox close as they shut down.

She handed the chain and jewel to Roni, who regarded it with the solemnity it deserved.

"I am a little nervous," she said. "I've never done anything until I passed out before, certainly not willingly."

Zara squeezed her hand. "I'll take care of you."

"I never doubted that," Roni said with a grin. "I wouldn't be this vulnerable in front of anyone else."

Touched by the trust, Zara lifted the back of Roni's glove and kissed her hand. Another thought occurred to her, and she brightened. "I'll finally get to clearly see one of the Vox's mythic shapes. Thanks for that."

Roni rolled her eyes but gripped Zara's hand, too. "Always a silver lining." After another deep breath, she placed the jewel on her wrist and wound the chain into a glove.

The Vox stirred. Zara nodded to them both, and the Vox leaped out of the cave mouth, flapping their wings and gliding out from the cliff so they could arc around to the scaffolding.

"Wait," Zara said, her hand still on Roni's. "Not yet."

"Gods," Roni whispered. "I love flying." She clutched Zara's hand again, her eyes slightly unfocused as the Vox wheeled like a winged dancer.

"Pay attention," Zara said gently. The flying was a rush, but at the moment… "Not yet, not yet." When the Vox was only a few wingbeats from the cliff, Zara said, "Now."

The Vox shimmered, growing, their form blurring, and the air around them growing hazy with heat trails. With a pop, they burst into flames, only a vague bird shape encased in an inferno.

Roni drew in a sharp breath. "Easy," Zara said, keeping her eyes on the breathtaking, living flame.

The Vox only had to come close to the scaffolding, and the wood crackled and burned, catching alight with an incandescent glow. The Vox dove, slowing now and again so the fire could spread. Roni let out another little noise, her head almost meeting the floor of the tunnel.

"Just a little more," Zara said. "Down toward the ship." Roni was fading fast. Better for her to land the Vox as soon as possible rather than have them exchange the glove in midflight. "Get close to the ship, then land the Vox on the shore."

Roni groaned through a nod, her face pained as she stared into nothing. Firellian cries came from above, on top of the cliff, from the shore, and now from the ship. Zara grimaced as people fell or leaped from the scaffolding, trying to get away from the flames. She tried to tell herself this was on their commanders for ordering them here, but her stomach still turned.

A cloud of arrows came from bowmen on the ship, but they turned to ash when they reached the Vox's cloud of heat before they even came near the burning heart. Gods, they were beautiful and terrible at the same time, like a ruler of hell.

"Almost," Zara said, keeping hold of Roni. "Nearly there."

The Vox flew among the ship's sails, and they roared into orange and scarlet flame. Zara opened her mouth to tell Roni to land the Vox, but something shot from the ship, a lance of blue and white light.

Streaking toward the Vox and leaving stars in its wake.

"No," Zara cried. She didn't even have time to reach for the glove before the lance blasted into the Vox and smothered the flames in one strike.

Roni shrieked. The Vox's small metal body fell toward the ship like a lead weight. Zara ripped the glove from Roni's hand and wrapped it around her own as the Vox struck the ship with a crash that she felt in her chest.

The gem was on her wrist, the glove complete.

Nothing responded.

"Vox," Zara whispered.

Nothing. No words, no sensations, no hint of life.

It had to be the distance. The Vox was hurt, needed her help. She had to get down there. With her heart in her mouth, Zara hugged Roni close. Her eyelids were flickering, but she was awake, alive. "Stay here. I'll be back."

Roni made some noise of protest, but Zara was already standing, then running out of the cave, hurrying along the ledge until she saw the first way up. She clambered up quickly, refusing to think of anything except the task in front of her.

On top of the cliff, the Firellians were in chaos. Zara waited behind a clump of spindly bushes. She slipped the chain and her left fingerless glove off, then donned the chain again, pausing to reach for the Vox.

No response.

That meant nothing. She put her fingerless glove on top of the chain, hoping no one would notice the sparkle near her fingers. It wouldn't do to disguise herself only to have the chain give her away.

Now for the disguise itself.

When a Firellian ran by alone, looking around as if bewildered about what to do, Zara yanked them into the bushes, knocked them out, and took their uniform. She hated wearing the dark gray of the enemy, but the Vox needed her. "I'm coming," she thought as loudly as she could, whispering the words for good measure.

She shouldered through the Firellians clustered around the top of the scaffolding. Some of the ropes remained intact, and the Firellians pulled up those who'd managed to climb toward safety. Before she could look at the long, gut-twisting drop, Zara took hold of one rope and swung out over nothing. Her stomach tightened and flipped. The Firellians cried out for her to stop, but she was already sliding, her feet hitting a knot. She spun slightly, the world becoming a whirl of green and blue.

She couldn't look, but she couldn't shut her eyes. The Vox needed her, even when she was hanging over nothing. She grabbed another rope to steady herself. The Firellians were trying to pull the other one up, gesturing for her to climb to them. She curled her foot in the second rope and switched to that one. It wound through a pulley overhead, and the Firellians wouldn't be able to get hold of it.

She began to ease downward, then gained speed. With a cry, she reached for the first rope again. The material of her glove peeled away as if burned, but the rope couldn't cut through the golden chain. With a cry that she swiftly stifled, Zara clung to both ropes until her stomach and head caught up with her. Gods, she couldn't give up now.

While her heart was still with the Vox, Zara lowered herself in spurts, quickly reaching the shore and hitting with enough force to rattle her teeth. She called for the Vox as she staggered toward the burning ship.

Nothing, nothing, nothing.

"Please," she whispered. Her wounded hand and hip ached, but she kept stumbling. One Firellian grabbed her arm, shaking his head. Zara punched him in the gut, and he backed off, staggering. Others called to her, but she hurried up the hasty-looking gangplank and plunged into the smoke.

"Vox," she yelled out loud and in her head. The sails rained fire from overhead, the flames eating down the masts. She tried to feel the Vox, even just a direction, but nothing answered her. They couldn't be dead, couldn't be, couldn't be...

The smoke grew thick. Zara coughed, fighting the urge to fall to her knees. Which way had she come from? She staggered, turning. "Vox?"

She slid, one foot going over empty air. Zara tried to right herself, but she tumbled down a short staircase.

Into fresh air.

Zara breathed deep, one hand on her aching, wounded hip as she got her feet back under her. Smoke swirled in the daylight coming down the stairs, but it rolled around her as if she stood in a bubble of air. Her mind wanted to rebel from this impossibility, but movement from the shadows caught her attention.

A woman walked into the light, the Vox cradled in her arms. Her eyes were wild, her hair unkempt, and her face frightened and marred by lines of pain. She wore plain clothes: trousers, shirt, and jacket. They looked rumpled and untidy but were clean of soot. The bubble of fresh air seemed to move with her when she took a step.

One of the Firellian mage monsters.

Zara glanced at the Vox. The lance that had felled them had probably come from this woman. Zara ached to draw her saber, but if the mage died, no doubt this bubble of air would go with her, and Zara would never get the Vox out.

Would never get Roni out.

Tears rolled down the mage's face as she looked at the Vox and spoke in Firellian. "Is...your friend? I didn't know what they were." She spoke slowly, and Zara managed to understand most of it. "I'm sorry."

Zara held her hand out. "Give them to me," she said slowly, knowing her accent was terrible.

The mage looked at the Vox again. This close, Zara should have sensed something but heard only awful silence in her head.

Zara struggled with her own tears as she held out both hands now. "Please." The least she could do was bury them properly, with all the honors they deserved.

"I'm sorry," the mage said again. She put a hand on the Vox's chest, and her eyes slipped closed.

A thrum of electricity shuddered through Zara's body. She gasped, one hand to her chest as her stomach went topsy-turvy again. An echo built in her mind, as if the wind was blowing through her skull. "Vox?"

"Unit activated," a single voice said in her head, a copy of her own voice. "Speak command."

Zara put a hand to her mouth. Gods and devils, was this all that was left of her friend? Loss pressed her down like the hand of a powerful ghost. What was she going to do? What was life without the Vox?

It was almost enough to bring her to her knees.

Almost.

The Vox was alive. And while they lived, she could help them. She wouldn't give up on an injured comrade, an injured friend. No one who needed her would ever go wanting. She staggered but didn't fall. She couldn't fall now. She held out a hand, ready to order the Vox to return to her.

The mage was staring at her curiously and held a hand up, too. "Wait."

Zara paused, her hand curling into a fist. Another jolt went through her when the mage wrapped both arms around the Vox again. The wind blowing through Zara's skull became a roar, a counterpoint to the pulse in her chest. Her knees sagged. She couldn't take much more—

"What the hell was that?" the Vox's many voices said in her mind.

Zara cried out and raised her fists in victory. "Vox?"

"Of course," they answered. "Who did you expect?" They righted themselves, head twisting to look at the mage as they perched on her arm. "Tell her I said thanks. And don't kill her, please, Zara."

Zara nodded, wiping at the tears dribbling down her cheeks. She'd pay any price for the Vox's return, would have paid it before, but now, to have them fully back with her... "Thank you," she said to the mage. "I...will not hurt you."

The mage smiled before wincing, and the lines of pain between her eyes deepened, the pale skin turning white. "Please help me." She took a step as the Vox flew from her arm to Zara's shoulder. "Please... please help me," she said again.

In Sarrasian.

Zara gasped. "Are you from Sarras?" Had she been right when she'd thought one or more of the mages had been kidnapped? "Come with me." Zara gestured toward the staircase, her other hand out. "I'll get you out." Gods knew how, but she had to try.

The mage shook her head and backed up, the smoke clearing where she stepped. Zara strode after her, rushing when part of the flaming deck collapsed behind her. As the smoke billowed, she spotted another slash of sunlight, a hole that went through the deck and out the side.

Zara hurried to the hole, pointing. "Come on. We can get out here." The river swept by outside, and the water would be as cold as a devil's heart, but they could make it. "I'll help you swim. The Vox can keep you afloat."

The mage shook her head, her dark hair swinging wildly. In the brighter light, she seemed very young, reminding Zara of Gisele, making her heart hurt.

"I can't," the mage said. "They're killing us. Hurting us. We can't live long with the magic they make us use."

"Then come," Zara said, waving. "The army can rescue the others. Come now."

"I can't abandon them." She wrung her hands. "My name is Vale. If I can free the others and come to the city, will you help us?"

"Of course, but you should come now, Vale, and then we'll rescue the others together." She put a hand to her chest, secretly bracing herself to grab Vale's arm and drag her out. "My name is Zara del Amanecer." She didn't ask how Vale knew she was Sarrasian, guessing it was something to do with the ways of mages. "You can trust me."

"Thank you." She smiled as tears flowed down her cheeks.

Zara lunged for her, but a gust of wind blew from Vale, carrying her cry as it came. Zara grunted as she and the Vox flew backward, out of the hole and into sudden brightness. The Vox managed to take wing, but Zara held her breath as she plummeted toward the rapidly moving waters of the river.

CHAPTER TWENTY-FIVE

Roni had willed herself to stay awake as Zara climbed down over oblivion and ran onto a burning ship. She'd screamed at herself to keep her eyes open, but it had come out as grunts. How could she be falling asleep when her stomach was bottoming out, and her heart was clenching, and she wanted to hug Zara tightly and wring her neck at the same time?

When the burning ship began to collapse, Roni tried to get up but couldn't even push on her arms. Her limbs were like lead, and she would have sworn her head was tied to the ground. She could only sob between her teeth and watch the ship through her flickering eyelids.

Something strange caught the last bits of her consciousness: a bubble appeared in the smoke on the side of the ship, smoke and cinders flowing around it. What the hell? She blinked, then tried to force her eyes wide as something went shooting out the side of the ship as if thrown.

A person? But...

Something flashed above it, catching the light like metal as they hovered.

Metal wings. The Vox. Then the person had to be...

"Zara," Roni said with a sigh. A rush of joy filled her before consciousness fled completely.

When someone touched Roni's shoulder, she turned her head toward the warmth of a hand. Someone said her name, and she hoped it was Zara, that they were waking up together like in her dreams.

"Hey, babe," she said dreamily.

"Well, hello, sweetheart." A man's voice.

Roni rolled over and opened her eyes. Cortez's smirking face stared at her, his features distorted in lantern light.

"What the hell?" She sat up slowly, her head aching like she'd taken a few good knocks. "Cortez?" Her memory came back in a rush: Zara, the fire, the river. She twisted to see, but everything outside the cave was dark. "What happened?"

"You'll have to tell me." Cortez peered at her face and tilted his head as if to see her jaw or neck.

She felt the scabs there. "Hacha. Don't worry. He's dead."

"Good news." He helped pull her to her feet and steadied her. "Come on. I've brought reinforcements from the watchtower." He helped her out of the cave, onto the ledge, then up to a host of soldiers in Sarrasian uniforms, many of them with lanterns. Roni had no idea how long she'd slept, but every inch of her ached.

"The Firellians appear to have scattered," Cortez said.

Roni nodded. When a pissed-off looking sergeant came striding toward them, Roni launched into her story without being prodded, ending with Zara flying into the river.

The sergeant made a face like a lemon and nodded once, sharply, before barking at her troops to head back to the watchtower.

Roni looked to Cortez, her gut icing over in fear. "We can't leave Zara," she said.

"If she went down the river, she's far from here by now," he said. "I haven't heard about anyone being spotted on the shore, but the soldiers we left at the watchtower might have more information." He glanced around and lowered his voice. "And these woods might still be crawling with too many Firellians for us to take. The rest of the army is coming to clear them out. We just came for more intel. And you," he added hastily.

She gripped his shoulder. "Thanks."

"Don't get sentimental," he said, brushing her off, though the way he avoided her eyes said he was touched.

"Did you get word about the rest of the squad?"

"Not by the time we left." He passed her a canteen.

She drank greedily as they began walking back through the woods. Her stomach was in knots, and every time they paused, she edged closer to the cliffside, hoping to somehow see a glimpse of Zara even in the darkness.

"We'll find her," Cortez kept saying quietly.

His squad made camp not long after. Roni considered going ahead on her own, desperate for news of Zara, but Cortez told her not to be stupid. He all but muscled her into sitting down. A medic examined and rebandaged her wounds, rubbing some kind of smelly salve into the stitches on her belly and the cuts on her neck and hand. It burned like a devil, and she nearly cursed the medic out, but Cortez kept nudging her.

After the medic had done their job, Roni thanked them brusquely before squaring off with Cortez. "You elbow me one more time—"

"And you'll what?" he asked. His mouth turned down in a comical pout. "Does this mean I'm not your babe anymore?"

She breathed a laugh that wanted to become a sob, but she managed to hold it in. "She has to be all right."

"If anyone can survive a dunk in the Kingfish, it's her. Now, come on, sweetheart, get some proper sleep rather than trying to kill yourself by heading out alone."

She rolled her eyes, deciding one more lie wouldn't hurt if it meant she could help Zara. "I wasn't going to. And I'm awake enough to take a watch so…" She trailed off as he stared at her, his eyes half-lidded and his flat expression saying he didn't buy her bullshit for one moment.

"Oh, fine. Asshole." She ducked into a tent and stripped to her long underwear, certain she'd get no sleep right until it hit her like a hammer.

When she woke at dawn, she was up and dressed in record time. The squad hurried all through the day and didn't reach the watchtower until after dark. When they piled into the squat, ugly tower, the sergeant climbed the stairs while everyone else stowed their gear. Roni jogged after the sergeant before Cortez could stop her. She passed through a room of bunks and up into a large room that had maps tacked to the walls and several desks cluttered with paper.

"…reports several members of Commander del Amanecer's squad arrived," someone was saying to the sergeant.

Roni breathed out, glad the rest of the squad had gotten to safety. Hopefully, Claudia and Jaq were safe, too. "What about Zara?" she asked.

The sergeant looked at her incredulously, blue eyes wide in her lean face. "Did I ask you to accompany me, Recruit?"

Oh, not this shit again. She wanted to shout, "Fuck you," and make her thoughts very clear, but she swallowed that, sensing that would get her locked up. She had to be soldier-y about this. "Sergeant, please," she said quietly. "She's my commanding officer, and she... did all of us proud, made sure we were safe."

The sergeant relaxed slightly, and Roni held in a cheer. "Corporal?" the sergeant asked. "Any news of Commander del Amanecer? Last seen in the river."

The corporal looked between them and shook her head. "Sorry."

Roni ground her teeth, fighting the despair that wanted to take over. Zara was okay. She'd be all right. "I volunteer to climb down to the shore and search, serrah."

The sergeant frowned. "We wait for orders in this tower, Recruit. If we get orders to search the shore, I'll keep your offer in mind." She gestured back down the stairs. "Report to Ramirez. You'll be on duty here until the infantry collects you and takes you back to base."

Well, if talking like a soldier didn't help...

Roni had a small speech prepared about where the sergeant could shove her orders, but Cortez grabbed her arm. She jumped. Devils, he could be quiet when he wanted to. The sergeant gave him another of those wide-eyed looks, but he spoke before anyone else could.

"I am commandeering Recruit Bisset on behalf of Sarrasian intelligence," he said. He pointed upward. "Send a message back to the city, and they'll clear us to operate on our own. Code is: shadow, seven, zero, zero, six, five, pale." He pointed to the corporal, who grabbed a piece of paper and wrote furiously. "That's p-a-l-e."

The sergeant stepped closer. "That's not an army code. Who do you think will *clear* you to work on your own?"

"Field Marshal Fabian Ortiz."

The sergeant and corporal gasped. Roni looked from one to another, biting back the urge to ask who the hell that was.

The sergeant frowned hard. "How in the devils do you know—"

"That's not up for discussion. Put the message through, or you'll answer to General Garcia after Field Marshal Ortiz gets done yelling at her."

The sergeant took a deep breath, no doubt counting to ten before she turned. "Corporal, go ahead and light the signal fire and ready the shutters for this message."

Roni held back a smirk. The field marshal's name had obviously put the fear of the gods into her.

But the sergeant turned back to Cortez with an evil smile. "Then have these two locked in the larder. When a reply *fails* to appear from the illustrious field marshal, put together an official charge of attempted desertion."

Well, shit. At least Cortez didn't lose his confident look, even when they were locked in the larder.

"Who's Field Marshal What's-their-name?" Roni asked when they were alone.

"Fabian Ortiz. One of the field marshals that the general of the army reports to. And they report to the oligarchs."

"Fuck me," Roni said quietly, unable to even imagine such corridors of power. "I bet they've got some good loot."

He snorted. She hadn't even realized she'd said that aloud. Great, her mouth had reached a new level of running away. At least it had kept mum for a little while.

"Is Ortiz the head of your agency?" she asked.

He yawned while making eye contact, a clear sign that he wasn't going to answer.

She sighed but smiled. "That's fine. I'll just ask Jean-Carlo when we all get home."

Cortez pointed at her. "Don't forget your promise to brag about me to him."

With one hand over her heart, she said, "I swear so to do, serrah. As soon as we find Zara."

He nodded. Roni tried to settle in to wait, snacking on some jerky, but before she could worry herself into a lather, the larder door opened.

The corporal from before stood there, a fearful look on her face. She saluted Cortez, who waved the gesture away. She stood aside. "You're free to go, serrah. Sergeant Chambre wanted me to apologize—"

He waved that away, too, and helped Roni to her feet. "We're going to need some supplies."

Roni stuck the rest of the packet of jerky into her pocket and tried not to look smug as she followed Cortez. She was finally *officially* on the way to get Zara back.

"You're heading out in the dark, serrah?" the corporal asked.

Cortez paused as if just realizing how late it had gotten. "Ah."

Roni snorted dismissively. "This won't be the first difficult climb I've made at night."

"In the city," Cortez said. "It's pitch-black out there."

Damn. He was right. But somewhere out there, Zara might be suffering, waiting for someone to come looking for her. Roni was pretty certain she could make the climb, any climb, blind, but she'd have to do it alone. When she reached the bottom with her one lantern, she might walk right by Zara and never know it.

"First light?" Cortez said.

Roni had to nod, knowing she'd get no sleep tonight, not while waiting for dawn.

"Zara, wake up." It was the Vox's many voices again. But they didn't sleep, couldn't know how important it was for humans. "Zara, now."

She groaned. She'd never had trouble getting out of bed except when she'd been sick as a child. And she felt ill now, so why couldn't Adella let her rest?

"That's just the kind of confusion we're trying to avoid. Wake up now."

The Vox. Again. Maybe she could take the chain glove off for a little while. She reached for it, but a pinch from a cold metal beak made her jerk upright.

"That's better." The Vox sat near her left hand, their back to the fire at the entrance of this shallow excuse for a cave. Zara drew her feet up and shivered in her damp long underwear. Daylight shone outside. Maybe her clothes were dry by now.

The thought was enough to get her moving. "Thank you, Vox," she said, her teeth chattering around the words and her throat sore from trying to breathe river water. "I'm sorry." She crawled toward where her clothes lay on a jutting rock. Her useless right arm was tucked in the front of her undershirt, but it still sent agony rolling through her when she moved.

"You don't have to apologize for anything," the Vox said softly. "Take it slow."

The stolen uniform was dry, thank the gods. Slowly, wincing and groaning from the pain, she pulled the uniform on. The Vox helped where they could. They'd done so much for her already: fetching kindling, helping light the fire, prodding her to undress and secure her screaming arm, and keeping her from falling asleep and from there into oblivion.

"It's a shame you have to keep us both going," the Vox said. "Everything I do takes a little of your strength."

A small price.

"For you to live?" the Vox asked. "I agree."

For both of them to live. She couldn't help recalling her anguish when she'd thought the Vox was dead, and that thought led to memories of tumbling about in the cold river, struggling to stay on the surface in her armor. The Vox had to pull on her helmet, her shirt, whatever they could reach, to keep her afloat. Especially after she'd caught hold of that log that had rolled on her, a broken branch pinning her arm as she sought to push away. The crack had sounded *inside* her body. Gods, the pain. Her stomach roiled.

"Easy, easy," the Vox said.

They'd had to drag her the rest of the way to shore. She had to keep wearing the chain glove, keeping them awake to keep her awake.

"There," the Vox said, pulling the jacket over her shoulder and broken arm. The jacket and the shirt hung open. It would have to do, regulations be damned. She wasn't going to try to tackle the arm holes on her right side.

"And now..." The Vox stuck a metal talon into the fire and pulled a blackened fish from the ash. "I can't applaud my skills as a cook, but it's something."

Zara's stomach turned, but she reached for the fish with a shaky hand.

"Let me." The Vox came to her rescue again and pulled the fish apart with their claws and beak.

She looked away, the sight too much for her nausea. When she looked back, the meat sat in a shredded pile. She ate slowly, carefully, tasting nothing but pain. Her appetite returned a little as she went. The Vox watched, their talons and face grubby from helping. Zara managed a smile. "If any birds see you, they'll be appalled at your table manners." She swallowed, trying to ease her sore throat.

The Vox turned their head up proudly. "Let them think what they will."

Her heart warmed. She couldn't believe she'd almost lost them. She *had* lost Vale. And maybe Roni.

"None of that," the Vox said. "The sooner we find help, the sooner we can send someone back for Roni. She's probably waiting in that cave, safe and sound."

And cold and hungry.

"And," the Vox said loudly, "waiting for you to sweep her up in your arms. So put on your boots, and let's get moving."

"Arm," Zara croaked. "Singular. And at this rate, she'll have to sweep me." She threw sand over the fire and began staggering along the shallow beach on the Sarrasian side of the border. When spring came, even this spit of land would be underwater. In a way, she was lucky to have fallen in at the tail of winter.

Her frozen extremities did not agree.

She couldn't focus on her body right then. Not the leaden feeling or the pain. Roni needed her. Her sisters needed her. Mages like Vale needed her. And the Firellians needed to be kicked out of her homeland.

The Vox encouraged this thinking as they hopped from perch to perch in front of her, making her stagger toward them again and again. A ringing sound built in her ears, drowning out even the Vox's voices inside her skull.

Just a few more steps and she could rest. Then a few more. And a few more than that.

When she stumbled and fell, she rose again, wobbling. The Vox was saying something, but she didn't have the energy to walk and listen. She couldn't fall, could she? After everything she'd been through, a mere trip down the river would be the thing to lay her low?

It was proof at least that the world was a logicless place.

Ah well. At least the army would recover the Vox when they found her body.

Roni glanced back the way they'd come again. There were so many large rocks about, and any of them could be hiding Zara. Her frustration grew every time she had to lean around another gods-forsaken boulder or poke her head into another shallow cave or wonder if Zara was even on this side of the cursed river. This whole damn armpit-of-nowhere-ness could go straight to hell.

And Cortez wasn't helping by being slow.

Roni looked back to where he was lagging. "Come on."

He frowned as he caught up to her. "Not so loud. You don't know who might be lurking on that side." His finger jabbed at the Firellian forest, which was too far away to worry about, and the noise of the river made quiet conversation impossible in any case. But he couldn't seem to fight his paranoia. Hell, they probably taught paranoia at Sarrasian intelligence.

"You want to know what's over there? Trees." She put her hands on her hips. "There aren't Firellians lurking behind every fucking tree in the hope that a Sarrasian will wander by on this side." She put a hand up to shade her eyes and looked at the forest. "And what would they do if they did spot us? Build a ship and sail over to get us?"

He glared. "The fire was bound to draw attention."

"Days ago," Roni said as she started walking again. "And now even the trees think you're moving too slow." Gods and devils, what if they weren't even going the right way? What if Zara had floated past already and was lying farther downriver, desperate for help?

"I'm going to kiss her," Roni mumbled to herself. "Then I'm going to tie her up so she can't keep throwing herself into danger."

"I don't think she'll care for that," Cortez said.

"You waited until I was talking to myself to keep up with me? Great." She wasn't even angry with him, but it was nice to have someone to snap at. Angry was so much better than worried.

"We'll find—"

"Less placating, more looking," she said.

He sighed dramatically but followed her anyway.

The day was getting on. If they didn't start back soon, they'd be camping down here or risk climbing the cliffside in the dark. Roni was certain she could make it, but Cortez had almost fallen several times on the way down. She'd had to tie them both to the guide rope and help him find every handhold. She was definitely going to give him some training of her own when they got home.

All of them. Because she wasn't leaving Zara behind. Ever.

A noise came from ahead, a metallic ting. Roni froze, her mind going to weapons, but they weren't the only things made of metal. When the sound came again, she ran. Cortez called for her to stop, but she couldn't, especially after she saw a flash of metal.

The Vox, active, moving. Zara was alive. Roni cried out in happiness and put on a burst of speed, rounding a boulder to see Zara lying face-up, her shirt and jacket only draped around her right side where her arm had been tucked into her undershirt. She wore no helmet, and her dark hair blew across her face. Roni moved it gently, noting the lines of pain near her fluttering eyes and the dark circles above her cheeks.

"Oh, Zara," Roni whispered. "It's all right. You're okay now. And you're going to let someone else take care of you for a change *while* you're conscious." She reached for the Vox's chain glove and moved it to her own hand so she could find out just how badly Zara was hurt and then wake her up.

And kiss her well again in order to yell at her properly.

❖

The Vox went silent. That meant something, but Zara needed to rest in order to figure it out. A small thought wormed through her. She couldn't sleep. Not here. Not while she was…something.

The explanation didn't matter. She needed to get up, but how? Maybe if she just opened her eyes, she'd be able to sit up.

When Roni's face appeared above her, Zara blinked, happy. This was a nice dream. Maybe she could manage to steer it the way her sisters could. Roni kissed her softly, just like she wanted. Good, she could write her own dreams after all.

"Stay awake, Zara," Roni said. "Open your eyes. Can you sit up?"

Why would she want to? It was so much nicer lying down.

"Stay."

"I'm here, babe. I'm not going anywhere, but you need to sit up, then get up and walk. We have to get you to safety before nightfall."

Zara felt safe enough where she was.

Roni drew in a sharp breath. "I'm sorry for this."

Pressure on Zara's arm made her gasp, eyes flying open, and the world returning in a snap of pain. She cried out.

"I'm sorry, I'm sorry, I'm sorry," Roni said. "But you can't sleep out here, Zara. You have to walk."

Zara blinked at the shore, the rocks, the river. Roni. "You're... really here?"

"And so are you, and we're both staying that way." Roni turned away. "Cortez, get your ass over here."

Cortez, too? Zara tried to stand, not wanting to seem weak, but she quickly dismissed that notion. She was hurt; there was a difference. But when Roni and Cortez pulled her up between them, and she put her uninjured arm around Roni's shoulders, she made herself walk. Cortez sprinted away.

"He's getting help," Roni said, her own breathing labored.

Zara snorted. "We'll be back up the cliff by the time they get here."

Roni laughed and kissed her cheek. "That's right. Because the squad is waiting for us, Zara, waiting for you. They're okay. I'm okay and so is the Vox. You did it. You got us out alive and got the information you needed. You completed the mission."

She had, hadn't she? She felt absurdly proud, even with the pain, even with everything. "And I have you."

"Yes." This close, Roni's smile lit up the whole world. "And I have you, too."

CHAPTER TWENTY-SIX

Zara stood before Colonel Lopez's desk and looked him in the eye as she reported everything she'd learned during the mission.

Well, almost everything.

She'd left out a little bit about Roni, like stealing the Vox and being the reason Hacha had followed them. She'd only said he'd come after them in order to capture the Vox. Part of Zara wondered why she bothered omitting the truth. Cortez was still *commandeering* Roni, as he put it—never mind that Zara had told him that word didn't normally apply to people—so the army couldn't punish her if they wanted to.

But Roni had asked her to leave it out, and so…

"It's not bad if she rubs off on you a little," the Vox said in Zara's mind.

She spared a glance for where they rested on Lopez's windowsill. She'd claimed she needed their help remembering everything, but the truth was, she still had a hard time being apart from them after what they'd endured.

"Commander," Lopez said, bringing her attention back to him. He'd been pondering for the last several minutes, but now he gestured to a chair, an invitation to sit.

Normally, she would have refused, but her hip was beginning to ache, and her arm always felt better if she could rest the sling on the arm of a chair. "Thank you, serrah."

"The infantry is already headed into the woods," Lopez said, "alerted by the watchtowers. They'll clear the Firellians out. I'm sure the general will want to give you a commendation."

She winced. "I beg your pardon, Colonel, but that's not right. Ernesto died under my command."

"That didn't stop you from burning that scaffolding and the ship. Or from killing one of their mages."

Zara winced at that, too. The mage who'd died might have been Sarrasian like Vale, but damn it, she hadn't known. "Still, if anyone deserves a commendation, it's my squad."

He nodded. She'd been singing the same tune since she'd found out that Jaq and Claudia had also made it to safety, but ultimately, it wouldn't be up to her or Lopez. If they wanted to give her some kind of ceremony, she was determined to ask Gisele how to fake being sick.

Or Roni might know. Zara hid a smile behind her left hand. They had so much to teach each other.

"And we'll be bringing in some mages from the guild to ask about the magic you reported, this spike that affected the Vox, and how these 'monster mages' might be forced to use their power. Though I don't know why the Firellians would treat their mages so harshly."

"Because they're captives?"

He shrugged. "I think the guild would have noticed if a great many of their own had been kidnapped. Of course, we still don't know for sure why the Firellians have never produced many mages of their own. All we have are rumors about how they disapprove of magic." He seemed to lose himself in his thoughts again. Zara coughed slightly to draw his attention back to her. He smiled. "Anyway, our mages will sort that out. And you might get to work with your sister."

Zara tried to hide her grimace with the same hand. Asking Gisele for advice was one thing, but working with her…Zara shuddered. Gisele would be fracturing protocol all over the place.

Lopez gave her a sympathetic smile, and she wondered if he also had a difficult home life, but he said, "I'll be delivering the news to Ernesto's family."

Her heart sank, bouncing all over the place today.

"Just breathe," the Vox said, an order she'd given many a recruit.

"I should...should I..." She couldn't say she'd go, though she would obey if he ordered it.

"No," Lopez said firmly. "If anyone should go, it's Hoffman for forcing your squad to test the prison recruitment scheme."

Zara shook her head. "Ernesto was killed by Hacha. The recruits did well. They just need more training." Gods, what a turnaround from her former opinion. But Roni was right. The prison system in Sarras did need reforming. "What about Julia Esposito in Haymarket Prison? By sending Hacha after the Vox, didn't the Newgate Syndicate declare hostilities against the army?"

"I can talk to the warden, but the prison isn't in the army's jurisdiction whether they declare hostilities or not. They're not a foreign power."

True, but the thought of a prisoner running a prison made no sense. It was almost enough to drive her mind off the well-worn path again. She would have to speak to Cortez about it since his agency appeared to operate along the fringes of law. Or maybe Jean-Carlo could do something. Roni could probably pit them against each other to get something done, though she hadn't gotten the chance yet.

And while she was at it, Roni could find out how this intelligence agency knew about the Vox in the first place and how a criminal syndicate had acquired those anti-Vox spikes.

The list of questions seemed destined to keep growing.

"What of Tati and Leo?" Zara asked.

"They'll be going to basic training, though they should fly through it now. Do you want them for your squad when your arm heals?"

Thinking of their parting words to her, she nodded. "Loyalty like that is hard to come by," the Vox said, echoing her thoughts.

He gestured to the door. "Well, if that's all, Commander."

Zara stood, used to the vague dismissal. She saluted and turned.

"Happy to have you back in one piece," Lopez said.

"Thank you, serrah." She left after a nod, too tired to be choked up by more sentiment. And she still had one more parting today.

The Vox landed on her uninjured shoulder once she was outside. "We only have to say good-bye for the moment. You're off-duty because of the injury, but that doesn't mean you can't come see me every day."

"I know," she said with a sigh. "It's illogical, but…"

"Nothing's going to happen to me in the meantime." Their cold beak rested against her temple for a moment. She'd left the gold helmet at home today, also too tired to be bothered about salutes.

"I know."

"So brighten up. Roni stayed at your house last night, yes?"

She smiled and recalled the feeling of sitting next to Roni in front of the kitchen fireplace, their warm hands intertwined. "Yes."

"But you were too tired for anything but sleep."

"You already know that."

"And today you're tired of lots of things, but perhaps, for other things, you might find some energy."

She chuckled. "You can be as bad as Adella. If you mean sex, just say so."

"I didn't want to pressure you."

She didn't feel pressured. She'd been thinking of lovemaking a lot lately without any prodding. Or maybe the Vox was trying to irritate her so she'd be happier to leave them in the armory.

"Whatever works," they said with a chuckle.

She walked into the armory and picked up the box that normally held the chain glove. She took the Vox back inside their little room. It had been hard enough leaving them yesterday when she'd arrived back at the base, but she'd been dead on her feet then. Now it seemed doubly difficult.

"Then don't say good-bye," the Vox said. "How about, see you later?" They sat on their perch, and the sun streaming in the windows gleamed off their golden body. "I'll be here if you need me. Always."

She smiled, hoping all her gratitude came through their connection. "I'll see you later. If someone tries to steal you, come find me."

They laughed in her mind, a chorus of happy voices. "Definitely."

Once the chain and jewel were under lock and key, Zara walked home, feeling lonely without the Vox, but her heart picked up when she thought about whom she'd be going home to. She didn't know how long Roni was going to stay with her. She hadn't asked, fearing

Roni would see that as a request to leave. Technically, Roni should be staying wherever Cortez and Jean-Carlo did, if they had a barracks for their spies, but Zara supposed Roni could stay wherever they put her. And it had been wonderful to see her smiling face at the del Amanecer breakfast table. Even if she did put the milk in the wrong place. Zara needed to make those labels sooner rather than later.

Funny, she'd always thought Gisele would bring in the next houseguest. But she'd only peppered Roni with questions, her and Adella both, while Bridget and Zara had tried to change the subject and give Roni a break.

They needn't have bothered. Roni only shared what she wanted to, as if she knew Zara wouldn't want to give out salacious details. She really was a rare find.

Even if she was one more person in Zara's space.

Who didn't know where everything went.

Voices caught Zara's attention when she walked in the front door. Roni was chatting to Jean-Carlo in the kitchen, completing her promise to Cortez, it seemed.

"He's also really good at climbing. Well, mostly." Roni glanced up at Zara and smiled as if her salvation was at hand. She looked radiant. Her red hair fell in soft waves to her chin, and her dark eyes seemed to sparkle. "Hello, you."

"Hello," Zara said, grinning back at her, Jean-Carlo be damned.

But the look he gave her said she'd saved him, too. "Good morning, Zara. I don't suppose Bridget is with you?"

"Good morning. And, no. I've just come from the base."

His hopeful look fled, and he glanced at Roni again.

She barked a laugh. "All right, you're paroled. You don't have to listen to me brag on Cortez anymore. Unless he drops by."

"Perish the thought," Jean-Carlo muttered as he sipped from a mug. He tossed his long black braid over one shoulder as if banishing Cortez's presence from the room.

Zara wished he'd banish himself, too. She wanted to be alone with Roni, to talk or kiss or even go upstairs so Zara could learn more about what made people in novels go weak in the knees. She was just about to suggest Jean-Carlo wait for Bridget in the sitting room, when the front door opened and closed again, bringing more voices.

Gods.

Adella and Bridget came in with Serrah Nunez behind them like a colorful cloud. She wore a pale blue gown and matching wig, the braided ends of which bore tiny bells. She had to have the loudest wardrobe in all of Sarras.

"All my favorite cupcakes in one place," Serrah Nunez said, beaming at them. She put a basket on the table. "I've brought some goodies for the invalid."

Zara managed a smile. "Thank you." She hoped she wasn't expected to eat them now. She hated eating food made by people she knew. No one ever took her criticism well.

Thankfully, they all fell to chatting instead. Bridget and Jean-Carlo talked near the fireplace. Adella spoke to Serrah Nunez and Roni, and Gisele joined them not five minutes later, raising the volume even more.

"I'm going to keep working for Cortez," Roni was saying. "He wants my help gathering info on the city's crime syndicates. He's already working on a way to get Julia Esposito transferred to a prison in another city." She rolled her eyes. "And some of my salary has to go toward the people I've…" She glanced around. "Whose goods I've liberated."

"You can say stole," Zara said around her mug.

Roni shrugged. "I already returned the last jewels I took. Everything before that should be old news."

Serrah Nunez laughed. "Not to the people who first owned it, treacle. They're not likely to forget."

"They'll get their money." Roni sounded a bit petulant until Zara caught her eye, then she winked.

Zara smiled back. She might not understand what Roni was talking about at times, but she knew Roni was on her side just like the Vox was. Always.

"Zara said you might get involved with the prison reform project," Roni said to Adella.

She nodded. "It goes hand in hand with my crusade to help the homeless. We've built a few shelters already. We could have reform houses for nonviolent prisoners or low-income housing for those who feel like they have to steal to live."

Zara gave her a smile, too. Growing up without much money had taught Adella how to stretch every coin. Zara had spent some of last night explaining her past to Roni, but they had so much more to say. If they could get some gods-forsaken peace in this house.

Gisele laughed loudly at something Bridget said. Zara couldn't help a frown. She looked to Adella for help, and Adella gave her a nod. "Serrah Nunez, come this way. I want your advice on redecorating the sitting room." She slipped an arm through Bridget's as she went. "Gisele, what was the name of that color you fancied?"

Just like that, Adella had gathered almost everyone and moved them out of the room. Even Jean-Carlo trailed in her wake.

"She's a marvel," Roni whispered in Zara's ear.

"She was a diplomat, trained to marvel." Zara leaned her forehead against Roni's. She could still hear the chatter from the other room but not what they were saying. If she pretended, the voices could be nothing more than the wind in the trees.

Roni kissed her softly. Zara leaned into the small movement, enjoying the way it sent tingles through her belly. "You're marvelous, too," Roni whispered when she pulled away slightly.

"I think we all are in our own way."

Roni's smile took up the whole world. Zara kissed her this time, daring a deeper contact. Roni made a little noise of pleasure. "Well, Mistress of the Sneaky Arts, can you spirit us upstairs?"

Zara exhaled, so glad Roni had asked. She'd been trying to think of a swoon-worthy way to say just that but didn't know how to be anything other than direct. The Vox would no doubt tease her by saying, "If you mean sex, why not say so?"

Because Roni said it so much better.

And she'd provided an interesting challenge.

"Hmm. The others will see us if we simply climb the stairs."

"Mm-hmm," Roni said, kissing Zara's neck, a further distraction to make the challenge harder.

"We could sneak out the back and try for a window, but at this time of day, they're probably still locked."

Roni nibbled her ear, making her gasp. "And so?"

"And so…" Zara's thoughts deserted her as Roni caressed her thigh. "We walk right past them, and if they ask where we're going or what we're doing, we tell them to go to hell."

Roni's husky chuckle sent the weakness Zara had read about straight to her knees. "On your orders, Commander."

Zara stood and pulled Roni up with her good arm. "I'm not your commander anymore."

"That's right," Roni said cheerfully. Her eyes went half-lidded, and she ran a finger down the sling that held Zara's broken arm. "And with this, you'll have to be careful, make sure to lie back and relax." She leaned close, her touch igniting Zara's skin. "And take orders from me for a change."

Zara shivered. "As you will, serrah."

Roni took her arm and led her upstairs. If the others noticed, they said nothing. Or they had noticed and Adella had a hand clamped over Gisele's mouth.

Either way, it was perfect.

About the Author

Barbara Ann Wright writes fantasy and science fiction novels when not hoarding glitter. She has been a finalist in the *Foreword Review* Book of the Year Awards, the Goldie Awards, and the Lambda Literary Awards. Her first novel, *The Pyramid Waltz*, was one of Tor.com's Reviewer's Choice books of 2012 and made *BookRiot*'s 100 Must-Read Sci-Fi Fantasy Novels by Female Authors. *Lady of Stone*, the prequel to *The Pyramid Waltz*, was recommended on Syfy.com. Her work has also won five Rainbow Awards.

Books Available from Bold Strokes Books

A Convenient Arrangement by Aurora Rey and Jaime Clevenger. Cuffing season has come for lesbians, and for Jess Archer and Cody Dawson, their convenient arrangement becomes anything but. (978-1-63555-818-0)

An Alaskan Wedding by Nance Sparks. The last thing either Andrea or Riley expects is to bump into the one who broke her heart fifteen years ago, but when they meet at the welcome party, their feelings come rushing back. (978-1-63679-053-4)

Beulah Lodge by Cathy Dunnell. It's 1874, and newly engaged Ruth Mallowes is set on marriage and life as a missionary...until she falls in love with the housemaid at Beulah Lodge. (978-1-63679-007-7)

Gia's Gems by Toni Logan. When Lindsey Speyer discovers that popular travel columnist Gia Williams is a complete fake and threatens to expose her, blackmail has never been so sexy. (978-1-63555-917-0)

Holiday Wishes & Mistletoe Kisses by M. Ullrich. Four holidays, four couples, four chances to make their wishes come true. (978-1-63555-760-2)

Love By Proxy by Dena Blake. Tess has a secret crush on her best friend, Sophie, so the last thing she wants is to help Sophie fall in love with someone else, but how can she stand in the way of her happiness? (978-1-63555-973-6)

Loyalty, Love, & Vermouth by Eric Peterson. A comic valentine to a gay man's family of choice, including the ones with cold noses and four paws. (978-1-63555-997-2)

Marry Me by Melissa Brayden. Allison Hale attempts to plan the wedding of the century to a man who could save her family's business, if only she wasn't falling for her wedding planner, Megan Kinkaid. (978-1-63555-932-3)

Pathway to Love by Radclyffe. Courtney Valentine is looking for a woman exactly like Ben—smart, sexy, and not in the market for anything serious. All she has to do is convince Ben that sex-without-strings is the perfect pathway to pleasure. (978-1-63679-110-4)

Sweet Surprise by Jenny Frame. Flora and Mac never thought they'd ever see each other again, but when Mac opens up her barber shop right next to Flora's sweet shop, their connection comes roaring back. (978-1-63679-001-5)

The Edge of Yesterday by CJ Birch. Easton Gray is sent from the future to save humanity from technological disaster. When she's forced to target the woman she's falling in love with, can Easton do what's needed to save humanity? (978-1-63679-025-1)

The Scout and the Scoundrel by Barbara Ann Wright. With unexpected danger surrounding them, Zara and Roni are stuck between duty and survival, with little room for exploring their feelings, especially love. (978-1-63555-978-1)

Bury Me in Shadows by Greg Herren. College student Jake Chapman is forced to spend the summer at his dying grandmother's home and soon finds danger from long-buried family secrets. (978-1-63555-993-4)

Can't Leave Love by Kimberly Cooper Griffin. Sophia and Pru have no intention of falling in love, but sometimes love happens when and where you least expect it. (978-1-636790041-1)

Free Fall at Angel Creek by Julie Tizard. Detective Dee Rawlings and aircraft accident investigator Dr. River Dawson use conflicting methods to find answers when a plane goes missing, while overcoming surprising threats, and discovering an unlikely chance at love. (978-1-63555-884-5)

Love's Compromise by Cass Sellars. For Piper Holthaus and Brook Myers, will professional dreams and past baggage stop two hearts from realizing they are meant for each other? (978-1-63555-942-2)

Not All a Dream by Sophia Kell Hagin. Hester has lost the woman she loved and the world has descended into relentless dark and cold. But giving up will have to wait when she stumbles upon people who help her survive. (978-1-63679-067-1)

Protecting the Lady by Amanda Radley. If Eve Webb had known she'd be protecting royalty, she'd never have taken the job as bodyguard, but as the threat to Lady Katherine's life draws closer, she'll do whatever it takes to save her, and may just lose her heart in the process. (978-1-63679-003-9)

The Secrets of Willowra by Kadyan. A family saga of three women, their homestead called Willowra in the Australian outback, and the secrets that link them all. (978-1-63679-064-0)

Trial by Fire by Carsen Taite. When prosecutor Lennox Roy and public defender Wren Bishop become fierce adversaries in a headline-grabbing arson case, their attraction ignites a passion that leads them both to question their assumptions about the law, the truth, and each other. (978-1-63555-860-9)

Turbulent Waves by Ali Vali. Kai Merlin and Vivien Palmer plan their future together as hostile forces make their own plans to destroy what they have, as well as all those they love. (978-1-63679-011-4)

Unbreakable by Cari Hunter. When Dr. Grace Kendal is forced at gunpoint to help an injured woman, she is dragged into a nightmare where nothing is quite as it seems, and their lives aren't the only ones on the line. (978-1-63555-961-3)

Veterinary Surgeon by Nancy Wheelton. When dangerous drugs are stolen from the veterinary clinic, Mitch investigates and Kay becomes a suspect. As pride and professions clash, love seems impossible. (978-1-63679-043-5)

A Different Man by Andrew L. Huerta. This diverse collection of stories chronicling the challenges of gay life at various ages shines a light on the progress made and the progress still to come. (978-1-63555-977-4)

All That Remains by Sheri Lewis Wohl. Johnnie and Shantel might have to risk their lives—and their love—to stop a werewolf intent on killing. (978-1-63555-949-1)

Beginner's Bet by Fiona Riley. Phenom luxury Realtor Ellison Gamble has everything, except a family to share it with, so when a mix-up brings youthful Katie Crawford into her life, she bets the house on love. (978-1-63555-733-6)

Dangerous Without You by Lexus Grey. Throughout their senior year in high school, Aspen, Remington, Denna, and Raleigh face challenges in life and romance that they never expect. (978-1-63555-947-7)

Desiring More by Raven Sky. In this collection of steamy stories, a rich variety of lovers find themselves desiring more, more from a lover, more from themselves, and more from life. (978-1-63679-037-4)

Jordan's Kiss by Nanisi Barrett D'Arnuck. After losing everything in a fire, Jordan Phelps joins a small lounge band and meets pianist Morgan Sparks, who lights another blaze, this time in Jordan's heart. (978-1-63555-980-4)

Late City Summer by Jeanette Bears. Forced together for her wedding, Emily Stanton and Kate Alessi navigate their lingering passion for one another against the backdrop of New York City and World War II, and a summer romance they left behind. (978-1-63555-968-2)

Love and Lotus Blossoms by Anne Shade. On her path to self-acceptance and true passion, Janesse will risk everything—and possibly everyone—she loves. (978-1-63555-985-9)

Love in the Limelight by Ashley Moore. Marion Hargreaves, the finest actress of her generation, and Jessica Carmichael, the world's biggest pop star, rediscover each other twenty years after an ill-fated affair. (978-1-63679-051-0)

Suspecting Her by Mary P. Burns. Complications ensue when Erin O'Connor falls for top real estate saleswoman Catherine Williams while investigating racism in the real estate industry; the fallout could end their chance at happiness. (978-1-63555-960-6)

Two Winters by Lauren Emily Whalen. A modern YA retelling of Shakespeare's *The Winter's Tale* about birth, death, Catholic school, improv comedy, and the healing nature of time. (978-1-63679-019-0)

Busy Ain't the Half of It by Frederick Smith and Chaz Lamar Cruz. Elijah and Justin seek happily-ever-afters in LA, but are they too busy to notice happiness when it's there? (978-1-63555-944-6)

Calumet by Ali Vali. Jaxon Lavigne and Iris Long had a forbidden small-town romance that didn't last, and the consequences of that love will be uncovered fifteen years later at their high school reunion. (978-1-63555-900-2)

Her Countess to Cherish by Jane Walsh. London Society's material girl realizes there is more to life than diamonds when she falls in love with a non-binary bluestocking. (978-1-63555-902-6)

Hot Days, Heated Nights by Renee Roman. When Cole and Lee meet, instant attraction quickly flares into uncontrollable passion, but their connection might be short lived as Lee's identity is tied to her life in the city. (978-1-63555-888-3)

Never Be the Same by MA Binfield. Casey meets Olivia and sparks fly in this opposites attract romance that proves love can be found in the unlikeliest places. (978-1-63555-938-5)

Quiet Village by Eden Darry. Something not quite human is stalking Collie and her niece, and she'll be forced to work with undercover reporter Emily Lassiter if they want to get out of Hyam alive. (978-1-63555-898-2)

Shaken or Stirred by Georgia Beers. Bar owner Julia Martini and home health aide Savannah McNally attempt to weather the storms brought on by a mysterious blogger trashing the bar, family feuds they knew nothing about, and way too much advice from way too many relatives. (978-1-63555-928-6)

The Fiend in the Fog by Jess Faraday. Can four people on different trajectories work together to save the vulnerable residents of East London from the terrifying fiend in the fog before it's too late? (978-1-63555-514-1)

The Marriage Masquerade by Toni Logan. A no strings attached marriage scheme to inherit a Maui B&B uncovers unexpected attractions and a dark family secret. (978-1-63555-914-9)

Flight SQA016 by Amanda Radley. Fastidious airline passenger Olivia Lewis is used to things being a certain way. When her routine is changed by a new, attractive member of the staff, sparks fly. (978-1-63679-045-9)

Home Is Where the Heart Is by Jenny Frame. Can Archie make the countryside her home and give Ash the fairytale romance she desires? Or will the countryside and small village life all be too much for her? (978-1-63555-922-4)

Moving Forward by PJ Trebelhorn. The last person Shelby Ryan expects to be attracted to is Iris Calhoun, the sister of the man who killed her wife four years and three thousand miles ago. (978-1-63555-953-8)

Poison Pen by Jean Copeland. Debut author Kendra Blake is finally living her best life until a nasty book review and exposed secrets threaten her promising new romance with aspiring journalist Alison Chatterley. (978-1-63555-849-4)

Seasons for Change by KC Richardson. Love, laughter, and trust develop for Shawn and Morgan throughout the changing seasons of Lake Tahoe. (978-1-63555-882-1)

Summer Lovin' by Julie Cannon. Three different women, three exotic locations, one unforgettable summer. What do you think will happen? (978-1-63555-920-0)

Unbridled by D. Jackson Leigh. A visit to a local stable turns into more than riding lessons between a novel writer and an equestrian with a taste for power play. (978-1-63555-847-0)

VIP by Jackie D. In a town where relationships are forged and shattered by perception, sometimes even love can't change who you really are. (978-1-63555-908-8)

Yearning by Gun Brooke. The sleepy town of Dennamore has an irresistible pull on those who've moved away. The mystery Darian Benson and Samantha Pike uncover will change them forever, but the love they find along the way just might be the key to saving themselves. (978-1-63555-757-2)

CPSIA information can be obtained
at www.ICGtesting.com
Printed in the USA
LVHW030711271021
701607LV00001B/2